ACCLAIM FOR TAMERA ALEXANDER

"Tamera Alexander is one of my favorite authors, so I expect a lot from her novels. *To Win Her Favor* is captivating beyond expectation! This novel has everything readers are looking for—rich characterization, page-turning intrigue, a heartwarming romance charged with tension, and more!"

—Cindy Woodsmall, *New York Times* and CBA bestselling author of Amish fiction

"I have rarely read a more wonderful book than *To Win Her Favor* by Tamera Alexander. Rich with historical detail and fully developed characters, this novel held me spellbound until the last page. If you read one historical novel this year, make it *To Win Her Favor*. It will linger with you long after the last page."

—Colleen Coble, *USA Today* bestselling author of the Hope Beach series and *The Inn At Ocean's Edge*

"Marriage of convenience stories are my favorite and *To Win Her Favor* by Tamera Alexander is no exception. The challenges and dynamics of the unlikely relationship between a southern lady and handsome Irishman sizzle with tension and passion. The plot is as powerful as the magnificent thoroughbreds the heroine rides. A moving story of overcoming post-Civil War obstacles and racial discrimination, readers won't be able to put down the book until the last page."

—Jody Hedlund, bestselling author of *Love Unexpected*

"*To Win Her Favor* is a beautiful love story, not to mention a story of faith that shines through in the darkest circumstances. From the very beginning, I lost my heart to Cullen and Maggie and yearned for the moment when they would lose their hearts to each other. Add to everything else a sleek thoroughbred named Bourbon Belle, and this novel quickly galloped its way onto my list of favorite books."

—Robin Lee Hatcher, bestselling author of *Love Without End* and *Whenever You Come Around*

"Tamera Alexander has done it again! *To Win Her Favor* is peopled with fascinating, richly drawn characters that drew me into their very hearts and souls. Maggie and Cullen's story captures the drama and tragedy of the post–Civil War era, but more importantly, it captures the humanity of those who triumphed after a dark time in our nation's history to rebuild lives marked by joy and anchored by faith."

—Deborah Raney, author of *The Face of the Earth*
and The Chicory Inn Novels series

"Tamera Alexander delivers a beautifully realized novel of love, faith, and redemption. Brimming with rich historical detail and populated with compelling characters both real and imagined, *To Win Her Favor* is certain to find favor with Ms. Alexander's fans and to win her many new ones."

—Dorothy Love, author of *The Bracelet*

"Tamera Alexander has done it again. Her imagination and skillful pen intertwined with history takes the reader on a beautiful journey. *To Win Her Favor* is sure to stir the heart and open the mind."

—Jenny Lamb, Director of Interpretation &
Education Belle Meade Plantation

"Already a *USA Today* bestseller, [*To Whisper Her Name*] draws a fresh thread in this author's historical fiction tapestry. Tamera Alexander's painstaking research into the people, places, and times of which she writes is evident on every page, and she depicts the famous residents of post-bellum Nashville with great detail and even greater affection."

—USAtoday.com, Serena Chase

"Alexander writes a beautiful story of love, friendship, and finding purpose."

—*RT Book Reviews*, four stars (for *To Whisper Her Name*)

". . . pure reading pleasure."

—Liz Curtis Higgs, *New York Times* bestselling author
of *Mine Is the Night* (for *To Whisper Her Name*)

"Two-time Christy Award winner Alexander continues her historical series with this sweeping Southern romance that is engaging and full of hope. Recommended for fans of Robin Lee Hatcher and Francine Rivers."

—*Library Journal* (for *A Beauty So Rare*)

"Bestseller Alexander will delight fans . . ."

—*Publishers Weekly* (for *A Beauty So Rare*)

"Better than sweet tea on a veranda, *A Lasting Impression* is a winner!"

—Francine Rivers, *New York Times* bestselling author of *Redeeming Love*

"To put it simply: This book is a full-on HIT."

—*USA Today* (for *A Lasting Impression*)

". . . Making an impressive debut, Alexander has written a charming historical romance that features well-drawn characters and smooth, compelling storytelling that will have readers anxiously awaiting the second installment of the Fountain Creek Chronicles. Highly recommended . . ."

—*Library Journal*, starred review (for *Rekindled*)

TO WIN HER FAVOR

Books by Tamera Alexander

Belle Meade Plantation Novels

To Whisper Her Name

To Win Her Favor

To Mend a Dream (novella)

Women of Faith Fiction

The Inheritance

Belmont Mansion Novels

A Lasting Impression

A Beauty So Rare

Timber Ridge Reflections

From a Distance

Beyond This Moment

Within My Heart

Fountain Creek Chronicles

Rekindled

Revealed

Remembered

A Belle Meade Plantation Novel

TAMERA ALEXANDER

TO WIN HER FAVOR

ZONDERVAN

To Win Her Favor

Requests for information should be addressed to:
Zondervan, Grand Rapids, Michigan 49546

Library of Congress Cataloging-in-Publication Data

Alexander, Tamera.
To win her favor / Tamera Alexander.
pages ; cm. -- (A Belle Meade plantation novel ; 2)
ISBN 978-0-310-29107-7 (softcover)
1. Horse racing--Fiction. 2. Belle Meade Plantation (Tenn.)--History. 3. Tennessee--History--19th century--Fiction. I. Title.
PS3601.L3563T665 2015
813'.6--dc23
2014044831

All Scripture quotations are taken from the King James Version.

Printed in the United States of America

15 16 17 18 19 20 / RRD / 20 19 18 17 16 15 14 13 12 11 10 9 8 7 6 5 4 3 2 1

To Polly Chandler Alexander
I'm so grateful our together forever started here

For thou hast been a shelter for me,
and a strong tower from the enemy.

Psalm 61:3 (KJV)

Preface

During the nineteenth century Tennessee dominated the thoroughbred racing industry in the United States, with Belle Meade Plantation in Nashville serving as the preeminent stud farm in the nation. Does the name Secretariat sound familiar? What about Sunday Silence and Seattle Slew? Those champion thoroughbreds and countless others all trace their lineage to this estate, the setting of my Belle Meade Plantation novels.

The first time I stepped foot onto the Belle Meade grounds and learned about the Harding family, "Uncle" Bob Green, and so many others who lived and worked at Belle Meade in the nineteenth century, I knew I wanted to write stories that included them, the magnificent property, and this crucial time in our nation's history.

While this novel is peopled with characters who lived during that time, as well as real historical events, their overarching personalities and actions as depicted in this novel are the product of my own imagination.

Thank you for entrusting your time to me. It's a weighty investment, one I treasure and never take for granted.

Blessings from Belle Meade,

Tamera

Chapter One

Nashville, Tennessee
May 4, 1869

"Steady, girl," Maggie whispered, peering down from the bluff, leather reins held taut. The thrum of spectators on the field below rose on the cool morning breeze, and she leaned forward to stroke the thoroughbred's neck. "Wait," she gently coaxed, anticipation sparking the air. "It's coming . . ." But even as she said it, her own pulse edged up a notch.

Bourbon Belle pawed the dirt, and Maggie sensed the mare's restraint growing thinner by the—

The gunshot sounded. The horses on the racetrack below bolted from their marks, as did Bourbon Belle, and exhilaration fired through Maggie's veins.

Belle surged to life and Maggie gave the horse her head, allowing the mare to surrender to every instinct the animal's sleek-muscled body commanded. To *run*.

Belle's hooves pounded the smooth dirt path, and Maggie imagined that this was what Willie experienced when he raced Belle around the track below. Except the boy was less than half Maggie's weight, so he and Belle all but flew, just as she expected the pair to do again at the heat later this week.

One and a quarter miles, barely a two-minute race. But the thud of Maggie's heart marked the time as Belle rounded the familiar curve in the path, the mare's powerful stride devouring the distance.

Crouching forward, as she'd trained Willie to do, Maggie felt the wind whipping the pins from her hair, and she relished the freedom that only this kind of riding could bring. And though she knew the peace was temporary at best, she embraced it.

Belle thundered down the path and Maggie urged her on, the starting point looming just ahead. At that moment a chorus of cheers rose from the field, and Maggie looked to see a thoroughbred flashing across the finish line below. Belle powered onward, slowing only when Maggie tugged the reins.

Breathless, Maggie paused and let the pungent sweetness of the field grass fill her lungs. She reached to scratch the place between Belle's ears. "You did well, girl." Maggie took another needed breath. "I was the one who slowed us down."

Belle whinnied as though acknowledging the fact, and Maggie smiled.

The winnings from the upcoming heat—*if* Willie and Belle won, which they would, Maggie felt certain—wouldn't come close to paying the back taxes owed on Linden Downs, but she hoped it would be enough to pacify the Tax and Title Office. Again.

Belle had won her last five heats, and considering the number of races scheduled at Burns Island Track, that meant a fairly reliable source of income for the next few months. But what Maggie's sights were set on—if Linden Downs could survive that long—was the inaugural Peyton Stakes to be run that fall, the largest race in the country with the highest earning purse in history. And it would be run right here in Nashville at Burns Island.

And her own Bourbon Belle, the three-year-old she'd raised from a foal, would win that, too, barring any unforeseen competition. The mare's race times demonstrated that without question.

So why did the next few months seem like an insurmountable hurdle? She couldn't bear to imagine that, after holding on for so long, she and her father might lose the only home either one of them had ever known.

Maggie dismounted, welcoming the chance to stretch her legs and let Belle cool down before starting for home. But as the moments passed and the excitement of the race ebbed in the field below, the reality of her situation returned.

How had it come to this? Such a jagged end to something she'd worked so hard to hold together. Yet she refused to give in to the despairing thoughts. Not while she still had breath . . .

And a jockey ready to race only four days hence.

She would succeed. With Belle, and with Linden Downs. She had no other choice. Her father had been her shelter and strong tower for so long; now it was her turn to be his.

Maggie retrieved the pack she'd laid aside earlier, along with her rifle. The pack she stuffed into the saddlebag, and her rifle she secured in the sheath tied to it. Racing and shooting all in the same day. The term *blissful* came to mind, but didn't quite seem befitting of the activities.

She climbed back into the saddle and nudged Belle toward home but quickly realized Belle wasn't interested in trotting. Or even cantering. The thoroughbred wanted to do what she did best.

And Maggie happily obliged.

⁂

Kneeling on the riverbank, Cullen McGrath stared into the murky waters of the Cumberland, yet saw only shadows of the briny deep that had swallowed his world whole. Never a man to question his own judgment, he'd been bested by doubt more times than he cared to admit since he'd first planted a sodden boot on this country's soil a year ago.

Regret had proven to be an equally brutal companion. But of one thing he was certain . . .

"I'll be keepin' my promise to you," he whispered in the humid morning air, "no matter what the cost." Were vows spoken aloud in this earthly realm heard in the next? He hoped so. In this moment, at least. His grandfather, who had spoken oft of such things, had assured him of it.

Aye, Cullen, me boy. 'Tis naught but fools who believe this life is all there be. The world comin' after 'tis far greater. And the secret of livin' this life to the full is to do it in light of the next. Never forget that you're—

"Hey! You over there. The horse is ready."

Cullen grimaced at the sharp rein to his thoughts, his grandfather's brogue still thick within him like mist on the heathlands. People used to tell him as a lad that he sounded like the man, but not until recent years had he fully appreciated the comparison.

He rose to full height, but as he turned, movement in the field across the river caught his eye. A horse and rider passing in a flash. Nay, more like a streak of lightning. But was it really a—

He squinted. Surely not . . .

Yet the skirts flapping behind the slip of a girl—or was it a woman, hard to tell at this distance—left no doubt. She rode with a freedom and passion that reminded him wistfully of another lifetime. And she rode astraddle to boot. He felt the start of a smile. He hadn't seen that kind of speed and grace in a horse's stride since watching Bonnie Scotland race the wind back in—

"Hey! Are you listenin' to me, boy?"

Boy? Bristling, Cullen looked back and directed his gaze to the tree trunk of a man who stood waiting, reins in hand.

It wasn't the blacksmith, the owner of the livery, who had accepted his offer earlier—begrudgingly, if the blacksmith's reluctance to shake his hand indicated anything. But Cullen remembered this fellow all the same. Younger than Cullen by a few years, and cocky, from the looks of him. He'd come in shortly after the blacksmith had agreed to the deal and had stood off to the side watching and listening.

Cullen crossed the distance, sensing challenge roll off the man in waves. Back in the day he would've planted a fist upside the fellow's head just for looking at him sideways, much less for doing so with such disdain. But Cullen doubted that a blow, even square on, would take down a man this size.

Yet with his own stature and strength being a fair match, he gauged that one well-placed jab would at least shake a few bolts loose. And considering the anger that had been building inside him in recent months, it would feel good to knock the fool's head clean off his shoulders. Along with that silly smirk.

But he needed what he'd come here for today, so instead of giving in to old instincts, he met the man's stare straight on. He withdrew a wad of bills from his shirt pocket and counted them out, reaching for a civility that had been all but stripped clean in his months of working on the docks at Brooklyn harbor.

He held out the bills.

The man shook his head. "This horse is worth two hundred dollars."

Cullen eyed him. "And yet I'll be payin' a hundred and fifty, like the blacksmith agreed upon not an hour back."

A dark look hooded the man's eyes. "Dixon's changed his mind. Guess he decided he don't want to sell this horse for that amount. Leastwise, not to you."

From his peripheral view Cullen caught the blacksmith peering from inside the doorway, and he quickly gained the truth of the situation.

He'd been in Nashville only two days, but already he'd faced the less than enthusiastic reception most Southerners extended to people from his homeland. And if by some miracle he'd managed to miss that, the countless HELP WANTED: NO IRISH NEED APPLY shingles hanging outside nearly every blasted shop he'd seen thus far told the story well enough.

It would seem the tales of hospitality he'd heard told back in Ireland weren't quite on the mark. But this was the New World, and a free one. He had every right to be here. And he'd come too far to turn back.

Cullen looked at the money in his grip, then at the man. "If this is to be the way of it, then you best tell Dixon he's decided to lose the sale."

"He don't care about the sale."

Cullen feigned surprise. "He sure enough seemed to care when he shook my hand on the deal." With effort he averted his eyes from the magnificent animal he'd spent the last two days scouring Nashville's liveries to find. A Percheron, one of many fine specimens he'd seen. But none like this. A black stallion standing nineteen hands, with a sharpness to his gaze that betrayed a keen mind with strength enough to build a dream. Or so Cullen hoped.

"Or maybe," Cullen continued, further testing the waters, "a handshake doesn't mean anythin' to you Southern gents."

"Oh, it means somethin' to us. We just don't like bein' cheated."

"Cheated?" Cullen gave a sharp laugh. "That's a mighty stout word to be bandyin' about, friend. 'Specially when you're the one shiftin' the deal here."

"I ain't your friend. And we ain't got no deal. Not with you. Not with your kind."

Again Cullen bristled. "And exactly what 'kind' would you be referrin' to?"

A sneer lifted one side of the fellow's mouth. "The way I see it, you're just like them darkies. 'Cept lighter. Out to cheat and steal, to take whatever you can. But we're teachin' them a thing or two. Same as we'll do with you."

"Like them darkies, you say?" Cullen blew out a breath and tucked the money safely back into his pocket. "So, in addition to bein' blind as a beggar, you're also dumb as a cockeyed post, is that it? Or do you really think you can tell the make of a man by the color of his arse?"

Cullen managed to dodge the fellow's first swing—and the spooked Percheron's nervous sidestep. But the second blow landed like an anvil to his gut, and his breath left in a rush. The punch reminded him of his older brother's, only Ethan's blows packed twice the wallop.

Winded, but still steady, Cullen managed to drive his fist square onto its mark, and the man teetered—Ethan would've been so proud—and a trickle of blood edged down his chin. He blinked as if dazed not only by the blow but by the one who'd delivered it.

On the street passersby slowed their pace to gawk, children among them. A tiny girl, her expression stricken, stared wide-eyed, and Cullen—his fist still stinging—swiftly soured on the fight. He saw the moment for what it was—the chance to end it, and perhaps knock some sense into one of these hayseed hoopleheads.

A swift right hook, lightning fast with nothing held back—just as Ethan had taught him—and the tree trunk fell with a thud.

Cullen spied the blacksmith backing farther into the shadows. "I've no desire to quarrel with you, Dixon," Cullen called out, flexing his hand, "but I do aim to have this horse. And for what we shook on. A man's word is his bond. If you don't have that," he said, more to himself than to the other man, "then you've got nothin'." He took a deep breath, and the ache in his side told of soreness that would set in by morning. He looked back again. "So tell me, are you comin' out? Or am I comin' in?"

The blacksmith, a short boulder of a man, came bustling out faster than his trim height would have portended. "It weren't my idea, McGrath. Y-you—" Stammering, he glanced down at his friend, who was still out cold. "You gotta know that."

"All I know is that you and I shook hands." Cullen tugged the bills from his pocket again. "Now in my book, that means we have us a deal. What say you?"

Dixon hesitated. His gaze flitted about, first to his friend, then up and down the street. Finally he snatched the money and stuffed it into his grimy apron pocket. "The horse is yours. But don't come 'round here no more." His gaze ventured past Cullen a second time. "I won't sell to you again."

Cullen glanced over his shoulder to see what was of interest, but spied nothing in particular. Even the curious onlookers had moved past. "And why won't you be sellin' to me again, Dixon? My money's as good as the next."

"It ain't about your money."

"If that's the case, then why won't you—"

"'Cuz buyin' a horse like that—" The blacksmith gestured toward the Percheron, frustration outweighing the hesitance in his voice. "It says you aim to stay here, get yourself some land, maybe start up a farm."

"So?" Cullen shrugged. "What if I do? It's nobody's business but my own."

Huffing, Dixon peered up at him. "That's where you're wrong, Irishman. You're in the South now, boy. There ain't no such thing as your own business. Not for me, and 'specially not for the likes of you. Now take the horse and go, before I change my mind. And if anybody asks"—Dixon moved to help his friend, who was finally coming to—"you didn't buy that horse from me."

The man's warning sat ill within Cullen, and was only made worse by the dismal prospect of future business dealings in this town. But having learned the importance of timing—be it in a physical confrontation or otherwise—Cullen did as the man asked and gathered the Percheron's lead rein to guide the draft horse down the street. The effort took some coaxing, and he quickly added *strong-headed* to the animal's admirable qualities.

He made his way toward a saddlery shop he'd passed earlier. He only hoped the owner of that establishment would prove to be more open-minded than the others.

He held a similar hope for at least one of this city's landowners. Although, up to now, that hadn't been his experience. Without exception, every farm he'd visited yesterday with an inquiry about land advertised for sale had earned him the same response: Irish need not inquire. But he'd inquired anyway. Determination had given him no choice.

But determined or not, he'd come up empty-handed and had twice been threatened at rifle point for trespassing. He gave a frustrated sigh.

His pockets held the same currency as theirs, yet his apparently wasn't good enough. At least he didn't need a loan. No bank would loan "to the likes of him," as Dixon had put it. But no matter. Cullen had funds enough to purchase one of the smaller properties he'd seen listed in the newspapers—if only they would sell to him.

Several were set to go up for auction within a fortnight, but his visit to the courthouse yesterday morning had provided a swift answer to the question about whether or not a bid from him would be accepted. No, he would have to find someone willing to sell to him outright. Which at this point seemed next to impossible.

But perhaps one of the property owners close to going to auction, if desperate enough, might be persuaded to take less than the asking price.

Cullen slowed his steps, his attention snagged by the distant roar of cheering and by another sound he could never mistake, not in a thousand lifetimes . . .

The telling, rhythmic pounding of hooves.

As though guided by some unseen hand, his gaze trailed the length of the street to a field at the far end. Seeing the twentysome-foot banner stretched across the entrance, he felt a wake of memories break inside him, and he paused on the sunbaked road.

BURNS ISLAND TRACK, the banner proclaimed, with the smaller title NASHVILLE THOROUGHBRED SOCIETY printed beneath.

Merely reading the words tempted him to turn and run while he still could, even as the tug of the familiar baited him closer. But he knew better. And besides, he'd already chosen to run. That's why he'd left England to come to America. To start over.

A question occurred to him then that was neither new nor kind, but he still wished he knew the answer. Was what had happened on the voyage across the Atlantic his punishment for what he had—and hadn't—done in London? Had the Almighty been paying him back?

If so, God was crueler than he'd imagined. Could heaven not see that he'd had no other choice?

Cullen's grip tightened on the lead rein. If he had come forward with the truth, it wouldn't have made any difference. People had already made up their minds. Much as they'd done here, in this town, as soon as he opened his mouth.

He'd never been ashamed of his heritage, and he wasn't now. But he *was* ashamed for having believed, for so many years, in the goodness of the Father God his grandfather had spoken of so many times. Turned out, maybe God the Father was more like his own *da* instead of the just and benevolent being Grandfather Ian had followed with such allegiance and affection.

From down the street, cheers swelled to a roar, and Cullen felt a thirst begging to be slaked inside him. But that part of his life was dead and gone now. As surely as were his precious Moira and their wee Katie . . .

A needlelike sharpness pricked the back of his throat.

If he could have given his life for theirs that day, he would have. He swallowed with effort. But God hadn't listened to his pleas. Not in the small hours of that morning, and not in the dark, empty hours that followed that night when the precious life he'd cradled in his arms reached out into eternity for the comfort of her *ma*. With heart ripped open and laid bare, Cullen had petitioned heaven for help. But God had turned a deaf ear.

The last time he'd attended Mass seemed a lifetime ago. On one of his first nights in Brooklyn he stumbled upon a church, heard the familiar prayers, and ventured in, something within already telling him it would be futile. He sat in the pew and gazed up at the blurry form of the crucified Christ and asked—nay, begged—God again to tell him *why*. To show him the way to go, tell him what to do next.

But no still small voice answered. No whisper, not even a wisp, had heaven spared for him. So he'd left, vowing never to return again. The Almighty wanted to remain silent? Fine by him. He'd return the favor.

The Percheron shifted beside him and pawed the ground.

"Easy, boy," Cullen whispered, reaching up to give him a rub. If he had any hope of a future in this town, or any other, it was up to him alone, and his past must stay buried.

But was an ocean vast enough to keep hidden the weight of his sins? Especially when one of the men Ethan had wronged was an American. Cullen had been told the scandal was reported in the papers here as well. No surprise, considering what horse had been involved, and what it had cost the American businessman. Cullen exhaled, exchanging the stale air in his lungs for fresh.

Surely his past demons—and those that likely still hounded Ethan, wherever his brother was—had grown weary and given up the hunt. If not, Cullen knew that if they caught up with him, they would eat him alive, gnawing on his bones 'til there was nothing left but dust.

Determined to keep running, he continued in the opposite direction down the street toward the saddlery shop. He was a long way from the rule and reach of London's Thoroughbred Society, and he intended to keep it that way. That, and stay as far away from thoroughbreds—and that racetrack—as possible.

He knew just how to do it too. Tuck himself away on some quiet little farm on the outskirts of town. A world away. Alone. That's what he wanted. Maybe then he'd find the peace he sought.

Once in the saddlery shop, he made his selections, choosing the finer but simpler leatherwork from among pieces more ornate yet not as well crafted. A fancy saddle caught his eye, and he knew which one Ethan would have chosen if there.

Ready to pay, he approached the counter, nodding to the young woman watching him attentively.

"Good day, sir," she said softly, smiling at him, her eyes sparkling. "Perhaps you need help finding something else?"

Checking his gear, Cullen ignored the invitation in her tone and shook his head. "I believe I've got everythin' I need, miss. But thank you just the same."

Like snuffing out a candle, the light fled the woman's eyes. She looked at him as though he'd grown a second head, one she found significantly less attractive.

And as she silently, stoically summed up his receipt, Cullen thought back to a night with Ethan in an English pub when a tavern wench had reacted much the same.

Cullen, you sorry bugger. Ethan had lifted his ale, laughing. *If only you'd taken after our father like I did and had the mark of the Irish atop your head for all to see, that wouldn't happen. As it is*—Ethan let out a hearty burp—*you can thank our mother, God rest her, for those pale green eyes and dark curls atop your head that draw the ladies . . . leastwise 'til you open your mouth!* More raucous laughter had followed.

Cullen smiled to himself, remembering. But apparently Southern women held the same opinion of Irishmen as did English barmaids. Through the years, Ethan had ribbed him mercilessly about not having "the look of the Irish." But for that distinction alone, he and Ethan could've passed for twins. Aye, Ethan had slightly more brawn to him, but in countenance they were brothers through and through.

Half an hour later, Cullen had the horse nearly saddled and ready when he sensed, rather than heard, someone behind him. And he knew who it was. Wishing now that he'd finished the fight while he'd held the advantage, Cullen turned at the ready.

But the person he came face-to-face with wasn't the one he expected.

Chapter Two

The gent, a real dandy from the looks of him, eyed the Percheron. "That's quite an animal you've got there. But are you certain you wouldn't prefer one of our fine Tennessee thoroughbreds to this . . . Goliath of a beast?"

Cullen regarded the finely tailored suit and fancy top hat. And the fellow's boots—so shiny and ornate in detail, they looked better suited to a maiden than a man. The gent's smile was slick, much like his dark hair combed back in neat, even waves. It took Cullen all of two seconds to form a first opinion. And his first opinions, once set, rarely budged.

He managed an obligatory nod then returned to tightening the stirrup straps. He had three more farms to visit this afternoon, and he needed to get a move on.

"You may not know it, being new to the area as you are," the man continued, and Cullen stilled. "But unlike other cities, Nashville didn't lose all its blood horses to the war. So . . . in case you're interested, there are others from which to choose."

The stranger ran an assuming hand over the Percheron's quarters, and the horse's muscles contracted in response. Cullen straightened and turned back a second time. Was the man foolhardy—or just a fool? Either one, a swift kick from this beast would be the end of him.

Yet the man didn't strike him as the foolish sort. Not with his keenness of manner and the hint of cruelty about his eyes. Cocky? Aye. Pushy? Without question. But foolish? Nay, not a wit's chance of that, as his grandfather would've said.

Cullen faced him, their gazes almost level. "Thank you for takin' such an interest in my affairs," he said evenly. "But I purchased the exact horse I wanted."

The man's smile widened. How did these Southerners do it? Smile so nicely when their true feelings, written so plainly for all to see, were quite the opposite.

"And where did you purchase him, I wonder? I've been looking for such an animal myself now for some time."

Cullen knew when he was being baited. Dixon's parting warning returned to him, and though he felt no loyalty to the blacksmith, the man had sold the horse to him in the end. "Several liveries in town have Percherons. I'm sure you won't have any problem findin' one to suit your needs."

The man stepped toward him, and his eyes narrowed. "Speaking of needs, I'm curious. For what purpose did you purchase this animal? Surely you don't plan to run him at Burns Island Track. Now that"—his hearty laugh wasn't the least convincing—"I'd pay good money to see."

Four men standing off to the side laughed beneath their breath, and Cullen met each of their stares, not missing the one whose hand rested on the gun at his hip. Cullen focused again on the gent before him. For not liking the Irish, these folks sure went out of their way to start a conversation.

Cullen smoothed a hand over the massive neck of the Percheron. "I'm not lookin' for speed, or for one of your fine thoroughbreds." He tried for a touch of humor. "Don't tell me you Southerners haven't heard of the tortoise and the hare? It's not always the swiftest that wins the race."

"It is around here," the man answered, his voice gaining an edge. "But I wouldn't expect a simple . . . potato farmer like yourself to know that. Isn't that what you people are?" Polite facade gone, cruel intent sharpened his features. "Though not quite successful at it, I'd say, considering the curse you suffered."

Cullen heard laughter off to the side again but didn't acknowledge it. "The curse?" he asked, wondering if the man would take the bait. "And what curse might that be?"

"The blight the Almighty sent to your country two decades back. Your people's punishment for not accepting him when you had the chance."

"Ah . . ." Cullen nodded slowly, as though he hadn't heard the conjecture a hundred times before. "So you believe God's a Protestant then."

"What I believe"—the stranger's look held venom—"is that God is not a pagan lover. Nor is he fond of white niggers." He spat out the term. "So you would do best to move on. There's plenty of land east of here yet to be settled. In the Carolinas, perhaps, or south on into Georgia. It matters not to me where you go, as long as you don't stay here. Am I making myself clear? Or do I need to speak in plainer terms?"

Cullen met his stare unblinking, half wishing Ethan were there. Five-to-two odds would be just about even, with his brother in the thick. If not for the gun. "I understand perfectly what you're saying."

"Good, then." The man clapped him on the shoulder in the manner of old friends. "I'm glad we had this conversation, Mr . . . ?"

"McGrath is my name," Cullen said, wanting him to remember it. "Cullen McGrath. And you are?"

Challenge flickered in the man's expression. "Stephen Drake. A name you'd do well to put to memory. And a word to the wise, McGrath. The quicker you leave town, the better. We've had our share of unfortunate occurrences lately, and I'd hate it if you got caught up in any of that ruckus. Believe it or not," Drake said, shaking his head, "there are those who, sadly, might wish to do you harm. And we wouldn't want that, now would we?"

A sheen of friendliness, beguiling though it was, lit the man's expression, and anyone looking on would have thought they were the finest of friends.

Cullen watched the men walk away, wondering if Drake had the least inkling of how ineffective his little speech had been. He heard his mother's sharply teasing voice clearly in his memory. *Whatever it is you want to get an Irishman to do, just tell him that he can't.*

He gathered the reins and swung up into the saddle—no small feat—more determined than ever to buy land and make a way for himself. He could scarcely remember a time when his heritage or religious upbringing—no matter how far he'd strayed from it—hadn't invited trouble. When his family moved to England when he was fifteen, he'd daily been reminded that his people weren't welcome there any more than they seemed to be in this city.

But he had a reason for being here, as well as a right.

He flicked the reins, and the Percheron plodded on. If there was one thing he'd learned in his near thirty years, it was that no matter how desperate the circumstances, there was usually someone else worse off.

He just needed to find that someone.

Where was Willie?

Maggie looked out the open double doors of the stable again. Already half past twelve, and still no sign of him. They'd agreed to work here at Linden Downs today, so her father could see the progress Willie and Belle were making together. The boy was never late. Perhaps he had forgotten.

Belle whinnied and nudged Maggie's hand, and Maggie leaned close, recalling what she'd overheard at the racetrack last week despite Belle's recent wins. "Don't you listen to them, girl," she whispered. "Some say you can't do it. But they're wrong. You were born for this, I know it."

Just as she knew what she was born for. Even if people said it couldn't be done by a woman. Or *shouldn't* be. Which is what her mother, God rest her soul, had said more times than Maggie could recall, and with a sharpness to her tone that stung even now. It was a hurtful thing for a mother not to be proud of her only daughter.

Footsteps from behind drew her attention.

"Thought I'd save you a trip, Maggie." Her father carried in a bale of hay, Bucket padding loyally along beside him.

How was it that she'd rescued the black-and-white collie, had nursed the sickly little pup back to health, only to have the dog bond with her father instead of her? Yet seeing them together, and knowing how much Bucket had helped ease Papa's pain when Mother had passed, Maggie wouldn't have wished it otherwise.

Her father hefted the bale into one of the stalls then paused, his breath coming hard. He braced a hand against the stable wall. Despite the cool air, sweat glistened on his forehead. He rubbed his left arm, the muscles apparently complaining from use.

Maggie felt a tug of concern, especially after what had happened last week. "I've told you, Papa. I can do that. I don't mind."

"I know you don't. But neither do I." He swabbed his forehead with a handkerchief then quickly looked away. He reached for the pitchfork. "Did you have a good ride this morning?"

Recognizing avoidance when she saw it, Maggie moved to take the pitchfork from him, but he held fast.

"I'm fine, Margaret."

Maggie started to press the issue; then, recognizing the accustomed determination and gentleness in her father's expression, she reluctantly acquiesced.

"I know I can't do what I once did . . ." Frustration—or was it worry—shadowed his faint smile. "But I can still heft a bale of hay for my daughter."

He held her gaze, unblinking. At his feet, Bucket stood stock still, as if sensing the change in temperament.

Her father had always been more than able-bodied. Of average height, he had especially broad shoulders, which made him appear larger somehow. Maggie had ridden on those shoulders as a little girl and oh, the view from that perch. The world had looked so different. Bigger somehow, and wilder.

Yet she'd known that nothing could hurt her because her father would never have allowed it. Her strong tower. Whatever bad was coming would have to get past him first, and that could never happen.

At least, not in the mind of that little girl.

But time had a way of eroding such innocence. And as she'd grown, Maggie had often wished that the world were more like the one she'd viewed from that lofty height.

She eyed her father as he spread the hay. As strong as he'd always been, he was equally kind and good-natured. Her four brothers, all of them older than she, had been just like him—perhaps a bit more rowdy—God rest them all. Not a day went by that she didn't miss them.

And while she *could* well imagine her world without her father, she didn't like to. He was all she had left.

"When Dr. Daniels was here to see you yesterday, Papa . . . You're certain he told you everything was fine."

"Like I said. Nothing to worry about." Her father shoved the pitchfork into the hay and gave the load a toss then repeated the process.

"When you see the doctor next, please remind him to keep his regular appointment. He's been showing up at odd times, and I want to be here for his visits."

"You and Willie were over at Belle Meade working with Uncle Bob. I know how important that time is to you, especially with a heat coming up this week. I saw no need to disturb you."

"Disturb me?" She scoffed playfully, but touched his arm, letting him see she was serious. "Next time send Cletus for me. Or Onnie. All right?"

He chucked her gently beneath the chin the way he'd done as far back as she could remember.

"I will, sweetheart. Next time." He glanced out the open door. "I thought you said Willie was coming."

"I did. But I'm wondering now if he's forgotten."

"Do you have appointments later today?"

Maggie resisted the urge to sigh. "Yes, three. And all new students."

"That's a good thing."

She nodded. "Yes, it is."

"And yet . . . it's not what you wish to be doing."

It wasn't a question, she knew. Still, she shook her head. "But we need the money, so I'm grateful." As soon as she said it, regret moved into his eyes, and she wished she could take back the remark. "Papa, I—"

He lifted a gentle hand. "If Belle doesn't win the heat later this week—"

"She *will* win. I know it."

"But if she doesn't"—he lowered his head briefly before looking back at her—"then you know what we must do. We'll have no choice, Maggie. Stephen Drake was very clear on that point."

Stephen Drake . . . at the Tax and Title Office.

Maggie would have thought the childhood friend of her eldest brother would be more understanding. Yes, Mr. Drake had granted them an extension—two, actually—but couldn't he offer to do so again, under the circumstances?

She remembered his coming to the house when she was younger. Twelve years her senior, he was now as he'd been then—handsome, successful, and well thought of by all who knew him. And no wonder, when the Drake family owned so many businesses in Nashville. He was now the object of pursuit of nearly every unmarried woman in town, especially the wealthy ones. These women were regularly seen on Mr. Drake's arm at social gatherings.

Not that Maggie attended such events. Those invitations had ceased coming over three years ago. Which was about the time she'd given up the girlish dreams that no longer fit with her lowered place in society.

Most of the young men her age had been taken by the war, and those who had not had their pick of either wealthy widows or women younger than she, with far more promising assets.

"If the worst happens," her father continued, pulling her back to the moment, "if Bourbon Belle doesn't win . . . everything we have is scheduled to be sold at auction two weeks hence." His gaze moved beyond her to Belle. "Everything," he repeated quietly, as his focus trailed out the open double doors to their family home—a shadow of what it had once been.

"We'll need every penny we can manage in order to"—his voice broke, his composure faltering—"to secure a place in town."

In his eyes Maggie saw years of pain and disappointment well up. Her own throat tightened.

"I'm sorry it's come to this, Maggie." Hollowness filled his voice. "I wish I could change it. I've searched, I've prayed, I—"

"We're going to be fine, Papa. Don't you worry." Maggie forced a bright countenance to veil what felt like a lie, even though she wanted to believe it. "Belle will win, and we'll get another extension. I'll call on Mr. Drake myself this time."

Is this how her friend Savannah Darby had felt when she'd lost her family's land only months ago? Along with their home and the majority of their belongings? And Savannah was on her own besides, with two younger siblings to care for. Maggie had held her friend as Savannah wept, thinking she understood. But she hadn't.

Until now.

So many fine families, once landed gentry, first families of Nashville's settlement nearly a century ago, now near destitute.

Her father leaned down and gave Bucket's head a gentle rub. "I've already spoken with a woman at a boardinghouse. We'll need to stay there. Only temporarily," he added, straightening again, "until we find something suitable."

By suitable Maggie knew he meant affordable. The concern in his expression caused a tightening in her chest. Not wishing to add to his worry, she managed a weak nod. Yet the looming possibility of losing Linden Downs tore at something deep inside her.

It wasn't that she loved the land itself so much, although she did feel an affinity for it, especially the bluff that overlooked the river in the distance. She appreciated that the near four hundred acres had been in the Linden family since Nashville's settlement. Land that her grandfather had farmed, along with his only son, and after that her father and his sons. Land that—except for the small garden they still tended—had lain fallow for the past two years.

And yet, her own love for Linden Downs—guilt nipped her conscience—was slightly less altruistic. She wanted to save the family land for her father, yes, because it meant so much to him. But mostly she was fighting to keep it because without Linden Downs, *her* dream was dead.

As was her chance to prove—if not to her mother, then to others, maybe even to herself—that a woman really could ride, race, and win—and still be a lady.

In the past she'd tried to imagine her mother peering down from heaven and smiling as her only daughter rode the fields, jumping fences and creeks and anything else in her path. But Maggie gradually accepted that the daydream was only a foolish attempt to fill a void that could only be filled with a mother's pride. Which was an impossible wish.

But regardless of that, she *had* to keep this land. She couldn't raise thoroughbreds, much less train them to race, while living in a boardinghouse. She needed to be here, near Belle Meade and Uncle Bob. She loved the land because it allowed her to keep Bourbon Belle.

And as it turned out, Bourbon Belle was going to be the answer to keeping both the land and her dream. *If* Belle won the Peyton Stakes.

She looked over to find her father still, his eyes closed, his grip tight on the pitchfork. "Papa . . . are you sure you're all right?"

He blinked. "Yes . . . yes, I'm fine."

A thought occurred to her. "If you don't feel well enough to go to Burns Island for the race this week, then maybe I—"

"I'll be there. I wouldn't miss it." He looked at her as though peering over his reading spectacles. "Besides, you know how the club members feel about women poking around in their business."

"If I made excuses, perhaps—"

"I said I'll be there. Like I always am."

Maggie nodded, grateful, but wishing the all-male members of Nashville's Thoroughbred Society would be more open-minded.

On the ledgers her father was listed as the owner and trainer of Bourbon Belle, and he officially entered Belle in the races. The men in the club had never questioned him about it, and their not knowing the truth didn't bother Maggie. Much. But those closest to her knew.

And while her father was supportive of her aspirations, she wondered deep down if he would've preferred her to have chosen a different path for her life. But she was meant for this.

She'd felt that affirmation yet again as she'd ridden Belle on the outskirts of town that morning.

Her father moved to the next stall, and Bucket followed obediently.

Aware of the hour slipping away, Maggie glanced out the window again, her annoyance slipping into concern. Where was Willie?

The boy loved time with Belle as much as Maggie enjoyed teaching him. He was a natural, as Uncle Bob had said so many times. Thin and wiry of build, Willie, nine years old as of last month, was like a feather astride Bourbon Belle, and together horse and rider sped like a bullet around the track.

Other thoroughbred owners had tried to talk Willie into riding for them, but the boy told them he wouldn't ride any other than Belle, or for anyone other than Miss Maggie. She appreciated his loyalty and rewarded him accordingly.

"I read the most recent letter from Mrs. Watson."

Maggie turned at her father's voice.

"You left it on the table." He offered a shrug. "So I assumed—"

"It's fine." She nodded. "You're always welcome to read them."

"It was kind," he continued, "what she wrote about you. She's grown quite fond of you through the years, you know."

Maggie offered more smile than she felt. "As I have of her."

"I'm proud of you for continuing to keep in touch with her despite her moving to South Carolina. Other young women whose beaus died in the war have quickly forgotten and moved on." He laughed softly. "Hard to believe you were only fifteen at the time."

"Mrs. Watson had no one else here in town, and"—Maggie briefly bowed her head—"I had promised Richard. Now his mother is happily situated with her sister on the beaches of Charleston. He would have liked that."

After a long silence her father returned to his task, and she did likewise.

She drew the curry brush over Belle's coat with smooth, practiced strokes, trying to recall the details of Richard's countenance as she'd seen him that very last time, going on five years ago now, only days before the Battle of Franklin. But all she could recall was the portrait of him Birdette Watson had kept on the mantel.

That, and how he looked as a boy standing by the creek with a fishing pole in his grip.

Mrs. Watson had lost her husband and only son in the same battle. How was it that some women grieved and yet moved on with their lives, while others, like her own mother—Maggie felt a sting at the memory—were weighted down by the severity of it, until they finally succumbed?

Apparently the daughter who remained hadn't been enough to sustain her following the loss of her sons. The thought pricked at an old wound, and for the thousandth time Maggie wondered what she could have done to have been more for her mother.

Or at least to have been enough.

Yet it was a futile thread at which to pick, she knew, so she tucked it back beneath the blanket of memories.

She hoped her new riding students proved promising. One of the girls had apparently not ridden a horse since being thrown some years earlier, which didn't bode well for today's first riding lesson. Yet the best way to beat a fear was to face it.

Maggie had learned that well enough through the years.

She stood back to admire her work. Belle's coat shone a deep reddish brown, the color of the whiskey Maggie's grandfather used to bring out on special occasions. When Belle was born, her father had commented on the likeness of the smooth amber color, and the mare's name had swiftly been decided.

Recalling Belle's birth and what hopes they'd had back then made Maggie think of the land again, and she sighed.

After the war, she'd thought life might gradually take an upward turn. But it hadn't. Another war had simply taken the former's place. One fought not with cannons or guns or bayonets but with bullets just the same, relentless and aimed at the heart.

Empty places at tables, never to be filled again. Fields lying fallow beneath the hot summer sun. Brokenness everywhere a person turned. Northerners soon arrived and started buying up the land, moving into deserted shops to sell their overpriced goods. Foreigners swiftly followed.

When she went into town these days, she scarcely heard English being spoken. She heard German and Italian in abundance. Then there were the Irish, who supposedly used the King's English. But not very well, from what she'd overheard. They were a lazy and violent lot, given to heavy drink and wantonness. At least that's what she read in the newspapers.

And in what part of heaven was it acceptable for a foreigner to come in and—for only pennies on the dollar—buy up farmland that had been cleared, tamed, and tended by the same family for nearly a hundred years? It wasn't right.

And she determined again not to let that happen to Linden Downs.

Movement from beyond the open barn doorway caught her attention, and Maggie looked up. A sigh of relief escaped. "Finally . . ."

It was Willie, still some distance away. And bless the boy's heart, he was running full out. He probably felt bad about being late and was—

Maggie stilled, squinting, certain that what she thought she saw couldn't be.

But as Willie came closer, the tears streaking his face came into focus, as did the blood soaking his shirt and trousers.

Chapter THREE

"Willie!" Maggie called, running to meet him, her father following with Bucket at his heels. "What happened? Are you all right?" She knelt by the corral and touched the boy's head then inspected his face, neck, chest. His breath came staggered. No cuts, no injuries that she could see. Yet blood stained his shirt and pants.

Her father knelt beside them, his breath almost as labored as the boy's.

"They kilt—" Willie hiccuped a sob, fear in his eyes. "They kilt him, Miss Maggie. Strung him up." He bit his lower lip, but a cry still slipped past. "Right there . . . in front of the shanties."

"Who, Willie?" Maggie's voice came out firm, steeled with fear over how the boy might respond. "*Who* was killed?"

"M-Mister Rawl . . . Man who lived next door to us." Willie shuddered. "They beat my pa, too, when he tried to stop 'em. Beat him bad."

Maggie's father slipped an arm around the boy's shoulders. "Who did this, Willie? Do you know?"

The boy shook his head. "Ain't got no names. Their heads, they was covered up like ghosts. Mama say Missus Rawl kept screamin'." He closed his eyes as though trying to block out the memory. "Her husband was just hangin' there. Swingin' back and forth."

Maggie cradled his cheek in her palm, and Willie's thin shoulders shook.

"When did this happen?" her father asked, the quiet of his voice belying the anger in his expression.

"Early this mornin', sir. I weren't there. I's gone to the store." Willie drew back, his lips trembling. "To spend the pay you give me last night, Miss Maggie. I's buyin' the things from Mama's list. But then when I get home I saw—" His face crumpled again.

"Come on into the house," Maggie urged, rising. "We'll get you cleaned up."

Willie resisted. "No, Miss Maggie. I can't. Mama says I got to get right back." He looked first at her father then back at her. "We's leavin' here, ma'am."

The blow of his statement landed square in Maggie's midsection. "What?" she whispered. "Leaving town?"

"I's sorry, ma'am. I am. But my mama says we done had enough of this. Papa said it too. Them men that did it—" Willie sniffed. "They said they's comin' back. They say this town don't want us niggers livin' here no more, Miss Maggie."

He looked up at her with eyes so full of innocence, yet tarnished by evil.

Forcing herself to think of the boy and his family instead of her own situation and the fate of Linden Downs, Maggie felt a jab of shame that it took some effort. "When are you leaving, Willie?"

He bowed his head. When he finally looked up, she saw the answer to her question.

"If Papa's able, they say we goin' first thing come mornin'," he whispered, as if saying it softly might ease the blow. "We headin' north, ma'am. To some place called Chicago. Other families, they goin' with us. I's sorry, Miss Maggie." He grimaced. "I don't want to, but—"

"Shhhh . . ." Seeing his renewed tears, she patted his back then let out a gasp as his thin arms came tight around her waist. She stared down, not knowing what to do. In the past year of working with Willie day in and day out, never once had she touched him. Nor he her. Not like this. And it felt . . . awkward, to say the least.

Yet, hearing his sobs . . .

Maggie gently cradled his head. "You have to do what's right for your family, Willie," she heard herself say. "Do what keeps you all safe."

Based on recent events—the burning of freedmen's schools, the midnight raids on shanties huddled at the edge of town—keeping safe was becoming next to impossible. But this . . . in broad daylight. These acts of violence were growing bolder.

Willie looked up. "Papa says we wouldn't even have money to go if not for you payin' me like you do, Miss Maggie."

The irony wasn't lost on her. "Your parents want what's best for you and your sisters." She met her father's gaze. "That's what Mr. Linden and I want too."

Willie's focus shifted from her to the stable then back again. Understanding his silent request, Maggie nodded, the scene he'd described still crowding her mind. The violence, the hatred.

So much blood had already been spilled over this issue, and yet it only seemed to get worse. Brutality escalating to a degree that made her want to run at the merest mention of it, even as something deep inside her, something she couldn't begin to understand, much less explain, demanded that she not.

She looked over at her father to find him kneeling beside Bucket, staring out across the land as though taking it in for the very last time.

Which, she guessed, was close to the truth.

⁂

Passing the entrance to the farm, the last on his list, Cullen glanced at the modest wooden shingle that at one time had likely borne the name of the estate. The rocks from the limestone walls that had once bordered the property, so common in this countryside, lay in ruins in the dirt, weeds long since having made their home in the cracks and crevices.

On a whim he nudged the Percheron off the main road, deciding he wanted to see the land before the house or anything else. Although he doubted this meeting would prove any more successful than the two he'd just come from.

As it turned out, the properties he'd visited earlier—properties listed as being for sale in that very morning's paper—were apparently not available after all. He gave a sharp exhale, knowing what each owner had meant when they'd told him, "I've decided not to sell."

They just wouldn't sell to *him*.

Wondering if he would have to move on after all, to find land in another area, he continued across the grassy meadow until he happened upon a well-worn path tucked alongside a creek. It seemed to beckon, and he nudged the Percheron to follow.

The fine animal needed a name. Goliath was out of the running, to be sure, not only because of what had happened in town earlier but because Cullen knew the fate of one certain giant who'd borne that moniker. Defeated by a mere lad, and with a slingshot and stone, no less.

No, this kingly beast deserved a nobler name.

The beauty of the woods—the canopies of oak and pine stretching overhead, the sunlight sneaking past poplars and maples, the trickle of water over smooth rock—was intoxicating and formed a perfect accompaniment to the quiet of late afternoon.

I have read of a place called Tennessee, Cullen. In the New World. They say its hills are as green as those of home.

Cullen's grip tightened on the reins. It had been Moira's dream to come here, not his. She'd spoken of it oft enough. But he'd told her time and again they could make a life together in England, despite the lack of welcome.

When she finally stopped bringing it up in conversation, she began praying about it, which had worried him far more. Because once Moira McGrath began seeking the Father's face on something, it was pretty much determined. In the end God had listened to his wife, and rightly so. For a godlier woman no man would find. Why she'd loved him, Cullen didn't know. And hadn't questioned. He'd just been grateful.

But when the scandal had broken and Ethan fled, leaving him alone to give answer, Cullen finally listened to her, and they left.

But he wondered . . .

If he'd heeded her advice earlier, if they'd left England before all that happened, would she and Katie still be alive? Would God have still exacted such a price?

Up ahead the woods opened in welcome to another meadow, and through the filtered light Cullen spotted something. A man standing—nay, kneeling—beneath an ancient oak, a dog close beside.

Cullen slowed the Percheron's gait. Surprised to find someone out here, he squinted in the dappled sunlight, and that's when he saw the graves.

Seven in all, lined neatly in a row, rough-hewn wooden markers silently, boldly staking their victory.

He reined in, no more than twenty feet away, watching.

The man, his head bowed, shoulders stooped, never turned as he stood, moved a couple of steps, then knelt again, going from one grave to the next. The dog followed suit.

Something about the man's posture felt uncannily familiar, recalling the tang of salt in the air, the lap of angry waves against the hull of the ship, the heaviness in his own chest. Shaking off the memory, Cullen held the reins taut, not wanting to intrude on the moment but unable to continue on.

Finally the man rose then went perfectly still, his gaze warily fixed in Cullen's direction.

Cullen urged the horse forward then dismounted. "Good day to you, sir," he said, taking a slow approach.

The older gentleman—well into his sixties, Cullen guessed—gave the dog a pat on the head and whispered something to it, then gave the Percheron a thorough going-over before focusing on Cullen again. "For a moment there, I thought I was seeing Alexander the Great astride his magnificent Bucephalus."

The subtle humor in the man's voice, combined with his deep Southern drawl, coaxed a smile from Cullen. "Not even close to the truth, sir. Just an Irishman enjoying your lovely woods."

"They are most certainly that." The man peered up, his expression absent of judgment. "As my father always told anyone who would listen, that's why he and my mother chose this land. And if you think this is pretty, you should see the meadows by the house. Or the bluff overlooking the river." His humor faded. "In my estimation, it's the finest acreage in all of Tennessee."

Cullen nodded, allowing for bias in the man's opinion while also agreeing with his assessment. "It's fine land, to be sure."

Gauging how to proceed, Cullen's gaze fell upon the assembly of graves tucked beyond the seven he'd already seen, hidden from his earlier vantage point. The family cemetery. Beautiful setting, and neatly tended. Exactly what he would have chosen for Moira and Katie, if God had allowed him a choice.

Feeling the man's attention, he extended a hand. "Cullen McGrath is the name, sir."

The man's grip was firm but lacked the strength Cullen suspected it once had.

"Gilbert Linden, Mr. McGrath. Good to make your acquaintance."

"Fine to meet you, Mr. Linden. I'm sorry if I gave you a start just now."

The man shook his head. "That's what I get for reading the classics before retiring. I see them in my dreams. Both sleeping and waking, apparently."

An educated man, Cullen noted, yet he tried not to attach too much hope to that fact.

Mr. Linden gestured to the collie at his side. "This fine companion of mine is Bucket."

Bucket? Wondering at the name, Cullen leaned down, extended

a closed hand, and let the dog sniff him. The collie's brown eyes warmed, and the animal licked his hand. Mr. Linden chuckled, obviously pleased.

Cullen took it as a good sign.

"So tell me, Mr. McGrath . . . What is an Irishman such as yourself doing wandering my lovely woods?"

No accusation weighted the question, only curiosity. "I was on my way to pay the owner of this farm a visit. Which, as it turns out . . ." He gestured then let the sentence fall away.

Gilbert Linden said nothing, holding his gaze and proving himself a patient man, if not a bit intimidating, despite his standing a head shorter. Reminded Cullen of the way his grandfather used to look at him when the man knew he'd done something wrong.

Quickly remembering how he'd found Mr. Linden, Cullen gestured to the graves, able now to read the names and dates carved into the various wooden markers. The marker farthest left bore the name *Laurel Agnes Linden* and the inscription *Heart of my own heart* carved beneath. Looking to the right, Cullen read six names, one after the other, all male, and all with various dates of birth.

But four claimed the same month and year of passing. *December 1864.* "I'm so sorry for your losses, Mr. Linden."

Linden's gaze trailed the grave sites. "Are you well acquainted with grief, Mr. McGrath?" he asked without looking back.

So blunt a question, and intimate, from someone he didn't know. Yet Cullen found himself responding. "Aye, sir, I am. Though . . . not as well as you."

Linden took in a breath, held it, then slowly exhaled, and Cullen would've sworn the woods around them did the same.

"You've lost a child then?" Linden said softly.

"Aye," Cullen whispered.

"A son?"

The memory of Katie's birth resurfaced, as did the first time she'd ever called him da, and it took Cullen a moment to find his voice. He shook his head. "My daughter was three. She died with her ma."

Seconds passed before the older man reached over and placed a hand on Cullen's shoulder.

"I used to think the heart could be broken only once, Mr. McGrath, and that after that it would somehow be easier to bear life's pains. But in truth, losing those you love is a little like falling on the same bruise over and over and over again." Linden swallowed, the sound audible in the quiet. "The pain goes deeper each time. Deeper than you thought it could, and than you ever thought you could bear. And yet"—a flicker of light slipped in behind the sadness—"you can, and you do. And although life is never the same again, you find happiness again too. With the Lord's mercy, of course."

Linden gave his shoulder a fatherly squeeze, but Cullen looked away.

"You don't believe in his mercy?"

"I believe if he were as merciful as people said, he would answer a man's humble question when asked."

Linden nodded slowly, regarding him. "He's disappointed me on that count, too, son. Many a time."

Cullen looked back.

"Don't hear me saying the deficiency is with him, Mr. McGrath. But I do understand what it's like to lay a petition before him only to have it ignored . . . time and again." He looked back at the graves.

The lamenting coo of a mourning dove floated toward them from deep within the dense woods.

"And yet . . . you still choose to trust, sir."

The older man smiled. "Let's just say that as I've gotten older, I've learned that there's always a conversation going on. It's just me who's sometimes stubborn of hearing." His gaze lowered. "Either that or I simply don't like the direction the conversation has taken."

With a somewhat sadder smile, Linden moved away.

Cullen's mind awash in memory, he looked again at the graves and felt a kinship with this man. But not of anything having to do with the Lord's mercy.

Eventually he lifted his face and saw Mr. Linden leaving, Bucket in tow. Then the man paused and looked back. Reading invitation in the gesture, Cullen followed, leading the horse behind him.

He caught up easily and fell into step with the older man. "Mr. Linden, I have a question I'd like to—"

"You're here about the land." Linden didn't look at him when he spoke.

"Aye, sir. I am."

"You read about the auction in the newspaper and figured you might come and offer me a deal beforehand. Hoping to get it at a greatly discounted price, would be my guess."

Cullen caught the first hint of displeasure in the man's demeanor and felt the door of opportunity closing. "No, Mr. Linden, that's not true at all. But I would appreciate the chance to talk with you about—"

The crack of a whip followed by a primal scream tore Cullen's focus from the man beside him, raising the hair on the back of his neck.

On a road that ran alongside the meadow, two men flanked an enclosed wagon, yelling at each other and at whatever was inside. One of them brandished a whip. A ramp extended from the back of the conveyance, and Cullen had a good idea what the wagon held. Especially seeing the rectangular windows cut out along the top.

The man with the whip cracked it again, and a second scream rent the air. The mares pulling the wagon tried to bolt, but the wheel brake canceled the effort.

"Those foolish, ignorant—" Gilbert Linden firmed his mouth.

But Cullen was already astride the Percheron.

Chapter Four

The Percheron ate up the distance like Leviathan slicing through the ocean waves. Cullen reined in at the road and dismounted, the horse's massive hooves sending rocks and dust flying.

The man wielding the whip raised it a third time, but Cullen plowed into him and sent him sprawling.

The fellow looked up, his face going red. "What in the—"

Cullen dragged him up by the collar and squeezed the man's fist until he cried out and dropped the whip. Then Cullen brought him close. "*Never* use anythin' on a horse you wouldn't want used on yourself."

Cullen shoved him back hard then bent to retrieve the whip, sending the other man a look of warning. Apparently somewhat brighter than his partner, the second man backed away, hands raised in truce.

"We was only tryin' to get him out, mister. Somethin' spooked him, and he keeps kickin' the wall. General's gonna have our hides if that horse is all cut up."

"If that horse *is* injured . . ." Out of breath, Gilbert Linden joined them, his face drained of color, and the collie, ever loyal, sticking close. "I'll make certain he knows who's at fault."

Cullen hesitated, concerned by the older man's pallor. "Are you all right, sir?"

Linden waved him off. "I'm fine. Just . . . a little winded, that's all."

Not fully convinced, Cullen handed him the whip then moved around to the back of the wagon, careful to keep a safe distance from the ramp. One look inside told him he'd guessed correctly, but also told him the situation was worse than he'd thought.

The stallion—magnificent, even at a glance—was tethered to the front of the wagon. So each time the thoroughbred reared, his fetlocks scraped the wood. From where he stood, Cullen spotted blood.

"Easy, boy," he whispered, inching closer, sizing up his options.

The stallion bucked, doing a better than fair job of showing what damage a single kick from his massive hindquarters could render. Cullen recalled as a boy seeing a man get his head kicked in. He'd died instantly. Here one second, in eternity the next. Cullen would never forget it.

He moved to the window on the far side where it was just him and the stallion. "You're strong and courageous, boy." He spoke softly. "I can see that." The horse watched him from above, the whites of his eyes pronounced in the dim light of the trailer.

"What's his name?" Cullen called out.

"What does it matter?" The man who'd held the whip rounded the corner, revenge in his eyes. "They can't understand things any more than I'm guessin' your kind can—"

His patience gone, Cullen landed a blow to the man's rib cage. Not even that hard, but the fellow dropped like a gunnysack at harvest.

Cullen stood over him. "What's *your* name, you sorry piece of—" Seeing Mr. Linden from the corner of his eye, Cullen dispensed with the remaining pleasantries. Working the Brooklyn docks had stolen so much of the good Moira had planted within him.

"Your name," Cullen said again.

"Grady," the man ground out, still holding his belly. "Grady Matthews."

"And whose stallion would this be?" Cullen asked.

"The horse belongs to General William Giles Harding," Mr. Linden supplied, joining them. "Of Belle Meade Plantation." He motioned to the land on the other side of the road. "And this man here knows full well the general doesn't hold to whipping horses. Nor does the general's head hostler."

Neither the name of the man nor the estate sounded familiar to Cullen, but if this General William Giles Harding didn't hold to whips, the man was already a step up from the hoopleheads.

Grady Matthews's partner approached. "The horse's name is Bonnie Scotland, sir. He arrived this mornin' by train."

Cullen couldn't help but stare. Bonnie Scotland. It couldn't be. He peered back up into the window only to find the thoroughbred staring back.

He'd seen a horse by the name of Bonnie Scotland chase the

wind—and win—another lifetime ago in England. But how long had that been now? Thirteen years? Fourteen? He'd been not a boy anymore, yet not quite a man, when his family had been forced to move from Ireland to England, and one of the first places his da had sought out had been the racetracks.

"What do you know about this horse?" Cullen asked, still watching the stallion.

"Only that they say he was somethin' back in the day," the same man answered. "Won a few races in England, I think."

Cullen smiled to himself, feeling as though he were looking at a piece of his past resurrected in the flesh, living and breathing right before him. "Bonnie Scotland made four starts at the age of three, after bein' injured the year before." He could still see it in his mind's eye. "He won the Liverpool Saint Leger, placin' fourth in the Great Yorkshire Stakes, then managed a second place dead heat at Doncaster. So, aye," Cullen laughed. "You might say he's won a few."

Maybe he was imagining it, but Cullen would've sworn he glimpsed acknowledgment in the stallion's eyes.

And to think he'd been reminded of this very thoroughbred earlier that morning when he'd seen the horse and rider across the river. That horse had moved with such speed and gracefulness, just like Bonnie Scotland had run back in the day.

"You two—" He motioned to Matthews and the other man. "Unhitch the mares and lead them a stone's throw down the road." He looked back at Bonnie Scotland. "No man likes to be afraid. Especially not in front of a woman."

Once they'd done as he bade—Grady Matthews begrudgingly, judging by the fellow's scowl—Cullen moved to stand at the end of the ramp.

Mr. Linden came alongside. "You're not going in there."

"Someone has to. Eventually. Besides . . ." He looked over at the man whom he already felt he knew better than everyone he'd known back in Brooklyn. "Haven't you ever come upon moments in life when you simply knew you were supposed to do something?"

Gilbert Linden didn't respond immediately. "Yes," he said quietly. "I've experienced such times."

Cullen shrugged in response then gestured for the older man to step aside. "But just in case he kills me . . . you can have my horse."

With nary a blink, Mr. Linden nodded. "Much obliged. I'll take good care of him too. What's his name?"

Sensing the man's seriousness behind the humor, Cullen glanced back at the Percheron—and knew. "Levi. It's short for—"

"Leviathan." Linden nodded, then whistled at the collie as it crept closer to the trailer. Bucket reluctantly returned. "It's from the Bible. Well chosen, Mr. McGrath."

Leviathan was from the Bible? Cullen took a deep breath, readying himself for what was ahead, even as he was heartened to find there was a bit of Moira left in him after all.

With the mares unhitched, he didn't have to worry about the wagon taking off with him inside. He had enough to worry about with the stallion alone. He moved to the side so Bonnie Scotland could see him unhindered. The stallion turned his head, watching as closely as Cullen was watching him.

Arms relaxed at his sides, yet with heart pounding, Cullen was careful not to match the horse's gaze as a predator would. Instead he looked down and away as he inched forward, watching the horse's hindquarters for any hint that he would buck.

"'Tis the last rose of summer . . ." He softly sang the ballad he'd known since childhood, as much to calm his own nerves as the thoroughbred's. "Left bloomin' alone . . . All her lovely companions . . . are faded and gone."

The horse reared and the trailer shook.

Cullen managed to keep his balance, but a rush shot through him as if he'd downed a pint of stout ale. Which didn't sound half bad at the moment. He waited before moving forward again, almost inside the trailer now.

"No flower of her kindred . . . No rosebud is nigh." Funny how a song his own ma had sung—and that he'd sung to his precious Katie—would return at such a moment. "To reflect back her blushes . . . or give sigh for sigh."

The thoroughbred struggled, straining against the tether, then bucked as Cullen had feared. But he was past those powerful hooves and inside now. Still, the animal could crush him if he had a mind to.

He couldn't believe he was standing this close to a horse he'd seen race all those years ago. "Liverpool Saint Leger," he whispered. "You ran that day like the champion you are."

Ever so slowly, so the stallion could see him, Cullen reached out and laid a hand on the thoroughbred's withers.

At once the stallion reared, then sidestepped, smashing Cullen into the wall. The back of his head connected with a thud, and pinpoints of light obscured his sight. He heard a voice in the distance, but it took a few seconds for the fog to clear.

"Mr. McGrath, are you all right? Can you hear me?"

With jarring pain spreading from ear to ear, Cullen finally realized who it was. "I'm fine, Mr. Linden," he said evenly. "Stay back."

Remaining perfectly still and keeping his hands to himself, Cullen took inventory. No injuries that he could tell. Just pain. But it would pass. For the longest time he stood unmoving, the tense silence a third companion in the crowded space.

Meanwhile, Bonnie Scotland snorted and pawed at the trailer floor.

"You and me both, boy," Cullen whispered. "I know what it's like to feel trapped." He sighed. It must have been around '57 or so, but he remembered reading in the newspaper about the sale of this thoroughbred to someone in America. "So you've been standin' stud all these years, I take it. Not a bad job all in all, I'm guessin'. Though I'm sure it gets tirin' from time to time."

The stallion looked back at him, and Cullen couldn't help but smile.

"You're safe now," he said softly, over and over, inching forward.

Hoping the stallion wasn't a biter, he untied the first tether, keenly aware of how massive this horse was. And how handsome. Not as enormous as Levi, but a full sixteen hands high to be sure. And with the longest shoulder, deepest heart-place, best forehand, shortest saddle-place, and the most powerful quarters of any thoroughbred he'd seen.

With the second tether free, Cullen held the lead rein. "I saw you beat Ellington that last day. You flew around that track. If not for the dirt you kicked up, I would've sworn your hooves never touched the earth."

The thoroughbred shook his head from side to side.

"Aye. You're free. And your new home awaits." What a comforting thought that was. *Home.* But also a lonely one when such a place didn't exist.

Cullen applied the slightest pressure with the lead rein, and the stallion backed out of the trailer as though they'd done that together a thousand times.

Half an hour later, with the mares again hitched to the wagon and a much calmer Bonnie Scotland tethered to trail behind, Cullen stood with Gilbert Linden and watched the wagon and prized stud pull away.

Grady Matthews glanced back, a cigar wedged between his teeth and challenge in his eyes. But Cullen had met his sort before. The type of man who thought far more of himself than he ought. The type of man other men enjoyed seeing put in his place. Especially when the putting was so rewarding.

The wagon disappeared around the bend.

"So . . ." Mr. Linden sighed. "I take it this means I don't get your horse."

Cullen laughed. "I think I'll be keepin' him for now, sir."

"He was a little nicked and scraped"—Linden's focus was still on the road—"but it wasn't nearly as bad as it could have been. And would have been, if you hadn't intervened."

"I was happy to do it. And would do it again . . . in another hundred years." Cullen strode to where Levi was grazing. "Mind if I water him at the creek?"

Linden gestured. "Not at all."

They walked the short distance, Bucket reaching the creek first, and as the collie and Percheron drank, Cullen knelt and splashed water on his own face and neck. He cupped his hands and drank to his fill, the water cool as it went down. "Truly a fine piece of land you have here, sir."

"Yes, it is. And I believe you had a question you wanted to ask me about it, Mr. McGrath."

Cullen rose to find the gentleman watching him. He hadn't intended for his statement to be interpreted as a springboard, but—

"Aye, sir. I do. You were right about me seein' your property listed in the newspaper as goin' to auction soon." He glanced away. "But you're mistaken about my reason for comin' to see you about it before that. The reason I'm here today is . . ." He hesitated.

"Go on," Linden said softly.

"Well, sir . . . In case you haven't noticed, I'm Irish. So I'm not allowed to bid, much less apply for any job in town. But I don't want a job in town. I want land. I want a farm. My da was a farmer until the famine wiped us out, along with everyone else. He moved the family to England, and there we made the best of it. But . . ." Cullen shook his head. "In the end, it wasn't where we were supposed to be."

"We," Linden repeated, question in his tone.

"Moira and me. And our Katie." Cullen bowed his head. "Typhoid.

On the voyage over. Moira passed one mornin' before sunrise, and Katie followed her that eve."

For the longest moment Linden regarded him, his expression inscrutable. "Walk with me."

As they made their way back across the field, Cullen listened as the man shared the history of the farm, what crops had been planted through the years and which had done best, along with how the farm had fallen into ruin after the war.

The field widened and up ahead, situated in a meadow, sat a white two-story farmhouse, a barn, a stable, and various outbuildings. Cullen paused to view the idyllic scene—the collie bounding toward home, a dairy cow grazing near the house, chickens pecking about the roost, and laundry drying in the breeze.

"Straight from a picture book," he whispered.

Linden laughed softly. "A touch of heaven, my friend." Grimacing, he took a sharp breath, and his shoulders pitched forward.

Cullen grabbed hold of his upper arm. "Sir—"

Linden lifted a shaky hand. "It will pass," he said, breathless. "I just . . . need a moment."

"Could I get somethin' for you?"

He shook his head, his face bathed in sweat. "Just . . . wait with me."

Moments passed, and with them whatever the trouble had been. Finally Linden breathed easier. He looked over at Cullen and smiled, though his grayish complexion wasn't reassuring. "Shall we journey the rest of the way?"

Cullen occasionally peered at him as they went, watching for signs of another episode. But as they drew closer to the house, the surroundings begged his attention, and the scene he'd considered so idyllic from a distance took on a slightly different cast.

The roof on the far side of the barn sagged with the passage of time, as did that of the stable, which was empty from what Cullen could see. Numerous plank wood boards forming the stable walls had bested the nails once driven through them and now pulled away in rebellion. The house, too, needed repair. Shutters on the second floor hung at dissonant angles to the windows, the railing along the front porch bowed outward, and in more places than not the white paint—long since defeated by relentless summer suns—had retreated to reveal the bare wood.

Still, even with all the maintenance it would require, Linden Downs was worth every penny Cullen had in his pocket. And more.

"I can see what you're thinking, Mr. McGrath."

Cullen realized the man had been watching him.

"You're thinking there's plenty of work to be done. And it's true. I can't do what I used to. After losing my sons, and after the slaves went free . . . well, that was the beginning of the end."

"I'm not afraid of hard work, Mr. Linden. Anythin' worth havin' is worth workin' hard for."

The squeak of ill-tempered hinges complained somewhere behind them, and Linden raised a hand in greeting.

"Cletus," he called out.

Cullen trailed his gaze and saw an ancient-looking man, shoulders stooped, gait measured, exiting the barn. He wore an old slouch hat, and at first glance Cullen would have thought him feeble if not for the cinder blocks he carried. One in each massive grip.

"Afternoon, Mister Linden," Cletus answered in a voice as deep and dark as the color of his skin. "You have yourself a good visit, sir?"

"Yes, I did." Linden paused briefly on the bottom porch step, the collie already waiting for him by the front door. "The last remnants of winter have been cleared away from the graves. Spring flowers will be making their way soon enough."

Cletus nodded, glancing at Cullen beneath the rim of his hat, then just as quickly looking away. "Miss Laurel, she was always partial to keepin' things in they place."

As Cletus passed, Cullen sensed a silent exchange between the men and felt certain Cletus was the one responsible for tending the graves. Just as he was certain Mr. Linden had been thanking him for it.

Cullen tethered Levi to a post and followed Mr. Linden inside.

He found the home neat and tidy with fine furnishings that, though showing their age, still had plenty of life in them. But no doubt Mr. Linden would take those with him when he left. It was a good-sized house, but how lonely it must be with the rest of his family gone on before.

They entered a small library whose book-lined shelves bore testimony to a man who treasured their company. Just as the handsome Sharps rifle hanging above the hearth—a pristine .52-caliber with extended barrel and breech loading mechanism—spoke to another of the man's admirations.

"Have a seat, Mr. McGrath."

Linden claimed the chair behind the desk while Bucket stretched out at his feet. Cullen took the chair opposite, trying not to let his hopes rise.

"As I said before, sir, I'm interested in buyin' your land. More than interested." He reached inside his jacket pocket and withdrew a thick leather pouch. "I'm prepared to offer cash."

A knock sounded on the door behind him, and Cullen paused as a woman carrying a tray entered the room. He laid the pouch on the desk.

"Mister Linden," she announced. "Some tea for you and your guest."

Despite being older, the woman served the hot tea with quick, efficient movements, and Cullen wondered if she was any relation to the gentleman he'd seen outside, Cletus. They were married, perhaps?

"Onnie, I—" Mr. Linden hesitated, then leaned close to whisper to her.

Almost before he drew away, the woman produced a folded piece of paper and emptied its powdery contents into Mr. Linden's cup, then stirred. Cullen watched as the briefest meeting of their eyes conveyed both thanks and acknowledgment.

So different, these people.

He was accustomed to saying what he thought and showing what he felt. But that seemed unwelcome here. Even looked down upon. No matter what anyone said, he preferred his own way of things. It was cleaner. Clearer. Even if it did lead to arguments on occasion. He and Moira had had their share of going at it. But oh, the making up part. That had been sweeter than anything he'd imagined.

He missed her closeness. Her touch. Knowing her womanly ways as he had. And her, in turn, knowing him.

A good while after she'd passed, he'd found himself looking upon other women and responding to their overlong glances, to the way the bolder ones would lean close and offer him a generous view of what was cinched beneath tightly fitted bodices.

Yet he'd not been with a woman since Moira, no matter how much at times he desired to. He wouldn't tarnish her memory that way. Not after what they'd shared.

The closing of a door brought him back to the moment. Onnie had left, and Mr. Linden held a cup aloft. "Shall we?"

Cullen drank from the delicate china cup, finer than anything he'd been able to buy Moira. The tea was strong and pungent with an herb he didn't recognize, but liked.

"You know your thoroughbreds, don't you, Mr. McGrath?"

"I grew up on a farm. So aye, sir. I know horses. And as I said before, my da was fond of the track. Too much so. And of gamblin'. Not a good union, those two."

"I agree with you. Though horse racing can be a lucrative business for some. General Harding, for instance. The man whose thoroughbred you rescued earlier."

Cullen stared, feeling a stir of caution.

"He owns Belle Meade Plantation and Stud." Linden smiled. "Which encompasses the fifty-three hundred acres south of here and the finest stable of racing thoroughbreds you'll find in the southern United States. Once he learns about what you did for him today, I'm certain he'll want to show his appreciation."

Cullen shifted in his seat. "There's really no call for that, sir. What I did, I did for the horse, not for the man." And the last thing he needed was a connection to thoroughbred racing.

With a faint smile Mr. Linden reached for a piece of paper and pen and wrote something down, then angled the page Cullen's direction. "This is my asking price for Linden Downs."

Cullen read the figure. Then read it again. Fifteen hundred dollars? Why, he had nearly twice that in his pouch and had been prepared to offer most of it. But Linden's asking price didn't make sense. The newspaper listing indicated the property was worth well over three thousand. "I don't understand, sir. I've seen every farm—either on paper or in person—that's for sale in this area, and your land is worth—"

"More than that. Yes, that's my opinion as well."

"So why are you pricin' it for so much less? Surely you'd fetch more than that at the auction, if it comes to that."

Linden gave him a thoughtful look. "If you'll allow me, Mr. McGrath, there's a . . . stipulation I'm adding to the sale."

Stipulation? Now Cullen's curiosity was thoroughly piqued. "And what would that be?"

Linden leaned forward. "You're a good man, Cullen McGrath. I raised four sons. Fine, true, and strong, every one of them. So I can read a man's character. And as my daughter says—"

"You have a daughter?"

Mirth lit the man's eyes. "Indeed I do. Margaret is my youngest child, as well as my only remaining kin."

"Seein' you today at the cemetery, sir, and with what you said about your sons earlier, I—" Cullen attempted to soften the words. "I assumed you'd buried all your children."

"All but one. And she is most dear to me, as I'm sure you understand."

"Aye," Cullen said softly.

"As I was saying . . . my daughter, Margaret, says that horses see things in people that we often miss. Much as dogs do." Linden leaned down and stroked the collie's head. "Has your experience taught you the same?"

The man's line of thought had his curiosity in knots, but agreeing with the daughter's conclusion, Cullen nodded.

"One final question for you, Mr. McGrath, then I'll tell you the stipulation. Is there anything you would not have done to save your daughter?"

Having asked—and answered—that question a thousand times over, Cullen responded without hesitation. "No, sir. I would have given my very life in exchange for hers. And for my wife's."

Understanding shaded the older man's expression. "My own heart's desire as well, Mr. McGrath. And hearing that it's yours makes me even more certain of my course." With a faint smile, he leaned forward again. "The amount I wrote down is the debt of taxes currently owed on my farm, including interest, plus a loan I took out to help us through the past two years. Pay that, which will bring Linden Downs back into right standing, and the land and everything on it—the house, the outbuildings, what animals there are, everything is yours . . . provided you agree to marry my daughter."

Chapter FIVE

Maggie!"

Hearing her name, Maggie looked toward Mary Harding's house and saw her friend standing on the edge of the lawn. "Father would like to speak with you before you leave."

Maggie cringed. She was eager to return home and see to her own father, who'd promised to rest for the afternoon, but she knew she had no choice. When General William Giles Harding requested one's presence, the only response was, "Thank you, I'll be right there."

Turning back, she found Martha Blankenship, the mother of her newest pupil, Lucy, descending from the carriage, reticule in hand.

"Thank you, Miss Linden, for agreeing to work with my daughter. I fear she can be rather dramatic at times."

"It's I who am grateful, ma'am, for your trust." Maggie sneaked a look at the young girl already seated inside the carriage. She could still make out the girl's red-rimmed eyes. "Our lesson went well, considering this was her first time back on a horse. With time and experience, I'm confident she'll warm up to them again."

"I sincerely hope you're right, Miss Linden. That you were able even to get her on the horse was a huge feat!" Mrs. Blankenship pressed the money into her hand. "There's a little extra for your trouble. And for your patience. Same appointment next week?"

Maggie nodded. She'd sincerely enjoyed her lesson with the woman's daughter. Lucy Blankenship, eleven years old, was petite for her age, and even the smallest mare at Belle Meade dwarfed her lithe frame. A challenge to which Maggie could relate.

As the carriage pulled away, young Lucy leaned out the window and waved, and it did Maggie's heart good to see her smile.

She hurried up the walkway to the mansion, her thoughts returning to Willie and his family. She couldn't get the scene he'd described out of her mind. Sometimes it seemed the world was coming apart at the seams. All the hatred, the violence. Would Willie's family ever find a place free of such trouble?

As she neared the front steps, her gaze drifted upward over the massive limestone columns—six in all—that framed the front of the home. She knocked on the partially open door, glancing upward. The transom above was fitted with ruby glass that likely cost more than her entire house at Linden Downs.

"Mary?" She peered inside.

Having been friends with Mary Harding since they were girls, Maggie still felt comfortable at Belle Meade, even while being keenly aware of the ever-widening gap between her own station in life and Mary's.

"Come on in, silly!" Her friend appeared from around the corner. "Father's in his office." Mary linked arms with her. "How were your riding pupils today?"

"Everyone did well, for the most part. I do appreciate your father allowing me to conduct the sessions here." She hoped that wasn't what General Harding wanted to talk to her about. Not only did she no longer have saddle horses, but the stables and corral at Linden Downs didn't come close to matching the amenities of Belle Meade.

"Have you spoken with Savannah this week?" Mary asked, lowering her voice.

Maggie shook her head.

"I saw her in town earlier today." Mary opened the door leading to a side porch and to the entrance of her father's office, then paused just outside. "She heard someone bought their family home at a recent auction."

Maggie felt a pang of empathy. "Does she know who it is? Or if it's someone local?"

Mary shook her head. "But I was thinking we could get together, the three of us. Maybe go into town for lunch one day next week. An attempt to cheer her up. My treat," Mary added quickly, as if reading Maggie's mind.

Maggie gave her hand a quick squeeze. "You're sweet, Mary, but I'm not comfortable with you paying for me."

She knew Savannah shared her feelings about the disparity between Mary's situation and her own, even though they both loved Mary and her family.

In light of the upcoming auction of Linden Downs, Savannah had written the kindest note last week, and Maggie appreciated every word of encouragement and reassurance . . . while still praying for a way out.

"Why don't the two of you come to my house instead?" she continued. "Onnie will be happy to prepare a luncheon for us."

"Well, as long as it's Onnie doing the cooking, and not you." Mary gave her friend a playful nudge.

"Mary? Is that you? Is Miss Linden with you?"

Hearing General Harding's voice through the closed door, Maggie quickly sobered. "Why does your father want to speak with me?" she whispered.

Mary shrugged, then grinned. "Good luck!"

The door opened before Maggie could respond.

"Miss Linden!" General Harding motioned her inside. "Please have a seat. This won't take long."

Maggie did as invited, finding her surroundings—and this man—rather intimidating. She reminded herself not to stare at his beard, which nearly reached the waistband of his trousers. He'd vowed not to shave it until the Confederacy won the war, and she wondered now if he would have that beard until he died.

She spotted a miniature portrait of Mrs. Harding on the general's desk and found it difficult to believe that this August would make two years since her passing.

"Miss Linden, I'll keep this brief." General Harding eased into the leather chair behind his desk. "Two of my workers experienced difficulty in transporting a most expensive thoroughbred from the train station to Belle Meade this morning. A gentleman came to their aid and rescued the blood horse—as well as my investment," he added with a humorless laugh. "I'm determined to discover the name of this gentleman so I can thank him properly, and was told he was in the company of your father."

"My father? But that's impossible. My father's been at home all day . . . resting."

He peered at her over steepled hands. "According to my men, who know your father, Miss Linden, he was on the turnpike to Belle Meade with this gentleman."

"I see." She tried not to let her frustration with her father bleed through. "I'll do my best to find out the gentleman's name."

"By week's end would be appreciated, Miss Linden."

He rose from his chair, so she followed suit.

"I trust that hosting your riding lessons here at Belle Meade is still a satisfactory arrangement?"

"Oh, yes, sir. Very much so. I'm grateful for your generosity in allowing me to use your facilities."

"I'm equally pleased that you're satisfied. And . . . that you're willing to help me with this little endeavor."

Hearing what he was saying, and what he wasn't, Maggie nodded.

He opened the door for her. "Is your father entering Bourbon Belle in the heat later this week?"

Maggie's thoughts went again to Willie and his family. "No. She won't be running this heat."

"Well . . . perhaps Belle Meade has a chance of winning then." General Harding's beard trembled when he laughed.

"Actually, our jockey is—" The images the boy had described returned in vivid detail. "He and his family have decided to move north. They're leaving this week."

"Oh . . ." The man quickly sobered. "I'm truly sorry to hear that. A good jockey is a rare find."

"You don't happen to know of any needing work, do you?"

"I don't at the moment. But I'll keep on the listen. Even if that does mean I'll have more competition on the track." His stare lengthened. "I don't suppose your father would be interested in selling Bourbon Belle, would he? I'd appreciate having such a fine filly sired by my own stallion Vandal."

While Maggie wasn't surprised at the man's proposal, the idea of parting with Belle made her heartsick. "You graciously purchased our stable of horses last year, General Harding. And I'm grateful for that. But no, sir. Bourbon Belle isn't for sale."

"Trust me, Miss Linden, there was nothing gracious about my gesture. I simply know fine horse flesh when I see it. As does your father, apparently. He's done a remarkable job with Bourbon Belle." Smiling, he offered a perfunctory nod. "Until the week's end then, Miss Linden. And give your father my best regards."

∞

Cullen was certain he'd misheard. "You want me to do what?"

Mr. Linden offered a look of patient understanding. "It's not that uncommon of an arrangement, Mr. McGrath. Certainly marriages in Ireland are decided upon, at least in part, by the parents of the couple?"

"Aye, but . . ." Cullen shot him a stare. "This . . . *stipulation,* as you call it. It's quite a ripper!"

"Yes, I realize that," Mr. Linden consented, his tone humble. "But I know from personal experience that a man and woman who scarcely know each other can join together and become as one. It doesn't happen in a day. It takes time and commitment, patience and forbearance, but it can happen."

Remembering what was inscribed on the wooden marker belonging to Linden's wife—*Heart of my own heart*—Cullen found he couldn't argue with the man's personal experience. But his and Moira's own coming together had been far different.

Almost from the moment he met her, he'd loved her. And she'd felt the same, though she hadn't told him until a good while later, sweet and shy as she'd been at first. Two months after meeting her, he'd asked her to marry him, and she'd accepted almost before he got the question out.

So marrying a complete stranger wasn't appealing. Not after what he'd known.

"As you've witnessed," Linden continued, "I am not a well man. Already I've surpassed my father's age when he died, as well as that of his father before him. So to say that I feel a pressing need to get my affairs in order is putting it lightly. I am most determined to make certain my daughter is provided for, Mr. McGrath."

"That I can understand, but—" Cullen found he could no longer stay seated. "Askin' *me* to marry her? A man she's never met, and that you yourself have only this day made as an acquaintance?" Cullen laughed at the absurdity. "You don't know me, Mr. Linden. I could be anybody. A blackguard, a scoundrel. A rogue, even."

Linden peered up at him, shades of humor in his expression. "You're no blackguard or scoundrel, Cullen McGrath. Although I would find it believable that you possessed some . . . roguelike qualities in your past. But I think those traits have been tamed—to a great degree, I suspect, by your late wife." He spoke the words softly. "And perhaps even by your precious daughter. Becoming a father changes a man. It brings into focus what's truly important in life. As does the love of a good woman."

Linden's words struck a chord within Cullen. Still, he had to make the man see reason. "I have a temper, sir. You've already been witness to that. Surely that's not a trait you desire in your daughter's husband."

"I witnessed righteous anger today, Mr. McGrath. Anger at injustice. That's something to be affirmed, not ashamed of. I want to know that after I'm gone my daughter will still be protected, along with the farm. Her future is tied to this land in a way she doesn't even understand right now. But you do. You know the importance of owning land. And I'm convinced you're more than capable of protecting both."

Cullen thought he heard something the man wasn't saying outright. "Have you had trouble on your land, sir?"

The rhythmic ticktock of a clock counted off the seconds as the question hung between them.

"In a manner of speaking. It started about two years back. I was approached at that time by someone requesting that an old hunting cabin on my property—a plot of land that borders the Belle Meade Plantation—be donated for use as a freedmen's school. I agreed. But not long after, someone set fire to the building . . . with the teacher and the freedmen—men, women, and children—inside. They managed to escape, though not without injury."

Cullen listened, questions springing to mind. But he'd learned long ago that being a patient listener had its rewards.

"Following that"—Linden sipped his tea—"certain things would go missing from time to time. Animals, mostly pigs and chickens. I reasoned that a wolf could have gotten them." He frowned. "Then farming equipment began disappearing too. However, it's been quiet in recent months. Probably because there's so little left to take, or maybe . . . since I'm about to lose it all anyway."

"You don't know who was responsible for the fire? Or for the theft?"

Linden shook his head. "But many others have suffered far worse than we have, even with the challenges that lie before us now."

The man's gaze moved to a window overlooking the meadow they'd just traversed, and Cullen sensed he'd been speaking of someone he knew.

A moment passed before Linden spoke again. "The time is coming, Mr. McGrath, and in fact is already upon us, when a man will have to boldly stand for what he believes, or everything he holds dear will be taken from him. And from those he loves. I don't want my daughter facing that kind of world alone."

Moved by the man's statement and the depth of his love for his daughter, Cullen rubbed the taut muscles at the base of his neck. He wanted this land. It was within his grasp, he could feel it. But to marry in order to get it . . .

A late afternoon breeze drifted through the open window along with the chirrup of a lone cricket getting an early start on evening.

"Sir, I know you've seen the signs in town: NO IRISH NEED APPLY. My people aren't accepted here. As my wife, your daughter would no longer be accepted either. She'd be an outcast. Is that what you want for her?"

For the first time Linden winced and bowed his head, and Cullen could see his arguments were finally getting through.

"My daughter's station in life has already fallen far below what it once was, Mr. McGrath. And though I have known the pain of losing children in death, there is a special pain in seeing your child's life become shackled, pared down. To see her choices, her future . . . stripped from her, piece by piece."

Cullen exhaled. So much for getting the man to see his side of things. He could feel Linden watching him, willing him to say yes, but he just couldn't see his way through the fog of it all.

"I'm sorry, Mr. Linden, but I can't do it. It's not right. Me marryin' a woman just to get her land."

"But that's not the case, Mr. McGrath. Or at least it doesn't have to be. Meet my daughter first, and then decide. She should be home soon. Margaret's a good girl. Though . . ." Melancholy touched his expression. "You must bear in mind, she was raised with four older brothers. Two of my sons went to be with the Lord shortly after their birth," he added softly. "But Oak, Ezra, Ike, and Abe—they doted on their baby sister even as they taught her how to climb trees and how to ride and shoot with the best of them."

A young girl who had climbed trees and fired guns? The man's description hardly painted an appealing image. But Cullen was careful to keep his opinion from showing.

"When Maggie was young, her mother, God rest her, used to worry that our daughter would grow up so wild no man would want her. But that certainly wasn't the case. Maggie did have someone special. Once."

"What happened?" Ordinarily Cullen wouldn't have asked so personal a question, but considering the circumstances . . .

"He was killed in the war. As were so many other boys Maggie grew up with. Gone. All of them."

As hard as he tried, Cullen couldn't get the deal to work in his mind.

Slowly, Mr. Linden stood, using the desk for support. The collie rose with him. "Mr. McGrath, I can see none of my arguments has proven successful in persuading you. But you have given ear to an aging father's request, and I appreciate that. As I appreciate our time together and the opportunity to get to know you. Now, allow me to see you out."

Uneasy in a way he couldn't describe, Cullen returned the leather pouch of money to his pocket and followed Mr. Linden and the dog back through the house, viewing it in quite a different light from before. He found himself searching what he assumed were family portraits adorning the walls, but in none of them did he see a young woman.

Not that it would have mattered what Margaret Linden looked like. Still, he was curious.

Once outside, Cullen looked for Levi where he'd left him tethered, but the horse wasn't there.

"Not to worry, Mr. McGrath. Your Leviathan is safe in Cletus's care, I'm certain."

As though he'd overheard their conversation, Cletus rounded the corner of the house. "I get your fine mount for you, sir."

"Much obliged for your kindness," Cullen said, noting Cletus's brief backward glance.

Cullen once again found his gaze drawn to the land. The sun was slowly making its way behind the hills, bathing the fields in a golden glow.

"Lovely, isn't it?" Mr. Linden said with feeling.

A little too much feeling, Cullen thought, and eyed the man beside him. "You still haven't given up, have you?"

"There are many forms of persuasion, Mr. McGrath. Stating one's case is only one of them."

Cullen had to smile at the man's cunning.

He sighed. All of this could be his. No one else in this city—or state, for that matter—was going to sell him property. That had been made doubly clear. But one thing he didn't know . . .

"What happens, sir, if my answer remains no?"

Linden looked at him with what appeared to be cautious hope, yet with the weight of the burden still heavy. "The property will go to auction as advertised. The land should bring substantially more than the amount for which I offered to sell it to you. Though with the abundance of property available and people's shallow pockets, one never knows. Whatever sum remains once the back taxes are paid will, hopefully, be enough for my daughter and me to arrange for another living situation in town."

The disappointment in his voice matched the disappointment Cullen felt. Then an idea came.

"What if I were to buy your land but agree that you and your daughter could continue to live on here as long as you like. From what I've seen, this is a large house with plenty of rooms. Eventually I could afford to build a cabin nearby and live in that."

Mr. Linden leveled a stare. "And what about when I'm gone, Mr. McGrath? Will you continue to live beneath the same roof with my daughter without benefit of marriage? Or beside her in a cabin? The two of you out here all alone. What would such questionable behavior do to my daughter's reputation?"

Cullen had never heard so deafening a silence as that which followed, nor could he remember a time since boyhood when he'd been so thoroughly reprimanded. And appropriately so, as he reflected on his proposition. Yet even in the face of such reproof, he still sensed the man's gentleness and acceptance.

What difference would it have made to have had a man this like for a da? A man of integrity and kindness, instead of one given to drink and to gambling.

Thinking about his past, he wondered . . . what if, somehow, it crossed an ocean and caught up to him? Then again, if he stayed tucked away on the outskirts of town, minding his own life and business, what was the likelihood of that happening?

I don't want my daughter to have to face that kind of world alone.

Linden's plea for his daughter returned and tugged at Cullen's conscience. He knew what it was like to have a protector. He also knew what it was like to be a father and to be helpless to protect.

"Have you given thought, sir, as to what your daughter would say about the proposition you've made to me?"

"Oh yes . . ." Mr. Linden gave a perplexed sigh. "I've given it much thought, Mr. McGrath. And she will *not* be for it. At least not at first. She can be headstrong, like her mother. But she's also a practical-minded young woman. In the end I believe she'll see this is the best way. The only way."

They stood in companionable silence as the lone cricket, nestled somewhere in the hedge below, continued to call for others to join him. Mr. Linden, appearing wearier by the minute, gripped the bowed porch railing for support, and Cullen looked out across what could be his future, if only he could accept the terms.

If he were still a praying man, he would've asked the Almighty for a sign to show him which way to go, what to do. Just as he'd done that night in the church in Brooklyn. Or perhaps he would've visited a priest to gain a bit of wisdom and perspective.

But his praying and priest-going days were over. It was up to him, and him alone, to make this decision.

Cletus exited the stable, leading Levi behind him, and Cullen—his thoughts racing—extended his hand to Mr. Linden.

"Sir, it's indeed been a pleasure to meet you."

All traces of playful cunning aside, Linden met his grip and held on tight, the earlier disappointment in his voice now accentuating the deep lines of his face. "And you as well . . . Cullen McGrath. Go with God, son."

Sensing a stirring within him, Cullen hesitated, then gave the collie a last rub before descending the porch steps. He accepted the reins from Cletus and swung up into the saddle, then paused again to take in his surroundings for one last time.

They say its hills are as green as those of home.

The breeze on the back of his neck felt like a whisper from eternity, and it slowly fingered its way down his spine. Hoping he was doing the right thing, Cullen swiftly dismounted, took the porch steps in twos, and offered his hand again.

"My answer is aye, Mr. Linden. I'll marry your daughter. If she's willin'."

Chapter Six

Smiling at her father from across the dinner table, Maggie lowered her fork to her plate, waiting for the humor he so skillfully hid at times to bloom at the corners of his mouth. When it didn't, her own smile faded.

"An agreement?" She heard the wariness in her own voice. "Exactly what kind of 'agreement' are you suggesting that I enter into with this man, Papa?"

"Precisely the kind you think I'm suggesting." Her father tucked his napkin beside his plate, his dinner only half consumed but the gesture announcing he was finished. Bucket started to rise from where he lay in the corner, but a single look from Papa convinced the dog otherwise. "I'm proposing that you marry him, Margaret. In fact, I've assured him that you'll seriously consider the idea."

She wanted to laugh, the idea was so preposterous. But the seriousness and loving concern in her father's eyes wouldn't allow it. Nor would the dire state of their circumstances.

"So the man you were with on Harding turnpike today, the man who tamed the wild thoroughbred, the same man who—"

The door to the kitchen opened and Onnie entered, carrying a pitcher of water. Maggie smiled up at her, deciding to continue the conversation after she left.

As Onnie refilled their glasses, Maggie caught the worried glance she gave first to Papa's plate and then to Papa himself. Maggie remembered asking Onnie once how old she was. The woman had said she wasn't rightly sure when she'd been born, but she figured, based on the ages of her brothers and sisters, that she had to be at least fifty. That was well over a decade ago.

But looking at the dear woman now—part family, part servant—Maggie thought she looked every day of her sixty-plus years.

Onnie retrieved Papa's half-eaten plate of food but didn't turn to leave. "Got some news just now, Mr. Linden." She dipped her head. "Miss Maggie. It come by my youngest sister. She say Willie and his family, they leavin' tonight. Goin' with a passel of others. Marna and her husband and children, they travelin' with 'em too. She come to say good-bye."

"Your sister and her family are leaving?" Maggie asked. She looked at her father for his reaction, but she couldn't read his expression as she usually could. Marna and her family had lived and worked on a neighboring farm for years.

"Yes, ma'am. Marna say it got to be better up north than here. And I reckon she right."

For a moment no one spoke, the horror of what had happened that morning, what was happening all too frequently these days, filling every corner of the room.

The silence lengthened until finally her father looked up.

"Onnie." His deep voice seemed oddly fragile against the quiet. "As you know, our situation here is . . . uncertain at best. If you and Cletus would like to go with your sister and her family, please know that you'll have our blessing."

Maggie didn't know if the knot at the base of her throat was due to the emotion in her father's voice, the glistening in Onnie's dark eyes, or the fact that she couldn't imagine life without this woman she'd known for all of hers.

"Yes, sir," Onnie responded softly. "I know that. But I's too old to start over someplace else. I reckon I stay here long as I can. 'Sides, who gonna take care of you two if I go?" She laughed in a way that wasn't fully convincing. "Cletus, he feel the same. I's born here on Linden Downs. Then Cletus and me, we wed here. We aim to stay on right here, too, long as God wills."

Her father opened his mouth as if to say something more, then firmed his lips and nodded instead. Onnie closed the kitchen door behind her, leaving a starker reality in her place.

Grateful for Onnie's admission, and relieved at the same time, Maggie folded her napkin and tucked it neatly beside her plate, the polite gesture seeming trivial in light of all else.

"To continue our conversation," she offered softly, eager to get the idea her father had put forth settled between them, "the man you were with on Harding turnpike today, the same man you met earlier in the cemetery . . . this is the man you're suggesting I marry?" She huffed a laugh she didn't feel. "All because he showed up here this afternoon with a pocketful of money and promises. Like some carpetbagger or foreigner who thinks he can—"

"No, Margaret. It's not because of anything remotely like that." Her father's tone gained an unaccustomed edge. "It's because within two weeks' time my father's farm, the land he bought and toiled for all his life, the land I've been unable to keep for my family"—he winced, his breath catching—"for *you.* No matter how I've tried, that land and everything on it is going up for auction, and I will have no place for my daughter to live. Do you know what that does to me? To know I've failed you so miserably?"

"Papa, no . . ." Maggie moved to kneel by his chair. "You haven't failed me. This isn't your fault."

He shook his head. "Bourbon Belle will be gone. Everything we've worked for will be—"

He took a sharp breath and grimaced, gripping his arm against his chest. He couldn't seem to catch his breath.

Maggie put an arm around his shoulders. "Breathe, Papa. Just *breathe.*"

He paled. His lips moved but no words came.

"Onnie!" Maggie screamed, aware of Bucket beside them. She tried with shaking hands to unbutton her father's collar.

In a heartbeat Onnie was there, a cup of water in one hand and a powder in the other.

"What is that?" Maggie watched her swirl the mixture.

"Mister Linden." Onnie held the cup to his mouth. "You gotta drink this medicine, sir. Just like the doctor said."

"The doctor gave him that?"

Onnie's telling glance said it all. "There you go, sir. That's it now, that's it."

Her father gulped the mixture, water trickling down his neck and beneath his open collar.

"A little more, sir, then we done."

With Onnie's help her father drained the contents of the cup, and Maggie watched through tears.

Later that evening, seated at her father's bedside with Bucket keeping guard nearby, Maggie observed her father as he slept, watching the labored rise and fall of his chest.

They'd sent for Dr. Daniels, and he'd brought more powders. Digitalis, he called it. Maggie had pounced with questions, but didn't like the answers.

"It will help with the pain, and the recurring incidents," he'd told her before leaving. "He'll have good days and bad. But I'm sorry, Miss Linden. There's nothing else to be done. Rest is vital. That, and a calm and serene environment. Which I know, understanding your present circumstances, will be a challenge. I wish there were more that could be done, but his heart is simply giving out."

Her father's eyes fluttered open then shut again.

"Papa?" She leaned close and slipped her hand into his. "Are you awake?"

He moaned. Or was it a sigh? "I am now, Maggie."

She smiled, then tears welled. "Why didn't you tell me?"

He squeezed her hand. "Because of the way . . . your voice sounds right now."

She kissed his forehead and smoothed his thinning hair. The breathlessness he'd been experiencing, the fatigue. She had thought he'd simply been overexerting himself. He *was* getting older. But this . . .

"He's a good man . . . Maggie."

It took her a second to realize whom he was referring to.

He pulled in a breath. "I wouldn't lead you down this path if . . . he were not."

"Let's not speak of this now, Papa. We'll—"

His grip tightened. "Promise me you will do this." His gaze sought hers. "*Promise.*"

Not wanting to upset him further, she nodded. "I promise . . . to meet him. To speak with him. I'll seek him out in town and—"

"No need, my dear. He'll be back in the morning." He closed his eyes, and tears traced his temples. "I have considered every possibility. This is the only way."

Using a fresh cloth, Maggie dabbed the moisture from his face. "Did you tell him?" she asked quietly. "About Belle and our plans for her? And . . . about me?"

Her father's sheepish smile told her much. "I intended to, but—" He drew air into his lungs then slowly exhaled, the act causing Bucket's ears to prick. "He does not hold a . . . favorable view of thoroughbred racing, my dear. He made that entirely clear. It seems his"—he held his chest as he coughed, the air rattling dull in his lungs—"his father's . . . overindulgence in the sport . . . left a bad mark on him."

Maggie dabbed his forehead with a cool cloth. "But simply because you race horses doesn't mean you gamble. Quite the contrary. You can't afford to gamble with something so precious. Only fools would do such a thing."

"And he is no fool, Maggie," he said with surprising strength, peering up at her.

And neither am I, she wanted to say.

Her father reached for her hand. "Sometimes in life, when what we want most is just beyond our reach . . . and the ground beneath us gives way, we must grab hold of the nearest branch." He closed his eyes briefly. "And hang on."

Emotion tightened Maggie's throat. Her father had a habit of waxing poetic on occasion. And that was only one of the things she dearly loved about him. "Papa, I—"

He shook his head. "Listen to me, child. Your dream is still within reach. You simply must . . . find a different way to lay claim to it."

He grimaced as another bout of coughing tore through his chest. Maggie helped him sit up, then held him until the spell passed. Finally she eased him back against his pillows. His eyes fluttered as though he was fighting to stay awake, and she too felt a wave of fatigue.

She wished she could press him for more information, but she knew better. He needed to rest.

At her urging he drank several more sips of the horehound and boneset tea she'd made earlier, then slipped into sleep again. She leaned forward, arms wrapped around herself, and studied the yet strong features of her father's face, while clearly seeing evidence of time's relentless pursuit.

Please don't take him. Not now. Not yet.

It wasn't so much a prayer as it was a desperate plea. But maybe, in the end, those two things were more akin than she thought.

Finally she dozed in the chair beside him until sometime after midnight, when Onnie came to relieve her.

But once Maggie was in bed, sleep wouldn't come. She lay in the darkness recounting all the reasons her father had given when he told her about this "arrangement" at dinner, and she wrestled to refute them. And couldn't.

If only they had more time. But they didn't.

If only she could find a jockey. But she hadn't.

If only Richard had lived. But—

If only, if only, *if only.*

She realized her father had done what he'd done as much for her safety and security as for her aspirations for Bourbon Belle. And she was grateful. So why these stirrings of resentment? Not at her father. But at the man, whoever he was.

This man had leapt at the chance to marry a daughter of Nashville's landed gentry, however distant the gentry distinction seemed at present. He'd likely heard the family name, then decided to swoop in and lay claim before the property went to auction.

And he didn't know about Bourbon Belle . . .

What if he saw Belle, and instead of seeing her for the champion the mare was, he saw a quick way to get money for the farm?

Maggie rolled onto her back and kicked off the sheets, the room suddenly warm. Knowing how men in general felt about women and thoroughbred racing, she would have to tread carefully. And now, knowing this particular man's disdain for the sport, well . . . She sighed.

He'd been married before, Papa said. Did that mean he was old? Twice her age? Maybe more? She didn't wish to marry an old man. She'd always dreamed of being a wife, not a nursemaid. Guilt chided her at the thought. She was happy to take care of her father this way.

But a husband? That was different.

How was it her father had described him earlier? *A proud man, but in the best sense of the word.* What did that mean?

"Some might consider him a little rough around the edges," Papa had added. "But he's a man other men respect, even if they wish they didn't."

So he was old *and* a bully. Maggie shoved her hands through her hair and stared up at the ceiling.

Even though she didn't know this man, she knew her father. And her father—her safe haven and strong tower for as long as she could remember—would never lead her down a path he wasn't certain of.

But what if it was desperation or his deteriorating health influencing his decision? Then again, as he'd said, what other choice did they have?

She'd had such different plans for her life. And as much as she wanted to believe that God wanted them to stay on this land and for her to keep Bourbon Belle, to do what she'd set out to accomplish, she wasn't quite so sure anymore. She'd seen so many people who trusted him brought low.

So why should she expect to escape a similar end?

Maggie curled onto her side, cradled a second pillow to her chest, and did what she always did when she couldn't sleep. She tried to recall every detail about the faces of her mother and each of her brothers, while wishing that the world—and her future—still looked as it had when she'd ridden upon her father's shoulders as a child.

It wasn't until she awoke the next morning, the sky tinged with pink, that she realized she'd never even asked her father her would-be suitor's name. No matter. She was going to make it perfectly clear to the man exactly what she thought of him and his designs to get Linden Downs. Before she reluctantly said . . . *I do.*

Chapter Seven

Cullen prodded Levi up the road leading to Linden Downs, seeing the land in a different way this morning. All this was his. Or soon would be. If Margaret Linden said yes.

As tired as he'd been last night, he still slept fitfully, unable to get comfortable. Unable to keep from thinking about today, about what he was doing and how his life was about to change.

"I'm keeping my promise to you," he whispered, staring up into the cloudless blue, remembering Moira's last requests. *Promise me,* she'd said, voice thready, tears trailing her temples, *that you'll take our Katie and make the life we've dreamed about. Don't give up, Cullen.*

He wasn't giving up. But keeping this promise was coming at a far greater cost than he'd imagined. And was being fulfilled in a far different way, he was certain, than Moira had ever dreamed when she'd asked it of him.

He hoped that if she could see him today, she would understand. But better yet if heaven would simply keep the veil between this world and that pulled taut.

It was a moot point, but a majority of his sleeplessness had been devoted to Miss Linden. How he wished he'd made a better effort to seek out her portrait in the house. Surely, with her being the only daughter, there were portraits. What was she like?

Was she short? Or tall? Lithe? Or curvy? Those things mattered to a man when he was marrying. Actually, they mattered all the time, but especially with a wife.

That truth swiftly faded as reality reminded him that this marriage wasn't like his first one. This union was not borne of love. Not the vows they'd take during the ceremony, whenever that might be in the days ahead, nor the husband and wife union that would follow later.

Surely though, with time and getting to know each other, he and Miss Linden could grow to have something, at least.

If she said yes.

He'd passed the Tax and Title Office earlier and was eager to return later that day with the signed deed to pay off the debt that was owed. He looked forward to presenting the "paid in full" receipt to Mr. Linden. But taking that step would definitely mean he'd be all in. No turning back.

The farmhouse came into view, and he reined in.

He checked the time on his pocket watch, a gift from his grandfather before he died. Half past eight. Earlier than he thought. Linden had asked him to return that morning at nine.

Not wishing to arrive before the Lindens were ready, he guided Levi across a field to the east in the opposite direction of where he'd ridden yesterday. Everywhere he looked were gently rolling hills and fields bordered by thick stands of pine and poplar.

He imagined the fallow fields come July, knee high with stalks of corn or covered with the hearty growth of sweet potatoes, those green-leafed vines spreading out and taking over as they grew.

Linden said they'd also planted white potatoes in the past, but—Cullen huffed—with what happened to his own family and their potato crop in Ireland, he wasn't willing to throw away good soil on white potatoes that rotted as soon as you looked at them.

Linden also said they'd grown cotton, but Cullen had no experience with the plant. For that he'd have to rely on Gilbert Linden's knowledge.

He spotted a bluff a half mile or so away and remembered Linden remarking on it. He urged Levi to a canter, then to a gallop, and the Percheron ate up the distance. Even the steep incline leading to the bluff was no match for his strength.

The view from the bluff was indeed breathtaking—and instructive.

From this vantage point the layout of the fields and the various plots of land was plainly evident. And true to Linden's word, Cullen could also see the Cumberland River in the distance and the city of Nashville some six miles east.

If Mr. Linden hadn't had the opportunity to ride up here in a while, Cullen would offer to bring him. They could discuss plans for what to plant and also—

Just then, on the ridge due south, a rider crested the hill, the horse covering the ground at breakneck speed. Watching them, Cullen couldn't shake the uncanny sense that he was reliving a moment he'd already experienced. Yesterday, by the river.

He leaned forward in the saddle, watching the pair's progress, and for a moment, as the girl gave the mount its head—her skirts whipping behind her—he was a boy again, back at the London track, seeing Bonnie Scotland race like the wind with the same speed and gracefulness. And win.

A minute later, rider and horse disappeared back over the hill, headed in the direction of Belle Meade. A member of the Harding family out with one of their champion thoroughbreds, no doubt. He guided Levi back down the hill and toward the farmhouse.

He'd thought a lot about General Harding last night too. Just because people were neighbors didn't mean they had to be neighborly. He planned on treating Belle Meade Plantation just as he would the Nashville Thoroughbred Society.

Give both a wide berth.

The house was quiet when he arrived. After Mr. Linden's enthusiasm yesterday, Cullen half expected the man to be standing here waiting for him. He tethered Levi and climbed the steps to the porch, the worn wooden planks already feeling somewhat familiar, tempting him to dream of home and of a place to belong.

He knocked on the door, softly the first time, more pronounced the second. The soft tread of footsteps, then the door opened.

"Mister McGrath." The servant from yesterday had apparently learned his name.

"Miss Onnie." Cullen smiled when her eyebrows shot up. Expecting her to smile in turn, he was surprised when her countenance remained somber.

"Mister Linden, he still be abed, sir. And *Miss* Linden, she—" Onnie looked beyond him, and at the same time Cullen heard the drum of hooves. "There she come right now, sir."

Cullen turned and walked to the edge of the porch, focusing on the rider still some distance away. *That* was Miss Linden? Feeling as if something blurry were now coming into focus, he watched her progress as she flew astride the handsome bay thoroughbred across the field. The same thoroughbred she'd been riding earlier on the ridge and, as it turned out, by the river yesterday morning.

He couldn't decide which was more graceful—the horse or the rider. Miss Linden slowed the mare to a canter then reined in by the porch, eyeing him with every bit of the curiosity he was certain showed on his own face.

Her gaze moved over him in a manner he was certain wasn't customary for a lady. But he wasn't bothered in the least, especially when the tiniest smile touched her mouth. When her gaze met his again, a blush rose to her cheeks, but he found her perusal—and apparent approval—more than a little heartening.

She dismounted, and he could understand now how he'd mistaken her for a slip of a girl. She was a tiny thing and looked even more so next to the thoroughbred. But seeing her up close left no doubt.

Margaret Linden was *woman* through and through.

Where Moira had been blond and tall, this lady was brunette and petite. Moira had had full curves, but Margaret Linden's were far less pronounced. Still, on her lithe frame, they made an impact.

Cullen quickly dismissed the thought and descended the porch steps, having rehearsed what he wanted to say. Cletus approached for the horse, and Cullen waited until he'd led the thoroughbred away.

Pleased when Miss Linden curtsied and offered her hand, he took it in his, and only then realized how nervous she was. Her slender hand shook, and he gently tightened his grip to reassure her.

When she returned the gesture, the mixture of fear and hope, of panic and relief blooming in her expression moved him more than he would have expected in such a moment.

"Miss Linden, I know this is a difficult position for a lady such as yourself to be in." Her brow furrowed, and he rushed to continue, not wanting her to mistake his meaning. "But I want you to know that I pledge to—"

She pulled her hand away. "You're Irish?"

The tone she used to say the word wasn't a polite one. Nor was it promising. The warmth in her eyes just seconds before disappeared so swiftly Cullen questioned whether he'd imagined it to begin with.

"Aye, ma'am, that I am." He studied her. "I take it your father didn't mention that detail."

"No." She swallowed, her chin jutting the tiniest bit. "He did not."

She glanced beyond him to the door, and he could see her thoughts spinning, her expression revealing all. She was working to figure a way out of this, and her reaction stabbed at his pride. But he held the advantage in the moment, because he knew something she apparently didn't as yet. She didn't have another way.

And when her gaze finally slid back to his, he could see that she knew it too.

She bowed her head.

"Is this a problem for you, Miss Linden?" His voice came out more smoothly than the words felt leaving him.

If gauging her response by her slowness to answer, he'd have untethered Levi right then and been on his way. But the struggle mirrored in the tightness of her shoulders, in the firm knot of her tiny hands at her waist, kept him grounded where he was—while not softening him toward her in the least.

She lifted her head and looked toward the house again, her eyes glistening, then back at the stable. Then finally at him again, appearing as though at any moment she might need to empty her stomach.

"No," she said quietly. "It isn't a problem, Mr. . . . ?"

"McGrath," Cullen said, certain he understood why Gilbert Linden had left that part out. "*Cullen* McGrath."

"McGrath," she repeated, as if trying out the name. The downward turn of her mouth told him how she felt about that too.

Wordlessly, she entered the house, leaving the door open behind her. That was something, at least, he thought. Following her inside, he paused on the top step. If there were any other way . . .

He walked into the house and closed the door behind him, certain of two things. In Margaret Linden's eyes he rated somewhere far, far beneath her love and devotion to a father she adored—and a horse.

As Onnie buttoned Maggie's best dress from behind, Maggie held her breath, determined not to cry. The pastor had arrived shortly after she'd returned from her ride, and Cullen McGrath seemed as shocked to see the man as she was. Her father had sent Cletus into town earlier to fetch him.

"It ain't white or fancy," Onnie said, working to fasten each tiny pearl button on the back of the dress. "But it'll do real nice."

The cream-colored calico was one Maggie hadn't worn in a while, and it didn't fit as it once had. The bodice wasn't nearly as snug, and where the cotton material once hugged her waist, it now hung loose.

She stared out the window. Her view overlooked the stable and meadow, but all she could see was her life and dream of marriage coming to a hasty and final end.

Papa's confidence in the rightness of this arrangement and his obvious certainty that she would go through with it were both comforting and alarming. He would never do anything to hurt her, and this *was* the last resort.

But did that make it right?

She'd tried to discourage Papa from coming downstairs, even told him they could hold the ceremony in his bedroom if need be. But after he managed to sit up in bed and eat something, he insisted they convene downstairs in the parlor.

"Right where your mother and I married," he'd said. "However different this day is from what I imagined it would be."

She'd helped him get ready for the ceremony and was accompanying him downstairs to the parlor when Mr. McGrath saw them on the stairs and insisted on helping. From all accounts and for whatever it meant, the man seemed genuinely concerned about Papa's well-being.

"There you go, Miss Linden." Onnie touched her shoulder. "Now turn around and let's have a look."

Maggie turned and read approval in Onnie's understated nod. Having her here was a comfort. But Papa was right. Today—her wedding day—was nothing like she'd imagined either.

An Irishman. That's who her father had chosen.

When she'd first ridden up and had seen the man standing there on the porch, she'd blinked to make certain her eyesight wasn't playing tricks. Handsome was a word often used to describe the masculine gender, but in this case it fell far short of the mark. Mr. McGrath had a look about him that made a woman's eye linger. And hers had done just that and more, much to her chagrin.

His features weren't the suave, cultured sort belonging to Southern men she'd known. They were rougher. *He* was rougher. And she'd found herself fascinated by him. With dark brown hair worn longer than fashionable, pale green eyes, and a lean-muscled physique, Cullen McGrath looked more suited to the wild than he did to Nashville. And certainly to Linden Downs.

Twenty-five years old, she guessed, maybe one or two more, he was the kind of man women stopped to look at on the street. But only because they'd never seen anything like him. They never would have whispered about him at parties, because his sort were never invited. More suited for tavern brawls than ballroom dancing.

And yet she'd found herself altogether captivated as she'd stood there staring at him. Until he opened his mouth.

She cringed. Everyone knew what the Irish were like. No one in town would hire them, much less keep company with them. They were lazy, eager to fight, had no morals. Selling Linden Downs to that man wasn't saving the farm; it was only delaying the inevitable. And yet . . .

He was the nearest branch, as Papa had said in so many words. And she was grabbing hold.

Maggie turned and caught a glimpse of herself in the mirror. Not exactly the image she'd pictured when dreaming of her wedding day. No gown of white silk with high-fitted bodice, or long delicate veil of white tulle reaching to her feet. No wreath of maiden-blush roses with orange blossoms gracing her head. Nothing a real wedding would have.

Then again, this wasn't a *real* wedding, in that sense.

She reached for her scent on the dresser, the glass bottle long since empty. She removed the decorative stopper and held the bottle to her nose. The faintest scent of lilac and something else too far gone to remember with clarity tugged at her sensibilities. Perfume was a luxury. One she'd done without for well over three years now.

Most days she smelled of fresh hay, leather oil, and horses. Not exactly a feminine scent, nor one befitting a bride. But it wasn't as though she cared what Cullen McGrath thought. Still . . .

She pressed the underside of one wrist to the bottle's opening and rubbed, then did the same with the other, then sniffed. Scarcely a trace. She placed the empty bottle back on the dresser, remembering the last time she'd worn this dress, and what she'd been doing. Dancing. With Richard . . . She clenched her jaw in an effort to quell the emotion.

"Don't you go cryin', Miss Linden. Now ain't the time."

Surprised by Onnie's uncustomary admonishment, Maggie looked at the woman's reflection in the mirror.

Onnie moved closer. "Day I meet Cletus is the day I married him." She nodded as if acknowledging Maggie's surprise. "Cletus and his family, they was bought by your grandfather and brought to Linden Downs long 'fore you was born. Soon as my papa clapped eyes on Cletus, he went and made a deal with Cletus's pa. Next day we's jumpin' the broom. I's hardly a woman then. But Cletus, he was already a man."

Maggie stared at Onnie's reflection in the mirror then bowed her head. She was familiar with the custom practiced by the former slaves. As girls, she and Savannah and Mary used to borrow her mother's broom and go play in the barn, jumping over the broom again and again, making up stories of who they'd someday marry.

So far none of their dreams had come true. Not even today, on her wedding day. Savannah and Mary didn't even know. What would they say when they found out? Once they learned who her husband was.

Maggie slowly lifted her head. "I always thought from watching you and Cletus that you'd—"

"I know what you thought. Same as others did. But just 'cuz you thinkin' it don't make it so. You feelin' trapped right now, child. Like you wanna run to the hills, and yet your feet, they's mired deep in the mud. You can't move. And ain't nobody can get you out."

Hearing the finality in Onnie's voice, Maggie felt tears rising again. Onnie had described how she felt so perfectly.

"I know that feelin', Miss Linden. I done lived with that all my life."

The tears froze in Maggie's throat, her love for this woman rubbing up against the only life she'd ever known until after the war. Some days it still felt like they were trying to find their place with each other.

Onnie's eyes softened. "You always been a good girl, Miss Linden. Even as a child, you was thoughtful and kind."

Maggie felt a smile.

"But you ain't never had life tell you what you is and ain't gonna do. Not like it's tellin' you now." Her expression sobered. "I's by your mama's bedside when she breathed her last, and I reckon if she was here today she'd have all sorts of things to tell you. But she ain't here, Miss Linden. So I gonna tell you what my own mama tol' me on my weddin' day. She say, 'Child, in hard times more than any other, you gots to remember that the Lawd is maker of both the joy and the pain.'"

A single tear slipped down Maggie's cheek, but she quickly brushed it away.

Onnie smoothed the back of her dress. "As for Cletus and me—" She gave a soft laugh. "I done told the Lawd to take me long 'fore he takes that man. 'Cuz when he die, he gonna take half of me with him."

Onnie turned away and busied herself with folding the skirt and shirtwaist Maggie had worn earlier.

Unable to speak, Maggie finished tucking strands of hair into place atop her head. She was grateful Onnie and Cletus had enjoyed so special a closeness after such a beginning. But she remembered what her own mother had said about Negroes, more than once. *They're different from us, Margaret. Not only in temperament, but in how they see things. In how they look at life.*

So even though Onnie said she understood what marrying this man meant, Maggie knew she really didn't. Because Onnie didn't comprehend life in the same way. The woman couldn't begin to understand how drastically Maggie's world would change.

And not for the better.

Chapter EIGHT

"Dearly beloved, we are gathered together in the sight of God, and in the face of this company, to join together this man and this woman in holy matrimony . . ."

Maggie clutched the bouquet of freshly bloomed magnolias, certain their sturdy stems would snap at any moment. She looked down to see the thick white petals trembling in her grip, then caught Mr. McGrath's eye and realized he was watching them too.

She quickly stared ahead at the pastor, a younger man recently hired after their pastor of decades died last summer. She'd seen the man on occasion when she and Papa attended services, which was infrequent these days, considering her father's health. This pastor scarcely knew her family, a fact for which she was most grateful at the moment.

Maggie looked at her father seated in the chair by the empty hearth, Bucket lying at his feet, then at Onnie and Cletus standing on either side. They all wore a similar expression. Not a smile really, and not a frown. It was as though they were waiting for her to decide for them.

"This union, instituted by God—" The pastor's notes slipped from his Bible and floated to the floor. "Oh, I beg your pardon." Face flushing, he bent to retrieve them, then proceeded to try and put them in order again. Finally he cleared his throat and started again. "This union, instituted by God, is not to be entered into lightly, but reverently, discreetly, advisedly, and solemnly."

Mr. McGrath shifted beside her.

Maggie bowed her head and sneaked a look his way only to see his hand balled tightly into a fist at his side, his knuckles white. *He* was nervous? She trailed her gaze up the length of him, his height challenging her discretion, and she saw the muscles tensing in his jaw.

Cullen McGrath wasn't nervous. He was angry. And she felt her resolve to go through with this slip another notch. To be married to such an ill-tempered man . . .

The pastor hadn't even asked them to kneel at the first, as was custom. Then again, there was no altar in the parlor, there were no attendants, no groomsmen. The regular order of things had been set aside. As was just as well, she guessed.

"Who gives this woman to be married?"

The pastor's question jarred her, but it was the sheen of affection and earnest hope in her father's gaze when he nodded his consent that was nearly her undoing.

"Marriage is the union of a husband and wife in heart, in body, and in mind . . ."

Maggie felt weak in the knees. Two of those unions—interminable as they were—she could live with, under the circumstances. But that of the body? She gulped. She could no more be intimate with this man beside her than she could any stranger on the street. And he'd been married before, which meant he knew all about . . .

Well, everything. And she knew next to nothing.

Then again, his being an Irishman, he'd likely already known about all of that long before marriage.

The pastor went on and on, and the longer he went, the more Maggie realized she couldn't do this. She'd thought she could, but she couldn't.

"I do," came a deep voice beside her.

What? Mr. McGrath had taken his vows? Already? And precisely what had he vowed? She hadn't been listening.

She peered over to see him looking down at her, his eyes a pale, almost grayish green, and—surprisingly—she found not a trace of anger in them. Only what looked to be . . . understanding?

"Miss Linden?"

Maggie turned back.

The pastor offered a smile that said he clearly thought her a sweet but nervous young bride. At least he was partly right. "I'm going to read your vows now, and all you need do to indicate your willingness to accept them is to say 'I do.'"

"Do you, Margaret Laurel Linden, take Cullen Michael McGrath to be your husband, to live together after God's ordinance . . ."

Mr. McGrath shifted beside her again, this time brushing her arm, and the solidness of him sent a shiver through her. Not an altogether pleasant one. Once she said *I do* to this man, this Cullen Michael McGrath, he would have control of Linden Downs, of *her,* and no telling what he would demand.

"Will you love him, comfort him, honor him, in sickness and in health, for richer, for poorer, for better, for worse, in sadness and in joy . . ."

Were those the same vows he'd taken on her behalf? But even if he had, he hadn't meant them. He couldn't have. He didn't even know her. He would never be standing here beside her if not for Linden Downs. He was only marrying her to get the land.

If she were to speak up right now and end this charade, she knew exactly what the outcome would be for her and her father. The auction, then moving into town. Yet considering the man beside her, that alternative was becoming more desirable by the minute. But for her father, her saying no to this marriage would mean the loss of a family legacy. And that heartache alone, not to mention the transition of the move itself, would likely cut short the number of months—or weeks?—he had left.

By saying *I do* she would fulfill her father's wish and they would keep the home, the land, her Bourbon Belle. The two possibilities wrangled inside her until an unlikely adage rose to offer counsel. *For he who fights and runs away, may live to fight another day.* She didn't know who had said it or remember where she'd learned it, but she was grateful for it now, because it helped her realize her father was right. This was the only way.

". . . and forsaking all others, keep yourself only unto him as long as you both shall live?"

Realizing the moment had come, Maggie opened her mouth to respond, but her bravado left in a rush and took her voice with it. She couldn't say the words. She closed her eyes, breathed in and out, and tried again. With the same result.

For courage she looked at her father, and this time tears welled in his eyes. She turned back.

"I do," she whispered and would've sworn she heard a sigh of relief beside her.

"Do you have a token of love to offer your bride, Mr. McGrath?"

Maggie shook her head, trying to save them all some embarrassment.

"Aye, I do." Mr. McGrath pulled something from his pocket, already looking at her when she turned. He held it out. "It's your grandmother's ring," he said softly. "Before you came down, your father gave it to me . . . to give to you."

Her paternal grandmother's ring. The one her mother had also worn.

"Very nice," the pastor said, beaming. He thumbed through his notes. "Ah, here we are." He cleared his throat again. "Mr. McGrath, if you will place the ring on Miss Linden's finger and then repeat after me."

Mr. McGrath held out his left hand and Maggie, not wanting to, slipped hers into his. His grip tightened ever so slightly as he fitted the ring onto her finger. She made the mistake of looking up at him and felt a twinge of whatever it was she'd felt when she first rode up to the house and saw him standing there—before he opened his mouth.

Keenly aware of the warmth from his hand, she forced her gaze downward as the pastor began reciting the vows.

"With this ring," Mr. McGrath echoed, "I, Cullen, wed thee . . . Margaret."

His deep voice dropped nearly to a whisper, and Maggie's pulse quickened. But she kept her gaze on the ring. And on his hands—hands that dwarfed hers. Hands that, surprisingly, appeared to be accustomed to hard work, judging by the calluses on his palms.

His hands and forearms were tanned and dark next to hers, except for a thin white scar that stretched across his knuckles.

"And with it, I bestow . . ." His grip suddenly firmed on her hand, and he hesitated in repeating the last part of the vow. ". . . all my worldly goods," he finished, his voice falling off at the last.

Maggie lifted her face then, wanting to see the look in his eyes, but his gaze was conveniently occupied elsewhere. She gently pulled her hand away.

"Well done," the pastor said, a hint of relief in his voice. He closed his Bible with a flourish. "By the power invested in me as a minister of the gospel of Jesus Christ, I now pronounce you man and wife. And now, if you wish, Mr. McGrath"—the clergyman gave a nervous laugh—"you may take this opportunity to kiss your bride."

Cullen McGrath turned to her, and Maggie tensed. He leaned down, and all she could think about was the memory of her first and only kiss, and how she didn't want that to be—

He kissed her forehead, lingering only a second. Yet even after he drew back, she could still feel the unexpected tenderness of his lips on her skin.

But knowing the kind of man he was and why he was standing here to begin with, she knew better than to trust him. And she planned on telling him exactly that at her first opportunity.

"That was a fine dinner, Miss Onnie." Cullen tucked his napkin beside his plate, discreetly taking his social cues from Mr. Linden, who'd done the same thing a moment earlier.

Cullen looked across the table at Miss Linden—he simply couldn't bring himself to call her Mrs. McGrath, regardless of what had transpired between them earlier that day. But as was the case since the ceremony concluded, she kept her gaze occupied elsewhere—on her place setting, the tablecloth, looking about the room . . .

"You welcome, Mister McGrath," Onnie said softly, removing his plate and not looking at him either. Apparently it was a common theme. Not that he faulted them.

At least the canine member of the family seemed eager enough to welcome him. Bucket watched him intently from the hallway, wagging his tail every time Cullen looked in his direction.

Cullen glanced back across the table. Putting himself in Miss Linden's place, he knew he wouldn't have liked the situation any more than she did. In fact, standing beside her earlier as the pastor droned on and on, he'd worried that she wouldn't go through with it.

Saying his own vows had proven more difficult than he'd imagined. Especially while remembering the first time he'd made those promises to a woman. He'd meant them then with all his heart, mind, soul, and body. He'd meant them today, too, only not with the same fervor. Or emotion.

But how could he, when he didn't even know the woman? And when her eyes held such reservation?

He'd been glad a pastor had married them rather than a priest. Having a priest preside over the vows would have made what he'd done that much harder.

"So, Mr. McGrath—" Mr. Linden fingered the rim of his water glass. "Cullen," he added with a smile. "Did you enjoy riding the property this afternoon? I wish I'd felt able enough to have gone with you."

"Aye, sir, I did. Linden Downs is just as beautiful as you said, and then some."

Mr. Linden gave a satisfied look, but Miss Linden's expression communicated anything but satisfaction.

Cullen had asked her to accompany him on the ride, thinking it would give them an opportunity to talk, which seemed a good idea considering they were now man and wife. At least on paper. But she had declined.

Cullen pulled some notes from his pocket. "While I was out I drew up a plan about what to plant in each field, as you suggested, sir. Perhaps we could sit down and discuss it."

Miss Linden frowned in his direction.

"Once you're feelin' better, of course," he added quickly.

Though Mr. Linden looked considerably stronger following his afternoon rest, Cullen shared Miss Linden's obvious concern for her father's health. Linden had described the "incident" from last evening to him, and Cullen knew it must have been frightening for them both. No doubt the man's distress over back taxes and the pending sale of his land had contributed to his ailing heart.

Hopefully now, though, if things went as Cullen planned, Gilbert Linden would be able to regain his strength even as he watched his farm take on new life again.

"I also have the deed to the land here, Cullen." Linden removed a pouch from his coat pocket. "I'll go ahead and sign this over to you, and then—"

"Papa, don't you think it would be wiser to do that tomorrow? After Mr. McGrath has the receipt confirming he's paid off the back taxes?"

Cullen looked across the table to find Miss Linden's heretofore elusive gaze now riveted to his, her suggestion thick with accusation. Did the woman really think that lowly of him? That after all this, he would attempt to take the property and . . . do what, sell it at auction and abscond with the difference? As if any of the powers-that-be in this town would allow an Irishman to get away with such a thing.

"Margaret." Subtle disapproval tinged Mr. Linden's tone. "I don't think it's helpful to—"

"No, sir, that's fine," Cullen interrupted, offering a reassuring glance. "I don't mind waiting. And perhaps, M—" He'd nearly called her Miss Linden, which didn't quite seem proper now either. He tried again, watching for her reaction. "Perhaps . . . Margaret might wish to go along with me. In fact, I think that would be a very good idea."

Her eyes narrowed the slightest bit. "I'll happily accompany you . . . Cullen."

And so it begins, he thought to himself, not really tempted to smile but finding her response a touch humorous all the same. She'd said his name as though it were an off-color word. He already knew from having seen her ride that the woman was a fighter, not fond of losing. And that was good. She'd met her match.

"We're going to need workers, Mr. Linden." Cullen shook his head when Onnie returned and offered him more water. "Some of the crops require greater care than others, but by my figures we'll need at least twenty men to start out. Men with experience are preferred. But I won't turn away a hard, honest worker."

A soft huff came from across the table, and Cullen looked in Miss Linden's direction, only to find her head bowed.

"Good workers are hard to come by, Cullen." The gentleman rose slightly to nudge his chair back, and the simple exertion caused his breath to quicken. "I can give you some names of people to contact in town. Men I've done business with in the past. Our families go back quite a ways. I'm certain they'll be willing to help you. *Us*," he added, his excitement evident.

Cullen thanked the man, but already knew from recent experience that whatever contacts Mr. Linden had from years back would not welcome a contact from *him*. Best go directly to the source of the hardest workers he'd ever seen. Men who worked from sunup to sundown with nary a complaint.

And he knew just who to talk to about that at Linden Downs.

"Well, it's been a long day. I think—" Mr. Linden started to rise then leaned heavily on the table.

His daughter jumped to his aid, the same time as Cullen.

"I can help him!" She wrapped an arm around her father's waist.

"Best let Cullen do this, my dear." Her father patted her back. "He all but had to carry me down the stairs this morning."

Miss Linden finally stepped back, and Cullen took hold of the man's arm. But he saw the hurt and anger in her eyes.

A while later, when Cullen returned downstairs, Miss Linden was nowhere to be found. He'd been gone longer than he'd expected due to her father's fondness for conversation. He appreciated the older man's company, so it was mutual. However . . .

He and Margaret Linden needed to have a conversation of their own. Preferably *before* retiring. He wanted to say some things to her, and he was certain—based on the woman's facial expressions alone—that she had things to say to him.

He wanted to reassure her of his intent, to tell her that despite their less than amiable beginning he held hope that in time they would grow to care for each other. Same as so many other couples in similar situations had done, as her father pointed out. Even though, at present, he didn't see how that was going to happen.

In all his life he'd never imagined a wedding day like this one. Nor a wedding night where he couldn't even find his bride.

The sun had set when he walked outside to the porch. The fragrance of lavender scented the breeze, and he breathed in the night air. The meadows and fields lay pale, almost alabaster, beneath the moonlight, and above him a million stars shone with bright abandon.

Where do stars come from, Da?

Cullen's throat closed. As much as he cherished his memories, sometimes he wished he could close himself off from them, so painful they were. Especially in light of his current situation and how unwelcome he was in this house. At least by the one who would matter most.

Well, my sweet Katie, the stars are diamonds that God himself cast across the night sky so you, me, and your ma would have somethin' to look at as we lay atop this blanket.

He closed his eyes and could almost imagine the way she'd laughed at his story. He was back in the moment with little Katie's head on his shoulder and her tiny hand tucked safely—

"As you're obviously aware, Mr. McGrath, my father is vulnerable and desperate, and eager to trust you. But please don't make the mistake of applying those same attributes to me. Especially not the latter. I see this situation for exactly what it is."

Torn from his memories and half grateful for the rescue, Cullen looked down and barely made out Miss Linden's silhouette at the base of the steps. Yet despite her tone being sweetly cordial, at least on the surface, he sensed his pretty young bride was itching for a fight.

Chapter Nine

Furthermore, sir, I believe it would be best if we could come to an understanding from the outset. We both are well aware that the—"

Cullen lifted a hand in truce, feeling as though he'd been dropped headfirst into a conversation that had left the station without him. "Back up a wee mite, if you would, ma'am. Just what 'situation,' may I ask, do you think you see? And so exactly."

"This." She exhaled, gesturing between them. "Our . . . *marriage*. To pretend that this is anything other than a . . . a business arrangement is absurd." She gave a laugh, but the sound held no humor.

Cullen blinked. "A business arrangement?" He heard the surprise in his own voice.

"That's precisely what it is, Mr. McGrath," she said, her voice evenly demure. "You would not have married me, and I most certainly would never have married a man like you, if you hadn't decided you wanted Linden Downs."

"How do you do that?" he asked almost without thinking.

"Do what?" Wariness edged her tone.

"Say somethin' so mean-spirited with such politeness to your voice. It must be somethin' you people teach each other when you're young."

"You people? Are you intentionally trying to insult me now?"

It was his turn to laugh. "Isn't that what you just did to me? Tell me you'd never, not in a hundred lifetimes, ever choose to marry a wretched bloke such as myself? Because that's precisely what I heard."

"W-well, that's . . . not what I said."

"What did you say then? Or more importantly, what do you wish you could say to me, Miss Linden? Maybe that's where we should start, ma'am. Forget all this polite savagery and just get on with it."

She scoffed. "That's how *your* people do it, I presume."

"Aye, it is. We know how to fight. But we come at each other straight on, ma'am. No knives in the back."

He would've sworn he sensed *her* back go rigid.

"Mr. McGrath." She raised her chin, the thinnest veneer of civility skimming her tone. "I believe it would best serve us both to keep our—"

"Aren't you the least bit mad at me?" It was clear the woman needed some priming, and he was happy to oblige. Best get this out now, so the thing could heal. If it was going to. "What would best serve us both," he said, imitating her hoity-toity tone as best he could, "is if you would stop shootin' daggers at me every time you look my way. Just go ahead, take aim, and throw."

"That's what you want? For me to say exactly what I think?"

"Aye, ma'am." He sighed. "Me, and all the angels in heaven. The whole lot of us would be pleased."

She took a step forward. "I do not appreciate being spoken to in such a condescending manner."

"Do you appreciate me standin' here now on what'll soon be *my* front porch?"

That did it. He could feel her anger from where he stood.

"You wanted our land, Mr. McGrath. You saw an opportunity to take it from us, and you did. So yes, I'm angry. I realize, however, that you likely see your role in this as a benevolent soul. Buying the land and then allowing the poor widower and his destitute daughter to stay in their own home."

She said it with all the flair of a street actor back in London, but with that Southern touch. But he decided now might not be the best time to make such an observation.

"What I see most when I look at you, Mr. McGrath, is a man who took advantage of a father who, yes, is desperate to make certain his daughter is provided for. I see a man who pounced on the opportunity to marry a woman of landed gentry, somehow thinking that his purchase of such an estate would fill the deficit of his own lack of family breeding while bolstering his social status." She took a quick breath. "But I can tell you right now that your plan, on that last count, will not work. Right or wrong, you will never be accepted in this town."

Feeling the cut of her words, and the sting of truth scattered among them, Cullen was grateful Mr. Linden was already abed. Only a short while ago the man had said how well he'd thought today had gone and how he believed his daughter would adjust given time. Cullen briefly closed his eyes.

And to think he'd held a sliver of the same hope. Especially when looking into her expression today as they stood together before the pastor. Aye, she seemed nervous, even frightened, but for half a heartbeat, after he placed the ring on her finger, when he leaned to brush a chaste kiss on her forehead, he thought he'd seen a possibility of . . .

Well, no matter. He'd hoped Margaret Linden was more like her father and less like everyone else in town. But it seemed he was mistaken. And if he was hurt by anything she'd said just now, he had only himself to blame. After all, he'd egged her on.

Regardless, she was right, especially in one sense. They needed to get some things straight between them. And now it was his turn. "Miss Linden—"

He descended the porch steps, and she took a quick backward stride. Was the woman frightened of him? Cullen stopped where he was.

"To be clear, ma'am, I did not *take* your land. I bought it, as you said yourself. Or I will, tomorrow. And as for marryin' you today, you're right. Without this land between us, you and I would never have crossed paths, of that I'm sure. And correct me if I'm wrong, but I'm not the only one who said 'I do' today."

"I had no choice in the matter."

"If there's one thing I've learned, ma'am, and it's a lesson that cost me dearly, it's that one always has a choice. You chose to marry me because if you didn't, in two weeks time you would've lost everything. So some might say it's you who used me—and my money. But now you get to keep your home, your horse, all your things. So the way I see it, we both did the marryin' today because we wanted somethin'. And for the both of us, that somethin' outweighed the cost of this marriage. It's as simple as that—" He hesitated. Did he dare? Aye, he thought he would. "Mrs. McGrath."

He couldn't see her face, but he didn't need to. Her slender shoulders tightened, and her hands curled into tiny knots as though she wished she could wallop him. The thought made him smile. Which wouldn't have gone over well, he knew. Fortunately for him, it was dark.

Her breath quickened as though she was gaining steam for a second round. "You're correct, Mr. McGrath, at least in part. I didn't want to lose my home, my family's land. My horse," she added softly. "And I'm . . . grateful to you for allowing us to keep Linden Downs." She ground out the words. "But the true motivation behind what I did today was for my father. After last night . . . seeing him like that, I—" Her voice caught. "I realized that if I didn't do this, if I didn't . . . marry you . . ."

The words came in a whisper. Not with disdain, as had colored her tone earlier, but rather with a deep vein of regret. Which somehow wounded him even more.

". . . then my father's distress about what would happen to me in the future, once he's no longer here to provide, would be too much for him. And coupled with losing this land he loves so much . . . Well, I don't think he would live through that. And he's all I have left."

She bowed her head, and even though she made no sound, Cullen knew she was weeping. And even though she'd been the one to pick the fight, he felt every bit the boorish fool he'd been.

"Miss Linden, I—"

"Please . . ." She looked up, her voice a whisper. "Don't patronize me. And please don't stand there thinking that you and I are the same. Because we are not." She exhaled a shaky breath.

Tempted to defend his actions, as well as to correct her misassumption about his pouncing on the chance to marry her, Cullen held his tongue. Nothing he said right now would be heard. She was hurt and angry, and he couldn't say he blamed her. But he also couldn't just tell her to go on her merry little way. Because he'd given Mr. Linden his word that, in exchange for the land, he would protect his daughter and would do the same with her home and everything else.

And he intended to keep that promise. No matter what. Just as he was keeping his promise to his first wife.

Maggie skirted around him but heard Cullen's footsteps close behind.

Heart pounding, she couldn't believe she'd actually said some of the things she'd said. In a way, she was glad. But in another . . . she regretted having revealed such fragile feelings to him. She'd kept telling herself not to cry, do *not* cry, and then she'd cried anyway.

The weight of the day had taken its toll, and she was ready to put it behind her. Sad to feel that way about what should have been a joyous occasion.

She paused in the hallway, the house still and seeming so empty.

As usual when she worked late in the stable, Onnie had turned down the lamps in every room on the main floor save one at the foot of the staircase. Right now Maggie wished that Cletus and Onnie lived in this house, instead of in a cabin some distance away with others that had stood empty since the war. She would have welcomed company.

Her father was upstairs, she knew, and already asleep, Bucket at the foot of his bed. And she suddenly felt very much alone with Cullen McGrath. And on this, their wedding night.

But surely, under the circumstances, and especially after their exchange outside, the man wasn't assuming that they would share a bed. Maggie flushed just thinking about it. She certainly had no plans for anything of the sort!

Her four older brothers had taught her many things, God bless them. Among the lessons was that the majority of a male's thoughts were centered upon one thing and one thing only—females, to put it delicately. *If ever you're in doubt about the direction of a man's thinking, Maggie,* Oak had cautioned her, especially after she finally got her shape and his friends started noticing, *just assume that's where their thoughts are takin' 'em, little sister.*

Deciding to head Cullen McGrath off at the pass, she retrieved the lamp from the side table and hurried up the stairs. "I'll show you to your room, Mr. McGrath." She didn't wait for a response.

Reaching the second-floor landing, she took an immediate left and paused outside Oak's old room, the one she'd asked Onnie to make ready earlier that afternoon. It was the larger of the two unoccupied bedrooms, but the main reason for her choice was its location—on the opposite end and side of the hallway from hers.

Oak's room was also right next to her father's, and she'd recently thought about moving into it. But she always left their doors ajar at night and was able to hear him should he need anything.

A lamp burned low on the bedside table, and what few belongings Mr. McGrath had retrieved from his boarding room in town before dinner had been deposited beside the bed.

"Here you are, Mr. McGrath." She kept her voice low so as not to waken her father. "I trust you'll be comfortable." She nodded. "Good night."

She was halfway down the hall when she heard him whisper, "And which one is your room, Miss Linden?"

She paused, then looked back to see him standing exactly where he'd been, and she panicked. "My room?" What if he did have . . . husbandly expectations?

She broke out in a cold sweat. And in a blink she was a girl again, and she and Savannah had "accidentally" been snooping in one of her brothers' bedrooms when they found a stack of drawings. Drawings of scantily clad women. Why her brothers would ever want such things made no sense. But what stood out in Maggie's memory most was the frank conversation Oak had with her afterward. *Knowing Ma, she's not likely to ever say any of this to you, and it's time you knew at least a little.*

Growing up on a farm, Maggie was familiar with how the animals often played with each other. But not until that enlightening conversation with her eldest brother had she begun to understand the full meaning of the word *play*.

Even now, some ten years later, she still had plenty of unanswered questions.

Cullen McGrath took a step toward her. "Aye," he said softly. "Your room. You know, where you sleep at night and waken come morn? I take it that room there is your father's." He nodded toward Papa's partially opened door.

She swallowed. "I-I'm on the other side of the hallway." She didn't bother pointing to which of the three remaining closed bedroom doors was hers, preferring to leave it ambiguous, at least for tonight. "Why?" she asked, immediately wishing she hadn't.

Even in the dim lamplight she detected a sparkle in his eyes, and something about him—his offhanded manner, perhaps, or the way he seemed not to care what others thought, her included—had an effect on her. Despite his being Irish.

He stood there watching her as if he had all the time in the world, and yet wasn't bothered by time at all. And those eyes. Eyes that saw too much, she feared. At times, when he looked at her, she got the impression he was laughing at her, even though not a hint of a smile touched his face.

Like now, for instance.

He took another step forward. "I'm curious to know which room is yours . . . in the event your father needs you during the night. My room is close to his. I might hear him when you might not."

Maggie started to respond that she slept with her door open, but quickly decided to keep that to herself. "My room is the last door on the right." She gestured. "But not to worry, I can hear my father perfectly well. We've managed to get along just fine without any help until now." Begrudgingly, though, she had to admit, his consideration was a kind one, even if out of character.

Mr. McGrath said nothing, only cocked his head and stared. And there it was again—that sense that he was laughing at her.

Maggie gathered her nerve. "It's late, Mr. McGrath. And I recommend we retire. Each to our own rooms," she added quickly, then had another thought. "Best we leave for town first thing in the morning. I have other errands to run, as I imagine you will as well."

"I can leave whenever you like."

She nodded. Going earlier would lessen the chance of anyone she knew seeing them together. She couldn't keep their marriage hidden forever, or even for long in this town, but she would appreciate the chance to get accustomed to the idea herself before having others offer their opinions. And with the Tax and Title Office on the same street as Miss Hattie's Dress and Drapery Shop, where Savannah was employed, the earlier in the day they left and returned the better.

She intended to tell Savannah about Mr. McGrath. And Mary too. But she preferred to do it without Cullen McGrath around, so she could answer the 101 questions Savannah and Mary would pepper her with.

Mary . . .

Maggie had almost forgotten about General Harding's request to meet Mr. McGrath. The general's pointed mention of her use of Belle Meade's training facilities for her riding lessons had made it clear his request was not to be ignored. And yet . . .

If Mr. McGrath met General Harding, and they began talking thoroughbreds and Linden Downs and Bourbon Belle, then—Maggie felt the size of her world shrink by half. No, that would not do.

She couldn't have Mr. McGrath finding out about her racing Bourbon Belle before she'd laid the proper groundwork. How she would do that, she didn't know. But she would, given time to—

"Or we could simply leave right now and get to town before sunup."

Realizing he was teasing her—as well as purposefully waiting for her to go to her room first—Maggie ignored his jesting. "Good *night*, Mr. McGrath." She strode to her bedroom and closed the door behind her.

But just before it latched, she heard, "Rest well . . . Miss Linden."

And would've sworn she heard him laughing.

Cullen closed his own bedroom door, still smiling, but bothered as well, though he couldn't reason exactly why.

The night had cooled but his room still felt warm, so he nudged the open window up a little farther, the chirrup of crickets growing louder. Grateful for the pitcher of water and a glass on the dresser, he poured and drank. His thirst slaked, he stripped to his drawers, turned down the lamp, and fell into bed, exhausted.

The sheets were cool against his bare back and chest, yet no sooner had he closed his eyes than the day began to replay before him in quick succession. Scarcely in bed a minute, he grew overwarm and threw back the sheets. He stood and crossed to the door.

Silently he turned the latch then eased the door open. *Ah* . . . The transom above the double doors leading to a balcony at the end of the hallway was blissfully open, ushering a breeze through.

He turned to head back to bed when the telling squeak of a hinge brought him up short. He stilled, then a smile came. Could it be that Miss Linden—

"Cullen?" came a whisper.

His smile widened, not in pleasure, but at his own foolishness. "Aye, sir?"

He stepped into the hallway to see the older gentleman standing in the doorway to his own room, dressed in a nightgown similar to what Cullen's grandfather had worn, the collie right by him.

Cullen kept his voice low. "Do you need somethin', sir?"

"I was warm. Just thought I'd open my door the rest of the way."

Cullen nodded. "I did the same." He glanced down the hallway only to find Miss Linden's door still closed.

"Could I . . . trouble you to get me some water from downstairs? My pitcher is empty, and that yarrow tea Onnie brewed me earlier always makes me thirsty."

"Not at all, sir. But I think I have some left in mine."

Cullen got the pitcher from his dresser and carried it next door, able to see his way into Mr. Linden's bedroom in the scant moonlight, mindful of Bucket lying watchful on the floor by the bed.

Cullen found a glass on the dresser, poured, then handed it to his father-in-law, when he noticed . . .

Mr. Linden's window that faced the front of the house was wide open—and directly above the porch steps where he and Miss Linden had had their exchange outside just minutes earlier.

Cullen turned back.

Mr. Linden handed him the empty glass and wiped his mouth then eased back into bed. "Thank you, son. I appreciate that."

"You're welcome, sir." Thinking about all the things he and Miss Linden had said to each other—about him having taken their land, how he'd said they were the same and she'd argued just the opposite, her saying this was a business arrangement.

"Sir . . ." Cullen sighed. It was late, and the fatigue he'd felt earlier settled over him double-fold. Yet he couldn't assume or pretend the man hadn't heard. Not with the promises Cullen had made to him that morning before the ceremony. "What you overheard from below earlier this evenin', Mr. Linden . . . I don't want you to think I've changed my mind or gone back on my promise to you. Because I haven't."

Maybe it was the quiet coupled with the dark, but the silence seemed to stretch on forever.

"I know you haven't," Mr. Linden finally whispered. "And I know it's going to take some time. And commitment. And . . . patience."

Cullen winced, remembering the tone in which he'd said *Mrs. McGrath*, and wishing he could take it back. "Aye, sir. I realize that. I am committed and I will be patient. More so than I demonstrated tonight, I give you my word. Again," he finished, his voice tight with unexpected emotion.

After a moment, a gentle chuckle lightened the darkness. "I told you she was headstrong, just like her mother."

Cullen felt the touch of a smile return, yet couldn't give in to it. "I won't let you down, sir. And I won't let her down either. At least, not intentionally. This isn't a . . . business arrangement to me. It's a marriage. And I'll work to make it one." Even if it wasn't sacred, as his first had been.

In the dim light Cullen saw Mr. Linden reach out a hand, and he met the man's weakened grip.

"Son, you've already won my favor. Now all you have to do is win hers."

Chapter Ten

Cullen was up and dressed before sunrise. A night as fitful as the previous one left him feeling at odds with himself and with his surroundings, and he wondered again if he'd done the right thing. Especially when he recalled what Mr. Linden had said to him late last night. He tucked the leather money pouch down inside his shirt, feeling the weight of his dreams within it.

On his way downstairs he looked back and threw a cursory glance in the direction of Miss Linden's closed bedroom door—which was surely locked and bolted, perhaps even nailed shut, for all he knew—and his doubts deepened.

It had taken the better part of the night to figure out what had bothered him so much after they'd said good night, and the more he thought about it, the more riled he got.

He hadn't held the least expectation of taking Miss Linden to his bed. What kind of man did she think he was?

Margaret Linden was a beautiful woman, and regardless of his knowing that nothing was going to happen between them last night, it still hadn't stopped him from imagining what their wedding night might have been like had circumstances been different.

Especially with her bedroom only yards away, and remembering how that cream-colored dress she'd worn set off the brown of her eyes, as well as other things he noticed. After all, the woman was his wife.

Correction, his *business* partner.

Rankled all over again, he eventually found his way to the dining room. His mood and outlook improved by the time he'd downed three cups of Miss Onnie's black coffee, along with a full plate of scrambled eggs with toast and ham, all served up silently but kindly enough by the woman.

With no sign of Miss Linden, he headed to the stable to hitch up the wagon, the sun still yawning over the eastern horizon, the air fresh with morning. He found Cletus already at work in the garden tending newly planted vegetables set in neat, even rows in the tilled soil.

"Mornin', Cletus." Cullen nodded as he passed.

"Morning, Mister McGrath."

Cullen slowed then retraced his steps. "A question for you this morning."

The man paused, hoe buried deep in dirt. "Yes, sir."

Cullen went as far as the fence bordering the garden plot, making note of the rotting wood and missing slats, and adding both to his mental list. "I'm lookin' for about twenty men. Strong, able workers, willin' to put in a full day's work for a fair day's wage. I'm thinkin' you would know where I could find such men."

Cletus ran a hand along his jawline, his gaze roving the fallow fields. "Sure do. Reckon you want me to ask 'em for you too, sir?"

"No, I'll do the askin'. If you'll give me the names and where I can find them, of course."

Cletus eyed him. "Ain't many white men be in that part of town, sir."

"Well, they won't have trouble seein' me comin' then, will they?" Cullen smiled, glad when the older man did too.

Cletus glanced over at the barn. "I know me some men who make wagons, too, sir. And tools. Better and cheaper than what you get in town."

"Good. I'll take their names as well." Cullen hesitated. "Would you like to tell them to me later, or—"

"I have Onnie write 'em down, sir. My wife, she smart. She got her letters and numbers young. Me . . ." He laughed. "I ain't never took to 'em."

"No shame in that. Plenty of things I never took to either." From the corner of his eye Cullen spotted movement in one of the second-story windows and recognized Miss Linden's form as she passed by.

"I have them names to you real soon, Mister McGrath."

"That'd be appreciated, Cletus."

Cullen discovered that Cletus had already tended to Levi, so he wasted no time in hitching the Percheron to the wagon, having clearly understood from Miss Linden last night that she wanted to leave early.

To his pleasure, he found the Lindens' one and only wagon more than serviceable, though it was a bit smaller than he would've liked. But seeing no tarp, he returned to the stable and found one.

He also found Miss Linden's thoroughbred to be as exceptional upon closer inspection as he'd thought at first glance.

"You're a pretty girl, you are," he whispered, stroking the bay mare and appreciating the way she nuzzled up to him. "Like to run, too, don't you? I've seen you out there." *With your mistress,* he added to himself. Odd for the Lindens to keep such a horse when surely she'd bring a handsome sum. Why keep such a fine thoroughbred when they could sell her to someone in the racing community? Why not keep a draft horse accustomed to working on a farm?

Of course—he gave the mare a gentle rub on her nose—this fine lady could do the work nicely, too, if she was well trained. Yet it would be a waste of her truer gifts. He knew, though, why Mr. Linden hadn't sold the blood horse.

His daughter loved this animal. Her bond with the mare had been evident the first time he'd seen her riding.

"I'm ready, Mr. McGrath."

Cullen turned to see the woman herself standing in the doorway. She wore a blue dress that hugged every curve, reminding him yet again of what he hadn't enjoyed as a new groom the night before. In an instant the frustration he'd awakened with returned, especially since she appeared so well rested.

Yet he determined, as he'd promised her father, to be patient, to try to smooth the road before them. Wherever it might lead.

"Miss Linden! I was just admirin' your horse. She's quite a beauty."

"Thank you. And yes, she is."

"How long have you owned her?"

She held his gaze. "I've raised her from a foal, Mr. McGrath."

"I'm impressed. What's her name?"

Her focus moved from him to the horse. "Bourbon Belle."

He nodded, giving Bourbon Belle a rub. "That's a good name. Where was she bred?"

Was it his imagination, or did her eyes narrow the slightest bit?

"At the neighboring stud farm, Belle Meade." Her smile was fleeting. "And now, if you don't mind . . ." She fingered the reticule dangling from her arm. "Shall we be going? It's getting rather late."

Hearing the impatience in her tone, Cullen glanced outside, knowing it couldn't be much past seven o'clock. It scarcely took half an hour to get into town, and doubtful any of the shops would even be unlatching their doors until at least eight.

"Aye, we can be goin', if you like."

Outside, Miss Linden started to climb into the wagon of her own accord, but Cullen tossed the tarp in the bed, came up behind her, and lifted her to the bench seat—with momentum to spare.

She landed a little hard and looked down at him as though questioning whether or not he'd ever assisted a lady before.

"My apologies," he muttered, the back of his neck heating. "You're even lighter than I figured."

He'd meant it only as an observation but could tell by her slight frown that she'd taken it for the worse.

Jaw tight, he strode to the other side of the wagon, remembering what she'd said about his "lack of family breeding." Likely she was recalling the same thing about now. But even more frustrating to him was how fine it had felt to touch her, even that littlest bit. His hands encircling her tiny waist, the pressure of her slight weight against him. And her scent—sweeter than lavender in full bloom.

He climbed up beside her, doing his best not to appear as unsettled as he felt. But the wagon bench proved a narrower width than he'd wagered, and the feel of her thigh pressed flush against his only taunted him further.

She, on the other hand, seemed oblivious.

She merely stared straight ahead, clutching that fancy little purse of hers. Which only vexed him more.

He released the brake, gently slapped the reins, and the wagon jerked forward, the Percheron pulling with greater force than required. A rueful smile tipped Cullen's mouth. He wasn't the only one miscalculating.

Passing the house, he glanced up and saw Mr. Linden staring down from his bedroom window. The older gentleman lifted a hand in greeting, and Cullen, hoping he hadn't made the man a promise he couldn't keep, nodded in return.

"So where do you need to go in town, Miss Linden? After we finish at the Tax and Title Office?"

Maggie took her time in responding, still stinging over the comment he'd made when assisting her into the wagon minutes earlier.

She'd been almost fifteen before she'd finally gotten any semblance of curves. And this, after the rest of the other girls had already budded, bloomed, *and* blossomed. She remembered walking home from school with Mary and Savannah, both friends already well into womanhood, and the boys having taken notice of that fact. One day they passed the mercantile where the boys gathered outside and, wanting them to notice her, too, she had pulled her long hair forward over her chest, arranging the curls just so, hoping to give the appearance of substance where there was none.

But as her brother Abe had told her in that teasing voice, "You can't hide what you haven't got, Little Mag."

But for Cullen McGrath to all but say as much . . .

Maggie firmed her jaw, focusing her gaze on the hard-packed dirt passing beneath the wagon. Papa said Mr. McGrath had been married before, and she wondered . . . what had his first wife been like?

She sneaked a look at his profile, her imagination filling in the blanks. No doubt she'd been a buxom Irish beauty, full-figured with fiery red hair and alabaster skin like the women in the dime novels. A woman who would never have been mistaken for a boy. At any age.

He turned and met her gaze, and Maggie quickly faced forward.

"I need to stop in Mulholland's Mercantile for a few items," she said. "Then the dry goods store."

"All right. I know where Mulholland's is. But you'll need to direct me to the dry goods store."

She'd already worked out the details for how to coordinate their various errands that morning, beginning with paying the back taxes. But she decided to wait until they were closer to town before mentioning it.

Persistent spring rains in prior weeks brought green to the area earlier than usual, and the trees were leafed out and full. The pungent scent of pine layered the air. But the relentless moisture combined with passing wagons had left claw marks on the road, and the wooden wheels jarred over sun-dried ruts and dips.

With each bump and sway Maggie became more aware of the man beside her.

She'd ridden beside her brothers all her life, so to have a man crowding the wagon bench, his muscular leg brushing against hers, wasn't anything new. And yet . . .

It was.

Because sitting next to Cullen McGrath wasn't the same at all. Nor did it feel like sitting next to Richard, the only boy she'd ever kissed. Being with Richard had been like being with her brothers—the same ease and playful banter, only with a sweetness that set him apart and made her feel safe and comfortable.

Cullen McGrath made her feel anything but safe. And sweetness was not an attribute she would assign the man.

You're even lighter than I figured. His words played over in her mind. She glanced down at her chest.

Why was it men preferred women with larger busts? In the drawings she'd found in her brothers' room, every one of those women had a bosom ample enough to suffocate a small child. Women with waists so tiny and middles corseted so tight everything spilled over the top like bread left too long to rise. Well, if that's what Cullen Michael McGrath liked in women, then he could just—

"I went to university, Miss Linden. For two years."

Maggie's thoughts skidded to a halt. Where had *that* come from, she wondered, and looked over at him. "The Irish . . . have universities?"

He laughed. And too late, she realized how foolish she'd sounded.

"Aye, we have universities. And though it's been years since I left, I hear horses and buggies should be comin' to the island soon too."

His laughter was deep and full and all but invited a person to join in. Maggie felt herself smile. Then before she knew it, a tiny laugh escaped.

He looked over at her, and a warmth that she hadn't seen before filled his gaze. And she realized again how attractive a man he was. Even though rough. And Irish.

"What did you study, Mr. McGrath?"

He smiled and gave a boyish shrug. "Agriculture. And actually I studied in England, where my family lived at the time. Only it wasn't . . . regular university."

"What do you mean?"

"It was a school in the Irish part of town run by professors who taught in Ireland before they left. They weren't welcome in the English universities. No Irish were."

He said it matter-of-factly, yet in the silence following, and in the way his grip tightened on the reins, she sensed some lingering bitterness.

"When did you and your family leave Ireland?"

"I was nearly sixteen," he answered after a moment. "So that was . . . almost fourteen years ago."

She didn't know which surprised her more. To discover he was nearly ten years her senior, instead of five or six as she'd thought, or that he'd left Ireland so long ago to live in England. "But you still have your accent," she noted.

He turned. "What accent?"

His expression was so somber, she almost believed him. She gave him a look.

"As I said, we all lived in the same area. It suited us. And . . . it suited them."

She tried to imagine him as a boy of sixteen, and surprisingly, she could. Oddly enough, the image of Oak came to mind, and she realized with a start that Cullen McGrath was the same age Oak would have been, had he lived.

She glanced down at her grandmother's ring on her left hand and could still picture it on her mother's slender finger. Following the Linden family custom, this ring should've gone to Oak to give to his wife. It felt strange for it to end up being hers.

"I didn't complete my studies."

The flatness in his voice drew Maggie's attention. The firm lines of his mouth told her he wasn't proud of the fact, and she wondered why he'd told her.

"I told you I went to university, but . . . I don't mean to give you the impression I finished. Because I didn't."

She looked at him for a moment. "What happened?"

He started to respond then glanced over. "I take it your father told you about my da?"

She frowned. "Your . . ."

"My father."

The seriousness in his expression, coupled with his scrutiny, conspired to make her look away, especially when she remembered what she'd said about his family upbringing. But she didn't.

"Yes," she answered softly. "He did. He said your father was . . . a gambler, and . . ." She tried to remember Papa's exact wording. "His overindulgence in the sport left a . . . bad mark on you."

He laughed again, but it sounded different this time. "That's an awfully pretty way to describe somethin' so ugly, but I guess that about sums it up. He was partial to the bottle, too, which only made the gamblin' worse. Or maybe it was the other way around. Hard to say, once things started careenin' downhill as they did."

Maggie opened her mouth to ask another question, then realized they were on the outskirts of town. Already carriages and pedestrians dotted the streets. So early. Her plan to escape the notice of acquaintances might prove more challenging than she thought.

Cullen brought the wagon to a stop outside the Tax and Title Office, and she wasted no time in climbing down of her own accord, acting as though she didn't notice the irritated look he tossed her.

But when she reached for the handle to the front door, he beat her to it.

"Allow me," he said softly, closer to her ear than etiquette allowed. Unless, of course, the man was her husband . . .

Wondering if the neatly scripted shingle above the door had caught his eye as it had hers, she preceded him inside. NO NIGGER OR IRISH NEED APPLY. She'd never liked those signs. And liked them even less now.

She hoped the entire office staff hadn't arrived yet. There was one employee in particular she wished to avoid, and when she glanced at the manager's office and discovered the curtains still drawn, she breathed a tentative sigh of relief.

The office brought to mind her father's library—the distinct smell of dried ink on paper, perhaps, the collection of words aging with time.

"May I assist you?" The clerk, an older woman with silver sprinkled throughout her hair, rose from behind a desk, her spectacles resting half-mast and her smile doing much the same.

Maggie recalled having seen her before, but couldn't remember her name.

Cullen stepped forward. "Aye, ma'am, you can. Thank you."

The woman eyed him as he pulled a leather pouch from inside his shirt, her scrutiny accentuated by a furrowed brow.

Cullen produced a folded piece of paper from the pouch and presented it to her. "This explains our purpose here today."

Maggie frowned as the woman accepted the document, wondering what it contained and more than a little bothered by Cullen's use of *our.* More conscious of her mother's ring on her left hand, she discreetly covered it with her right.

"Mmm hmm . . ." The woman pursed her lips as she read. She glanced up at Cullen before her gaze slid briefly to Maggie. "This addresses the Linden Downs property, Mr. . . ." She looked at the document again. "McGrath."

"Aye, ma'am, it does." Cullen nodded. "Mr. Gilbert Linden penned that in his own hand."

Her father wrote it? It was all Maggie could do not to grab the piece of paper and read it for herself.

"And do you have the necessary funds with you, Mr. McGrath, to satisfy the outstanding debt? Because we don't make loans to—"

"I do." He touched the pouch. "So I won't be requirin' a loan."

She looked from him back to the letter. "I'll need to confirm that the amount listed is, indeed, the required sum. And that the signature for Mr. Linden agrees with the one on file."

The woman's gaze connected with Maggie's again, and Maggie saw recognition this time. And something else.

"Miss Linden . . ." The woman nodded once. "Nice to see you again, miss. I trust your father is well?"

Certain she heard a question within a question, Maggie hesitated, intending to answer honestly, yet not wanting to say anything that might cross purposes with the reason for their visit. "Actually, my father's constitution has weakened recently, which is why he's not here himself today. He'd be the first to tell you he's not as spry as he once was, as much as that annoys him."

Compassion shadowed the clerk's expression, followed by clarity. "A sentiment to which I can wholly relate, sad to say. Please give your father my best. Now if you'll both wait here, I need to pull records from the back."

As soon as the woman disappeared through the doorway, Maggie reached for the letter she'd left lying on the desk.

"Don't trust me?" Cullen whispered.

"I never said that."

"No . . . you didn't. Say it, I mean."

Determined not to take the bait this time, Maggie read the letter. Her father's script, as familiar to her as her own, confirmed the missive's authenticity. The message was brief and unequivocal.

All back taxes and loans owed by the property of Linden Downs will be paid in full by Cullen Michael McGrath. Therefore, with any and all outstanding debts satisfied, the property of Linden Downs as legally described below–including all livestock and horses–will be forthwith removed from scheduled auction and will, in turn, be assigned to its rightful possessor.

Carefully worded, the final sentence. It avoided stating outright who the owner would be, and Maggie wondered if her father had chosen that wording with intent. To delay the news from spreading around town, perhaps. She would remember to thank him.

The front door opened behind them and Maggie turned, bracing herself.

A man entered, about her age, and Maggie let out her breath. He nodded briefly in their direction as he shut the door behind him, and then walked to a desk in a far corner. Only then did she realize her stomach was in knots. The sooner this transaction was completed, the better.

"Here we are," the woman said, returning. She smoothed a folded document out on the desk before them. "The amount listed here is what is due. So if you'll present the full payment, Mr. McGrath, we'll sign the papers and the debt will be satisfied."

Cullen handed the woman a stack of bills, and she, in turn, counted them. Even though Maggie had never known a hungry day in her life, she'd never seen so much money in one place before. How did a man like Cullen McGrath have access to that amount of cash? She wished she'd thought to ask.

On second thought, she probably didn't want to know.

"I'll need to keep Mr. Linden's letter and place it in the file. If you'll sign here, Mr. McGrath"—the woman pointed—"and here, then we'll be done."

Feeling even more finality in the moment than she'd anticipated, Maggie sensed her world shift as Cullen signed the papers. She stared at the man beside her. A stranger. And yet . . . her husband.

For so long she'd tried to live right, to do as a God-fearing person should. And look where that had gotten her. Did God even see her anymore? Did he see her standing here now? Was this some kind of discipline, perhaps, for her pushing her father, as she had, to pay the stud fee to breed their best mare with Vandal, a Belle Meade champion? Then to let her race Bourbon Belle?

Despite her mother's adamant opinion to the contrary, Papa had told her she seemed born for riding. And for training horses. Granted, he'd added about the latter, *Born a little before your time, perhaps.*

Cullen McGrath chose that moment to look over at her, and she was certain she read triumph in his eyes. Then he blinked, and it was gone.

If he thought paying her family's debt and signing that piece of paper gave him the right not only to own Linden Downs but to dictate her future, she knew a certain Irishman who was going to be very disappointed.

Because she *would* race Bourbon Belle in the Peyton Stakes come fall. And she would win. She just didn't yet know quite how.

Chapter Eleven

Once outside, Mr. McGrath assisted her into the wagon again, more delicately this time. The smell of freshly baked bread wafted toward them from the open door of a nearby bakery, making breakfast feel more distant than it actually was.

Aware of people watching them, and certain it wasn't her imagination, Maggie spotted the sign for Miss Hattie's Dress and Drapery Shop and again imagined crossing paths with Savannah while in Cullen McGrath's company. Her body flushing hot, then cold, she attempted a casual tone.

"Where do *you* need to go in town this morning, Mr. McGrath?"

He released the wheel brake and urged the Percheron down the street. "To the saddlery, then to a feed store. I'd also like to stop by a bank, if the other errands don't take too long."

"I'm certain we can get it all done," she said with more brightness than the moment called for.

The sideways look he gave her said he noticed it too.

From an alleyway, a freight wagon cut into their path, and Cullen reined in sharply, sending Maggie pitching forward. He stretched an arm out in front of her, catching her across the chest and pinning her back. Though the wagon bench had already felt crowded, Maggie learned a new meaning of closeness.

"Are you all right?" he asked after a few seconds.

She nodded, keeping her focus ahead, keenly aware of his touch. "Yes, I'm fine."

He removed his arm and, once the traffic cleared, urged the horse onward. He'd meant nothing by the act, Maggie knew that. But her body was still reliving the moment.

Needing space between them, and trying to avoid the stares from passersby on the street, she saw the opportunity she'd been waiting for. "If you'll stop up ahead, I'll get out there."

He glanced over. "What do you mean?"

"I'll do my shopping and then meet you back here. That way I won't slow you down, and we'll finish faster."

He shook his head. "I'm in no hurry, Miss Linden. And Mulholland's Mercantile isn't that far from the saddlery, which is where I need to—"

"It's no bother. Really." She gathered her skirt and climbed down before he'd even brought the wagon to a full stop. Growing up with four older brothers had allowed her to hone her agility. She smiled up, her face feeling tight. "I'll meet you back here in . . . two hours?"

He said nothing, only stared at her, and she sensed he knew exactly what she was doing. His gaze went dull, then dark. A stab of guilt made the moment even more uncomfortable. But what did he expect her to do? Just arrive in town on an Irishman's arm and wave to all of her friends? And she the daughter of one of the founding families of Nashville?

What she'd been through in recent years had beaten her down. More than she'd realized. First, losing her family, save her father. Then the slow decline of Linden Downs. Losing one's place in society, one's station in life, was hard enough. But to do it with everyone watching . . .

Then came Bourbon Belle, and the dream of keeping their home had been given new life. Only to be snuffed out before it even had a—

He snapped the reins. "I'll see you in two hours."

The wagon pulled away and she watched Cullen go, his broad shoulders rigid. Standing there in the aftermath, she felt smaller somehow. Which only encouraged her to stand straighter. He simply didn't understand. How could he? They were from different worlds.

She removed her mother's ring and slipped it into her skirt pocket, determined to get her shopping done, then bide her time somewhere inconspicuous until he returned. She waited until he maneuvered the wagon around the corner before continuing down the street. But she needn't have bothered, because he never looked back.

She was so different from Moira.

Moira had been closer to his age; Margaret Linden was considerably younger. Moira had been gentle, loving, and wise; Miss Linden was sharp, antagonistic, and impatient. Even as the comparisons fought their way to the forefront of his thoughts, Cullen attempted to subdue them, knowing they wouldn't help his present situation.

Still, Miss Linden's opinion of him was undeniable: the woman barely tolerated him. When instinct kicked in moments earlier and he reached out to assure her safety . . . Well, her displeasure had been nearly as palpable as had been his instinctive gesture. Aye, the woman was petite, no doubt about it. But she was still woman through and through. However, best he not dwell on that for the moment. He was far from winning her over, as her father had kindly challenged, but he was still determined to do so.

After all, she didn't know him well enough yet to know she didn't like him. That would take at least a month. Maybe two.

For some reason, that thought made him smile.

Two hours later, after accomplishing everything he'd intended—with plenty of the backlash he'd incurred before from proprietors—he arrived back at the spot where Miss Linden had all but leapt from the wagon. Yet he saw no sign of her. The image of her climbing down filled his mind's eye again. That the woman had been raised with four older brothers was obvious. But to accomplish the feat with such finesse in a skirt!

He might have been impressed if he hadn't been so frustrated with her.

The streets were busy, and he waited for a carriage and freight wagon to pass before managing to pull the wagon off to the side and set the brake. That's when he saw her standing down the street, past the Tax and Title Office and near the corner in front of some boarded-up shops. He wasn't blind. He knew she didn't want to be seen with him. But as he climbed down to go fetch her, that was the least of his concerns.

He knew the moment she spotted him because she glanced about, presumably to see if anyone she knew was around. Which only made him want to throw her over his shoulder and carry her back to the wagon. Not a bad idea altogether, nor an unpleasant one. But he doubted it would help his cause.

"Miss Linden." He resisted the urge to offer her his arm. "Are you ready?"

She peered past him. "Where's the wagon?"

"I left it up the street a ways. Where you . . . liberated yourself from the wagon earlier and instructed me to pick you up."

Her lips firmed. "I simply decided to walk, and I ended up here."

He nodded, not buying it. Seeing two parcels at her feet, he bent to retrieve them.

"I can carry them." She managed to grasp one before he did, then reached out to take the other.

He pulled it back. "I don't mind helpin' you."

"That's very kind of you, Mr. McGrath. But I don't require your help."

The syrupy sweetness of her tone curdled beneath his skin. "You're doin' it again."

She peered up.

"That polite meanness you're so good at."

Her eyes darkened. "Well, if you would simply obey my wishes and let me carry my own—"

He let the parcel drop. It landed with a thud in the dirt. "Be my guest."

Her mouth slipped open then just as quickly clamped shut again. "If you only knew what—"

"Is this man bothering you, Miss Linden?"

Cullen heard warning in the voice behind him, but it was the utter embarrassment on Margaret Linden's face that knifed clean through him.

"M-Mr. Drake . . ." Miss Linden blinked, then smoothed her hair with a trembling hand.

It took a second for the name to register, but when Cullen turned he realized he'd guessed correctly. A telling glimmer sharpened the man's gaze, and Drake looked overlong at Margaret Linden, then back again at Cullen, a challenge in his eyes.

"We meet again so soon, Mr. McGrath." Drake bent to retrieve the package in the dirt and handed it to Miss Linden, moving closer to her as he did. "And here I thought we had an understanding that you were moving on."

"No. No understandin' that I recall." Cullen noted the men standing to the side. Only two this time. And no gun, that he could see. "But from what I hear there's plenty of land east, if *you're* interested. The Carolinas, perhaps. Or south on to Georgia." He smiled, enjoying the downward turn of Drake's expression as he repeated the man's own words back to him.

Clearly confused, Miss Linden stared between them, her expression anxious. "I'm fine, Mr. Drake," she offered, inching away from him as though sensing Cullen's displeasure. "Now if you'll excuse me, I—"

"No need for you to go anywhere, Miss Linden." Drake tucked her hand into the crook of his arm, and it was all Cullen could do not to plow straight into him.

"McGrath, if you need directions out of town"—Drake gestured—"my men here will be obliged to help."

The two fellows stepped forward, and Cullen grew aware of the space suddenly open around them. A handful of people had paused to watch, but most folks hurried past, giving them a wide berth and not looking back. Knowing how he would have handled this if Miss Linden weren't present, Cullen took a deep breath then caught a glint of indignation in her eyes. But he didn't think it was directed toward him.

"No need for that, Drake. I know the way . . . should I decide to leave."

"Which I trust will be soon. Because remember what we discussed could happen if you don't."

Cullen held his tongue, clearly seeing Miss Linden's embarrassment. But each time he looked at her hand on Drake's arm, his anger only burned hotter.

"Good, then." Drake's smile dripped with arrogance. "I'm glad we finally see eye to eye. Now . . ." He gestured. "Leave. And don't be bothering Miss Linden again."

Cullen smiled. "Botherin' her?"

Drake stiffened. "That's exactly what I said. Or do you have trouble hearing as well as speaking?"

Miss Linden's gaze met his, and Cullen had never seen eyes so expressive. She didn't approve of Drake's actions, that was clear. Still, he could all but hear her pleading with him not to make more of a scene than was already made. But if she thought he was going to tuck tail and run because of a man like this—

"I'll leave. As soon as you unhand Miss Linden."

Drake laughed. "Unhand her? The Lindens and I are old family friends. It's you, McGrath, who aren't welcome here. I think the lady has made that quite plain."

"Is that so?" Cullen waited, watching her, seeing the struggle in her eyes and yet knowing what a moment like this meant, even if she didn't. Life was full of them. Little turning points, is what his grandfather had called them.

A moment when a life was defined. Given direction. And once that direction was chosen, there was no going back. At least not easily.

And even then, if you could retrace the steps, the view was never the same. Nor the path ahead. Because every step changed the view. He'd learned that painful truth and was determined to make his path straight and true this time. No lies. No half-truths. He wasn't going to waste another moment living life the way someone else told him to.

He only had one life to live, and by God—or without—he would live it the best he could.

"As I said, Drake, I'll leave." He leveled his gaze at Miss Linden. "As soon as you unhand my wife."

Chapter TWELVE

Four days, and still she would scarcely look at him.

Cullen lifted the ax and brought it down with force, splitting the piece of wood clean in two. He set another log on the stump and repeated the process for the better part of the morning, welcoming the physical exertion and hoping it would ease his frustration.

Bathed in sweat, the morning air thick with summer and freshly laid hay, he shed his shirt and wiped down his face and neck. If he had it to do over again, would he handle the situation with Drake any differently? The man had all but called him out. What was he supposed to do? Walk away without saying a thing? What would Miss Linden have wanted him to do? But of course he didn't know, because she wasn't speaking to him.

He tossed his shirt over the corral and knifed his hands through his hair.

Deathly silence had accompanied them all the way home in the wagon. Miss Linden's back rigid, jaw set, eyes forward. And he would've sworn the bench seat had grown. Either that or she was hanging off the side—anything to touch him as little as possible. The woman was his wife, if only on paper. But what woman could respect a man who would cow to such arrogance? Such ignorance?

Nay, he'd done the right thing, even if her embarrassment kept her from seeing it at present. No woman wanted a man who wouldn't come to her defense.

"Mister McGrath?"

Cullen turned to see Onnie standing on the front porch, a glass in her hand, and Bucket running straight for him.

"For you, sir. If you's thirsty."

After giving the collie a welcome, he crossed to the porch. "Thank you, Miss Onnie." He gulped the sweet tea without pause.

She must have put the glass in the icebox beforehand, and he held it to his forehead, the cool feeling like a touch of heaven.

She took the glass from him and nodded toward the pile of wood. "Think we got us enough for two winters already."

He shrugged. "I like to be prepared. And it always goes faster than you think it will." Especially with the plans he had for this place. He glanced at the door. "Is she back yet?" he asked, figuring it had to be nearing noon.

"No, sir. But sometimes her ridin' lessons at Belle Meade, they take a while. You get that letter come from Belle Meade earlier?"

Having successfully put it from his mind until now, he nodded. But he didn't care who General William Giles Harding was, Cullen was in no hurry to cozy up to a man neck deep in horse racing. General Harding would forget soon enough what he'd done.

"You still goin' into town like you said, sir? With that list?"

Cullen nodded. "After I clean up at the creek."

"I fetch you clean clothes and leave 'em here on the porch."

She disappeared into the house with Bucket and returned a moment later with the clothes, along with a towel and soap. Cullen walked through the woods to the creek and rinsed the remnants of work from his body. He waded into a deeper pool, lathered his hair, and dunked several times.

The Lindens and I are old family friends. Drake's words returned to him, and so did Cullen's frustration.

Stephen Drake was no fool. The man had a streak of meanness in him, of the worst sort. The kind that gave a man like Drake a twisted sense of pleasure. Combine that twisted nature with power, which Stephen Drake certainly possessed as manager of the Tax and Title Office, as Onnie informed him, and you had someone who could sway decisions to get whatever he wanted. And if that didn't work, he'd simply threaten the person until he did.

Cullen strode to the creek bank and grabbed the towel, recalling the initial shock in Drake's expression when learning that Miss Linden was now Mrs. McGrath . . . then the slow way the man's face and neck had reddened when she nodded then looked away.

That had been the hardest part for him, seeing her embarrassment.

Embarrassment at being seen with him. At being singled out as his wife. Yet he'd also seen offense in her expression, which told him she'd personally felt the cut of Drake's prejudice. Which, in turn, meant a great deal.

He pulled on clean drawers then trousers, reminding himself again that Margaret Linden was young yet. When he was her age he'd thought he knew everything, and hadn't allowed anyone to tell him different. Only with time and living—and loss—had he learned how little he really knew. Odd how that worked. Backward, in a way.

They hadn't gone to church yesterday, which was fine by him. One less punishment. But following breakfast, Mr. Linden had read from his Bible at the table. When Cullen saw him produce the thick leather binding he'd gotten a trapped feeling, thinking a sermon was forthcoming. But the man had simply read. And read well, in fact.

As it turned out, the text wasn't half bad either. Not nearly as discouraging as Cullen had expected.

He wasn't certain what book Mr. Linden read from, but the words had to do with charity. Or love, as Mr. Linden said it meant. Something about charity suffering long and being kind. Not envying or being puffed up. And although Mr. Linden never looked at him, and Margaret's gaze never ventured across the table, Cullen somehow felt that Mr. Linden had chosen that section of Scripture special, for them both to hear.

Dressed, he made his way back to the house, his thoughts returning to his earlier concern. Stephen Drake wasn't a man given to weak memory or to turning the other cheek. He was the type of man who always needed to win. Which meant one thing—a reckoning was coming.

But it would have come sooner or later, whenever the man had learned about the marriage. Cullen's main concern was what form that reckoning would take.

And that *he* be the only one to pay the price.

An hour later, he prodded Levi down a side street on the east side of Nashville, following the directions Miss Onnie had given him, however odd they seemed. The list of names from Cletus was tucked in his shirt pocket, but he already knew from the older man's comments which man he needed to find first.

Shanties, clustered together, lined the maze of dirt roads that wound through this part of town. For as far as he could see, lean-tos made of orphaned plank wood, rotting boards, and remnants of old crates huddled together beneath a sweltering sun, the smell of humanity ripe on the warm breeze. Wadded-up newspaper stuffed into cracks served as mortar, and windows were scarce, which no doubt lent the insides a dark, fathomless feel.

One good storm would likely lay waste the structures, but he knew the residents would simply build them again. Because it was all they had.

The day's heat had driven most of the residents from their shelters, yet they kept to what scarce patches of shade could be negotiated between constructed overhangs and scant tree branches.

Cletus was right: not a white man to be seen. And even though Cullen had never owned another human being in his life, the unblinking stares of both young and old as he passed seemed to reach out and assign him guilt.

When you come to a busted-up old plow, sir, head south.

Spotting a plow, its gears missing, the metal spades worn to nubs, Cullen nudged Levi southward, as Onnie had said.

Go on a ways, sir, 'til you see a shanty on a corner what got three old milk crates piled up on one side. Head east.

The instructions making more sense now, Cullen followed them until up ahead, just as Onnie had said, the seemingly random pattern of makeshift houses stuttered to a pause. When he reached the clearing he reined in. From the sturdy branch of an ancient oak hung an empty noose, the coiled rope dancing far too innocently in the slight breeze.

A heaviness settled inside him.

He read the newspapers. He'd seen the pencil-sketched drawings depicting both Negroes and Irish as apes, a mug of ale typically distinguishing the latter from the former. The Southern inclination toward disdain ran deep and wide. Same as the British. Some things didn't change.

"You need somethin', sir?"

Cullen turned in the saddle to see a group of men gathered behind him. Two dozen at a glance, most bare chested, dark skin glistening beneath the sun high overhead. Some carried a hoe or shovel, though Cullen doubted gardening was their intent.

One man stood out from the rest, and not only because he was situated at the forefront. Tall and powerfully built, muscular arms resting at his side, the fellow met Cullen's stare without reservation. Everything about him declared strength, and judging by the steadiness of his gaze, Cullen figured he was the one who had posed the question.

"Aye, I do need somethin'." Cullen dismounted. "I'm lookin' for a man by the name of Ennis."

Not one of them reacted. Not a nod, not a sideways glance, not even a twitch. Cullen had to admire their unity, even if he hated the reason behind it.

"Cletus sent me," he continued. "From Linden Downs. Onnie, his wife, told me how to get here."

This time an all but imperceptible flicker of acknowledgment shone in some of their faces. But not the one man. His expression didn't change.

"You still ain't told us yet what you need here . . . sir."

Cullen could appreciate the strained control in the man's voice as well as how the other men seemed to look to him for what to do next. Which, when remembering what Cletus had said, made him certain he'd already found the man he'd come looking for.

Having bid good-bye to her final student for the day, Maggie turned and saw General Harding walking in her direction. She ducked back into the mares' stable, wincing, hoping he hadn't seen her. Because she knew what he would ask her if he did.

"Who you hidin' from now, Miss Margaret?"

Maggie looked back to see Uncle Bob, Belle Meade's head hostler, watching her, his mouth curving in a smile.

Uncle Bob had been at Belle Meade for as long as she could remember. And even though her parents had cautioned her, growing up, about becoming overly familiar with slaves—freedmen now—Uncle Bob seemed different.

First, he didn't work for her father. And second, he was Uncle Bob.

"Please." She put a finger to her lips. "I can't talk to the general right now."

"Why's that?"

Crouching, she peered through a space between the boards. "Because he's going to ask me a question I'm not ready to answer."

Uncle Bob's laughter helped lighten the moment. "He still comin' this way?"

She moved to the right a couple of boards, following the general's progress. Then sighed. "No. I don't think so."

"Seein' you like that puts me in mind of when you and Miss Mary were little girls, runnin' 'round in here, playin' and hidin'."

Maggie smiled, the memories of those times stirring emotions both happy and sad. It didn't seem that long ago, yet it felt like another lifetime.

"Hard to believe you girls is all growed up now." He wiped his hands on his trademark white apron. "Makes a man like me feel old."

Maggie straightened and smoothed her skirt. "As I remember, you used to make us work too."

His smile turned sheepish. "If you's gonna ride, it's only right you help take care of the horses. They give to us, and we give to them."

She crossed to the stall where Bourbon Belle stood, and rubbed the mare's nose. "I learned so much here. Mostly from watching you."

"You might'a learnt somethin' from me, Miss Margaret." Warmth touched his voice. "But most of what you got was born in you, ma'am. As I tol' a good friend a while back, 'fore he left to go out west to Colorado, some things with horses can be taught. The rest of it"—he touched the place over his heart—"is either in here or it ain't."

Maggie nodded, looking back at Bourbon Belle and realizing again why she couldn't give up on her dream. For herself or Belle. She'd wanted this for as long as she could remember. And they were so close. Or had been.

Maggie stood on tiptoe, pressed her forehead into the side of Belle's neck, and breathed deeply the scent of horse and hay. And her thoughts took her to the one place she didn't want them to go.

Cullen McGrath.

When she'd left this morning, he'd been chopping wood with more force than necessary. He was still angry with her, she knew. Which was fine. She was still angry with him.

He'd embarrassed her in town that day with Mr. Drake, and with everyone watching, listening. *I'll leave, as soon as you unhand my wife.* Yet as embarrassed as she'd been, a tiny part of her had been grateful, even proud of him, for standing up for her. The man was formidable.

Stephen Drake's reaction had been one of shock. And with good reason. But something else had been weighing on her . . .

The comment Mr. Drake had made that day about having an understanding with Cullen. It was obvious the two men had met before, but how? Stephen Drake's dislike of the Irish wasn't surprising. But his animosity toward Cullen McGrath was.

Because it seemed so personal.

She'd feared Mary might have heard the news about her marrying Mr. McGrath from someone in town. But apparently Stephen Drake hadn't spread the word, because Mary hadn't said a thing, even over lunch earlier. Surely she would have if she'd known.

If Drake had shown discretion in that matter—regardless of his personal animosity toward Cullen—Maggie needed to thank him. Surely his thoughtfulness was due only to their family connection.

She picked up a curry brush and ran it over Belle's coat in quick, smooth strokes, none too eager to return home. Not with Cullen there. But neither did she wish to run into General Harding.

During lunch with Mary she'd tried to work up the courage to tell her about Mr. McGrath, but each time she opened her mouth to say the words they'd evaporated, leaving only air in their place.

Mary was eager to be wed, Maggie knew, especially following the recent marriage of her older sister, Selene. Only Maggie sensed that Mary, unlike Selene, wouldn't mind leaving Belle Meade. In fact, at times Mary seemed almost eager to go. And yet no suitors came calling.

But they would, Maggie was certain. Mary Harding was sweet, kind, and generous. And most importantly, it seemed to men these days, she was wealthy.

Thinking of Mary's promising prospects for marriage made Maggie think of what hers had been. Far less promising by comparison. But for her to have been forced into this marriage as she had been—

Something within her stopped the thought cold. *If there's one thing I've learned, ma'am . . . it's that one always has a choice.*

She sighed, not knowing which bothered her more. Admitting to herself that she had, indeed, chosen to marry the man. Or that Cullen McGrath was right.

Both truths rankled at the moment.

"Quite a beauty you got there, Miss Linden."

Maggie looked up to see a stable hand peering over the stall. Only his attention wasn't on Bourbon Belle, and the keenness in his expression spoke of something other than admiration. She'd seen the man at Belle Meade numerous times. He worked with the stallions in the other stable, but had never approached her directly.

She glanced over to where Uncle Bob was. Or had been.

"Something to be admired, ma'am. Mind if I get me a closer look?" Without waiting for her permission, he opened the stall door and stepped inside. "She's been winnin' some races, I hear. Must be fast."

Belle shook her head and stomped the ground, and Maggie grabbed hold of the lead rein. "I would prefer you would stay outside the stall, sir. The mare can be a bit skittish."

He hesitated for a second then moved back to stand in the doorway. "She was sired by Vandal, wasn't she?" He whistled low, not waiting for an answer. "She sure got some good blood in her."

"Grady!"

Maggie turned at the sound of Uncle Bob's voice. As did the stable hand.

"What you doin' in here?" Uncle Bob eyed him.

"Just gettin' some horseshoe nails." The man held up a box in his hand. "Couldn't find any in the other tack room."

"Well you got 'em now, so get back to work." Uncle Bob motioned outside. "Lewis is lookin' for you."

She'd never heard Uncle Bob use so strident a tone, and certainly not with a white man. A shadow briefly clouded Grady's expression, then the man smiled, though it wasn't a pleasant look on him.

Grady nodded. "Good day to you, Miss Linden. And to you too . . . Miss Belle."

Uncle Bob's gaze followed him as he left. "I ain't one to question why General Harding do what he do," he said beneath his breath. "But that man there—" He huffed. "Grady Matthews's papa was a friend of the general's in the war. But I swear, there gonna come a day when even *that* ain't gonna be 'nough to keep Grady this job. The fool does more jawin' 'round here than workin'."

Hearing Uncle Bob's opinion of the man, Maggie quickly decided hers wasn't needed.

The two of them worked in companionable silence.

After a while she laid aside her brush and walked to where Uncle Bob was grooming one of the mares. She watched him, still learning.

"Sure is good seein' you and Miss Mary talkin' more these days, Miss Margaret. Like you used to."

"I'm glad, too, Uncle Bob. It simply felt . . . odd sometimes, coming here to Belle Meade over the past two years. General Harding had purchased all of our horses, for which Papa and I were, and are still, grateful. But seeing them here, with all of this"—she looked around—"only reminds me of what I don't have anymore. I know that must sound very selfish to you."

"Sounds like you's human to me, Miss Margaret." Kindness softened his expression. "It's hard lettin' go of things that was ours. And people, 'specially. You know that well as most, I reckon. After Missus Harding passed, God rest her, Miss Mary kinda closed up tight. Then when Miss Selene wed Mister Jackson, I think Miss Mary done went into hidin' even more. But you comin' 'round again's helped her."

Maggie smiled. "She's helped me too."

Through one of the open windows she spotted Jimmy, a young boy who lived at Belle Meade, riding one of the thoroughbreds. "Is he training to be a jockey?"

Uncle Bob trailed her gaze. "Sure is. He gonna be a good one too. The general gonna let him start racin' next spring." He paused from his work. "Sorry you ain't gonna be racin' Belle in the heat this week. I done heard about Willie and his family."

Maggie nodded. "I'm sorry too. And I hate what happened to them."

"Lotta meanness in this world, Miss Margaret. But there be lots of good too."

She hesitated. "You wouldn't know of any jockeys looking for work right now, would you?"

He looked over. "General already come to me askin' that question for you."

Maggie's face must have shown her surprise.

Uncle Bob returned the curry brush to the shelf. "The general, he likes to win, ma'am. Mmm hmm. That's for sure. But it don't sit too well with him that there's a horse right here in this county that could beat his best mare, if only there was a jockey to ride her. No ma'am. The general, he cares as much about the racin' as he does the winnin'."

Hearing that about General Harding softened Maggie toward the man, even though she still wasn't eager to speak with him. Not considering his outstanding request to meet Cullen McGrath.

Checking the time and finding it later than she thought, Maggie saddled Bourbon Belle then peered out the stable door, aware of Uncle Bob's soft laughter behind her. Seeing no sign of General Harding, she thanked Uncle Bob, climbed into the saddle, and urged Belle toward home.

Nearly across the meadow to the woodsy path connecting Belle Meade to Linden Downs, a path used only by the families, she heard her name and turned.

"Maggie!" Mary was running toward her. With Savannah. Their smiles bright. And Maggie's heart fell.

Savannah waved. "You'll never guess what we just heard!"

But Maggie didn't have to guess. She knew. And now, apparently, so did they.

Chapter Thirteen

Wishing she had cause to encourage her friends' excitement, Maggie accepted their hugs. Oh, how she loved these women. They'd grown up together. They'd laughed and dreamed. Not until this moment did she realize how much she dreaded telling them what she'd done.

They'd held such high hopes for marriage, each of them. They'd been taught to esteem the relationship between a husband and a wife. And even though Maggie could defend why she'd done what she had, she still felt as though she was letting them down.

"I can't believe we weren't the first to know!" Savannah tweaked her arm.

Mary squeezed Maggie's hand. "And you didn't so much as hint at it over lunch today."

Maggie did her best to curb the urge to cry. "I wanted to tell you both. And planned to, but"—she lifted a shoulder and let it fall—"I simply didn't know how."

Savannah took her gently by the shoulders. Her eyes grew watery. "I want you to know, Maggie, how truly happy I am for you." Savannah's voice softened. "No matter that it didn't work out for me and my family."

Maggie looked at her, not quite following Savannah's final comment.

"And I'm equally grateful that we're going to remain neighbors." Mary slipped an arm through Maggie's. "It just wouldn't be right for someone else to live at Linden Downs." She scoffed. "All the carpetbaggers moving in here, buying up estates at auctions and taking over family farms, acting like they belong here."

Savannah nodded. "When the only place they belong is back North where they came from."

Mary nodded firmly. And that's when Maggie realized . . . They knew about her not moving from Linden Downs, but apparently hadn't heard about the marriage.

"So tell us all the details. All the newspaper reported was that Linden Downs had been removed from auction." Savannah scrunched her shoulders. "But tell us quickly, because I have to be at Miss Hattie's in about an hour."

Aware that her friends knew only half the truth, Maggie took a steadying breath. They would learn the rest soon enough. Best they hear it from her. "Thank you both for . . . being such good friends to me."

Mary and Savannah beamed.

"But there's something else I need to tell you, and this part is especially hard." Maggie tried to smile and failed. "The reason I'm still at Linden Downs, that my father and I are still there, is because I agreed to—"

In the distance she saw a rider coming up the road to Belle Meade, and her breath locked in her throat. Her throat conspired with her lungs, and her chest squeezed tight. What was Cullen doing here? Further, what was she going to do now that he was?

"Please excuse me," she said quickly, reaching for Belle's reins. "There's something I need to do."

"But, Maggie, we want hear all about how—"

Maggie was astride the mare before Savannah could finish her thought. As if sensing her rider's urgency, Belle responded to her command and crossed the meadow in a flash. Cullen McGrath was halfway up the drive to the mansion when Maggie caught up with him from behind.

Apparently hearing her approach, he reined in.

"Mr. McGrath!" Winded, she urged Bourbon Belle to the forefront, effectively situating herself between him and her pending ruination. "W-what are you doing here?"

A roguish smile turned his mouth. "Nice to see you, too, Miss Linden. And to be on speakin' terms again."

In no mood for his taunting, Maggie realized she was also in no position to demand. "So tell me . . ." She hoped her smile didn't look as fabricated as it felt. "What brings you to Belle Meade?"

His eyes narrowed as he watched her. His dark hair looked freshly washed, but his stubbled jawline heralded the man's obvious disdain for the razor.

He leaned forward in the saddle. "Is there a reason you would prefer me not to be here?"

"Of course not." She laughed, the sound unnaturally high. "I'm simply surprised to see you, that's all."

He nodded. "Well, if we're bein' truthful"—his look told her he clearly thought she wasn't—"I really don't want to be here. But this General Harding sent a note to Linden Downs this mornin' requestin' a meetin' with me."

"But how did he—" Maggie caught herself. "How does he know who you are?"

He laughed. "What you mean is, does he know yet that I'm your husband?"

Hearing him state it so plainly, without hesitation, Maggie broke out in a cool sweat. It didn't help that Savannah and Mary were walking in their general direction, though still some distance away.

"And no, I don't think he does," he continued. "Your father said the general stopped by a few days ago to see him. While we were in town, I guess. General Harding wants to thank me for somethin'." He gave a little shrug. "When the note arrived earlier, your father encouraged me to come. Well, he challenged me, actually. Said it would be the neighborly thing to do. So . . . here I am."

Maggie could well imagine Papa doing just that, in his gentle but insistent manner. She hadn't forgotten the general's account of how Mr. McGrath had saved his new blood horse, as well as his investment, nor how the general had asked to meet him.

But there was no way General Harding and Cullen McGrath could meet and not discuss horses, and she hadn't had time yet to broach with him the subject of racing Bourbon Belle. Nor was she eager to do so. Not with knowing how Mr. McGrath felt about horse racing and gambling.

And *her*, at the moment.

But what would she do if he did decide to sell Bourbon Belle? Or decided, for whatever reason, not to allow her to race Belle anymore? *If* she could find another jockey.

Seeing the space between her two worlds—the one before Cullen McGrath, and the one after—swiftly shrinking, and feeling helpless to do anything about it, Maggie accepted her options for what they were.

"If you truly don't want to meet with him . . . Cullen," she offered, using his first name as an olive branch, and taking his smile as a sign it had worked, "then I suppose I could meet with him for you. If you want me to."

His laughter was immediate, and his gaze far too discerning. "I'm almost tempted to clap . . . *Margaret.* That was quite good."

Maggie's face went hot.

"Now my obvious question . . ." He studied her. "Why don't you want me to meet General Harding? Instinct tells me it goes beyond revealin' that there's an *us.*"

The heat in her face fanned out through her chest. "All of this may seem funny to you, Mr. McGrath. But I had a life here before you came."

"A life you were about to lose."

"A life that I've worked hard for. As my father has, too, and his father before him. And for you to waltz in and start dictating how we do things is—"

"Name one thing I've dictated for you to do, Miss Linden. Just one."

Emotion tightened Maggie's throat.

"Or for your father. What have I demanded of him?"

She opened her mouth to respond, but couldn't think of a single thing. Her eyes stung and her pride burned. It didn't help when the frustration began to drain from his face. Nor when she remembered how much her father had laughed in recent days.

Every evening Papa and Cullen sat outside on the front porch discussing planting and farming, the workers to be hired and where they would start, while she sat alone in the sitting room, listening. Cullen would never replace the sons Papa lost, she knew. But he was swiftly taking her place in her father's life.

Or at least that's what it felt like.

She clenched her jaw to keep from crying. Not this time. Not again.

"I'm weary of arguin' with you, ma'am." His deep voice went tender. "Do you think there's the least bit of a chance we could talk to each other anytime soon without comin' to blows? Because if there is, I'd give much to see that come about . . . Margaret."

He said her name softly this time, with a sweetness, not a hint of sarcasm, and Maggie felt the faintest unfurling inside her, even as she resisted it.

Seeing her friends coming closer—and seeing their stares—she thought of the boardinghouse where Savannah and her younger brother and sister lived in a not-so-good part of town. Their parents and older brothers gone now, taken by the war, and Savannah sewing oftentimes seven days a week to provide for their needs. At times her knuckles swelled to twice their size, but Maggie had never once heard her complain.

"Yes," Maggie heard herself whisper, partly from shame, partly in an effort to end the conversation before Savannah and Mary came within earshot. "There is . . . Cullen."

He smiled, but sincerely this time. "I'm mighty glad to hear it." He glanced behind him, then back at her. "Friends of yours, I take it?"

She nodded, preparing for the introductions he likely wanted her to make.

"Perhaps I could meet them." He gripped the reins then gave her a wink. "Some other time."

He prodded his horse on toward the mansion, and the tangle of emotions pulled taut inside her as she watched him go. Such an . . . unusual man. Maddening, certainly. Frustrating, without question. But also . . . kind, in his own way. Add to that *odd.* Most men in Nashville would have done almost anything to have General William Giles Harding beholden to them. Yet Cullen McGrath seemed nonplussed by it. Even . . . disinterested. She sighed.

"Who was that?"

Maggie turned at Savannah's question and saw curiosity plastered on her friends' faces. But also a funny sort of wariness in Savannah's.

Maggie dismounted and took a deep breath, then gave it measured release. "That, though I realize this will be hard to believe"—she trailed their gazes up the path, bracing herself—"is my husband."

Chapter Fourteen

"Say that again, please?" Savannah's tone mirrored a countenance of shock and disbelief.

Mary shook her head. "It can't be."

"It is," Maggie whispered, her face going warm. "It all happened rather quickly. Last week."

The curiosity in her friends' eyes narrowed, and Maggie read their identical, unspoken question.

"No!" she said quickly, scoffing as she did. "It's nothing of the sort. You know me better than that." Seeing relief in their subtle smiles encouraged one of her own. "It's more of a . . ." She gave an embarrassed shrug, recalling another conversation similar to this one. "A business arrangement."

"A business arrangement?" Mary repeated.

Now confusion muddled her friends' expressions.

"He wanted to buy the farm, and Papa didn't want to see the land auctioned off, so—"

"Your father *forced* you to marry?" Mary's tone leaned toward incredulity.

"No, Papa didn't force me. He wanted to make certain I was well taken care of and that we could keep the land, but . . . it was my choice." She stood a little straighter as she said it.

In the distance, Cullen dismounted as the three of them watched. He took the steps to the mansion in twos then knocked on the door.

"Is he kind?" Savannah's voice was soft.

"Yes." Maggie nodded. "He is."

"And from what I saw," Mary said, glancing back, "he's handsome too."

Maggie felt an odd sort of pride in the compliment. And possessiveness too. Yet she hoped against hope they wouldn't ask anything related to intimate details, or pointed questions about him. Including his name. One step at a time. She'd told them she was married. She didn't have to tell them he was Irish. Not yet, at least.

"So." Savannah turned to look at her, a shadow—barely there, then gone—eclipsing her smooth ivory complexion. "You not only get to keep your land, but you're married as well." She smiled. "That's wonderful, Maggie. I'm so happy for you." She drew Maggie into a quick hug then stepped back, her eyes unnaturally bright.

Maggie's heart squeezed tight. "Savannah, I—"

"I need to be on my way." Savannah hugged Mary. "I'm going to be late to Miss Hattie's if I don't leave now." She turned to go.

"Savannah . . ." Mary gestured to the carriage pulling up in front of the mansion. "Selene asked me to accompany her into town. We'd be happy to give you a ride if you'd—"

"No, thank you. I'm fine." Savannah's smile was tight, like her voice. "I prefer to walk."

Watching the dust swirling about Savannah's skirt hem, Maggie felt Mary's arm come around her shoulders.

"I'm truly happy for you, too, Maggie. I can't wait to meet him." Mary's face lit with mischief. "And to see him closer up once I'm inside!"

Standing alone in the center of the long drive leading to the mansion, Maggie watched her friends walk away. One to wealth and to the certainty of marriage and a bright future. The other to the life that—if not for Cullen McGrath—would have been her destiny as well.

A quarter past nine and still Cullen hadn't returned.

Maggie peered out the window past the darkened front porch into the night. Surely the meeting with General Harding hadn't lasted this long. Not knowing the outcome of the conversation between the men and what had been said—specifically about Bourbon Belle—had worn on her throughout the evening.

Had Cullen learned about how they raced Belle? Did he realize how valuable the mare was? And might knowing that somehow alter his aversion to the sport? She sighed. Thinking of racing Belle made her think of Willie, and she pictured the scene the boy's tragic account had painted in her mind that day.

She briefly closed her eyes, trying to erase the images, and prayed that Willie and his family were safe, wherever they were.

Peering out the window one last time, she buoyed her spirits with the hope that General Harding hadn't said anything about Belle. Or racing. Perhaps he and Cullen had spoken only of cultural events and the weather.

What were the chances . . .

At least she'd managed to tell the two people she cared about most, besides her father, about the changes in her life. Reliving the hurt in Savannah's expression this morning wounded Maggie all over again. Savannah was the kindest person she knew, which made her friend's pain at the news that much tougher to bear.

The two of them needed to talk further, and would. Soon.

Maggie made sure the front door was unlocked, then turned down all but one of the lamps in the central parlor, grateful for the lovely evening she'd spent with her father. Just the two of them, as it used to be. It had been so nice, talking about everything, and nothing.

Yet Papa's occasional glances toward the door hadn't gone unnoticed, his question unvoiced though not unseen.

He'd retired earlier, making it up the stairs and to his bedroom with her assistance. His breathing had been labored, and the effort had taken all of his strength. She'd brewed a strong batch of catnip and pennyroyal tea, which seemed to help his cough. She'd offered to make him a plaster of onion and butter to apply to his throat and chest, but he'd refused, simply wishing to go to bed.

At times she thought his color was improving. Then at others, she was certain it wasn't. But the thought of this house, of her life, without him was nearly unbearable, and she never allowed her thoughts to go there for very long.

The pale glow of lamplight ghosted the central parlor, and she retrieved the lamp on the side table and was starting up the stairs when the sound of footsteps on the porch brought her around. *Finally.*

Not wanting Cullen to think she'd been waiting for him, she also knew she wouldn't sleep a wink without learning the outcome of his meeting. Schooling a polite but, she hoped, a slightly disinterested smile, she opened the door.

But no one was there.

Certain she'd heard him, she stepped outside, the lamp enveloping her in a halo of light. "Cullen?" She lowered the lamp a little in order to see better, and looked toward the stable. But the yard was empty, the door to the stable closed. A breath of wind stirred the lilac at the far corner of the porch, and the sweetness of the scent seemed incongruent with the moment.

She turned, her pulse edging up a notch. "Cullen . . . is that you?"

Only silence answered back, and the surroundings so familiar to her suddenly seemed less so, draped as they were in shades of gray and black. A low growl issued from somewhere behind her, and she turned to see Bucket standing in the shadows at the top of the staircase.

The hair rose on the back of Maggie's neck, and she stepped back inside and closed the door.

She bolted the lock.

Bucket growled again, louder this time.

"It's all right, boy," Maggie said softly, not wanting the collie to awaken Papa, yet secretly grateful for the dog's presence. Not easily spooked, she told herself it was nothing, yet she couldn't shake the feeling that she wasn't alone.

With the curtains undrawn, the lamplight reflected off the bare windows, and she quickly extinguished the lamp in her hand and the one in the central parlor. She found the darkness reassuring.

She moved to the staircase and eased down onto the next-to-bottom step, hearing Bucket's soft tread. She turned, expecting to see the collie coming down the stairs. But . . . no Bucket. Apparently the dog had returned to Papa's bedroom. So much for helping her keep watch.

She wished Cullen would return, while at the same time realizing how ironic that wish was. Sitting close to the wall, she leaned into the shadows, the steady thrum of her heart overloud in the quiet.

Moments passed, and with them she caught every aging creak and waning sigh of the house. They were sounds she heard every day. So why did they prick at her nerves like—

A shadow crossed in front of the window, and Maggie bit her lip to keep from screaming. She didn't dare move as the shadow disappeared around the side of the house.

The back door!

Flying off the staircase, she half tiptoed, half ran down the hallway into the kitchen and flicked the latch on the door only seconds before the telling creak of a board sounded from outside on the back porch. Or was it simply the house again, and her imagination playing tricks on her?

Heart hammering in her throat, she hurried back into the hallway and pressed against the wall outside her father's library, eyes closed, straining to hear the slightest sound from either end of the house.

But it was the rattle of the *front* doorknob—easy at first then more insistent—that shot heat through her veins like fire through ice.

❧

Realizing the door was locked, Cullen used the key Mr. Linden had given him. He made a mental note to thank Margaret for turning down all the lights. The house was pitch—

"Take one more step and I'll shoot!"

Cullen went stock still, seeing the glint of moonlight reflecting off the barrel of a rifle. He didn't dare raise his hands in truce lest the gesture be misconstrued. "Margaret," he said firmly. "It's *me.* Cullen."

He waited as she slowly—*very* slowly from his perspective—lowered the gun.

"What are you doing, sneaking in here like that? I thought you were a prowler!"

Tempted to smile at her chosen term, Cullen found the aftereffects of what she'd been about to do suddenly less than humorous. Heat surged through him, replacing the calm of seconds before. "Sneakin'? Since when do prowlers use a key?"

"I . . . didn't hear the key. I guess I—"

"Was too busy aimin' for my heart?"

She stepped forward into the scant light slanting in through the window. "I'm sorry, I—"

He strode to her, held out a hand, and she relinquished the rifle. He checked the barrel. Loaded. "You were serious."

"Never aim a gun unless you intend to use it. That's what my brothers taught me."

"Did they also teach you to actually *see* what you're shootin' before you shoot?"

"I didn't shoot."

"You almost did."

"I gave you fair warning!"

He scoffed. "With your finger on the trigger?"

She started to say something then lowered her head.

Remembering again the fear he'd heard in her voice, and seeing her hands trembling even now, he took a calming breath. "You're quakin' like a leaf. What's wrong?"

She raised her head a fraction. "I heard something a while ago. I thought it was you so I went outside to the porch, but you weren't there." She looked past him toward the still open door. "No one was there." She looked back up at him. "But someone was out there. I felt it."

"Did you see anything?"

She shook her head. "Not until I spotted a shadow go around the side of the house."

"So you *did* see someone?" He turned and looked behind him. Heard the wind in the trees and saw the shadows playing across the windows.

"I—" she started.

He looked back to find her watching him, then she shrugged as if reading his thoughts.

"I thought I saw someone. And then . . ." She fell silent and wouldn't meet his gaze.

"What?" he said more softly.

"I thought I heard a boot step on the back porch just before you came in."

He didn't know Margaret Linden well yet. But he knew her well enough to know she wasn't a woman easily unnerved. "Is your father upstairs?"

She nodded. "With Bucket. Who was no help whatsoever."

"You're certain they're both upstairs?"

Another nod.

"I'll check around outside. Lock the door behind me."

"But what if you—"

"Lock the door behind me, Margaret."

Gun in hand, he paused on the front porch until he heard the click of the lock, then he moved off into the yard. He circled around the side of the house, remembering the first day he'd seen the Sharps rifle hanging over the hearth in Mr. Linden's library.

That Margaret could handle such a firearm was impressive. That she'd been about to shoot him with it was far less so.

He paused beside the back porch to listen.

The distant hoot of an owl carried toward him on the breeze, and he glanced over at a rustling in a pile of leaves blown up against the foundation of the house. A mouse or some other night scavenger. Certainly nothing that would cause a shadow in the window.

If there'd even been such a thing. He could see how she might have been mistaken.

He made a circle around the house then checked the stable and barn for good measure. A good piece down the road, he could see Cletus and Onnie's cabin. It was dark, as were the other former slave cabins down the way. Seeing the rustic dwellings brought to mind his earlier discussion that day among the shanties on the edge of town.

His initial guess about the man in question had proven correct. Ennis was an impressive fellow, though none too trusting. Cullen could relate. Now to get the workers out here as they'd agreed and begin clearing, tilling, and planting these fields. Judging by the almanac, he figured they were already two weeks behind.

The night all stillness and quiet around him, he started back toward the house and was nearly to the porch when he caught the first whiff. Tobacco, he thought. But . . . with a sweetness to it. Careful not to alter his stride, he continued on across the yard and stopped by the well.

He reached into the bucket and lifted the ladle to his lips, listening—and remembering what Mr. Linden had said to him about the trouble he'd had some time back after the old hunting cabin had been burned down. Stephen Drake's threat was also never far from his mind.

Standing in the shadows, Cullen faced into the breeze and tilted his head upward as though admiring the blanket of stars overhead, his gaze scanning the tree line opposite him. Nothing. The scent was gone.

He gripped the rifle and strode back to the house. He scarcely knocked on the door before it opened.

"Did you see anyone?" Margaret ushered him in, wide-eyed, then closed and locked the door behind him. The collie, apparently having had a change of heart, stood obediently by her side, tail wagging.

Cullen rubbed the dog's head. "Decided to be of help after all, I see."

Margaret exhaled, glancing down. "Only after the fact." She peered up again, question in her expression.

Cullen shook his head. "It's all quiet." The half-truth felt stilted leaving him, and he knew why. But telling Margaret someone had been out there would only cause her to worry. And she had enough to deal with considering the recent changes in her life, including her father's deteriorating health.

"Why are you so late? Coming home, I mean. Were you with General Harding all this time?"

Cullen couldn't say why her questions pleased him, but they did. He propped the gun in a corner. "Things simply took longer than I thought. And . . . no. General Harding and I only met for about an hour."

"So . . . where were you all this time?"

Looking at her, the shadows hiding all but the scarcest hint of her expression, he heard the worry, and curiosity, in her tone and knew now—after meeting with General Harding—why she'd been so hesitant for that meeting to take place. "After I finished at Belle Meade, I rode their land, at invitation from the general. He invited me to hunt at Belle Meade anytime. Nice man, all in all."

"All in all?"

Cullen smiled. "Rich and powerful men are not usually ones I tend to cozy up to. Nor they to me."

"Yes, but you're now the *owner* of Linden Downs, one of the first farms to be settled in Nashville."

Her emphasis on the word hinted at lingering animosity, but the fact that she said it at all told him acceptance might be on the horizon.

"And while it may not be one of the largest farms," she continued, "it's one of the most respected. Or . . ." Her voice fell away. "It once was."

"And it will be again, Margaret. I promise you that."

She looked up at him, and he wished he could read the look in her eyes. Was there hope in them? Or the least bit of softening toward him, perhaps?

"So . . . what did you and the general discuss all that time?"

There. Finally, the question she'd been waiting to ask him. He offered a nonchalant shrug. "Belle Meade, Nashville, horses, crops . . . the things men talk about."

She waited as if wanting him to say more. And he knew what she was really asking. Yet he wasn't about to answer her. Not here. Not now. That was a conversation he wasn't eager to have. Yet knowing Margaret even so little, he knew they would have it soon enough.

"Did you tell him about . . . us?"

"Not initially. He knew the farm was up for auction, and all I told him was that I'd bought it. But then I saw his daughter . . . one of your friends from earlier."

She nodded.

"And I realized you must have told them."

Her head tilted to one side. "Why do you say that?"

"Because she kept passing by the office window, looking in." He was curious as to what she'd said to her friends about him, but thought better of inquiring. "That's when I realized that Harding's daughter knew. And that the general would, too, as soon as I left. Better for me to tell him than for him to find out afterward. He might wonder why I hadn't been forthcoming."

She nodded slowly, as though agreeing with him but still not liking the outcome.

Cullen felt something brush his calf and looked down to see Bucket sitting beside him. Cullen smiled and bent to give the dog a rub. "You're a good lad, aren't you?"

A soft scoff issued from above.

Cullen lifted his gaze as he rose. "I'm assumin' there's a story behind this one's name."

Margaret eyed the dog with open suspicion. "I found him one day on the way home from town, not far out of the city. I heard something crying, so I got off my horse."

Her voice softened and Cullen could almost see the memory unfolding.

"I followed the sound over to a ditch, where I peered down and saw an old wooden bucket." The faint smile touching her mouth held a sweetness that challenged her former suspicion. "The pup couldn't have been more than four or five weeks old. It had rained that morning, so he was soaked clean through, and shivering." She shook her head, her mouth firming. "And someone had just left him there. On the side of the road."

"In a bucket," Cullen finished softly.

"At first I thought he was going to be *my* dog." She shrugged. "But the more time he spent with Papa, the more I realized I was wrong. Little traitor."

"Sometimes the way things start isn't the way they end up."

Her expression inscrutable, he took hope from the way she matched his gaze, unflinching.

"I'll put up the rifle," she finally said, reaching for it.

Cullen stopped her with a touch to her arm. "I'll do it." He retrieved the gun. "You go on up to bed."

"All right," she said, voice soft. "Come," she directed Bucket, and the dog complied before stopping at the base of the stairs and looking between them. Then at him.

Cullen would've sworn the collie was asking for permission to stay with him. "I'll bring Bucket up with me when I come, if you don't mind. I'll make sure he gets back to your father's room."

"That'll be fine." Starting up, she hesitated and glanced outside. "I don't often let my imagination get the best of me that way."

"It happens to all of us from time to time."

Halfway up the stairs, she turned back again. "I've been meaning to ask you something about that day in town. With Mr. Drake."

Finding her timing interesting, Cullen also found himself wondering if she had any idea how beautiful she was. "And what question would that be, Margaret?"

"Mr. Drake said he thought the two of you had an understanding. What did he mean?"

He crossed to the foot of the stairs. "Mr. Drake introduced himself to me in town shortly after I'd arrived. For the express purpose of invitin' me to live elsewhere."

"Elsewhere," she repeated.

"As in anywhere but here in Nashville. But this is where I wanted—and want—to be. So . . ." He shrugged. "Mr. Stephen Drake can just do with that as he likes." He peered up. "Anythin' else about that day you'd like to ask me?"

She studied him, then finally shook her head.

"Well then . . . Good night, Margaret."

She gave him the tiniest smile. "Good night, Cullen."

He waited until he heard her soft tread on the wooden floor above, then he walked into the central parlor and eased down into one of two fancy chairs situated in front of the hearth, Bucket following alongside him.

The furniture was a mite small, but Cullen stretched out his legs and attempted to get comfortable, the rifle beside him on the floor. Bucket conveniently chose to lie within easy reach, and Cullen succumbed to the soulful brown eyes staring up at him.

Rubbing the dog's head with one hand, he leaned back, sleep the last thing on his mind. Not only because of what he'd detected outside earlier, but because of what his meeting with General Harding had revealed.

Cullen didn't consider himself a man easily surprised, but Harding had managed to catch him off guard more than once.

"It was disappointing to learn," Harding had informed him, "that the Lindens lost their jockey last week. The race this past Friday wasn't the same without Bourbon Belle."

Cullen held the gentleman's gaze, trying to make sense of the comment. When he finally did, he nodded in hopes of smoothing over his delayed response. "I've seen Bourbon Belle run, so I can only imagine how the mare's absence was felt."

"Oh, indeed it was. Although it did mean that Belle Meade brought home another silver cup and a tidy purse."

Cullen returned the general's smile, wondering what amount of winnings qualified as a "tidy purse" in the estimation of such a man.

"Do you have plans to race her yourself, Mr. McGrath? I only ask because I understand Mr. Linden's health is in decline. I inquired of Miss Linden last week"—the older gentleman inclined his head—"now Mrs. McGrath, of course, if her father was interested in selling, and she assured me he wasn't. But if *you're* interested, my offer still stands. I'd be more than pleased to take Bourbon Belle off your hands. And at a very fair price, I assure you."

Sighing, Cullen gave Bucket's head one last pat and rose from the chair. He moved in the darkened parlor to the edge of the window, which allowed him a full view of the area in front of the house. He looked toward the barn, thinking of the mare inside.

He'd known Bourbon Belle was a valuable thoroughbred. But three thousand dollars? That's what Harding offered him.

Mr. Linden had failed to tell him Bourbon Belle was a champion racehorse, one with quite a winning streak. Cullen could guess why the man had left that part out, and couldn't blame him. He might've done the same, under the circumstances. Much as he'd done himself moments earlier with Margaret.

Not a lie, yet not the whole truth. Which wasn't strictly a lie. But it was, without question, not strictly the whole truth. He sighed.

Harding had invited him to attend an annual yearling sale to be held at Belle Meade later in the summer. Cullen shook his head, the irony of the situation still fresh. A thoroughbred sale drawing owners of the finest blood horses from all over the United States and now, in the past year, Europe as well. Including . . . England.

Harding had stated it so proudly, all while Cullen felt an ocean evaporating in a single moment. Of all the farms for sale in Tennessee, how was it he'd landed at the one with a thoroughbred champion, next to a plantation that, he'd learned, was the largest thoroughbred stud in the South?

The grandfather clock in the hallway chimed the hour, and by the twelfth strike, as the last chord settled into the silence, he knew what he'd said to Margaret earlier that afternoon wasn't true.

There was one thing he would dictate. And demand. And never

compromise on. If she had it in her mind for him to step into her father's place and take over as trainer for that horse, and continue to race Bourbon Belle, the woman was in for an enormous disappointment—and the two of them in for a rough road ahead.

He briefly closed his eyes, the day catching up with him. If the situation came to it, which he hoped it wouldn't, he would sell the horse in order to keep his secret. Because if his past in England ever came to light here, everything would be lost.

Not only for him, but for Margaret Linden and her father as well.

Chapter FIFTEEN

How many men did you say you've hired?" Maggie looked across the breakfast table at Cullen, her foolishness from the other night still gnawing at her pride. A prowler, indeed. She'd allowed her fatigue and imagination to run away with her. And in front of Cullen, no less. He'd not mentioned it since, but still . . .

"Twenty-three," he answered, glancing at the clock on the hearth. "And they'll be here soon." He downed the last of his coffee. "Are you goin' to Belle Meade again today?"

She nodded. "Only until noon. I should be back shortly thereafter."

"The men and I will likely be in the fields until sundown. We have some catchin' up to do in regard to plantin', so I won't be here for dinner." He looked up from his plate. "In the event your father asks," he added.

Maggie nodded, forking another bite of scrambled eggs.

Breakfast conversation without Papa present this morning wasn't as uncomfortable as she'd thought it would be, which is precisely what her father had told her earlier. She wondered now whether he truly wasn't feeling well, as he'd said, or if he'd taken his meal abed simply so she and Cullen would be forced to speak to each other. She wouldn't put it past him.

She and Cullen had actually gotten along fairly well over the past two days. Not a cross word between them.

Granted, she'd scarcely seen the man, what with his either being in town or riding the fields, or holed up with her father late into the evening discussing what had been planted in which field last, or how to rotate the crops, or one of so many other farming topics she found less than captivating. But she hadn't minded their being in league with each other last night.

The latest edition of *American Turf Register and Sporting Magazine* had arrived yesterday, and she'd devoured it in her room, poring over the latest articles, the notices of which stallions were standing stud on which estates, and the racing memoranda reporting last week's wins and respective purses. Bourbon Belle's name was nowhere listed, of course. But Maggie vowed to change that soon enough.

She simply needed to find a new jockey—and the opportune moment to broach the subject with Cullen of racing Belle again.

She could scarcely believe General Harding hadn't mentioned anything to him about Bourbon Belle in the course of their conversation. Although some of the traits typically assigned to the Irish didn't seem to fit Cullen, a boldness in speaking his mind certainly did. If he knew about Bourbon Belle, he surely would have said something.

She studied him across the table.

As Papa had warned her, she didn't expect Cullen to be enthusiastic about the subject, not when considering his own father's struggles with gambling. But she and Papa never gambled. And for that matter, neither did General Harding. She simply needed to persuade Cullen to see the issue from their perspective. And she would.

Having had four brothers, she knew enough about men to know she needed to catch him in a favorable mood. But exactly what "favorable" looked like for Cullen McGrath, she couldn't quite say. She'd have to think on that.

"General Harding told me he's glad you're offerin' ridin' lessons in his corrals. He says it's good advertisement for his estate's services."

Maggie paused. "He said that? That he was glad?"

Cullen nodded. "And havin' seen you ride, I imagine you're an excellent instructor. You must enjoy it."

Surprised by the compliment and the sincerity in his smile, she was a bit taken aback. Yet also encouraged. Was this the opportunity she'd been waiting for? "Thank you, Cullen, I appreciate that." She fingered the rim of her coffee cup, debating if she should bring up the subject of Belle. "While I do gain satisfaction from teaching the girls how to ride, I wouldn't say that's what I've always dreamed of doing."

His gaze locked on hers and held, then swiftly broke away. He stood, tucking his napkin by his plate. "Well, you certainly are gifted at it all the same. Now if you'll excuse me, I need to be goin'. I've got a lot to do before the workers arrive. I hope you have a good day, Margaret."

Maggie stared at his back as he left, wondering if she'd ever seen a man clear a room so swiftly.

A few minutes later, changed from her day dress to her riding habit, Maggie retrieved her gloves from the side table and slipped them on, assessing the jacket and skirt. Both the sleeves and hem showed signs of wear. Not surprising, the garment having seen its fifth season. Savannah's skillful dressmaking guaranteed the garment would last, but even her friend's expert handiwork couldn't extend the life of the material.

But for now, funds didn't exist to commission a new ensemble. This one would have to do. At least the ivory point plat lace adorning the lapels—another of Savannah's skills—was still as beautiful as the day her friend had first sewn it on.

Maggie opened the screen door to the front porch and found Cullen standing motionless at the edge of the steps, staring out past the stable. She joined him, curious as to what held his interest.

Coming down the road, en masse, was a throng of people. All Negroes. Not only men, but women and children. Lots of children.

"I thought you said you hired twenty-three men."

"I did." Cullen shifted on the porch beside her. "But I told the men to bring their families with them."

Maggie looked over at him. "Every day?"

He turned. "What do you mean every day?"

"You told the men to bring their families with them every day?"

He eyed her. "I told the men to bring their families with them because they're going to live here. With their families. At Linden Downs."

Maggie stared. "I understood you to mean they would come and work here, then return to their homes in the evening. As a lot of the other farms are doing now. It's simpler, people say. And less expensive."

He smiled as though finding that premise—or perhaps, her—intriguing. "That may be true. But we're going to do things a little differently here."

She found his use of *we* slightly annoying. First, because he hadn't discussed any of his plans about the farm with her, never mind that she hadn't asked. And second, because he already seemed so comfortable in his role as owner. Yet she smoothed her frown and tried not to let her frustration show.

After all, they'd been getting along so well, and she needed to keep it that way if she was going to win him over to racing Belle again.

He offered his arm and, realizing his intent, she slipped her hand through and followed him down the stairs to stand beside him in the yard. To greet the newcomers, she guessed. What she hadn't counted on was how he covered her hand with his on his arm. And kept it there.

"You changed." His gaze roamed the length of her then leisurely wove its way back up again. "In case I haven't said this yet . . ." He leaned closer. "You're a beauty of a woman, Margaret Linden."

Moved by his hushed tone and the thoroughness of his attention, she found her frustration quickly fading—and her riding habit growing overly warm. "Thank you . . . Cullen."

Mary Harding was right. He was a handsome man. Even if not in the traditional sense. His eyes, so pale a shade of green. His dark hair, longer and—how had she missed this before—touched with streaks of silver at the temples. Even the perpetual stubble that graced his jaw was peppered with the same. But that was to be expected, she guessed. After all, he *was* older. Almost thirty.

Even the way he stood carried authority, and challenge. Yet when he moved, as she knew from watching him, he had an easy grace about him, one that said he didn't much care what people thought about him. And his mouth . . . Lips closed, though not set in a firm line, just waiting for the slightest excuse to—

His mouth tipped in a languid smile, fulfilling the thought she'd just had, and Maggie, growing aware of her actions, lifted her gaze to find him watching her. Amusement accented his features, all except for the not-at-all-humorous intensity in his eyes. She blushed to her toes. He'd caught her staring. And not only staring. *Admiring.* Though judging from the pleasure in his expression, he didn't mind in the least. But she did.

Because it felt as if he could read her every thought. Even the ones she preferred be kept tucked away.

Finding it harder to breathe, she removed her hand from the crook of his arm and focused again on the multitude of people moving as one up the road.

"Where will they all live?" she asked after a moment, her composure returning.

"In the cabins." His voice still harbored a smile as he gestured in the direction where Cletus and Onnie lived.

Maggie scanned the imminent throng. "But there are only four empty cabins. That's not enough room for all those people."

"I know. That's why we'll build more."

"More cabins," she repeated.

He nodded.

"But . . . that takes money."

"Which we have."

Again, that annoying *we*. Figures started populating her head, money she needed for Bourbon Belle. Entry fees for races, the higher grade feed, finer tack, the cost of paying a jockey. All of that mandated cash. And what she earned from riding lessons scarcely covered a fraction of it. Although she did have a little saved.

"Does Papa know about this?"

Cullen smiled. "In fact . . . he does. He knows about the saddle horses I'm purchasin' too."

"And he approves?"

He opened his mouth to respond when a somewhat feeble-sounding voice chimed in from above.

"I most certainly do."

Maggie turned, along with Cullen, to see her father sitting by his bedroom window on the second floor. He looked between the two of them, a smile on his face the likes of which she hadn't seen in a very long time.

"Cullen and I discussed all this at length," Papa continued, resting an arm on the sill. "I admit I had questions at first. All of which he answered more than to my satisfaction. Not that you had to," he said, the statement directed to Cullen. "But I appreciate your taking the time to discuss your plans with me."

Cullen shook his head. "*Our* plans, Mr. Linden."

Papa offered a smart little salute, a gesture Maggie remembered him using with her brothers, and a pang of loss tightened her chest as it did from time to time when life chose to remind her of what her world used to be like. Before the war.

Then just as swiftly, that pang took a different twist, and she recognized only too well the taint of bitterness inside her. While she'd not been especially close to her mother, she'd always been so to her father, and to see Papa interacting with Cullen this way, so accepting, so eager to trust, so proud . . .

"Mister McGrath, sir."

Maggie turned at the gentle thunder of a voice behind her and found herself looking into a sea of faces. All of them staring back.

A tall and exceptionally muscular black man, his expression fierce, stepped forward. "We here like we agreed, Mister McGrath."

The man's enunciation was distinct, and the strong undercurrent of his tone communicated volumes more than his words. Whatever Cullen had agreed to do, this man was reminding him.

Cullen stepped forward, and to Maggie's surprise, offered his hand to the man, who accepted without hesitation.

"Welcome to Linden Downs, Mr. Ennis." Cullen peered past him. "Welcome to you all."

Uneasy with Cullen's familiarity toward the man, Maggie searched her memory, trying to recall if she'd ever seen her father shake Cletus's hand through the years. Or that of any former slave. And she couldn't.

Odd, how something she'd never given thought to before could cause such a stirring inside her now.

As Cullen and Ennis spoke, her gaze wandered the crowd, and she found the women watching her. She took in their tattered clothes and the items they carried—bundles wrapped in threadbare blankets and old wash bins filled with sundry items—and became keenly aware of how she herself was dressed and of the kid leather gloves in her hand. And of the breakfast she'd eaten earlier.

Some of the children looked especially thin, the smallest ones peering wide-eyed from behind their mothers' skirts. There had to be at least a hundred people standing in the yard. So many, for Cullen having hired only twenty-three men.

"I'd like to introduce you to my wife, Mr. Ennis."

Cullen's statement pulled her back, as did his gentle grasp of her elbow, and Maggie looked to see the two men watching her.

Uncertain what Cullen expected her to do, she schooled what she hoped was a kindly expression. She'd never been formally introduced to a black man before, much less as Cullen's wife, and she wasn't certain what etiquette demanded. Or if etiquette had even been written to cover such situations.

"Missus McGrath . . ." Mr. Ennis dipped his head. "Honor to meet you, ma'am."

"And . . . you as well, Mr. Ennis." Curtseying to the man would have been inappropriate, Maggie knew that much. Still, the moment felt robbed of something. "I-I'm glad you and your—your *people* have come to work at Linden Downs."

Mr. Ennis and Cullen exchanged a look she almost missed and couldn't define, but the seriousness in Mr. Ennis's expression softened by a degree.

"Me and my people are glad, too, Missus McGrath."

Cullen's smile and gentle squeeze to her elbow told her she'd done well. Still, she felt awkward and exposed, standing there as she was. Suddenly remembering, she checked the chatelaine watch pinned to her waist. Half past eight! Her first pupil arrived at Belle Meade at nine. And she'd forgotten to ask Cletus to saddle Bourbon Belle.

"If you'll excuse me . . . Mr. McGrath," she said more formally, remembering how her parents used to address each other in public. "I need to be off to my appointments for the morning."

Turning where only she could see—and Papa, too, if he was still looking, which she felt certain he was—Cullen winked. "I'll do so most happily . . . Mrs. McGrath." He nodded to the stable. "Belle is saddled and ready."

Chapter SIXTEEN

Maggie sat up in bed with a start, her breath coming hard. The dream, so vivid, still seemed present and ready to pounce from the darkness. A sense of foreboding prickled her spine, and she pressed a hand to her chest, her heart thumping a steady staccato against her palm.

She kicked off the sheet, the humidity causing her nightgown to cling to her. Her windows were open, yet not a breath of wind stirred outside. How could it be so hot? If it was this warm with June only two days away, what merciless heat did summer have in store?

Knowing her room as well in the dark as she did in daylight, she crossed to the dresser, lifted the water pitcher, and poured, only to discover it empty. With a sigh she slipped into the hallway, her bare feet silent on the wooden floors.

She heard her father's deep snores coming from across the hall and slipped into his room. Bucket instantly rose from his place at the foot of the bed, but Maggie motioned the collie back down.

She could scarcely distinguish the outline of her father's form in the bed, but the sound of his breathing gave her comfort. Tears rose to her eyes. *Please don't take him. You have the rest of them. Don't take him too.*

She wrapped her arms around herself, silent tears slipping down her cheeks. She closed her eyes, only to see the images from her dream slither to life again, so she quickly reopened them.

Oh . . . so horrible a way to die.

Pulling in a stuttered breath, she breathed a silent prayer for her father and then stepped back into the hallway, not wanting to awaken him.

In the past two weeks, the naps he used to take in the afternoons now extended to mornings as well. Some days she would find him asleep in the chair in his office by ten o'clock, his book still propped open on the desk. And the powders . . .

He took so many now. And laudanum, on occasion. But at least he didn't seem to be in as much pain. Better to sleep, she thought, than to suffer through those spells.

Thirsty, she moved toward the stairs, tiptoeing past Cullen's room. His door was open and she paused outside, his soft, rhythmic breaths soothing after she'd awakened in such a state.

About the only time she saw him these days was at breakfast. He took lunch and dinner with the men in the field, and often returned after she'd retired for the night. It was hard to believe they'd been married almost a month.

Although, it wasn't *really* a marriage, she reminded herself, stuffing down the restlessness that so often accompanied that thought these days.

Once downstairs, she hesitated for a second then moved to the window, edged back the curtains she routinely closed at night now, and scanned the darkened yard in front of the house, relieved to find it empty and still.

No more allowing her imagination to run away with her.

As though challenging that thought, a remnant of her dream tried to bully its way back in, but she resisted, clenching her eyes tight and centering her thoughts on what she always did when she needed to overcome a fear. She thought of racing Belle across the fields of Linden Downs, then on into town, the wind in her hair, the sun on her face, the singular sense of freedom and release only riding could bring.

She didn't bother lighting a lamp in the kitchen, but got a drink of water then refilled her glass. Turning to leave, she spotted a covered plate—the remaining apple turnovers Onnie had made for dessert the previous evening. She felt all of five years old again, sneaking sweets in the middle of the night.

Noiselessly she pulled a chair from beneath the small corner table—the one she'd occupied as a girl when helping Onnie in the kitchen—and she sat, a flood of years sluicing through her.

She remembered one night in particular, when Savannah had stayed at their house. Giggling in bed together into the wee hours of the morning was hungry work, and they'd sneaked down to the kitchen to find these little apple treasures waiting for them, along with two glasses, as though Onnie had anticipated their midnight caper.

Dear Savannah . . .

Maggie's heart ached at what her friend was going through, and at the pain her own good fortune was causing her friend. Maggie couldn't remember the last time two weeks had gone by without their speaking.

She took a bite, promising to remedy that in the coming week.

The flakiness of the pastry and sweetness of the apples seemed to encourage her memory, and she savored the moment, almost able to hear the echoes of laughter these walls had absorbed over the years. The conversations that had filled this kitchen. Nearly a hundred years' worth. And not only conversations . . .

She remembered well the ruckus her brothers created when brawling in the next room, the telling thud of their bodies hitting the floor, broadcasting the progression of the fight. All with Mother constantly bidding them to be quiet even as a sparkle lit her eye.

Another memory surfaced, and Maggie's smile faded.

You shouldn't wear your brother's overalls, Margaret! Not even when fishing. Someone will think you're a boy! Now walk upstairs right this minute, like a lady, and change into a dress. And try not to get dirty again.

Maggie took a long drink, the water cool and wet against her throat even as the reverberation of her mother's oft-issued warning chafed the pleasant childhood memories. Maybe if she'd been less like her brothers and more like a "lady," as her mother desired, the two of them would have been closer.

But it was observing her mother's strong affinity for her brothers that had made her want to be more like them. Well, partly. That, and she'd always preferred to do whatever it was her brothers were doing instead of the pursuits of a "proper young lady" such as sewing, knitting, learning to play the piano, or perfecting her French.

It wasn't that she'd loathed those pastimes. They simply hadn't kindled a passion the way her love of horses and riding had.

Maggie sighed and took another drink, a familiar sense of loneliness creeping over her as it always did when she thought about her mother and their differences. If only—

"Margaret?"

She gulped, then spewed, choking on the water. Coughing, she turned to see Cullen standing in the doorway.

"Are you all right?" he asked, his voice sleepy-sounding.

She reached for the cloth that had covered the plate and wiped her chin and neck, working to regain her breath. "I *was* all right." She swallowed, running a quick hand through her hair, loose about her shoulders. "Before you scared the living daylights out of me."

He laughed, the sound reassuring in the darkness. He lit a lamp and held it up, frowning. "Who said you could have another tart? Onnie said those were for me."

"They're turnovers, and she did not." Maggie held back a chuckle, enjoying when he sparred with her. "Would you like some water?" She held up the pitcher.

He nodded, and she rose to get him a glass, then froze, remembering she was wearing only a gown. And not her robe. She quickly sat back down and positioned the pitcher just so in front of her. Then crossed her arms. Seeing he'd had the presence of mind to put on his trousers and a partially buttoned shirt didn't help.

He set the oil lamp on the table and claimed the chair opposite her. "Is everythin' all right?" he finally asked.

"Yes, it's fine. It's just—" He'd seen her once before in her robe, but never in her gown. And even though she knew it wasn't true, she still felt a little . . . naked.

"It's just . . . what?" He looked at her.

She looked back, trying to think of what to say.

Then his gaze dipped. Swiftly down, then back up again. And slowly, he smiled, the gesture taking its own sweet time as the corners of his mouth turned and the gleam gradually found its way to his eyes, deepening her embarrassment.

He leaned back in his chair and sighed. "I'm suddenly very thirsty."

He said it with such seriousness, she almost giggled. But she couldn't. Because she truly didn't know what to do. She'd never been with a man while wearing so little. Well, at least a man she wasn't related to.

"I'm *so* thirsty," he whispered, drawing out the words and crossing his arms over his chest.

She shook her head at him. "You'll need to get your own glass, Cullen."

"But you're closer." He looked pointedly at the cabinet behind her, then back. "And it's on your side."

She leveled a stare, meeting the challenge in his eyes. "You know very well why I cannot get you a glass."

"Actually, I don't." He leaned forward, the gleam in his eyes turning devilish. "But if you'd like to stand up and take a twirl, we can talk about it."

Trying not to, she smiled the tiniest little bit, and triumph marched in behind his eyes.

"Did you know," he said, rising, "that we're comin' along well on buildin' the extra cabins?"

Wondering if this was a ploy, she kept an eye on him. "No, I didn't. I haven't been down there."

He turned, glass in hand. "Not at all?"

She shook her head.

He took his seat again. "You should let me show you tomorrow. They're similar to the other cabins but have two rooms instead of one, and a loft area above."

"I've never seen the inside of the other cabins."

He paused. "You've never been inside the cabins your grandfather built for his slaves?"

Had she imagined the hint of reprimand in his tone there at the last? "No, we weren't allowed to go down there. The closest I've ever gotten was when Savannah, Mary, and I hid in the woods to watch when couples jumped the broom together." She paused, seeing his inquisitive look. "Do you know what that means?"

"Why don't you tell me."

She leaned forward. "It's what Negroes do when they're married. When I was a little girl, Onnie told me that whoever landed on the ground first, be it the bride or the groom, would be the person who made the decisions in the marriage. Onnie said she tried not to jump too high so she could land first, but Cletus merely hopped over and beat her to it!"

Cullen smiled, watching her.

"But if Papa or Mother had ever caught us down there watching . . ." She shook her head.

"Come with me tomorrow." He bit into a turnover, his mouthful equaling at least two of hers. "I'll introduce you to Ennis's wife, Odessia. You'll like her. And their children too."

Maggie didn't respond at first, then realized she needed to, for his sake. Especially having seen him interacting with the workers over the past couple of weeks. "I don't know if that would be best, Cullen."

He paused from chewing. "What do you mean?"

"I mean . . . I realize you work with the men, so there's a certain . . . ease that develops between you. But . . ." She tried to put it as gently, yet as honestly, as she could. "I think there can be too much familiarity between an owner and . . . the workers. Which then . . . complicates the relationship."

"Complicates it?" he asked, setting his turnover aside. "Complicates it how?"

Definitely hearing censure in his tone this time, Maggie almost wished she hadn't brought it up. But she'd seen her father watching Cullen from his bedroom window in the mornings before the workers headed out. Even though Papa hadn't said anything to her, she'd read disapproval in his expression, yet she doubted he'd confronted Cullen about it. Papa continued to insist that Linden Downs was Cullen's farm now and should be run according to his wishes. But that type of closeness with former slaves went against everything her parents had taught her.

Her father *had* taken the stand since the war ended that freedmen should be offered the opportunity for schooling, and had even offered an old hunting cabin on their land for that purpose. But that undertaking hadn't turned out well in the end.

She wasn't naive. She knew the world had changed. But it hadn't changed that much. And perhaps with reason.

"All I'm saying is that it might be better if you weren't so . . . friendly with the workers. They have their role and you have yours, and keeping distance between the two would be beneficial."

"Beneficial for who?"

"For everyone."

He nodded, but she could tell by his darkened expression he didn't agree.

"Do you think them beneath you, Margaret? Is that it?"

"No. Not at all. I'm not one of those haters who believe in doing those awful things." She thought of Willie and his family being forced to flee with the others. "That's *wrong*. And those people should be stopped."

"We agree on that at least." His tone held mocking.

"Do you not believe there are any differences between us?"

"Aye, 'course I do. Plenty of 'em. But none that make any of us any better or higher than the rest."

"I'm not saying I'm better or higher, Cullen."

"What are you sayin' then?"

"I'm saying that we all have different roles in life, different responsibilities. And that those should be respected and adhered to. For the good of everyone."

He stared at her for the longest time, then leaned forward and rested his sun-browned arms on the table. "Would you have curtsied to me the first day we met, if you'd known I was Irish?"

Maggie blinked and looked away. "Such an audacious question to—"

"Keep your eyes on mine, please, Margaret. And I'd like an answer."

Exhaling, she dragged her gaze back to his, and her breath quickened at the fierceness in his look. Not that she was afraid of him. He'd never given her any reason to fear him. No, it was the fierceness of his belief, so evident in his expression, that acted like a fist around her heart. And it took everything within her to match his stare.

She swallowed. "What you're asking, Cullen, it makes no—"

"A simple yes or no will do nicely."

Her throat aching along with her chest, she pressed her lips together in an effort to quell the emotion roiling inside her. A shadow flickered behind his eyes as though he'd already heard her answer.

"No," she whispered as a tear escaped and slid down her cheek.

An audible breath left him. "Thank you . . . for your honesty."

He rose, the chair scraping the floor overloud in the silence, and she wanted to say something so he wouldn't leave. But to her surprise, he stayed.

He moved around to her side of the table and held out his hand. She looked at it, then up at him, wondering if he was asking what she thought he was asking.

"Take my hand," he whispered.

She thought she'd had trouble breathing a moment before, but it was nothing compared to this. Every muscle in her body went taut, and she tightened her arms that were already crossed over her chest, her fingers digging into her flesh. Deep down inside, she'd known the time would come when he would want to consummate the marriage, but—

Hating herself for crying, she looked up at him and shook her head. "I'm . . . not ready."

A shadow crossed his face. His expression grew pensive. And for an instant she wondered what she would do if he demanded it. Her body went weak. Then just as swiftly, his expression cleared and the shadow lifted.

"All I'm askin' is for you to take my hand, Margaret. Nothin' more."

She blinked, relief flowing through her like summer rains after a drought. Unclenching her arms, her muscles grateful for the relief, she slipped her hand into his, and he drew her up.

They stood in the faint light, bodies close but not touching, save for their hands.

"I'll never force you, Margaret," he whispered. He brought her hand to his lips and kissed it. "And when we finally do, it'll be because we're both ready. Not just because I want you."

Knowing better than to trust her voice, Maggie simply nodded, achingly aware of the tender circles he traced on the underside of her wrist and of his mouth only inches from hers.

"Now . . ." He reached for the lamp. "If you're ready to go back upstairs."

Letting go of his hand and already missing its strength, Maggie led the way. Cullen held the lamp out to the side as they walked up the stairs, and the burnished glow haloed the path.

He walked her to her bedroom and handed her the lamp. "Good night, Margaret."

"Good night," she whispered, watching his shadowed form move down the hall. "And, Cullen . . ."

He turned.

She placed the oil lamp on the floor and crossed the empty space between them. "Thank you," she said softly, rising on tiptoe to kiss his cheek. "For . . . waiting."

He trailed his fingers down the length of her arm, sending a shiver through her, and she stilled, staring up at him. The way he looked at her did something to her on the inside. His lips parted and, as if in answer, hers did too.

"Margaret . . ." He swallowed, the sound audible in the quiet. "*This* . . . is not helpin' the waitin'."

She responded to the roughness in his voice and stepped back. "I'm sorry. I didn't mean to—"

He took her in his arms and kissed her full on the mouth, his lips both tender and insistent. The solidness of his chest against hers sent a rush coursing through her while at the same time making her knees go weak. His hands moved over her back in a mesmerizing kind of dance, and when he parted her lips, Maggie realized she'd never truly been kissed before. Not like this.

He drew back, and Maggie, her eyes still closed, felt the cool come between them. Her lips missed the warmth from his, and she blinked to see him staring down at her, his own eyes dark, his breath raspy like hers.

Taking her by the arm, he walked her back down the hall to her bedroom. "Good night, Margaret."

Not waiting for a response, he retraced his steps, and as his door was closing she whispered, "Good night."

Chapter Seventeen

"You don't have to do this, Margaret." Cullen kept his voice soft. Mr. Linden was already asleep again in a chair in the central parlor. "Regardless of what we said last night."

"I know," she whispered. "But I've thought about it, along with what you said last night, and . . . I think I should."

Cullen tried to read her expression as she tucked a light blanket about her father. But he couldn't.

She'd been so quiet this morning. Preoccupied, even tense seeming, both throughout breakfast and during her father's customary Sunday morning reading of Scripture. Was her hesitance due to his kissing her last night? And her kissing him, as he remembered only too well. Or perhaps because of where they were going now?

She didn't look any more rested than he felt, and he wondered if she'd had difficulty going back to sleep last night too. Not that he'd minded the reason behind his sleeplessness. Remembering how she'd responded to him, the way she'd pulled him closer and encouraged his advances . . .

It's a wonder he'd gotten any sleep at all.

Mr. Linden stirred. "Thank you, Maggie. You're a good daughter." His eyes opened further. "Cullen . . ."

The older gentleman stretched out a hand, and Cullen gently held it. The man's strength seemed to be waning by the day.

"Where are you both off to on this bright Sunday morning?"

"We're going for a walk, Papa," Margaret answered quickly, casting a glance at Cullen.

"Well . . ." Mr. Linden nodded, looking toward the window where dust motes floated featherlike in the morning sun. "Soak up some of that sunshine for me."

"We'll do that, sir." Cullen leaned down. "Maybe you'd like to sit outside on the front porch later. Some of the men and I, we'll be workin' on the barn roof. We could use some supervisin'."

Mr. Linden laughed, but even that sounded weak. "I'll look forward to it. After a little nap, of course."

"We won't be gone long, Papa. Onnie will check on you. And she's bringing more horehound and boneset tea. That will help your cough."

Margaret kissed her father's forehead, lingering, Cullen noticed, a little longer than usual. She was worried about him, he knew. So was he.

The man's color was more ashen than pale these days. And from what Margaret told him, the doctor's visits were growing more frequent.

Yet even with Mr. Linden's weakened state, the man insisted on reading Scripture at the breakfast table every Sunday morning. Cullen had to admit, he didn't dread the readings as much as he'd thought he would. Maybe it was Mr. Linden's choice of passages, or maybe his fine reading voice. But Cullen actually found himself looking forward to it each week.

He opened the front door, then paused and glanced back at Bucket, seeing if the dog wanted to go. But the collie, lying at Mr. Linden's feet, settled its head down on its paws. Cullen took that as a no.

Margaret accepted Cullen's assistance as they descended the porch steps, and although he enjoyed the feel of her hand tucked in the crook of his arm, he wished he knew the reason for her reticence.

They crossed the yard in front of the house and headed down the road in the direction of the cabins.

The morning dew had long since evaporated beneath the sun's warmth, but clouds building to the north promised relief from the heat. And, from the looks of them, they would bring welcome rain.

He hoped Margaret didn't regret what happened between them last night, because he certainly didn't. No authority on the gentler sex, he did remember days when Moira would be unusually quiet. When he would inquire as to what was wrong, she'd smile and say it was nothing, simply a melancholy day.

Maybe that's what this was for Margaret.

Having risen early, he'd ridden to the top of the bluff and watched the sun come up, wishing she'd been with him. As he'd looked out over the four hundred acres of Linden Downs, he still couldn't quite believe this land was his. Just as she was his.

Well, if not his in the most intimate sense, at least she was his wife, with the promise that the other might come in time. Only not too much time, he hoped, after last night.

"Thank you for agreeing to my father's request about Sundays."

"My pleasure. We can all use the rest, I assure you."

No fieldwork on Sundays was Mr. Linden's solitary request regarding the farm's operation, and Cullen hadn't argued. There was plenty to do without venturing into the fields on the first day of the week.

Moving freight on the docks in Brooklyn had strengthened his back and shoulder muscles, but the heat and humidity here in the South, coupled with the backbreaking work of clearing fields, then tilling and planting, made a man welcome a day with less strenuous tasks.

"It's good to see the land coming alive again," Margaret said. "The apple trees blooming amongst the white clover. To smell the freshly turned soil after a rain. I'd forgotten how beautiful the fields are when they're plowed and planted."

He trailed her gaze, sensing her relaxing. "They are that. We'll clear the last of the lower fields in the next week and get them planted, weather permittin'. And it's about time, too, with summer upon us."

"All of the lower fields?" She turned to look at him, the sun revealing the deeper red in her hair.

"Aye. The more we plant, the more we gather. Why?"

She lifted a shoulder, then let it fall. "That's where I like to ride Bourbon Belle. You know the field that runs along the river?"

He nodded.

"There's a path through the woods that leads all the way to town. Most people don't even know it's there. But it's one of the prettiest rides in all of Nashville."

He smiled, remembering the first day he'd seen her riding the mare. He almost brought it up, then decided it best not to. He didn't want to encourage another conversation he was doing his best to avoid. "I might be persuaded to leave you a little path around the side, if you'd like. It won't be the same, I know. But at least you could still get to the woods without tramplin' my corn."

She nodded, smiling.

They rounded a bend, and the cabins came into view. And Cullen felt her tense again.

He paused on the path. "They're good folks, Margaret. And not all that different from me and you, I give you my word."

"It's not that. It's more that now I—"

He waited as she looked anywhere but at him.

"I think some of them may think about me as you did." She glanced briefly at the cabins ahead. "That I consider myself . . . better than they are. It stands to reason that if *you* think it, then perhaps—"

"I never said I thought that about you, Margaret. I merely asked you a question last night."

Her look said she begged to differ.

"I was tryin' to get you to see things differently from the way most people in your world see them, because—"

"My world?" She turned to face him, removing her arm from his. "And just what, exactly, is wrong with my world?"

The tone with which she parroted back the phrase said she'd taken offense, and Cullen chose his words carefully. "I simply think it's important, Margaret, for a person to realize, myself included, that we often make decisions based on a limited amount of knowledge when really there's—"

"So now I have a limited amount of knowledge?"

He exhaled. "Sakes alive, woman, would you let me get out a complete sentence before jumpin' down my throat? I'm on your side here. Can't you see that?"

Her lips formed a line as she stared up at him, her brown eyes flashing. And for all the world, he wanted to kiss her again as he had last night. Only longer, and with greater freedom to know her better than he did. And she him.

Seeing her next thought swiftly forming, he rushed to beat it. "You've been here all your life, Margaret. That's all I'm sayin'. And when the world you're born in is all the world you've ever seen, it's hard to see it for what it really is. Believe me, I know. It took goin' to England for me to see my people for who they really were, and are. Aye, we're a brash bunch at times. We like speakin' our minds. We like celebratin' life when life gives us somethin' to celebrate. And aye, we'll down a frothy pint every now and then. But that's only because we know, as a people, what it's like to have life kick you in the teeth, then shove 'em down your throat."

Unexpected emotion tightened his chest. "A million Irish, Margaret. A million. All of them, starved to death. I was only six when the famine began, but I remember it as well as last week." He swallowed. "My three sisters, all younger, went first. Ethan, my older brother, and I were stronger. Always were, so we managed better.

"But we ate things not fit for beast, much less a man. I watched my ma waste away to nothin', even as my da spent what little we had on the bottle, tryin' to drown his grief and guilt." He shook his head, looking at the fields around them, wondering how they'd wandered into a part of his life he'd sworn he'd put behind him.

"All I'm sayin' to you is that people are rarely what they seem." He looked at her, seeing the fight leave her expression only for it to fill with something else he couldn't define. "Not from the outside. There's always somethin' more. But even after you know that, even after people have shown you who they really are, both for the better and the worse, we still somehow seem bent on decidin' who everyone is at a glance. I'm as guilty of it as any man.

"The British"—the very word left a bitter taste—"all high and mighty with their stuffed white shirts and their lofty rules for livin'. The way they looked down on us all. Treated us like trash, or worse. Laid the blame on us for things we never did. So we decided to come here, Moira and me, to make a better life for us and our daughter." His voice thinned as grief freshened within him. "Do you know what some Southerners call the Irish, Margaret?"

Her eyes watered, and she shook her head. "Don't," she whispered, her voice surprisingly fierce. "Don't you dare say that hateful word."

The conviction in her eyes, in her voice, tied a knot at the base of his throat, making it nearly impossible for him to continue. "Those people down there," he whispered, glancing at the cabins. "They hear it every day. Not from us. But from people who look just like we do. And you're right." He wiped a tear from her cheek and cradled the side of her face. "Some of them, certainly not all, look at you, and *me*, just as you said. But we all stand back and look at each other that way sometimes, don't you think?"

She held his gaze, her answer clearly written in her eyes.

"For me," he continued, "it was only once I admitted I was guilty of doin' that, that I could begin to change. And that's what I want this to be . . ." He looked back at the house, then to the fields, and all around them. "I want Linden Downs to be the place I wish the world was." He laughed softly. "Foolish as that may sound."

Which was just as he felt right then. More than foolish. Standing here in the middle of the road, jabbering away like a—

She took hold of his hand and grasped it between hers. "You had a daughter," she whispered, not a question so much as a newfound truth.

He nodded, her touch, her softness, having a greater effect on him than she likely knew. "Your father didn't tell you that?"

She shook her head.

"Her name was Katie Lynn. She was three when—" He looked down at their hands entwined together, her grip strong and steadfast, just like the woman she was. "When she died. On the ship. On the voyage here. Typhoid. It took nearly a hundred people."

"Your wife too?" Maggie said softly.

He nodded. "Moira went first, during the mornin' hours. Then little Katie, the spittin' image of her ma, all blond and blue-eyed, followed that night."

Fresh emotion brimmed in her eyes. "I'm so sorry, Cullen." She took a quick breath. "I'm so sorry."

She kissed the back of his hand and held it against her cheek, and Cullen drew her to him, cradling her head against his chest. Her arms came around his waist, and he knew that if anyone was watching, it would look as if she were holding on to him instead of the other way around.

But he knew the truth.

Chapter Eighteen

"And this is Odessia, Mr. Ennis's wife," Cullen said. "But everybody calls her Dessie."

Maggie caught the look he tossed her and exchanged greetings with the woman, aware of how much Cullen thought of her husband. It occurred to her how well suited Mr. Ennis and his wife seemed for each other. Both tall and commanding, their gazes clear and direct.

"Which do you prefer," Maggie asked her, keeping a safe distance from the washpot, mindful of the open flame and of the other cook fires dotting the common area shared among the cabins. "Odessia? Or Dessie?"

Keenness lit the woman's expression as she stirred, sweat glistening on her skin. "I prefer Odessia, Missus McGrath. Thank you for askin', ma'am."

Maggie caught Cullen's subtle nod of approval and appreciated his staying with her as he'd promised. He'd introduced her to so many people thus far, she knew she'd never remember all the names. Yet as much as she was enjoying doing this with him—and she was, surprisingly—the weight of her thoughts was still with him back there on the road from a while earlier.

He'd had a daughter . . .

She wished she'd known that about him before now. She couldn't pinpoint why, but it changed him in her eyes somehow. The crackle of flame devouring wood drew her attention, and she looked at the pot full of clothes, the bubbling water dark and murky.

"Only way I get this Tennessee soil to let loose of my husband's clothes is to boil 'em." Odessia's laugh was deep and rich like her voice. "You got good land here, Missus McGrath. Dirt that's dark and full'a life. It been restin' awhile, too, which does it good."

"Yes, it has." Maggie wondered if the woman knew that Linden Downs had almost gone to auction, then remembered how swiftly news traveled from other farms to Onnie and Cletus. Of course she would know. "We're grateful to your family, Odessia, and to the others, for coming to work at Linden Downs. My father and I were close to losing everything, so it's wonderful to see the fields all planted and slowly turning to green again."

She glanced at Cullen, wondering if he'd taken offense at the comment, but he seemed unbothered by it. Likely Odessia already knew about her and Cullen too. Why she'd married him. Why he'd married her.

Maggie looked around the common area at all the faces and felt as though they were all watching her. Imagining that everyone here knew the truth about her, she only grew more self-conscious by the minute.

Cullen introduced each of Odessia's children by name. "Jobah, Micah, and Kizzy, please meet my wife, Mrs. McGrath."

"Missus McGrath," the children said almost in unison.

Maggie smiled. "It's nice to meet you all."

She guessed the oldest boy, Jobah, to be about eleven, and the younger within a year or two of that. Maggie found it harder to peg the girl's age. Maybe seven or eight.

"Jobah here—" Cullen playfully grasped the oldest boy by the shoulder. "He picked up forty-seven bags of rocks in a single day following behind the plow last week."

Jobah grinned, and Maggie found herself doing the same.

"That's quite impressive, Jobah. You should be proud of yourself."

The smile he gave her warmed her heart. The boy was lean in build, though by no means scrawny. Still, forty-seven bags of rocks in one day.

"Mister McGrath, sir!"

Cullen and Maggie turned.

A man approached. "We gots a question for you, sir, on one of the cabins." He gestured behind him. "About bracin' up a loft . . . If you got the time."

Cullen turned to her, and Maggie read his unvoiced question. She smiled and mouthed *I'll be fine*.

As the children played a game in the dirt, drawing pictures of some sort, Maggie watched Odessia stir the clothes over the flame, the sun's heat beating down. If heeding her own body's complaint about the heat, she would've retreated a few steps back. But seeing Odessia's pleasant countenance as she stirred, the hem of the woman's skirt singed in more places than not, Maggie didn't dare.

She chanced a look about the open space and met far fewer stares this time. People had gone on about their business. Women stood over cookstoves, others tended washpots like Odessia. A handful of older men, part of extended families, she suspected, perched on overturned barrels beneath the trees and whittled, while every able-bodied man she saw was working on the new cabins in some capacity. Groups of women gathered beneath porches, involved in various tasks, their laughter lyrical and strangely carefree.

Yet not far from here, horrible, unspeakable things happened. Nearly every week a newspaper reported a death or hanging of some sort. Left unguarded, Maggie's thoughts drifted, and the darkness from the dream she'd managed to put from her mind crept close again, the images taking brutally vivid shape.

The origin of the dream was no mystery. Young Willie had described the scene so well. Only, in her dream—Maggie closed her eyes as though that would stop the scene from forming. She'd been standing below the tree branch, watching men without faces shove the noose over the man's head. She'd screamed until her lungs and throat burned as the faceless men had hoisted the man's body, higher and higher, his legs kicking, his feet trying to find purchase. But it hadn't made any difference, and she hadn't been able to save—

"You like to come up to the porch and sit, Missus McGrath? It's shady there."

Maggie blinked, then saw Odessia withdrawing the wooden paddle from the washpot.

The woman wiped her brow with her sleeve. "Just 'til your husband come back. I gots to go get laundry off the line."

Grateful for the interruption, Maggie nodded. "Yes, thank you. I would."

Odessia accompanied her as far as the porch then headed around back. Maggie climbed the steps, the wood giving a little beneath her boots. She found it surprising that Odessia and her husband—him being an obvious leader among the people—hadn't taken one of the newer cabins.

A lone chair occupied the porch, its slatted seat nearly worn through. She decided to stand.

She searched for Cullen in the direction he'd gone, but didn't see him. Standing in the shade, she thought again of his comment about her grandfather building the original cabins, and her curiosity got the better of her.

Feeling more like an intruder than wife to the owner, she peered inside.

Until last night she'd never given a thought to what was inside these cabins. But whatever she might have imagined, she would have been wrong. Because there was scarcely anything.

An ancient wooden table crouched in one corner with three mismatched chairs—similar to their forlorn cousin on the porch—huddling beneath. A rope bed absent its mattress occupied another corner, a threadbare blanket the only covering. Daylight streamed in through the walls and ceiling, ferreting out chinks in the logs and mortar and knifing through the roof overhead. And through the wooden planks of the floor Maggie easily made out the ground below.

Staring at the room, the stark contrast between these cabins her grandfather had built for his slaves and the house he'd built for his family and the generations of his family to come pressed down inside her, the weight of conviction coloring every moment of her life before this one and threatening to redefine the rest to follow.

The empty perfume bottle on her dresser bullied its way to the forefront of her mind and with scalpel-like precision sliced through some of the recent struggles in her life, laying them open for examination. And she didn't like what she saw.

In her world, not being able to afford her scent was a hardship. As had not being able to commission a new riding habit. For a while there, a year or so back, eating meat only once or twice a week had been a sacrifice. But compared to what she was looking at now . . .

I was tryin' to get you to see things differently from the way most people in your world see them . . .

Her world. All her life, she'd been only a stone's throw away, and yet—

"You like wearin' them kinda dresses?"

Slightly startled at the childish—yet decidedly confident—voice, Maggie looked down to see Ennis's daughter staring up, tiny hand on hip.

"I once heard tell of a white woman who done got one of them fancy dresses like that all wrestled up in a wagon wheel." The girl pointed at Maggie's skirt, a flair of drama in the act. "Horses spooked. Dragged her. Kilt her too." The girl shrugged matter-of-factly. "That's what folks say."

Curbing a grin, Maggie studied the child. "That's a very sad story—"

"Kizzy," the girl said, thin eyebrows arching. "I 'member your name, ma'am. It be Missus McGrath."

Maggie smiled. The girl was articulate for her age. And then some. "To answer your question, Kizzy, yes, I do enjoy wearing a pretty dress sometimes. But when I was younger, about your age . . ." Maggie leaned down and looked from side to side as though she were making certain they were alone. She lowered her voice. "When I'd work in the barn, I would wear my brother's dungarees!"

Far from the wide-eyed look of shock Maggie expected, the girl's eyes narrowed.

"How you kept them britches up if they was your brother's? Ain't they been too big for ya?"

Maggie liked the girl's spunk. "I used a length of rope, actually. Tied it in a knot, good and tight."

"Kizzy! You stop botherin' this fine lady."

Maggie straightened as Odessia gained the porch. "She's not bothering me at all, I assure you."

"Well, she talk your ear off, ma'am, if you let her." Odessia tugged one of her daughter's braids and gave her a look.

Little Kizzy gave it right back. "I'm gonna pick me up forty-seven bags next week, too, Mama. So I can get me as much as Jobah did."

Odessia deposited a basket of laundry on the table. "What your husband is doin' for the young ones, Missus McGrath . . . It's awful good of him."

Maggie stared.

"Payin' 'em like he do. A penny for every sack full of rocks they get."

"Oh . . ." Maggie nodded quickly. "*That.* Yes, well, I'm certain they're earning it." She looked down the way for Cullen again and was grateful to see him striding toward her. From now on, she intended to start listening more closely to the conversations he had with her father about the farm.

"My Ennis, he say Mister McGrath be a real good man."

Maggie glanced beside her to see Odessia looking at Cullen then back at her. "Thank you, Odessia. That's . . . very kind of you to say."

Maggie watched as he spoke to people as he passed, and she

leaned toward agreeing with the woman. Yet she wasn't fully convinced of the fact. He did have an ease about him, though, a comfort in his own skin, that was attractive.

She thought again of last night and how he'd kissed her, and how it had felt to have his hands on her. Her body flushed with warmth that had nothing to do with the heat of the day, and that only intensified when he looked up at her and smiled.

She wondered again what she'd wondered last night as she'd fallen asleep. Which was worse, the fact that she'd married a man she didn't love in order to keep her land and Bourbon Belle? Or that the man she'd married—the man she feared she was already growing to love—was the main obstacle standing between her and what she knew she was put on this earth to do.

Taking a different way home, Maggie urged Bourbon Belle across the creek behind the old Harding cabin where Uncle Bob lived, then guided the mare to the meadow beyond and urged her to a canter toward Linden Downs.

Helping Lucy Blankenship overcome her fear of horses had been a slow and painstaking process, but worth it in the end. In more ways than one. Thanks to Mrs. Blankenship's enthusiasm, Maggie's schedule for riding lessons was now filled to the brim. The jingle in her saddlebags felt good.

The month of June had settled in hot and heavy, ushering in new waves of daunting summer heat, and by the time Maggie reached the lower fields of Linden Downs she had to stop momentarily to remove her riding jacket. She stuffed it into a saddlebag then unbuttoned the collar of her white shirtwaist and fanned her neck. Even the slightest touch of cool was an improvement.

She gained the ridge a minute later only to see who she'd been wanting to see all day. She spotted him just before he looked in her direction, and she returned his wave.

She was thrilled to discover they hadn't cleared *her* field yet. Cullen had told her last night they should get to it today. And they might yet, with plenty of daylight left.

She leaned down and gave Belle's neck a good rub. "You ready, girl?" The mare pawed at the dirt. "All right then. Let's make this one count."

Maggie had never seen a horse with so swift a start as Belle. One minute you were sitting astraddle and the next you were flying on the back of Pegasus, sleek muscle and brawn carrying you through time and space so fast not even the wind could catch you.

Her focus on the well-worn path, Maggie heard the cheers and briefly looked up to see Cullen smiling and shaking his head, the workers whooping and hollering, and the children running through the field as though trying to keep up with Belle.

The moment was perfect, just like her Bourbon Belle, and Maggie couldn't contain the laughter inside her. Coming to the smoothest part of the path, she gently tightened her legs around Belle, let go of the reins, and stretched her arms out wide, lifting her face to the sun. Happy tears moistened her cheeks, and the image of her eldest brother came to mind.

The first time Oak saw her ride without reins as a young girl, arms outstretched, he'd been livid. Scared to death for her, she'd learned later from her father, who had always been her greatest support and encouragement. Oak had given a name to what she did: *soaring*. And he hadn't approved.

But he simply hadn't known horses the way she did. And she knew Belle. Like no one else.

Belle slowed as she always did when they approached the end of the meadow, and Maggie grasped the reins again. She turned around, the cheers of the workers now replaced by their applause. She took a bow atop Belle, and when she looked up again she spotted Cullen.

He wasn't clapping. And judging by his stance, he wasn't smiling anymore either.

He lifted a hand, not so much in a wave but as a we'll-talk-later gesture. She did the same, knowing he'd get used to seeing her soar. Or, like Oak, he would simply learn to accept it.

Her heart light, she directed Belle toward the creek. Once their thirsts were slaked, they continued on, Maggie letting Belle set the pace.

When they crested the last hill and home came into view, Maggie looked down to see her father seated in one of the rockers on the porch, waiting for her as he oftentimes did, with Bucket right beside him.

Even from a distance she thought she detected Papa waving, and she waved in return, big enough so he'd see her. Knowing how he enjoyed watching her ride, she snapped the reins, and Belle ate up the distance.

Chapter Nineteen

Maggie reined in and Belle skidded to a halt, sending dirt and pebbles flying.

Papa smiled, rocking slowly back and forth. "I never tire of seeing you do that."

"Do what?" She dismounted and removed the saddlebags, grinning as she did.

"Do what you love most. And what you're so gifted at, Maggie. Riding."

Cletus came for Belle and led her to the barn, and Maggie claimed the rocker beside her father, dropping the saddlebags at her feet. She leaned down and rubbed Bucket between the ears, smiling when the collie's tail thumped the floor.

She settled back. "I thought of Oak earlier when I was riding across the lower fields."

Her father gave her a knowing look, and she laughed. "I couldn't help it. The field was just so pretty, and they'll be tilling it tomorrow. But I don't think Cullen liked seeing me soar any more than Oak did."

"No." Her father shook his head, looking out across the fields. "I don't imagine he would."

Maggie briefly covered his hand on the arm of the rocker. "You've always believed in me, Papa. You've always trusted that I knew what I was doing with horses." She glanced toward the stable. "Especially with Belle. I appreciate your faith in me. So very much."

He turned and looked at her, the creak of the rocker falling away. His brown eyes, so much like her own, shone bright with emotion. "I do believe in you, Margaret. But it—" The break in his voice and slight tremble in his chin revealed his struggle. "It took me years not to be half frightened out of my wits every time I saw you ride like that. Arms stretched out with such abandon. So . . . fearless."

Maggie's smile faded. "Papa," she whispered, seeing his eyes glisten.

"That doesn't mean I didn't believe in you then," he continued hastily. "I did. And I still do. But even when you know someone can do something, even when you think they *should*, sometimes you're still a little frightened for them when they do." He sighed, his focus returning to the fields. "You're frightened because you love them so much, of course. And you can't imagine your world without them."

Staring at his profile softened by the late-afternoon sun, Maggie started to respond when he leaned forward, the rocker creaking as he did.

"Ah . . . look there!" A smile swiftly replaced his sorrow. "Here they come."

She looked up just as the wagons topped the hill. Cullen drove the first rig, pulled by Levi, the massive Percheron, and the wagon bed was filled with women and children. Ennis, his cargo the same, followed in the second wagon, pulled by two recently purchased mares. A throng of men walked behind them, their conversation drifting downhill toward the house.

"Look at the fields, Maggie," her father whispered after a few moments, settling back. "Can't you feel the life flowing back into the place?"

She smiled, hearing the hope in his voice. "Yes, Papa, I can."

Bucket rose and trotted to the edge of the porch as Cullen brought the wagon to a stop in front of the barn. Ennis guided the second wagon in right behind him. They assisted the women and children down, then Cullen made his way to the porch. His boots were caked in mud, his shirt and trousers stained with dirt and sweat.

He came as far as the bottom step then stopped. "Mr. Linden," he said, nodding and giving Bucket a firm pat on the head. "Margaret . . ." His gaze met hers, changing ever so slightly before moving back to her father. "It's good to see you sittin' outside again, sir. Looks like the fresh air suits you."

"I wish I could be out in the fields with you instead, Cullen." He breathed deeply. "The smell of freshly turned earth has always been as sweet as honeysuckle to me."

Cullen laughed. "I've got plenty of dirt on me now, but I promise you . . . I smell nothin' like a flower."

Her father laughed, the sound like a tonic to Maggie. But Cullen's less-than-warm greeting confirmed what she already suspected. They would have words later.

The squeak of the screen door brought them around.

Onnie stepped out. "Dinner be ready soon." She stopped to give Cullen a good looking-over.

Papa grinned at him. "You best go on and wash up, then we'll eat. And you can catch me up on the progress."

Cullen gave him a smart—and familiar—salute. "I'll enjoy that, sir. I have a lot to tell you."

"Mister McGrath . . ." Onnie held out an envelope. "This come earlier for you, sir."

Cullen started to accept, then glanced at his hands.

"Thank you, Onnie." Maggie rose. "I'll take it." The fine stationery looked familiar, and she soon realized why. "It's from Belle Meade." Addressed, she noted, to Mr. Cullen McGrath of Linden Downs. Not to her. Or to her father.

Her father resumed his rocking. "Probably an invitation to the yearling auction in August. General Harding was impressed with you, Cullen."

Cullen offered a look he likely intended to be amiable, but it was far from convincing. "I've got a couple of things to do in the barn, then I'll go wash up for dinner."

Maggie watched him walk away, fingering the envelope. If General Harding was extending an invitation to Cullen to attend the yearling auction, Cullen must have conveyed their financial standing to be quite good. Which made her wonder . . .

What exactly *was* Linden Downs's financial standing? During dinner tonight, she would do her best to find out. Linden Downs was, after all, her family farm. Or had been.

She stood. "I think I'll freshen up before dinner."

"And I think I'll stay right here with Bucket and enjoy the evening."

She leaned down and kissed Papa's forehead then grabbed the saddlebags. Inside, she laid the envelope on the side table, looking again at Cullen's name on the front. It shouldn't bother her.

But it did.

Upstairs, she changed into a fresh shirtwaist and, standing before the mirror, tucked the loose strands of hair back into her braid. Movement from outside the open window drew her eye, and she spotted Cullen, headed, presumably, to the creek. It was nice, in a way, considering what her father had said moments ago, that Cullen apparently wasn't pleased with how she'd ridden Belle. It would indicate that he cared about her, which she believed he did.

If not as a proper husband should, at least to some extent. Which boded well for a more favorable reaction from him when she finally found the right moment to broach the subject of racing Bourbon Belle.

Maggie emptied her saddlebags and looked at her reticule stuffed with coins and currency from the lessons she'd taught. Not even a fraction of the smallest fortune, but progress. For when she found a jockey.

Which would be soon, she hoped.

On her way down the stairs she caught a whiff of dinner. Chicken and dumplings, she thought—one of Onnie's specialities—and her mouth watered. She was famished. And tired too.

The screen door creaked as she opened and closed it, and she paused to admire the sun setting over the hills. "It's beautiful, isn't it, Papa?" she whispered. "So peaceful."

She turned to find him asleep in the rocker, and smiled. The hope in his voice earlier, the warmth in his eyes as he'd watched the workers returning home, did her heart good.

She crossed the porch and leaned down. "Papa." She laughed softly, touching his shoulder. "You need to wake up. Onnie's not about to let you nap through her chicken and dumplings."

He didn't stir.

She nudged his arm, a little harder this time, and knelt down. "Papa, it's time to—"

The slack of his jaw and slump of his shoulders drove her to her knees. The air around her thinned. She couldn't breathe. "Papa?" she whispered, eyes burning. She sucked in a breath and shook him again. "*Papa!*"

His arm, resting on his leg, slipped off to one side, and somewhere in the distance Maggie heard a woman wail. Deep, uncontrollable sobs. And not until strong arms lifted her from behind did she realize she was the woman.

Chapter TWENTY

Margaret cried and struggled against him at first, but Cullen held her fast, his own throat aching with unshed tears. Her sobs tore at his heart, and he turned her in his arms, away from her father.

"It's goin' to be all right, Margaret," he whispered. "It's goin' to be all right."

Her shoulders shook, and she fought to gain her breath.

Footsteps sounded from within the house, and Onnie came running. The screen door slammed behind her. At the same time, Cletus gained the porch, and the two of them stood staring at Mr. Linden. A deep sigh left Onnie, and Cletus slipped off his hat and bowed his head.

Onnie closed her eyes, her lips moving silently. The only sound, Margaret's soft, hiccuped sobs.

After a minute Onnie turned. "Why don't you take her to her room, Mister McGrath."

Cullen nodded, but Margaret drew back, shaking her head.

"No." She took a staggered breath. "I need to take care of him."

Her tears started afresh, and Onnie lifted her chin.

"Child, you done taken *good* care of your father all these years. Now it's time you let me do this for you. And for him. This one last thing." Onnie's lips trembled. "I be honored . . . if you let me."

For a moment Cullen thought Margaret was going to refuse. Then she bowed her head.

"Thank you," she whispered and turned to go inside.

Cullen opened the door for her and followed her to the staircase. She got to the second stair and her gaze slowly lifted, weariness in the act, and that's all the prompting Cullen needed.

He lifted her in his arms. She didn't fight him. He carried her up the stairs and into her bedroom, then laid her on the bed. She immediately curled onto her side and pulled the second pillow to her chest.

Cullen saw a blanket folded atop a cedar chest at the foot of the bed, shook it out, and drew it up over her, wishing he could do more.

"Is there anythin' I can get you?" he asked softly. "Anythin' I can do?"

She shook her head and buried her face in the pillow.

He reached out to stroke her hair then hesitated, not certain she'd welcome his comfort. He drew his hand back. "I'll check on you again shortly."

When she said nothing, he turned.

"Cullen . . ."

The fragile whisper brought him around again, the weakness in her voice touching something deep inside him.

"Would you . . ." She took a sharp breath and pulled the blanket closer beneath her chin. "Close the door . . . when you leave."

Rain pelted the heavy canopy of branches overhead, and Maggie held her mother's parasol closer, as much to shield herself from stares as to protect from the rain. Her gaze fixed on the coffin in the damp, dark hole at her feet, she heard the pastor's voice, yet didn't hear it at the same time.

Papa had looked so handsome in his suit and tie. She hadn't realized, though, how much weight he'd lost until she saw him after Onnie had finished. Maggie shivered despite the morning's warmth. She'd grasped Papa's hand one last time, but only for a second. Because it hadn't been his hand anymore.

Papa was gone. All that was left was a shell.

Cullen stood beside her, though not too close. She'd been grateful for the strength of his arm as they walked with Onnie, Cletus, Ennis, and Odessia to the family cemetery. And she would've welcomed his strength still, as she stood here, but the rain started right after they'd arrived, and she'd needed both hands to open the parasol. It had felt awkward, even a little presumptuous on her part, to slip her arm back through the crook of his arm again without him offering.

She was glad she'd insisted on a private burial. The last three days of well-wishers coming by the house to pay their last respects had exhausted her, even if the number of guests had been smaller than she'd expected.

The Hardings came, of course, as did Savannah and her siblings. Although Maggie and Savannah didn't speak much. Nothing beyond the softly whispered condolences friends offered on such occasions.

What was telling to Maggie was the absence of so many of their family friends. Oh, a few came, including the Petersons, the Barnards, and the Samuelsons. But in the end, the majority not attending was fine with her, because she suspected that at least some of those who came had done so out of curiosity. They wanted to see the Irishman who had bought Linden Downs—and Margaret Linden along with it.

Accepting well-meant words of condolence was hard enough when they came from someone she knew had loved her father. But hearing them from people who hadn't spoken to Papa or her since Linden Downs had fallen into financial demise . . .

Well, that was something she could have done without.

"Therefore we are always confident," the pastor continued, "knowing that whilst we are absent from the body, we are present with the Lord . . ."

Maggie wished Pastor Boddy—the man who'd known her family, who had preached at Mama's funeral and at each of her brothers' funerals—had still been alive to preach Papa's today. The man standing on the opposite end of the grave from her, the same one who'd officiated at her wedding, had met her father only a few times. The pastor hadn't truly known him. So however nice a man he was, and however kind and true the words he spoke, they sounded hollow and empty.

Grateful when the service finally concluded, Maggie was all too familiar with the next ritual. She knelt down, the frayed hem of her black dress damp with moisture, and scooped a handful of freshly dug earth, now mud, into her hand.

She looked at the clump in her palm, remembering.

Look at the fields, Maggie . . . Can't you feel the life flowing back into the place?

You got good land here, Missus McGrath. Dirt that's dark and full'a life.

Maggie stretched out her arm, turned over her hand, and the soil landed with a soft thud on the coffin below.

Later that night, waking from a restless sleep, Cullen heard the sound of weeping. He lay in the darkness, listening, knowing the pain she was enduring, the darkness in the midst of darkness, and he wished he could help her. Or hold her. Wished that she would allow him to do both.

The doctor had given her something to help her sleep, but apparently it wasn't working.

Twice he rose to go to her, and twice he lay back down.

He sat on the edge of the mattress and rested his head in his hands, knowing he'd never get that image of Mr. Linden out of his mind. The one from weeks ago, the afternoon he'd come upon Margaret's father in the woods, kneeling by the graves, almost as if the man had been waiting for him.

Yet Cullen knew better. Didn't he?

Margaret's crying quieted, so he lay back down, and as he sometimes did, he could feel the deep rocking motion of the ship even as he lay still in the bed, as if the ancient rhythm of wave and wind had somehow seeped into his bones. He closed his eyes, and the winds and waves grew more pronounced, as did the memories. And in the space of a breath, he was back on the bunk in the belly of the ship.

He held Katie close to his chest and breathed in time with her shallow, failing breaths, not caring if he lived or died since his world was all but gone. Even as she breathed her last, her tiny hand stayed curled around his index finger. In the moments following he memorized the sweet curve of her nose, her rosy cheeks, the way her blond lashes lay feather-soft against her skin. So peaceful in death, as if she were only sleeping.

He turned onto his side in the bed—the bed in the farmhouse that stood on solid land—and he wished, as he'd done many times before, that he had a likeness of her to carry in his pocket. But he guessed he did, in a way. The picture was just tucked away inside of him.

Hearing Margaret again, he sat up. But no longer were her sobs soft and muted. He rose and went to the hallway. And knew where she was.

He stepped inside Mr. Linden's bedroom and saw her curled up on the bed. Bucket lay by the empty hearth. A shaft of moonlight shone in through the open window, and the dog's dark eyes looked mournful and confused in the pale light. Cullen had tried earlier to coax the collie to sleep in his bedroom, but in the end Bucket had trotted back in here.

Cullen eased down beside Maggie on the bed and stroked her hair. After a moment she gave a shuddered sigh and reached for his hand, squeezing tight.

"I miss him so much," she cried.

"I know you do," he whispered. "I miss him too. Your father was—" His voice broke and he tightened his jaw, forcing the emotion back down. "He was a very good man."

After a while her grip on his hand lessened.

A few minutes more, and her breathing evened out.

He lifted her in his arms and carried her back to her own bed. He pulled the sheet up and leaned down and kissed the crown of her head.

"Thank you, Cullen," she whispered, reaching for his hand.

For the longest time he sat on the edge of her bed and watched her sleep, wondering if she would remember any of this when she awoke.

And knowing he would never forget it.

Chapter Twenty-One

Oh—" Maggie stopped short inside the stable, surprised to find Cullen still here at this hour of the morning. And Levi, in the stall behind him. However, seeing Bucket glued to the man's side wasn't at all shocking. During the past month the collie had found his new master. "I thought you'd be in the fields by now."

"And a good mornin' to you, too, Margaret." Cullen's smile seemed to come easily and held the same warmth as his voice.

The same warmth he'd shown her without fail in recent weeks. And though she was doing nothing wrong today, she still didn't want to tell him about her plans.

He gestured to the wagon out front. "An axle was comin' loose, so I stayed behind to mend it. I was just about to leave." He took a step toward her. "It's good to see you out of the house. And on a day when you don't have to give ridin' lessons. Are you takin' Belle for a ride?"

She hated to dash his hopes. "No, actually. I'm—" She didn't know how to say it without causing him hurt.

He'd been so patient, so kind and attentive in the past month, and she sensed he would be even more so if she encouraged him.

But as much as she enjoyed his company, and was especially glad to have him there for dinner each night, she couldn't bring herself to encourage him in that respect.

Because despite how moved she'd been when he kissed her—and how, even now, she would sometimes lie awake at night thinking about how safe and protected she'd felt in his embrace—she remembered what Oak had told her all those years ago about the direction of a man's thoughts. And she couldn't risk that Cullen might misunderstand her desire for companionship for a different sort of desire. Especially since they were alone in the house now.

She felt far more vulnerable around him. And *aware* of him.

Whenever he was in the house, she knew exactly where he was. If he was in the same room with her, she found her attention returning to him repeatedly. And yet . . .

Despite sleeping long hours, she still felt weary. All the time. And so . . . alone. Onnie cooked her favorite dishes, but food held little appeal. Beginning last week, she'd returned to giving riding lessons at Belle Meade three days a week. Some people might criticize her for that, she knew, with her still being in mourning. But Cullen and Onnie had both encouraged her to do it. Somehow she felt it was what Papa would have wanted too.

And yet her heart wasn't in it.

Sometimes in the evenings she would slip out of her bedroom and across the hall to sit on the edge of her father's bed, and she would try to recall every conversation they'd ever had, until she could scarcely keep her eyes open. Then she would return to her room and lose herself in the brief but blissful oblivion of sleep.

Bucket had taken to sleeping on the floor in Cullen's bedroom, which was a good thing, she knew—even though it hurt her to see it. It meant time was moving on, and she felt as though it was moving on without her.

She told herself it wasn't true, but there were moments when it felt as though she was the only one who truly missed her father.

Aware of Cullen still patiently awaiting an answer, she cleared her throat and forced out the words. "I'm going into town today." Already anticipating the frown on his face, she watched it swiftly form.

"Why didn't you say so? I'll be happy to take you." He tossed aside the rag in his hand. "Just let me send word with one of the workers' family members that I'm—"

"No," she said a little too quickly. "I'm fine going by myself. Besides, I don't want to bother you."

He scoffed. "I was plannin' on goin' tomorrow anyway. This'll just make my trip a far more pleasant one."

The authenticity in his tone—in the man himself—made her feel even worse. "Cullen."

He looked back, then stilled.

"I . . ." She truly didn't want to hurt him. "I would prefer to go alone, if that's all right."

He held her gaze for a beat, then gradually his expression darkened. "Is that it, then? Still?" He looked away, the muscles working in his jaw. "Fine, then. Go."

He shoved the latch to the stall door with more force than necessary, and Levi spooked, snorting and backing up a step.

"Cullen, that's not the reason. Not this time. I simply want to go by myself."

His expression told her he didn't believe her.

"I'm going to see Savannah," she continued, hoping that might convince him. "If she's not at her work then I'll need to visit her at home. So it could take a while, and . . . I may not be back until shortly before dinner."

He led Levi from the stall, but stopped beside her, his face close to hers.

"You're tellin' me that no part of your desire to go into town without me is due to you bein' ashamed of bein' seen with me. Of bein' known as my wife."

She almost wished she could lie, if only to spare his feelings, but she knew he would see right through her. "I'm growing more accustomed to the situation, Cullen. If you'll just give me—"

"A little more time," he finished for her, his tone gaining even more of an edge. "Aye, I've heard it before. But the real truth, Margaret, is that givin' you this time doesn't change anythin'. Because the problem isn't with *us*. The problem"—he exhaled, the set of his jaw communicating more hurt than anger—"is with you." His voice dropped. "I'm not ashamed to ride down the street with you by my side. Or to introduce you as my wife. Can you say the same about me as your husband?"

Tears welling, she struggled to steady her voice before answering.

"No," he said, his laughter holding no humor. "I didn't think so." He walked outside and hitched Levi to the wagon, Bucket sticking closer than a shadow.

Meanwhile, Maggie saddled Belle, the process far more taxing than usual. She heard the wagon pull away, and the weight in her chest sank like a stone to her belly. She stopped for a minute, wondering if she really wanted to go see Savannah after all.

She needed to, but what if her friend turned her away? Or what if—

"Margaret."

Her breath catching, she turned to see Cullen standing just behind her.

"You'll be back by dinner?" he asked softly.

Still seeing a simmer in his gaze, she nodded. "I don't see why I wouldn't be."

For a moment he just looked at her. Then he stepped close and pressed a kiss to her forehead, firm and quick. "I hope you and Miss Darby have a good visit."

Maggie opened the door to Miss Hattie's Dress and Drapery Shop, and a tiny bell jangled overhead, announcing her arrival. The stagnant air inside the shop made her wish her only black dress was suited more for summer than winter. She debated on leaving the door open, but the glare from the woman behind the counter told her that was not advisable.

"Excuse me." Maggie approached. "Is Miss Savannah Darby working today?"

The woman huffed. "She was supposed to be, but her sister got sick. Or so Miss Darby told me when she dashed in here this morning and then right back out again. So now Miss Darby isn't sewing the draperies for my best client as she was supposed to do today. And if I lose this sale because of her, it's going to cost Miss Darby her job." The woman's eyes narrowed. "And let me tell you something, even if she *was* here, I don't pay her to sit around and gab with her friends."

Nearly speechless at the woman's reaction, Maggie grew sorrier for Savannah by the second. She'd read in the newspaper recently that Miss Hattie's had been purchased by a new proprietor, but this . . .

The woman was beyond uncivil, and Maggie certainly didn't want Savannah paying the price for her visit here today.

Maggie drew herself up and summoned her most authoritative voice. "I would hope you don't allow your employees to sit around and gab, because I certainly didn't come here to waste my money. I came here because I was told this is where Miss Darby is employed."

In a blink the woman's bravado disappeared. Her face went a little pale. "W-well, it is. She is employed here, Miss—"

"It's Mrs., actually," Maggie corrected. "Mrs. McGrath." She watched the woman for any negative reaction to the last name, and seeing none, continued, her confidence bolstered. "I've seen Miss Darby's handiwork. It's the finest in Nashville. But if you're telling me you're not certain she'll remain in your employ, then—"

"Oh, no." The woman gave her a gushing smile. "I never said that. Of course she'll remain here. Where else would she work? This is the finest dress shop in town. Now . . ." She grabbed a pencil and piece of paper. "If you'll simply write down your name and what it is you're interested in . . ."

Maggie exhaled pointedly to let the woman know she found the whole exchange tiresome. "I believe I'll come back another day when I can speak with Miss Darby directly. Good day to you, ma'am."

Maggie closed the door behind her and walked a good two blocks before stopping to take a deep breath. *Oh* . . . She didn't know what she would do if Savannah lost her job because of her. Hopefully, she'd made certain that wouldn't happen.

She stood for a moment and took in her surroundings. The squeak and creak of wagon wheels, the hum of conversation coming from the various shops and vendors along the street. Young boys hawking newspapers and a "spittin' clean shine" for a penny. Mothers hushing babies while hurrying toddlers along.

Music played from somewhere down the street. A banjo and guitar, she thought. She could hear the chords but couldn't make out the words that accompanied the upbeat tempo. A flyer tacked to a board outside the mercantile advertised a Fourth of July celebration—that had passed without her even thinking about the date.

For the past month, her world had all but stopped. Yet life kept right on going. No matter what happened to an individual, people never stopped.

She walked six blocks to the street where Savannah lived, located the boardinghouse, and climbed three flights of stairs. By the time she reached the third floor, she was winded and perspiring.

Wiping her brow with her handkerchief, she walked down the hallway, reading the numbers on the doors and thinking of her father. How grateful she was that they hadn't had to move into a place like this. But even more, that he'd breathed his last at the home he'd loved.

Even thinking the thoughts, she felt guilty. Because this was Savannah's life. Finding the right door, she dabbed her eyes and slipped the handkerchief back into her sleeve. Taking a deep breath, she knocked.

Footsteps sounded and the door opened.

"Maggie!" Savannah blinked as if making sure it was her. "W-what are you doing here? Is everything all right?"

Maggie nodded. She'd had plenty of time to think of what she wanted to say to her friend. And yet, standing here now, all she could think about was how much she and Savannah had been through together. And how much she missed her.

Maggie gestured. "May I please come in?"

Savannah hesitated, but Maggie recognized the humiliation on her face and understood.

"Of course you may." Savannah stepped back to allow Maggie entry, then closed the door. Giving a nervous laugh, she gestured. "If you'll follow me into the central parlor . . ." She motioned to two worn chairs situated only feet away in front of a window that was boarded up on one side. An unmade bed sat adjacent. "May I offer you something to drink?"

"No, thank you. I'm fine." Maggie took a seat, then saw the bundle of letters on the table between them. "Oh, I'm sorry, Savannah. I've interrupted your reading."

Savannah glanced at the table. "No, no, it's fine." She picked up one of the envelopes. "Mother kept all of Father's letters that he wrote to her during the war. I read through a few of them shortly after Mother died, but it was too hard. More time has passed now, though, so I decided to get them out again."

Maggie nodded, wishing she had such a treasure from one of her parents. "How is Carolyne? I heard she was ill."

"She is, but how did you know?"

Maggie quickly relayed the scene at the shop, and by the time she was finished they were laughing together. And it felt so good.

"Oh . . ." Savannah sighed. "I wish I could have seen Miss Hildegard's face."

Maggie smiled. "It wasn't pleasant, I can tell you that. I do, however, think your job is secure. But only if I never return there again."

Savannah laughed softly then glanced behind her. Her expression sobered. "Carolyne *is* sick. It's bronchitis. The doctor says she'll be fine, but—" Again, that hesitance. "Andrew found work delivering newspapers today, and someone needed to stay with her."

"Andrew is delivering newspapers?" As soon as she said it, Maggie wished she could take back the question. The boy was eleven years old, two years older than little Carolyne, which was certainly old enough to do the work. But with those braces on his legs, she wondered how he could manage.

"It's only temporary. We needed a little extra money to make ends meet, so Andrew is doing odd jobs as he can. He's tired when he gets home, but he's managing it all right. And again . . ." She shrugged.

"It's only for a short time." Her eyes brightened. "A new Widows and Children's Home opened here in town recently. There were several columns about it in the newspapers."

Maggie nodded. She had read about it, and had thought about Savannah, Carolyne, and Andrew at the time.

"They serve meals every night," Savannah continued. "We've eaten there a few times already. It's quite nice, and the food is delicious. I spoke with the director of the home last time, a Miss Braddock, and we put our names on the list to live there. But it's a very long list, as you can imagine. And we do already have a place to stay."

Maggie nodded and smiled, but on the inside she was still trying to picture young Andrew walking all over town on his clubbed feet. The doctors had done all they could to correct the boy's condition when he was born, but the way his feet turned inward had always made walking a challenge.

Not for the first time, Maggie tried to imagine what Savannah's life must be like. Taking care of two younger siblings while working to provide for them. Given the same circumstances, she wondered if she would have done as well. Which made her think of what her life would be like now if not for Cullen.

Suddenly she was more eager to return home. To Linden Downs. And to him.

The silence lengthened, and Maggie noticed Savannah eyeing her black dress.

"You sewed it well for me," Maggie said softly, fingering the sleeve. "Thank you." She remembered when Savannah had delivered the dress to her house days before her brothers' funerals, then how her friend altered it yet again when Maggie's mother passed.

Savannah's expression held the weight of memory. "I'm only sorry you've had to wear it so often." Sighing, she looked around the sparsely furnished room. "Life didn't turn out quite the way we thought it would, did it, Maggie?"

Maggie followed her gaze, seeing the room but thinking of Savannah's father and two brothers who were killed in the war. And then of her mother who died shortly thereafter. Maggie thought of her own family, too, and of Richard, and all the other boys she and Savannah had attended school with. Gone. All of them.

"No," Maggie whispered. "It didn't."

Her gaze fell upon a marble-top table in the corner. One fashioned by John Henry Belter, if she wasn't mistaken. Quite valuable. She remembered seeing the table in the Darbys' central parlor throughout the years. Savannah's family home had contained so many lovely antiques and heirloom pieces. And still did, she guessed, since the house had been auctioned as furnished.

"It's the only piece I brought from home," Savannah said softly. "I've come close to parting with it many times, but it was Mother's favorite. I've been able to keep it so far."

"I'm glad. You need something to remind you of home."

Savannah's composure wavered, and a shadow crossed her face.

A moment passed. The rumble of wagons and carriages making their way on the street below rose to fill the empty spaces between them. Spaces Maggie wished weren't there.

"So . . ." Savannah's expression grew more timid, as did her voice. "What is it like . . . being married? Or should I say"—a trace of mischief touched her tone—"being in a 'business arrangement' with such a man?"

Maggie smiled at her friend's gentle teasing, but her sense of discomfort grew with the heat warming her face. She knew what Savannah was asking. As girls, they'd discussed in hushed whispers the imagined intimacies between a husband and wife. Not only physically but what it would be like to live with a man who wasn't your father or brother.

Yet even pooling their knowledge, the three of them—Mary included—had still lacked the necessary pieces of the puzzle to see the whole. And Maggie hated to admit to her friend that, even after having been married for weeks, she still hadn't solved that mystery.

"Marriage is," she began softly, knowing she was walking a fine line, "not quite what I thought it would be." Seeing the furrow in Savannah's brow, she hurried to add, "We're taking time to get to know one another, which is good. Very good."

Coughing sounded from the next room, and a weak voice called out, "Savannah?"

"I'll be right there," Savannah answered, then looked at Maggie, apology in her eyes.

"I need to be going anyway." Maggie rose, relieved but trying not to show it. "Please tell Carolyne hello for me and that I hope she's better soon. And thank you for the visit."

"I'm glad you came." Savannah walked her to the door. "I know I've told you this already, but . . . I'm so sorry about your father. He was such a kind man and always treated us so well. Even after we lost everything."

"Thank you," Maggie whispered, the mention of her father reminding her why she'd come. The guilt she'd felt earlier returned with renewed vigor. "I feel as though I owe you an apology, Savannah."

"An apology? Whatever for?"

Maggie looked at her friend. "For still living at Linden Downs."

Savannah took hold of her hand. "Margaret Laurel Linden, don't you dare say that. I'm so happy for you that you're still there. Truly I am." Savannah's eyes watered. "And I'm sorry for how I reacted that day at Belle Meade. Finding out your farm wasn't going to auction was one thing. But then learning you were married too." She shook her head. "Well, it was a lot to take in, that's all." She smiled brightly. "But I'm thrilled for you, Maggie. Really, I am. Friends?" she said sweetly.

"Always," Maggie answered, returning her hug.

But Maggie knew her friend's smile as well as she knew her own. And the one she was looking at now clearly came with an effort.

Chapter Twenty-Two

Maggie found traffic on the streets much busier than when she first arrived, and it took her longer to walk back to the livery where she'd left Bourbon Belle.

Waiting on a corner to cross the street, she kept thinking of Savannah, Andrew, and Carolyne. Savannah was right. Life hadn't turned out the way they'd imagined. But could anyone not say the same? The world had changed so much in the past few years. The world she remembered as a girl and the one she knew now bore scarce resemblance to each other.

She crossed the street, and a flyer on a shop window caught her eye.

The Peyton Stakes
Burns Island Track
Nashville, Tennessee
Saturday, October 16

Her pulse skipped up a notch.

It wasn't as though she didn't already know about the race, but seeing it advertised made it all the more real. As did seeing the winning purse listed in heavy print at the bottom. $35,000. Linden Downs could have successful crops for a decade or more and still not see that amount of money.

Somewhere in this town there had to be a jockey looking for work. All she had to do was find him. And then broach the subject with Cullen, and win him over.

She continued down the street, pedestrians rushing past, intent on reaching their destinations. Most never looked her way. She searched the sea of faces, recognizing none. Many of the people were foreign. Maggie couldn't fathom traveling halfway around the world to live somewhere else. New language, new customs. Leaving everything familiar behind.

And yet, according to the newspapers, immigrants continued to pour into this city, this country, every day it seemed, eager for the chance to live here. To start life over again. Or perhaps, just to start.

Someone bumped her from behind, and Maggie scrambled to keep her footing. She would've fallen, if not for a steadying hand on her upper arm.

"Miss Linden!"

Maggie looked up to see a familiar face. "Mr. Drake." She got her balance with his help, then accepted the offer of his arm. He escorted her off to the side.

"The city is a busy place, is it not, Miss Linden? Or—I should say—" Embarrassment shone in his features, and he frowned as though attempting to remember.

"Mrs. McGrath," she offered, surprised he didn't recall the name, considering the scene he'd had with Cullen the last time they were in town.

"That's right, please forgive me."

"No harm done." Sensing a less-than-sincere apology, she decided to give him the benefit of the doubt. She glanced toward the street. "Thank you for helping me just now."

"My pleasure, I assure you. So many . . . newcomers among us." Distaste colored his tone. "I fear they do not share our sense of hospitality or tradition. Nor, frankly, do they respect the natural order of things. Or what is good and decent, as do we. Those of us of similar mind must rise up and band together, should we not?"

The intensity with which he voiced his opinions, and so freely, not seeming to care who overheard, set her ill at ease. Not to mention his assumption that she would agree with them. And she was slightly surprised that he would make such a bold and sweeping statement when he knew Cullen was her husband.

She was especially grateful now that Cullen hadn't come into town with her. If he were to see her at this moment . . .

The thought of which made her all the more eager to extricate herself from present company.

"Tell me, Mrs. McGrath"—Drake's eyes narrowed in interest—"how is life at Linden Downs?"

Maggie looked at him, wondering if perhaps he hadn't heard about Papa. "Life is . . . slowly moving from the shadows, Mr. Drake. You might not have heard about my father's death."

"Oh, yes." His expression turned pained, his gaze falling briefly to her dress. "Of course I heard. I'm so sorry." He took her hand in his. "I hope you received my written condolences?"

She shook her head, uncomfortable with the liberty he'd taken in holding her hand. But he had been a friend of the family for some time.

"I'm so sorry for your loss. Your father was a pillar in this community and will be sorely missed by all who knew him."

The keenness in the man's eyes sharply contrasted with his sympathetic tone, and a protectiveness over her father's memory rose inside her. She took that opportunity to relieve Mr. Drake of her hand, pretending not to notice his reluctance to let go.

"Thank you, Mr. Drake, for your kindness. Now if you'll kindly excuse me, I need to be going."

"Allow me to escort you to your wagon."

"No need. I have other errands I need to pursue."

He eyed her. "Very well then."

She turned to leave.

"Mrs. McGrath."

Hearing a subtle challenge in the way he said her name, Maggie looked back.

"Do give your husband my regards. I haven't had the pleasure of seeing him recently." His brow furrowed. "He is still in town, I take it?"

Though his tone was guardedly pleasant, the dark flicker in his gaze told the truer story, while also letting her know he already knew the answer to his question. Stephen Drake and Cullen McGrath shared a mutual dislike, that much was clear. But as she recalled Cullen's recent actions and his calm, measured response when she'd questioned him about Drake, then contrasted it with Mr. Drake's blatant antagonism, she was surprised to find which man came through the comparison showing greater restraint, kindness, and even . . .

Strength of character.

Maggie forced a smile, eager to be on her way. "Yes, Mr. Drake. My husband is still at Linden Downs. And rest assured, I'll be certain to ask him to accompany me the next time I come to town. Perhaps then you can deliver your regards personally. Good day."

She cut a path for the livery, her heart pounding harder than usual. She sensed Drake's gaze on her retreat but didn't look back.

After walking several blocks, she paused to check the chatelaine watch affixed to her bodice. Nearly four o'clock. Later than she thought. A train whistle blew, and steam from the locomotive engine rose above the buildings two streets over. She'd always loved the sound of train whistles. Found them adventuresome, in a way.

This side of town was even more crowded than the other now, and she frequently had to turn her shoulder as she walked to keep from colliding with somebody.

Swept up in a crush of people on a corner waiting for the street to clear so they could cross, Maggie recognized an approaching carriage and strained to see if Mary was inside. About to wave, she refrained when she saw only General Harding occupying the compartment. The carriage passed and—

She squinted.

Cullen?

She caught sight of him on the opposite side of the street. What was he doing in town?

The crowd surrounding her surged forward, and she had no choice but to follow. Glancing back over her shoulder every few seconds, she tried to find him again. But couldn't. She'd lost him in the bustle of traffic.

Had he followed her? Surely not. Maybe he'd needed a new part for the wagon. But the question she most wanted answered . . .

Since when had he started wearing a hat?

~

"You're certain you weren't in town today?"

Cullen looked up from his plate. "I've told you three times, woman. I was here the whole day."

Margaret held his gaze as though waiting to see if he smiled. Which only made him smile.

"See?" She narrowed her eyes at him. "It *was* you."

He laughed and shook his head. It was good to see her in a cheerier mood. It was just good to see her.

She cut up her roast, a task, he knew from experience, that would take her at least two minutes. So he enjoyed the chance to watch her as he ate. And as he did, he vowed again, deep within himself, to love and protect her as best he could. Just as he'd promised her father he would do.

He looked over at Mr. Linden's empty chair, able to picture the man sitting there, his smile at the ready, kindness instructing his words. Cullen would be sore to admit it, but he missed Sunday mornings and the man's readings. He'd seen his father-in-law's Bible on Margaret's bedside table, but he hadn't felt the freedom to pick it up and read it.

Cullen checked her progress across the table, her dicing nearly done. She'd changed from the black mourning dress she'd worn into town. She now wore a dark gray skirt and similarly colored shirtwaist—the latter fitting her nicely.

She'd left the top two buttons at the collar unfastened. Not something that would have normally drawn his attention, but the past few weeks of living alone in this house with her had sharpened his senses in that regard. He was fairly certain he could *hear* naked now.

When she briefly closed her door at night as she readied for bed, his imagination kicked in, and not even the Farmers' Almanac charted phases of the moon could put him to sleep once that started.

From the way she'd responded to him when he'd kissed her that once, he felt sure he could persuade his way into her bed. But he wanted her to want him there, not simply succumb to his desires. He just didn't know how long it would take for that to happen.

Or if there was enough patience left in the world to see him through the vigil.

"Tell me about the crops."

He blinked, realizing he'd been staring at the soft hollow at the base of her throat, all thanks to the work of those two devilish little buttons. He lifted his gaze. "You want to talk about crops."

"That's right." She took a bite of roast and chewed.

He sat back, trying to size up what she was doing. "What would you like to know?"

"Everything."

He smiled slowly.

She did the same.

Then he stood. "All right. We leave in ten minutes."

Her fork paused midair. "Where are we going?"

He held up both hands, fingers splayed. "Ten minutes, Margaret.

Meet me in front of the barn." He motioned for Bucket to follow him, and the collie fell into step.

The woman wanted to know about crops. He would teach her about crops. And a wee bit more, if she was willing.

Chapter Twenty-Three

Belle's going to be jealous, you know." Maggie looked at the Percheron, then back at Cullen already in the saddle.

Cullen sidled Levi closer to the hitching post then leaned down and offered his hand. "I'm thinkin' she'll cope."

Skirts gathered, Maggie grasped his hand and started to climb atop the hitching post when she spotted Mr. Ennis coming up the road.

She let go of Cullen's hand and was certain she heard him groan.

"Mister McGrath!"

Cullen dismounted, looking none too pleased.

Ennis nodded to them both. "I sorry to bother you, sir, but I need to talk with you 'bout them"—he briefly glanced away—"wolves, sir. Ones that been takin' the chickens. Seems they got 'em a cow last night too. One of the men found it in the field just now."

"Wolves?" Maggie looked between the men. "We're having a problem with wolves?"

When Ennis said nothing, she looked to Cullen.

"It's nothin' we can't deal with." Not meeting her gaze, Cullen handed her the reins to the Percheron. "Mr. Ennis, I believe what you're needin' is in the barn. I'll show you right quick."

Mr. Ennis took a step then looked back. "Missus McGrath." He ducked his head. "You got to know you's all our Kizzy be talkin' 'bout these days. How you done flew by on that fancy horse of yours."

Maggie smiled. "That's very kind. You have a very curious and smart daughter, Mr. Ennis. She's not afraid to ask questions."

"She ain't afraid'a much at all, ma'am." He laughed.

"She's so young for being so confident."

He nodded. "She turnin' ten next week."

Ten? Maggie had thought her much younger, based on her size. Something she herself was familiar with.

Cullen stepped forward. "Mr. Ennis, I hate to keep you from your family." He gestured toward the barn.

Maggie watched them go, thinking of another time, probably a year or so ago, when Papa had said wolves were picking off some of the animals on the farm. She didn't remember what he did about it, but whatever it was, the problem had stopped.

She looked at the gargantuan horse beside her, still amazed at how huge he was. And yet so gentle. "You're one big beautiful boy." She settled for rubbing his muzzle, unable to reach any higher.

A few minutes later Cullen returned.

Wordless, he took the reins and climbed into the saddle. "Let's try this again, shall we?"

Her hand in his, Maggie climbed atop the hitching post, balancing with ease, then slipped her foot into the stirrup. With Cullen's assistance, she quickly transferred to sit in front of him—closely in front of him, thanks to the saddle's contours—and situated her skirt, all too aware of the swirl of heat initiating inside her where their bodies met. Working to sort out her reaction to him, she kept her focus forward, certain her face was as flushed as it felt.

Cullen snapped the reins and, with a ponderous gait, Levi started down the road.

Remembering, Maggie glanced back. "Where's Bucket?"

"With Miss Onnie in the kitchen. She came waving a soup bone, and the dog couldn't leave me fast enough."

Maggie laughed. "So now you know how it feels."

She peered to the side and marveled at how much farther it was to the ground compared to when she was on Belle, and how different this was from Belle's fluid stride.

"We have about an hour of sunlight left," Cullen said behind her, his arm coming around her midsection and securing her against him. "Let's use it well."

He urged the Percheron to a trot, then a canter, which Maggie found surprisingly less jarring than she would have imagined. Or maybe it was simply the way Cullen was holding her.

He directed the horse down the drive that led to the main road then broke off into a cornfield, keeping to the side. It was then she guessed where they were going.

Levi climbed the rise to the bluff as though it were flatland, and as if she and Cullen were but tiny sparrows perched upon his back. Maggie moved forward as Cullen dismounted, then leaned down to accept his help. Hands about her waist, he lowered her to the ground, taking his time.

She braced her hands on his shoulders, appreciating the layered muscle beneath her fingertips even as that familiar awareness of him rose inside her. When her feet touched the ground, he leaned close, and she realized he was going to kiss her. Her mind went blank. How did they do this last time? What had *she* done? She couldn't remember and she didn't want to make any mis—

He reached beyond her into one of the saddlebags and pulled out a blanket. "How long has it been since you've ridden up here?"

Quickly closing her mouth, Maggie gave herself a mental shake. "Um . . ." She forced her gaze from his lips to his eyes. "It's been . . . a while."

He looped the Percheron's reins over a low tree limb then gave the blanket a good shake. He crossed the distance and spread the blanket near the edge of the bluff, then offered his hand as she sat.

Feeling deprived of his kiss and not liking the feeling, Maggie sneaked a look over at him as he stared out across the land. Perhaps he didn't want to kiss her again. But she didn't think that was likely. Not because she was so comely . . . far from it.

But because, more often than not, when she was working, perhaps in the stable or in the garden, and she happened to glance in his direction, she would catch him watching her. And even with her limited experience, she thought his expression certainly seemed to hold interest.

Another possibility occurred to her.

What if—when they'd kissed before—he hadn't enjoyed it as she had? That thought lasted all of three seconds before she swiftly dismissed it. The look in his eyes that night, his quickness of breath matching hers, the way he'd held her . . .

No, it had to be something else.

"See that section of fields over there? Toward the north?"

She followed his gaze.

"That's all cotton. Then to the left, includin' what we just rode past, is corn. Those are our two biggest crops. We're trying some tobacco in those fields over there. And finally"—he looked over at her—"you may not believe this, but to the east . . . are potatoes."

She eyed him. "Potatoes? I'd have thought that to be the last thing—"

"I know what you'd have thought, and I thought the same thing. But your father, bless his soul, convinced me to meet with a man in town a while back. A German fellow, actually. I did and was impressed by what he showed me."

Touched by his mention of Papa, Maggie found her own interest piqued.

"The man says he's created a potato that doesn't rot. Or at least, doesn't rot as badly as they usually do."

"You've seen it?"

Cullen nodded. "The man pulled one up from the ground while I stood right there. But whether we'll be able to make the same happen here, I don't know." He sighed. "The man, a Mr. Geoffrey, a gardener I think, and a good one, based on where he's workin', says no other farmers in the area would take his seedlin's. They flat refused."

She frowned. "Why is that?"

"They don't trust him. Him bein' from Austria, and bein' a foreigner."

He cut a look her way, a mischievous gleam in his eyes, and Maggie flattened a stare right back at him.

Smiling, he continued. "Geoffrey told me the men were afraid whatever caused the blight in my homeland might be in the potatoes he's plantin'."

"Is that possible?"

"I don't know . . . not for sure. All I know is that your father asked me to go see him. And that the potato Mr. Geoffrey pulled from the earth was like nothin' I've ever laid eyes on. Nary a blemish on it, nor a black spot either. And it was bigger too. So I told Geoffrey we'd try it and let him know how it does."

Maggie wished again that she'd taken a greater interest in the crops and their discussions about them before now, while Papa was still alive. She gazed out over the land that spread like a deep green ocean in all directions, the soft rise and fall of the fields so gentle and inviting. The sun, half hidden behind the hills, lingered to kiss the land one last time before journeying on.

Cullen laughed softly beside her.

She turned. "What is it?"

"I was just rememberin' somethin' else your father said to me. I think it must be what first persuaded him to seek the man out about the potatoes."

She waited, eager to hear.

"He told me about the men he'd known for years. His 'business associates,' I think is what he called them. Your father said that, for the most part, they all snubbed him once things at Linden Downs started goin' downhill."

Maggie remembered how much that had hurt Papa.

"Seems those same men told this Mr. Geoffrey that no way were they goin' to plant those bloody—" Cullen stopped short then gave her a quick wink. "Let's just say they refused the man's request in quite colorful terms, your papa said." He laughed again. "Which I think helped him make his decision." Cullen sighed. "Papa sure was good at tellin' stories, wasn't he?"

Maggie nodded but turned away, her throat closing up tight. Seconds later, she felt a gentle touch on her arm.

"Margaret . . ." Cullen covered her hand on her lap. "Forgive me . . . Should I not be speakin' of him so plainly yet?"

Grateful for the approaching dark, she shook her head, the tears coming. "It's not that," she whispered.

"Then . . . what?" Touching her chin, he gently urged her back toward him.

"The opposite, in fact. It's just so good to hear you talk about him."

Even the waning light couldn't conceal the concern in his eyes.

"And to hear you say *Papa*." She felt a warmth in her chest, like the sun had left a tiny bit of itself behind. "It makes me feel"—she gave a little shrug—"like I'm not so alone."

He drew her to his side, and his arms came around her. Tucked there against him, she felt the weight of grief inside her begin to lift. And float up.

"You're not alone, Margaret. And while I know I'm not missin' your papa like you are . . . he was your da, after all . . . I've not known a finer man in all my life." He cradled her cheek. "Nor one who took such pleasure in givin' of himself to others."

She slipped her arms around his waist, holding on to him as she'd been wanting to do, not caring now whether he mistook her gesture for something more. Because . . .

Something more with him was exactly what she wanted.

*

Cullen drew back slightly, and she lifted her face. It was too dark now for him to see the look in her eyes, but her hand moving over his chest said enough. He turned her in his arms and kissed her, gently at first, relishing the taste of her mouth, then the softness of her neck. He moved a little lower, and she let out a little gasp. He sought her lips again, telling himself to move more slowly.

But desire for her whispered otherwise. Especially when she wove her fingers through his hair and pulled him closer.

Tracing the curve of her waist, he deepened the kiss. She hesitated only a second before angling her body into his. Desire for her tensed through him, and he eased her down onto the blanket. She looked up at him, her breath ragged.

He leaned down and kissed her, but in short, soft kisses this time, wanting to give her the freedom to stop, even as he prayed she wouldn't. Her lips so soft, her mouth so sweet and lush, he caressed her shoulder, then—knowing only too well the number of buttons on her shirtwaist—he loosened them. One at a time. And as each slipped free, her kiss grew more fervent.

He slipped his hand inside her shirtwaist, and she sucked in a breath. His body already hating him for it, he drew back slightly and looked at her lying beneath him in the last light of day, her lips parted, her eyes dark. And he knew that no matter how long it took him, he would win this woman's heart. Just as he was determined to win her desire.

Slowly, she sat up, and Cullen—already feeling the loss of her—took a steadying breath. Seeking to douse the fire inside him, he tried to recall a page from the Farmers' Almanac—those blasted phases of the moon, tips on when to plant, how to know when to harvest—anything to ease his desire for her, all while telling himself it would simply take time for her to—

Without a word, she reached to unbutton the top button of his shirt, then the next, and his throat went dry.

He let her finish, relishing the way her shirtwaist lay open to him, her corset and chemise beckoning beneath. But he could feel the trembling in her hands. He lifted them to his mouth and kissed each finger.

"Margaret," he whispered. "Are you sure you're—"

"Yes," she said and lifted her mouth to his. She kissed him, her lips tentative at first, then becoming bolder. "I'm very sure."

She slipped her arms around his neck and pressed closer, and he touched her, caressing, exploring, her soft sighs warm against his ear. And yet . . .

He needed to say the words to her. Even more, he needed to hear her say them. Her skin like silk against his, he lay beside her, looking at her in the moonlight.

"You are my wife," he whispered, brushing his fingertips against her lips when she tried to kiss him. "You . . . are . . . my . . . wife," he said again, and this time he saw the silver light of night mirrored in her eyes.

"I am your wife," she said softly, and the words washed over him.

He kissed her.

"I am your wife," she whispered again, over and over, their breath mingling.

And as he drew her to him, the rough ground beneath his back, Cullen knew her need for him was surpassed only by his for her.

Chapter TWENTY-FOUR

Awakening to the sun on her face, Maggie wiped the sleep from her eyes and turned over in bed—straight into Cullen. He was on his side, facing her, and she waited for him to stir. When he didn't—his breathing steady and deep—she carefully adjusted the sheet and nestled into her pillow, appreciating the opportunity to watch him.

His dark brown hair and sun-bronzed skin contrasted with the white of the bedcovers, and she resisted the urge to run a finger along his shadowed jawline. The sheet down about his waist, his bare chest invited her gaze—and her memory—and she recalled what his muscled shoulders had felt like clutched beneath her hands.

She sighed, wanting to relive that feeling all over again, and wanting to remember every detail about last night. And about him.

They'd returned to the house shortly after midnight to find Bucket eager to greet them when they opened the door. Cullen had been hungry—and to Maggie's surprise, so had she—so they stayed up talking in the kitchen, sitting at the table and eating scrambled eggs and bacon until half past three. They'd also devoured a stash of freshly baked lemon cookies Onnie had made and tucked inside the cupboard. They were Maggie's favorite. A recipe from her Aunt Issy, passed down through her mother's family for years.

"Good morning . . ."

The familiar voice deeper than usual, she lifted her gaze to find him staring, and felt herself blush. She attempted to smooth her hair, but he caught her wrist.

"Don't," he whispered. "I like seeing you fresh with morning."

His touch reawakened desires she would have thought depleted, and she laughed to cover what felt like a thousand frenzied butterflies fluttering inside her. Even though she was wearing her gown, she felt naked beneath the sheet, and far less confident in the light than she had been in the dark on the bluff last night.

He leaned over and kissed her. And beneath the cover, he caressed her thigh, and Maggie wondered if this was what it would feel like to awaken next to him every morning.

"Would you like some breakfast?" she asked, feeling a sudden need to fill the silence.

He shook his head, his gaze taking in the length of her. "Breakfast isn't quite what I'm wantin' right now, Mrs. McGrath. What about you?"

As his hand moved upward her breath quickened, and she smiled and reached out for her husband. "My feelings exactly . . . Mr. McGrath."

They got downstairs for breakfast later than usual, and Maggie insisted Cullen wait outside the dining room and let her go in first.

"You've got to be kiddin' me, woman."

"Shhh . . ." She held up a hand, not wanting Onnie to hear. "I certainly am not."

"Do you think Miss Onnie won't know?" he whispered.

"I don't mind her knowing. Eventually. I just don't want her knowing that we—" She widened her eyes. "Last night."

"And again this mornin', love," he said, grinning.

Swatting him in the chest, Maggie walked into the dining room and took her seat.

Seconds later, Onnie pushed through the door, a pot of coffee in her hand. "Mornin', ma'am."

Maggie smiled. "How are you this morning, Onnie?"

Onnie glanced down at her. "I be fine, ma'am. How is you?"

"Very well, thank you."

"Well . . . that's real good."

Maggie heard Cullen's steps in the hallway and busied herself with creaming her coffee.

Onnie looked up. "Mornin', Mister McGrath."

"Mornin', Miss Onnie." Cullen took his seat while signaling to Bucket to stay in the hallway. The dog lay down, gaze still intent. "Sure smells good down here."

"Thank you, sir."

Maggie looked across the table. "Good morning, Cullen."

Cullen gave an almost imperceptible shake of his head. "Good mornin', Margaret."

Pouring Cullen's coffee, Onnie looked back across the table, and Maggie tried her best to appear normal. She crossed her arms, but that didn't feel comfortable, so she placed her hands in her lap. But that felt wrong, so she picked up her coffee cup again.

"I be right back with breakfast," Onnie said softly.

No sooner did the door close than Cullen smiled. "She knows," he whispered.

"She does not."

"She does."

Throughout breakfast Maggie only grew more convinced that Cullen was wrong—and that Onnie's hotcakes were the best the woman had ever made.

"They really are delicious, Onnie." Maggie helped herself to another when Onnie held out the plate.

"So you been sayin', ma'am. More bacon?"

Maggie smiled. "I think I will, thank you."

Onnie rounded the table. "More for you, too, sir?"

"I think eight hotcakes is my limit, Miss Onnie. But thank you." Cullen rose. "I need to get to the barn. The men will be here anytime."

Maggie looked up. "I hope you have a good day, Cullen."

Smiling, he tucked his napkin by his plate, came around to her side of the table, and kissed her full on the mouth. "I hope you have a good day, too, Margaret."

Stunned, Maggie heard Onnie begin to laugh.

"Thank you, Lawd, is all I got to say." She looked between the two of them. "It be 'bout time!"

∽

The next morning Maggie awakened to discover that she'd overslept, and Cullen was already gone. Before she was even out of bed, she saw the note on her side table.

Dear Mrs. McGrath,

You're beautiful when you sleep, do you know that? It's an early morning and I've got to run into town for supplies. We'll be in the lower fields today. And I'll be eager to see you at dinner tonight.

Your husband,
Cullen
P.S. I think Cletus knows too.

Maggie grinned and stretched, eager to see him again as well, but with a day full of tasks between this hour and that.

An hour later, dressed and having eaten a quick breakfast—all while enduring Onnie's knowing smile—she headed out the door to Belle Meade.

It still felt odd not seeing Bucket around the house during the day, but the collie seemed to live for the moment when Cullen whistled for him to jump into the wagon bed. And some nights, by the time the crew returned at dusk and the collie gulped down dinner, the dog seemed barely able to make it up the stairs before sprawling in a heap at the foot of their bed.

But she knew Papa would have loved the fact that Bucket went into the fields every day. *Papa* . . . Oh, how she missed him. Their conversations, his laughter. The way he saw good in the world even amidst the bad.

Maggie guided Belle down by the lower fields but didn't see Cullen anywhere. Nor did she see the Percheron. And usually the two went together.

Her riding lessons went well and the morning passed quickly. Her heart for teaching the young girls was slowly returning, though it still wasn't her first love.

After her last student left, Maggie led the saddle horse, Daisy, one of her favorites, back to the mares' stable. The pretty little black mare was smart as a whip and had a sweet disposition. The horse was on the smaller side, too, which made her an excellent horse for training young riders.

"Good lessons with them girls today, Missus McGrath. You sure a patient soul, ma'am."

Still growing accustomed to being called that, especially by Uncle Bob for some reason, Maggie looked down the way to see him peering at her over a stall. "I try to be patient, Uncle Bob, but I'm not always. I have to remind myself what it's like to be their age, and their size, and how intimidating it is to ride one of these marvelous creatures."

"I don't think you was ever afraid, ma'am." Uncle Bob shook his head. "If you was, I don't 'member seein' it. And I been watchin' you ride since you and Miss Mary was seven years old. But I tell you what, ma'am, you done made my hair gray a time or two back then." Uncle Bob laughed as he walked away.

Maggie did too, but on the inside her heart squeezed tight,

thinking of similar words spoken to her not that long ago. *Papa . . . I miss you so much.*

She unsaddled the mare and brushed her down, grateful for a few moments alone with her thoughts. If she'd known how much Papa had feared for her, if he'd shown her that fear, she might never have learned how to ride the way she did.

Yet, as grateful as she was to know how to ride and to train, what she truly wanted was still out of reach. The Peyton Stakes was scarcely three months away, and she had the fastest horse in the county, perhaps even the state, but still no jockey.

Thirty-five *thousand* dollars.

What she and Cullen could do for Linden Downs with that money . . . Everything Papa had wanted for the farm—whatever Cullen wanted—would be within their reach. Listening to Cullen the other night, she'd heard Papa's love for the land in his voice and had taken such comfort from it.

If she could ride Belle in the race herself, she would, but she knew that would never be permitted. Besides, she weighed considerably more than a lithe young boy, and Belle's times would be far slower than when Willie had ridden the mare.

Daisy's dark coat finally gleamed a blueish-black, and Maggie cleaned the brush and returned all the tack to its proper place. She checked her chatelaine watch affixed to her skirt band. Half past twelve.

Surely Cullen had returned from town by now. She only hoped he hadn't had any more encounters with Stephen Drake while there.

Two nights ago, when she and Cullen had stayed up talking in the kitchen, he'd asked her about her day. She'd told him all about her visit with Savannah, and about their friendship since childhood. Mary too. But she hadn't said a word about her encounter with Stephen Drake, not wanting to upset him. Now she wished she had.

Because if Cullen happened to run into Drake in town, and the man mentioned seeing her . . . that would not go well.

She wondered again if she'd credited the man's character too heavily due to his family's good reputation. The elder Mr. Drake, Stephen's father, several years deceased now, had been a fine man, and a friend of her father's. But Stephen . . .

"You hear about last week's heat, ma'am?"

Maggie looked up, noting Uncle Bob's cautious expression. "Do I want to know?"

He shrugged. "You in a good place of mind right now? Or poor?"

She smiled. "I think the answer to my question, then, would be no."

"All right then." He started to walk away.

"Uncle Bob!" She laughed. "You *have* to tell me now."

He turned back, grinning, then nodded toward the mare in the stall behind her.

Maggie turned. "No! Fortune came in first again?" She threw a scathing look behind her at General Harding's champion thoroughbred. The same mare Belle had beaten twice earlier that spring. "That's three weeks in a row Fortune's won the heat."

"Don't I know it." Uncle Bob eyed her. "I was there to watch."

"I bet it was a handsome purse too."

"Handsome enough, ma'am. The general, he always be happy to win. But I can tell the victory ain't as sweet with him knowin' Bourbon Belle should be out there runnin' with 'em."

Having no response to that, at least none that would contribute to the conversation, Maggie saddled Belle and led her from the stall. "Thank you again, Uncle Bob, for everything."

"You welcome, Missus McGrath." He looked over at her, wiping his hands on his white apron. "You doin' all right, ma'am?"

A gentleness shone in his eyes beyond what was customarily there, and knowing he'd already offered his condolences more than once on Papa's passing, Maggie realized he could only be asking about one thing.

"Don't get me wrong, ma'am," he added quickly. "I's real happy for you . . . if you's happy."

She appreciated this man more than he knew. "Thank you, Uncle Bob. I wasn't at first, but . . ." She thought again of how much she enjoyed being with Cullen. Not only as his wife but simply being with him. "I am now." She read uncertainty in Uncle Bob's eyes. "Cullen McGrath is a fine man. And a very good husband."

His smile came slowly. "He best be, ma'am." He nodded, raising his eyebrows as though to accentuate the point. "He best be."

By the time Maggie returned to Linden Downs it was midafternoon. She stopped by the cemetery to put the wildflowers she'd picked on her way home atop Papa's grave, only to find a single purple iris already there. Freshly picked, too, the delicate petals so beautiful. She had a good idea who had placed it there and would be certain to thank him.

Back in the saddle, she looked downhill toward the house and saw the empty rocking chairs on the porch. A bittersweet yet undeniable resignation settled her. All of them were together now. Only she remained.

She searched the cloudless blue overhead, wondering if souls in heaven could ever see glimpses of the world they'd left behind. Or if, once there, a person would even want to look back.

But if they did, if they could, and Papa happened to be watching . . .

She snapped the reins and Belle responded, and by the time they reached the house and Maggie reined in, she could feel her father's pride inside her. She hoped that if he were watching her now, Papa would also know how grateful she was to have Cullen in her life. And in her heart.

She dismounted and was nearly to the stable when a sassy little voice brought her up short.

"I got me a question, Missus McGrath. And I's needin' an answer."

Maggie turned, and seeing who it was, she grinned.

Chapter TWENTY-FIVE

"I want you to learn me how to ride." Kizzy's face scrunched up. "But not like them white girls. I wanna ride like *you,* Missus McGrath."

Tempted to smile, Maggie eyed her. The girl looked from her to Belle then back again. "Have you been following me over to Belle Meade?"

The girl shook her head. "I gots to leave way 'fore you do. But I done figured out what days you go. I seen ya there three times now. You ain't never seen me though."

Maggie read the seriousness in the girl's expression and remembered what Mr. Ennis had said about his daughter. "Have you told your parents you want to learn to ride?"

The girl's bravado slipped a notch. "They done tol' me not to be askin' you, 'cuz you's the boss's wife. But I seen you learnin' them others, ma'am, and I *know* I better than they is. I can pay too." She dug into her pocket and held out her hand.

Maggie looked at the pile of pennies and thought about how many bags of rocks this little slip of a girl had toted to earn that amount, then about how much it cost the girls she taught at Belle Meade. Or, rather, what their parents paid for them. The costs didn't even begin to compare. Kizzy's was far greater.

"I'll teach you how to ride," Maggie said, admiring her spunk.

Kizzy's smile broke free.

"But," Maggie quickly added, watching the girl's mouth turn down, "one of your parents needs to give me their permission. In person."

Kizzy's brows drew together then just as quickly smoothed. She held the pennies out further.

Maggie shook her head. "I don't get paid until I give the lesson."

Studying her for a second, Kizzy nodded and slipped the coins back into her pocket. "But if Mama and Papa say I can, you ain't gonna change your mind?"

Maggie smiled. "I won't change my mind. And we can start soon, if you want. Within the next two weeks. You can ride with me over to Belle Meade."

Her eyes lit. "You mean, you be teachin' me over there?"

"*If* your parents give their permission."

Kizzy tore down the road, her little legs pumping.

"Kizzy!" Maggie called.

The girl skidded to a halt, dust pluming.

"Have you ever ridden before?"

The girl looked at her like she was daft. "Why, o'course I have, ma'am. We gots us an ol' mule I ride all the time."

Maggie laughed softly as the girl rounded the corner out of sight.

One afternoon later that week, Maggie flipped through the scant stack of mail she'd received in the past month, remembering what Stephen Drake had told her about sending his written condolences. Granted, there had been days right after Papa died when she'd scarcely left her room, but she would have remembered a note from Drake.

She checked the drawer in the desk in the central parlor, then the one in the hallway table. And there, in that drawer, lay an envelope.

She picked it up and was just as quickly disappointed.

The invitation from Belle Meade. Remembering the day it had arrived, she fingered the envelope, also remembering how frustrated she'd been that it was addressed to Cullen and not to her or Papa. But now . . .

She smiled. That didn't bother her at all. After all, she was Mrs. Cullen McGrath now. In every way . . .

She opened the envelope, already knowing what was within. And sure enough . . . the invitation to the yearling auction being held next month.

The invitation's ornate script and deckled edge gave it an especially rich feel, which was appropriate, considering the event. Mary had likely chosen the stationery, no doubt from Williamson's Writing Supplies in Nashville. Maggie turned the card over to see if she was right.

A handwritten note was on the back.

Dear Mr. McGrath,

I appreciated our visit the other day and trust you will seriously consider my offer. In the hope of convincing you, I'll add two of my finest saddle horses to the deal and raise my offer to five thousand dollars. Bourbon Belle is worth every penny. After all, as we discussed, I've seen her race.

Yours most sincerely,
General William Giles Harding

The note shook in Maggie's hand.

She read it again, already knowing what it said. And the second reading only worsened her trembling. And ignited her anger. So Cullen had known about Belle racing all this time, yet hadn't said a word. And now he wanted to sell her? Maggie exhaled.

He wouldn't do this to her. He couldn't. Could he? Not after what they'd—

Remembering this note had been written well over a month ago, the pieces began to jar into place. Cullen had met with General Harding about selling Belle right before Papa died.

So he was simply biding his time now, waiting for the right opportunity. That day in town, the same day she'd seen General Harding's carriage, she had also seen Cullen. Even though he denied it.

Maggie took a sharp breath, events becoming painfully clear. But not as clear as they were about to get for Cullen McGrath.

Chapter Twenty-Six

Cullen slapped the reins, urging Levi up the hill toward home. The Percheron's massive hooves found easy purchase, and the animal pulled the weight of the wagon, including the dozen or so women and children seated in the back bed, with seemingly little effort.

Cullen always marveled at how, in early morning, the chatter of the women and children behind him all but drowned out the squeak of wagon wheels and the chirp of birds. But as nightfall crept closer . . .

He smiled. They were so quiet, most of the little ones sleeping. He would've sworn that if not for the wheels' complaint over the rutted road, he would hear the sun's gentlest sigh as it edged slowly down in the west.

How could so beautiful a place harbor such ugliness?

The "wolves" were growing bolder in their attacks. The cow found slaughtered in the field days ago was proof of that. But unless wolves had taken to brandishing knives and slitting a cow's throat before hacking it to death, his earlier suspicions had proven correct.

Who the men were that were doing this, if it was indeed more than one man, he didn't know. But he had a suspicion. He hadn't seen or heard from Stephen Drake since that day in town with Maggie. But from experience, he knew that men like Stephen Drake didn't simply go away. Nor would such a man give a second thought to slitting the throat of a heifer. Or of another man, if it came to it.

Cullen looked out over the land, *his* land. And his and Maggie's home. Be it right or wrong, he'd instructed Ennis and the handful of workers who knew the truth about the incidents to refer to them as wolf attacks, if any of the women or children asked. No need to upset them, or Margaret. She had enough to deal with right now.

Meanwhile, he was dealing with the problem.

Cresting the hill, he guided the wagon toward the house and spotted Margaret waiting for him on the porch. Even from a distance, the sight of her warmed him. And at least for a while the challenges currently facing him receded.

Earlier that week he'd written her a note before leaving one morning. Pen in hand, he'd paused for a moment, just to watch her. She bewitched him, even in sleep. Her brown hair, touched with auburn, lay loose and wild on the pillow, and the sheet formed to the contours of her body. Curves he was coming to know so well.

The thought warmed him further, and desire for her fanned out through him. Grateful didn't come close to describing how he felt about the way they were learning to be with each other.

As he guided the wagon to the barn he threw her a wave, indicating he'd be there shortly, then pulled to a stop. He climbed down and assisted the women and children from the back bed.

The crops in the field were planted and—thanks to the timeliness of gentle summer rains—were well on their way. There was no longer any need to follow behind plows and pick up rocks, but he'd overheard the men discussing what a difference it made in their families for them to work together, and what the extra income meant to them too. So he invested in a slew of flour sacks, and now the women and children—those who wanted to—picked weeds and any unwelcome insects they found from among the plants.

It was hard to grasp how much his life had changed in what felt like so short a space of time. He'd felt so empty inside. And angry. And now . . .

It was as though he was finding his life again, much like the fields of Linden Downs. Sometimes he wondered if he should have told Mr. Linden about what happened in England, and with his brother Ethan. But he'd been so eager to put all that behind him. And he truly thought if Mr. Linden had known the truth, the man would've understood.

At least, that's what comforted him in the moments when doubt resurfaced.

He thought about Ethan often, wondering where he was, what he was doing, and whether his brother ever thought about him. The chance of his ever seeing Ethan again was nonexistent, because he'd never told his brother where he and Moira were going. He'd been so angry at Ethan the last time they'd seen each other. And angry at himself for not figuring out beforehand what his brother had planned. If only he'd—

"We get both the wagons unhitched tonight, sir."

The sound of Ennis's voice urged Cullen back from another world. One best left behind.

"Jobah and Micah," Ennis continued, "they help me do it, sir. Be good practice for 'em."

Looking at Ennis's young sons and seeing their little chests puff out, Cullen nodded. "Much obliged, young men."

"A word 'fore you go, sir." Ennis waited to speak again until his boys were set to task. "'Bout them attacks, Mister McGrath."

Cullen nodded.

"Two more men come up today sayin' they's willin' to help."

"That makes fourteen altogether then." Cullen kept his voice quiet. "That's good. That means two men watchin' per night. Everybody knows when and where we're to meet this weekend?"

"Yes, sir. I told 'em. All 'cept one of 'em shot a gun before. But if it comes to it, I ain't at all sure how close to the mark they can get."

"That's all right. Shootin' can be taught." He exhaled, hoping it wouldn't come to that.

Aware of Jobah and Micah watching from across the barn, Cullen gave the boys a smart salute. Even before the gesture was complete, a twinge of loss tugged at him.

He wished Gilbert Linden could see the farm, the way the crops they'd planned together were starting to flourish. He also wished he'd prompted Mr. Linden to share in greater detail about the problems he'd had with the land a year or so ago. What were the odds that the same enemy that had plagued Linden then was the enemy behind the butchery now?

As Cullen walked toward the house, he saw Maggie waiting for him on the bottom step, and he sent a thought heavenward, for what it was worth. *I'm keepin' my promises to you, Mr. Linden. Both for your daughter and for your land.*

Mindful of the dirt covering his clothes—and himself—he leaned in to brush a soft kiss to her—

"How *dare* you," she whispered.

He stilled, a breath away from her lips. Confused, he glanced behind him to see if, by chance, Ennis and his sons were watching them. But the yard was empty.

He turned back to the steel in her eyes and the hard set of her mouth. "What's wrong, Margaret?"

"What's wrong?" she repeated. "When were you planning on telling me, Cullen?" Her voice steadily rose in volume. "Or did you simply think you didn't need to discuss such matters with me?"

Feeling his guard edge up, Cullen tried to read her expression. And couldn't. Yet, seeing the shadows in her eyes, the suspicion, a sickening dread crept up inside him. Did she know about England? About what had happened? He glanced behind him again to make sure Ennis and his sons were out of earshot. They were still down by the barn.

"Margaret." He gestured toward the screen door. "Can we please take this inside?"

Tears rose in her eyes—though not the kind he'd dare attempt to wipe away—and she strode up the steps and into the house. He followed after her, catching the screen door before it slammed shut.

She continued into the central parlor then whirled to face him. "How could you do this? It's beyond—"

"Margaret, I don't know what you're—"

She thrust a piece of paper at him. The invitation to the thoroughbred auction at Belle Meade Plantation. Inwardly, he winced. No matter what she said, under no circumstances was he setting foot on General Harding's estate when scores of thoroughbred owners from this country—and Europe—would be in attendance.

"If you're tellin' me you want to attend this, then—"

"Turn it over," she said, her voice hard.

He did, and his gut twisted. He grimaced, her anger swiftly making sense, and the increase in Harding's offer also making a substantial impression. "Margaret, this isn't what you think. I never—"

"You discussed selling Bourbon Belle to General Harding."

"Nay, I did not. He broached the subject with me, and I—"

"You knew about Belle too." Her eyes narrowed. "You *knew* we'd raced her, yet you never said anything about it. To Papa. Or to me."

The suspicion and hurt in her eyes were a dagger to his conscience. He realized she likely hadn't considered he could easily turn the tables and point out that she had purposefully hidden from him the fact that they'd raced Belle. But he couldn't. Not knowing his own reasons for being less than forthcoming.

He also knew that the outcome of this conversation—no matter what she said, no matter how she tried to convince him—would not end in her favor. Because if it did, if she raced Belle and won, drawing attention to Linden Downs and to him, then his past would come to light and they would both lose everything.

Yet, looking into her eyes, seeing seeds of distrust where he'd last seen love, he already felt a great loss.

"You're right, Margaret. I've known for a while now that you and your father raced Belle. But never, for one moment, have I considered sellin' her to General Harding."

"Good. Because she's *mine.* You have no right to sell her."

Cullen felt his own eyes narrow, yet reminded himself she was angry and still grieving the loss of her father. "The issue of who owns Belle isn't what's most important right now. Because the horse isn't bein' sold."

She met his stare, her brown eyes simmering black. "And what if I told you that I wanted to race Belle again?" Her chin lifted slightly. "Once I find a jockey."

He worked to keep his tone even. "Then I would tell you that I strongly object to that idea."

"And what if"—she swallowed—"I *insisted* on pursuing that path?"

He chose his words with care. "Then I would also have to insist most forcefully, Margaret, that you not act on that pursuit."

Her cheeks flushed. "But she's a winner, Cullen. She can win the Peyton Stakes. A race this fall that carries a thirty-five-thousand-dollar purse. Do you realize what that would mean for us? For Linden Downs?"

"We're doin' fine, Margaret. We don't need—"

"She was sired by the champion Vandal at Belle Meade. I spent months convincing Papa to allow me to breed our best mare with Vandal. Then spent another small fortune paying General Harding for the stud fee. Yes, I'd hoped for a colt. But when Belle was born, when I looked at her and saw her strength even when she was yet so young, I knew. Papa and I spent nearly everything we had on getting Belle this far." Her features softened, as did her tone. "I've raised her from a foal, Cullen. I've trained her every step of the way. I'm *good* at it too." Her eyes glistened. "You love this land, I see it in your face and hear it in your voice when you speak about it. That's how I feel about Belle. And about racing her. For as long as I can remember, this is what I've wanted. Please," she whispered. "Papa supported me in this. Can you not do that as well?"

The dagger in his conscience twisted a half turn even as self-preservation swiftly clotted the wound.

The fact that she was arguing with him, pleading her case, told him much. Regardless of when Bourbon Belle was sired or that Margaret had trained her, he owned the mare now. And Margaret knew it. It wasn't fair that his mistake in England would dictate this outcome to her dream—yet it wasn't fair what had happened to him there either.

But rarely did life deal from the top of the deck.

"My answer is no, Margaret," he said softly, feeling a severing deep inside him. He reached to take hold of her hand. "I'm sorry, love, but—"

She pulled her hand back, and her jaw went rigid. "Your father's problem with gambling, while sad and tragic in its consequences to you and your family, Cullen, has no bearing on this situation." Her breath quickened. "Neither Papa nor I have ever gambled. Not once. Neither does General Harding. And I'd—"

"It's not an issue of gamblin', Margaret. Thoroughbred racin' is not the kingly sport so many claim it is. And it's no place for a female, I can tell you that for sure. And certainly not a lady such as yourself."

"But I wouldn't be in the forefront, Cullen. *You* would. Just like Papa, you would be the owner on the Thoroughbred Society's ledgers. No one would need to know I was the trainer. I don't care about that. I only care about seeing Belle race."

Cullen looked at her and loved her, and seeing the frail hope in her eyes caused his own to burn with emotion. "I'm sorry, Margaret. But I cannot allow it. I—" His throat tightened. How to make her understand without telling her the truth?

He didn't think he could abide the disappointment in her eyes when she realized the kind of man she'd married. He knew how she felt about the Irish. Or *had* felt. She'd made that clear from the outset. And learning this about him would only confirm opinions he'd fought hard to change.

"I would never forgive myself," he continued, "if somethin' happened to you. And honestly, do you really think the Thoroughbred Society here in Nashville would recognize an Irishman as an owner?"

She hesitated, then her eyes lit. "General Harding would vouch for you! I know he would. And he's on the board of the society. He's a very powerful man, and—"

"My decision is made, Margaret." Cullen steeled himself to the anger sure to come. "Now please, respect it."

She stared up at him, unblinking, her expression one of disbelief. Then betrayal. Which swiftly gave way to fury. She skirted past him.

Hearing her muted boot steps racing up the stairs, Cullen felt each one driving the wedge deeper between them.

Later that night when he finally came upstairs, Cullen discovered Margaret's bedroom door closed. Or . . . *their* bedroom door.

Though they hadn't discussed the situation formally, he'd been staying in this room with her since that night on the bluff, and he wasn't eager to give up the privilege. Unless, of course, she demanded it.

But even then, considering how far they'd come together, he would fight to win her over again. He knocked.

No answer.

"Margaret?" he said softly, then reached for the knob, half expecting it to be locked.

The knob turned in his hand. He opened the door. The bedroom was dark.

In the half light of midnight he saw her silhouette in the bed, unmoving, covers drawn up around her chin, her body as far to the edge of her side as she could be.

He stripped to his drawers and climbed into bed beside her, the mattress feeling even smaller than usual. He touched her unintentionally but she didn't move. She didn't make a sound, yet he knew she was awake. He could feel her awareness of him as well as he could feel the warmth from her body.

No matter how he looked at this—and he'd spent the evening doing just that—there was no other way. It was too risky. And even though Margaret was confident Belle could win that race, he'd heard the same conviction a thousand times before from those who were as certain as the sun would rise that their horse would win.

And even if Belle were that good—which General Harding's increased offer led him to believe—it didn't change the fact that, if discovered, he could be sentenced to prison. All for what he'd done, and for what he didn't do.

"Please, my love," he whispered, the darkness all but swallowing his voice. "Know that I'm doin' this for the good of us both. Even if you don't understand."

He waited, wanting to touch her. To comfort her.

She didn't respond. Not even the steady, rhythmic breaths of sleep. Only deafening silence. And the memory of the steel in her eyes persuaded him to keep his hands to himself.

His body exhausted, his mind raced.

He turned onto his side away from her to face the wall, and at least an hour passed before sleep finally claimed him. But sometime later, when darkness had robbed even the faintest light from the room, he awakened to feel a gentle shudder beside him. Her silent sobs.

He lay awake for the rest of the night.

Chapter Twenty-Seven

She had to change Cullen's mind. That's all there was to it. But how?

Maggie hurriedly saddled Belle in the barn, intent on leaving for Belle Meade before Cullen came outside and before any of the workers arrived, same as she'd done for the past two weeks.

Living with the man in recent days had proven even more difficult than after they'd first wed, and she still wasn't certain which rankled her more: the fact that he'd been so unyielding in his decision not to race Bourbon Belle, refusing to even discuss the matter, or that she missed him despite still being so angry with him.

Please, my love, he'd whispered that first night. *Know that I'm doin' this for the good of us both. Even if you don't understand.* Although the sincerity in his deep voice had warred with her willpower, she hadn't responded. She still didn't understand his reasoning—which he refused to expound on. And yet . . .

When she'd awakened earlier, she'd lain in bed and watched him sleeping beside her, the memory of skin against skin intoxicating—and growing more distant each day. Everything about him exuded masculinity. And drew her. Half of her wished he would open his eyes and take her in his arms. The other half wanted to give him a good shove off the side of the bed.

Maggie led Belle from the barn, the thick of summer laying its stifling hand over the land. The air heavy and still, late July spared not even a whisper of wind. Already, beads of perspiration dampened her forehead, and her chemise clung to her beneath her riding habit.

Remembering she'd left her reticule hanging on a hook in the barn, she looped Belle's reins on a post and hurried back in to retrieve it. She'd promised Kizzy riding lessons two weeks ago, and Kizzy had made it her mission to remind Maggie. Every day. But Maggie wasn't about to proceed without speaking to either the child's mother or father.

She'd finally spoken with Odessia and, true to the girl's word, Kizzy had asked permission and Odessia had eagerly granted it. "Yes, ma'am, Missus McGrath." A sparkle had lit Odessia's eyes. "You could say our daughter broached the subject. 'Bout beat it to death would be a mite truer, though."

Maggie tucked her reticule into the saddlebag and glanced toward the ridge beyond the barn. Kizzy said she would be waiting there in order to ride with her to Belle Meade. Maggie was determined to teach the girl the basics of riding. Though, considering Kizzy's only experience to date was riding a mule . . .

The familiar creak of the front door issued warning, and Maggie spotted Cullen descending the porch steps by twos, his stride determined, his expression the same.

Silently scolding herself for having taken so long, she quickly climbed into the saddle. Looking down on him would help her to feel more in control. But deep down she knew better.

"Margaret?"

Belle sidestepped and pawed the ground, feisty and ready to run. Commiserating, Maggie held the reins taut. *You're not the only one, girl.*

"Mornin'." Cullen came alongside them.

"Good morning." Maggie looked down, wishing his eyes weren't so true a green.

To her frustration, Belle sidled toward him, and he reached up and scratched the mare's forehead. Belle snorted in satisfaction.

"I'm sorry, Cullen, but I'm late for my lessons, so I'd best be—"

"Margaret." He took hold of Belle's harness. "This needs to stop. This . . . silence between us. I'm your husband. You're my wife. And—" He blew out a breath. The gesture might have smacked of impatience, if not for the sincerity in his features and the yearning in his voice. "I'm tellin' you the truth when I say I'm sorry my decision disappoints you. But thoroughbred racin'—and trainin' the horse, to boot—is simply no place, or occupation, for a woman. I know because I've seen the truth of the business up close, with my own eyes. It can be ruthless."

"But I've told you, Cullen, I'll stay in the background. I don't care about being the one who gets the—"

He held up a hand. "Belle may have won a few heats, and aye, she's fast. But this race you're wantin' to enter . . . It's a whole different world of competition. And competitors. These men and their investors, they're serious about winnin'. And they'll do anythin' within their power to make that happen."

"Don't you think I realize that? I've already faced their lack of acceptance. Their arrogance. And I'm telling you I can manage whatever they dole out. And Bourbon Belle can beat every one of the horses on that track."

"Perhaps," he said, a depth of questioning in the word. "But what kind of husband would I be if I allowed you to take such a risk? I'm workin' hard to save Linden Downs, to save your home. *Our* home. And we're doin' that, Margaret. Together." His gaze grew tender. "Aren't we?"

Feeling ashamed, though not fully comprehending why, she nodded reluctantly. "Of course we are. But—" Something he'd said to her one night after they'd made love returned. She felt a stab of betrayal in bringing it up now. But what other choice did she have? "Cullen, you told me that buying Linden Downs, that seeing the land come back to life, and being part of that renewal, was a dream come true for you."

The tenderness in his eyes swiftly faded, and wariness took its place.

"Well, racing horses is *my* dream, and has been for as long as I can remember, despite being told countless times growing up that I couldn't do it. Or shouldn't. If not for Papa's support, my mother would never have even begun to tolerate it."

Maggie stopped short, her mother's disapproval gaining fresh clarity through the lens of the moment. It rose up inside her accusingly, as if coming to Cullen's defense.

But Cullen knew none of that part of her life. Best it stay that way.

"Cullen . . ." She took a needed breath. "I've worked hard to get to this point. To buy Belle, to train her. Do you have any idea what it feels like to give your heart so completely to something, only to have that treasure ripped right from you?"

He stared at her for a moment, the silence lengthening. "Aye," he said finally, the wariness in his expression giving way to regret. "I know precisely what that feels like, Margaret."

Realizing what she'd said and how he'd misconstrued her meaning, Maggie bowed her head, her body going warm. "Cullen, that's not what I meant." She lifted her eyes. "I meant no disrespect to you, or to the memory of your late wife and daughter."

"I love you, Maggie." The muscles tensed in his jaw as if part of him regretted the truth of the words. "But I cannot—and will not—allow this." He briefly looked away. "I hope that with time you'll be able to accept that. And that you'll be able to forgive me for causin' you such disappointment."

He strode past her into the barn, and Maggie sat motionless, her throat aching with unexpected tenderness even as the heat of anger all but burned a hole through her chest.

He'd said he loved her—which he'd told her once before, but in the darkness, in a husky whisper, as they'd moved as one. This had felt different. Not any more real. But strangely, more . . . intimate.

And he'd called her Maggie . . .

Hot tears pricked her eyes. So small a thing, really, considering everything else. But still . . .

She heard the sharp clank of metal against wood coming from within the barn and wondered if the action rendering the sound had been intentional.

She guided Belle through the field and up the ridge, then spotted Kizzy not too far away. The girl ran toward her for all she was worth.

Maggie waved, then glanced back toward the barn. It wasn't that she didn't appreciate Cullen's concern for her. She did. But she simply couldn't stand by and watch this opportunity go to waste. She had the answer to securing the future of Linden Downs in her grip. Even if he couldn't see it.

The root of his disapproval lay in fear for her, of what could happen. She understood that. But as Papa said . . . sometimes a person needed to let go of a loved one and let them follow the course for their life.

Cullen had already lost so much. Both as a son and a brother, then as a husband and father. She didn't blame him for being worried about her. She simply needed to prove to him that there was nothing to fear.

And she would.

"It look mighty simple to me," Kizzy said, hand on hip, squinting in the sunlight. "This ridin' a horse."

Bluster crisped the girl's tone, but as Maggie peered over the saddle, she noted the way Kizzy's gaze kept darting to Daisy, the mare she would be riding, then darting away again. The girl shifted from foot to foot. Another telling sign. She looked so small standing here in the middle of the corral.

"Riding *is* simple." Maggie lifted a brow. "But it's not easy. There's a lot to remember. And to learn."

"I can do it. I know I can."

"I believe you can too." Maggie gestured her closer, knowing only too well how overconfidence could work against a new rider. "And now . . . your first lesson. Kizzy, meet Daisy." Maggie scratched the mare on the bridge of the nose. "And Daisy"—she demonstrated how to extend her hand, palm open and facing upward—"this is Kizzy."

The mare nuzzled Kizzy's hand, sniffing and licking, which coaxed a flood of giggles from the child. Maggie laughed softly. Regardless of whether a girl hailed from one of the finest homes in Nashville or had once lived in Shantytown, the first lesson always drew similar reactions.

Maggie studied her newest pupil—the anticipation in Kizzy's eyes, the tattered checkered dress laced together in front by a frayed string of rope, her hair braided flat against her scalp. And her build, thin and wiry like her brothers, not a hint of womanhood about her. Instead of pantalets, she sported britches beneath her dress, turned up at the hem. Britches belonging to one of her brothers, no doubt.

"Horses are very smart creatures," Maggie continued.

"Like me," the girl chimed in, her grin pronounced.

Maggie schooled a sober expression, wanting the girl to take this seriously. "Even without being around a person for very long, a horse knows what that person is like. Simply by reading them."

"Readin' 'em?"

"Horses sense things. About people. About situations. Most times long before humans do."

Kizzy peered up, eyes narrowing. "What you mean?"

"What I mean is that even having just met you, this horse already has a sense about what type of person you are. Whether you're kind. If you'll treat her nicely. Or whether you might raise your voice, or take a whip to her flank. Or beat her with a stick."

Kizzy's brow knit tightly as her focus slid from Maggie back to the mare. Her gaze went somber. "You tell this horse for me, Missus McGrath . . . I ain't never gonna beat her or do any of them bad things you said." The girl reached up and stroked the mare's jaw. "Not *ever*."

she whispered, her dark eyes warm with affection, her soft voice lined with steel.

After a second or two, Kizzy looked back. "You gonna tell her for me, ma'am?"

Maggie gently squeezed her shoulder. "I don't need to." She glanced at the mare. "She already knows."

The mare snorted and inched closer, and Kizzy beamed.

"Now," Maggie patted her back, "let's get you in the saddle!"

Kizzy weighed next to nothing, which made assisting the child onto the mare much easier.

"You'll want to sit deep in the saddle," Maggie instructed, which earned her a wary look. "That means you want to press your bottom down so you don't bounce when you ride. Keep your back straight." She demonstrated from where she stood. "And keep your legs in contact with the saddle. *And* with the horse. That's part of how you communicate with her. Sitting evenly in the saddle is important too. Leaning your body one way or the other will throw off your balance. It'll make it more difficult for Daisy to carry you, as well." Maggie thought back to something Uncle Bob had said to her years ago, when she'd first started riding. "It's a privilege when a horse allows you to ride it, Kizzy. Never forget that. It's sharing its strength and power with you. That deserves your respect and admiration."

Kizzy nodded. "Yes, ma'am." She leaned forward and patted Daisy's neck. "I ain't forgettin' that."

The girl's demeanor endeared her to Maggie in a way few things could. But her posture . . .

"You need to sit up a little straighter. Imagine a string that starts down here." Maggie pointed to where the girl's bottom met the saddle. "And that string is pulled tight straight up through your spine and out the top of your head. *So* tight that you—"

Kizzy started to giggle, her eyes dancing.

Maggie stared. "What's so funny?"

"You is, ma'am. Talkin' 'bout some string goin' from my backside straight up and outta my head. I ain't never thought I hear the wife of the boss talkin' that fool way."

Maggie chuckled, appreciating the sparkle in Kizzy's eyes and impressed at how relaxed she seemed under the circumstances, and so attentive. Attitude was important when learning to ride, and when learning to communicate with a horse. Daisy was exceptionally calm, too, which was rarely the case with first-time students.

Encouraged, Maggie bent to adjust the stirrups to the proper length. "The bottom of the irons should be . . ."

The girl's boot, its sole worn paper thin, had a hole in the toe. But it was the marks on Kizzy's lower leg—thin, ropelike welts, long healed, wrapping halfway around her thin calves—that chased every other thought from Maggie's mind.

"What them irons you talkin' 'bout, ma'am?" Kizzy leaned to one side.

Regaining her composure, Maggie pointed. "The metal part here. They're called irons."

Imagining how the girl had come by the welts clenched Maggie's heart and churned at her gut. She swallowed, but the bitterness caught in her throat. "If your stirrups are too long, you—" She paused, straightening. Then tried again. "You won't be able to stretch your legs and put down your heels, which means you won't be able to sit deeply in the saddle."

"And what if they's too short?"

"Then you'll find yourself perched above the saddle, which can throw off your ride."

Expression alert, Kizzy nodded, as though taking it all in.

Maggie remembered the day Cullen had taken her to see the workers' cabins. What was it he'd said about his people? *We know what it's like to have life kick you in the teeth, then shove 'em down your throat.*

Kizzy knew what that was like, too, and at far too young an age. Same as Willie.

"Keep your legs slightly bent." She gently touched the girl's knee. "So that your heels, hips, and shoulders are all in the same line."

"Like that string goin' up from my backside?"

Maggie expected to look up and see the girl's grin. But Kizzy was all seriousness, her features keen. And her posture—perfect.

"Yes, that's right." Admiring the girl's predilection for learning, Maggie reached up and loosened Kizzy's grip on the reins, the straps of leather a tight wad in the girl's grip. "Hold the reins lightly," she said, demonstrating. "Keep your hands relaxed, and keep the reins a little above the saddle."

"Like this?" Kizzy worked to get it right.

"Good." Maggie nodded. "*Very* good."

Holding the lead rope, Maggie led Daisy around the corral, keeping an eye on Kizzy and stopping to give her pointers as they went.

Starting their fifth time around the circle, Maggie felt resistance in the rope and turned to see Kizzy wearing a quizzical grin.

"Can I take her 'round by myself this time? I do it just like you say. Nice and slow. Like we's on a Sunday stroll."

Sensing the girl's excitement, Maggie debated. "You'll take her around exactly as we've done. And do as I instructed? You remember how to stop her?"

"Yes, ma'am." Kizzy's eyes narrowed. "I ain't only supposed to pull on the reins to stop her, I's supposed to use . . . my body, my seat, my legs," she slowly recounted. "And . . . *then* my hand. And when I push my backside down in the saddle, the horse knows somethin's 'bout to happen, then . . ."

Maggie listened as Kizzy parroted back her instructions with surprising accuracy.

"And when the horse does somethin' we told 'em, we got to . . ." She hesitated.

"Reward," Maggie gently prompted.

"—*reward* 'em. Right then. I got to relax my hand too," she said, more to herself than to Maggie, and did just that. "And always . . ." The girl squinted as though trying to remember something. Then her head popped up. "Look where I's goin!" She let out a breath, her grin reaching her big, beautiful eyes and lighting her countenance from within.

Certain the buttons on her riding jacket were about to pop, Maggie gave an approving nod and stepped back. She waved an arm, and around the corral horse and rider went. Once. Twice.

On the third pass, Kizzy grinned big as she approached, then urged Daisy to a trot and squealed with excitement when the pace quickened. Maggie watched, heart in her throat. But not from fear. Daisy was a well-trained horse with a smooth gait, but Kizzy . . .

Maggie marveled. Kizzy was a—

A low whistle came from behind, and Maggie turned.

Uncle Bob nudged his black bowler higher on his forehead, his focus glued to the corral. "You got yourself a natural there, Missus McGrath."

Maggie smiled. "My thought exactly. She's amazing!"

"She's *you* made over, is what she is." Uncle Bob's expression grew sheepish. "If you don't mind me sayin' it that way."

"I don't mind at all, Uncle Bob. Quite the contrary, in fact."

"You took to it just like that, ma'am." He nodded. "Rode back after a few times around and asked me if you could try a bigger horse."

"I did not."

His eyes widened. "I swear on my sweet mama's grave."

Maggie smiled again, then turned back to watch Kizzy, thinking about the scars on her legs. "Do you know much about her family?"

"She belong to Ennis and Odessia, don't she?"

Maggie nodded.

"That family been in these parts for years. Worked on a plantation up north of town 'til the war. Ennis, he a good man. Workin' for your husband now, ain't he?"

"Yes, Mr. Ennis works for my husband."

"Won't find a better worker, ma'am. Same for his wife. They both be—" Uncle Bob stopped midsentence. "Lawd, would you look at her fly!"

Maggie turned. Kizzy had Daisy at a full gallop, the girl's seat deep and true, her body bent forward in perfect alignment.

"I didn't teach her to do that," she said softly.

Uncle Bob laughed. "Nobody taught you either, ma'am. You just knew it. God tucked that gift inside you 'fore you even got here." He grinned. "Just like he done with her." He sighed. "Too bad she ain't a boy. You'd have yourself a horse *and* a jockey nobody could come close to beatin'."

The truth of his statement struck like a hammer on an anvil inside Maggie, and sparks flew.

"O' course," he continued, "the rules don't say nothin' 'bout the jockey *havin'* to be a boy. Leastwise not that I ever heard."

Maggie turned. A trace of humor marked Uncle Bob's expression, but in his eyes she glimpsed a flicker of possibility. And even . . . challenge.

"No," she finally responded, the quickened pace of her heartbeat matching the pounding of Daisy's hooves. "The rules don't say that. Do they?"

Chapter Twenty-Eight

Cullen awakened to find the space beside him in bed empty and the morning light barely reaching through the open windows. Sighing, he raised up and surveyed the bedroom.

The dress Maggie had hung on the peg by the wardrobe last night was gone. As were her boots. As was she. *Again.* And apparently she'd taken Bucket with her this time too.

With a sharp exhale, he flung back the sheet. The plank wood floor creaked beneath his weight. Yesterday morning's exchange between them outside the barn hadn't produced the peaceable end he'd intended. When she'd returned home later in the afternoon, she'd seemed less tense somehow. But still unapproachable.

Each morning it seemed she rose earlier and earlier. Soon she'd just never come to bed. At least she hadn't moved into another bedroom or asked him to move. That was something, he guessed.

But he needed to mend this rift between them.

Hearing the familiar creak of the barn door, he peered out the window in time to see Maggie climb into the saddle. She paused and gave Bucket the command to stay, then gave Bourbon Belle the signal to do what the mare did best—give the wind something to envy.

Cullen watched horse and rider until they disappeared over the ridge behind the barn. Beauties, both of them. Aye, he had to find a way to mend things. But without giving in to Maggie's request. He grabbed his pants on the chair by the desk.

He'd considered simply telling her the truth. It wasn't as though he feared she would turn him in to the authorities. He was her husband, after all. And even if she didn't care for him the way a wife ought to love her husband, he knew Maggie wouldn't do that. The woman wasn't capable of such betrayal.

But if he did tell her, and then by chance the truth became public—if she happened to mention it to Savannah Darby or Mary Harding—and if what he'd been party to in England came to light, then he'd for sure lose Linden Downs, which meant Maggie would lose it too.

Along with everything she held dear.

And the promises he'd made to her father—and the vows he'd made to her—would all be for naught. Yet even as the scenario played itself out in his mind, he knew he wasn't being completely honest with himself.

In truth, he was afraid she wouldn't respect him, much less love him, if she knew the man he was. Or had been. He doubted she'd be able to see past her formerly held opinions. And could he blame her? Didn't he view the British with the same critical, unforgiving eye?

He retrieved a clean shirt from the wardrobe and caught her scent still clinging to her dresses. A sharpness clenched his chest. He didn't think he could bear the disappointment in her eyes. Not after having seen a similar disappointment in Moira's.

Oh, Moira had forgiven him, he knew that. She'd known his older brother, after all, and had understood what kind of man Ethan was. The same kind of man—Cullen paused as he buttoned his shirt—that he'd been himself. Until Moira. Until their precious Katie. They had changed him, each in her own way.

If he told Maggie the truth, might she even blame him for what happened to them? Just as he still blamed himself, at least in part?

He reached for his boots, sat on the side of the bed, and tugged them on. Then he paused and looked down at his hands.

They were his father's hands—large and strong—a similarity he'd never paid much attention to until the first time his father had beaten him as a boy. Or tried to. Ethan had been so brave, stepping between them, cursing their father to his face as he'd taken blow after blow, calling him names that Cullen had only mustered in his heart.

Cullen fingered the scar across his knuckles. With these hands he'd picked potatoes as a boy, played stickball in the streets, and stolen apples from the fruit stand in his childhood borough. He'd buried his younger sisters and smoothed the hair back from his mother's brow as she lay in the casket. He'd been in more barroom brawls than he could count, much less remember. He'd cradled his baby girl with these hands, then had secured her tiny body in her mother's arms and lowered them both into the sea, the thick rope rough and wet with salty spray.

He could still feel the soft silk of Maggie's skin beneath his touch, and remember the way she sighed against him. To know a woman's love, to experience the pleasure in it, was one of the greatest gifts given a man. But for her to return that love, and to experience a similar pleasure . . . Aye, that was a rare gift indeed.

So many things a man did with his hands in a lifetime. How could the same hands be party to such conflicting pursuits? It didn't seem right somehow. And yet, he guessed a man's hands were only a reflection of the man himself.

He rose and scratched his stubbled jawline, then glanced back at the bed. A soft indention marked the spot where she'd lain beside him last night, very close to the edge, he noted. He shook his head, expelling the air from his lungs. He would fix this.

Turning to go, his gaze fell to Maggie's bedside table, and to Mr. Linden's Bible that still rested, seemingly undisturbed, right where it had for weeks.

Cullen glanced behind him toward the hallway then silently chided himself, knowing she was gone. He picked up the Bible, the worn leather supple in his grip. He recalled Mr. Linden reading to them from the latter pages. He opened the book and thumbed through the pages, a little surprised at what he found.

Not only were verses on the pages underlined, but notes crowded the margins too. Some with dates beside them.

He held the Bible at an angle to decipher the man's handwriting. *Not in my strength, Lord, but in yours.* "The third of January, 1865," Cullen read aloud, then turned the book in his grip yet again to read the corresponding underlined verse: *And he said unto me, My grace is sufficient for thee: for my strength is made perfect in weakness.*

Cullen stared, trying to remember the date inscribed on the wooden markers belonging to Mr. Linden's four older sons. December of 1864, he thought. Only one month prior. No doubt their passings had been in the man's mind when he'd penned this note.

Cullen's gaze jumped to the top of the page. *II Corinthians.* The title of these chapters was familiar. Mr. Linden had read from this book before. But . . .

Strength being made perfect in weakness? A foolish thought, in Cullen's opinion.

He eased down on the edge of the bed and flipped through the next few pages, intending only to read a few of the notes in the margins, but what Mr. Linden had written compelled him to read the verses beside them as well. Odd to read a man's thoughts after he was already gone—even his prayers, Cullen soon discovered as he turned the pages. It made him wish again that he'd had the opportunity to know Mr. Linden better.

"Mister McGrath?"

Onnie's voice drew Cullen's attention.

She stood at the open door of the bedroom looking at him, then at the Bible in his hands. "Don't mean to bother you, sir. But some of the workers already here, and you usually out there by now."

He glanced out the window to find the sun fully risen. "I didn't realize the time."

He laid the Bible back on Maggie's bedside table, yet as he hurried downstairs and ate breakfast, then met the workers in the barn, he felt as if he were carrying a portion of the verses—and of Gilbert Linden—inside him.

"Uncle Bob, after working with Kizzy for the last week—" Maggie paused, noting how his attention suddenly shifted away from her. Perhaps he guessed her question and wasn't eager to answer it. But she needed to know his opinion. And the sooner she knew, the better. "Do you believe Kizzy has a—"

"Excuse me, Missus McGrath." Uncle Bob nodded past her. "I think you got yourself a visitor, ma'am."

Cullen.

Maggie froze, praying it wasn't him while simultaneously trying to think of how she would explain giving lessons to Kizzy if it was. But no matter what she said, he would instinctively know what she was doing. One look at her with those gray-green eyes, and the man could read every thought in her head. Bracing herself, she turned.

Relief cascaded through her when she saw Savannah standing at the edge of the corral. Savannah waved and Maggie did the same. Yet even from a distance, Maggie detected unrest in her friend's expression. Oh, she hoped whatever it was didn't involve Andrew or little Carolyne.

With a smile Maggie indicated she'd be right there, then slipped her pocket watch to Uncle Bob. "Kizzy has another six—"

"Six laps to go. Yes, ma'am." He took the watch. "I watch the time for you."

"Thank you." She turned, then hesitated, still eager to know his answer. "After seeing Kizzy ride"—Daisy rounded the corner at full gallop, the mare's hooves covering ground, while Kizzy sat easy in the saddle, looking like the happiest child alive—"do you think she has a chance, Uncle Bob? Not just at racing, I mean. I *know* she can race."

"Ain't no question 'bout that, ma'am."

"But can she win the Peyton Stakes?"

He smiled, his kind brown eyes shaded beneath the brim of his bowler. "You know good as I do, ma'am . . . Ain't nobody can answer that. Horses that should win races, don't. And those that ain't got no business winnin' . . ." He shrugged. "Well, sometimes they do."

Maggie nodded and turned to go meet Savannah.

"But I *can* tell you this—"

She turned back.

"That girl there, she got racin' in her blood. She fearless, just like you, ma'am." He grinned. "She got a heart these horses just seem to take to. They trust her. But the real test is gettin' her on Bourbon Belle."

Maggie nodded, already knowing that was the next step. But also knowing that Daisy's speed and power were nothing compared to Belle's. "I don't want to do anything that will endanger Kizzy. Or Belle, for that matter. But . . ." She bit her lower lip. "I think Kizzy's ready."

"Oh, she ready all right, ma'am. Don't you worry 'bout that none. Question is, will Belle take to her like Belle took to Willie?"

Maggie watched Kizzy fly. "We only have a few weeks to train her."

"But Belle, she ready, ma'am. You kept her in racin' shape. And Kizzy . . . my guess is that girl'll be ready to face just 'bout any jockey I seen yet."

Maggie hoped he was right. "If you have time this afternoon, we'll get them together. See how they do."

"That's a pairin' I wouldn't miss for the world, ma'am."

Maggie cast him a hopeful look, yet also felt a wave of dread. She still didn't know how to convince Cullen to side with her on the racing issue. But that would have to wait. She hurried to join Savannah outside the fence.

Savannah met her, reaching for her hand. "I'm sorry to bother you, Maggie." She squeezed tight. "I know you're busy."

Maggie shook her head. "Never too busy for you. Andrew and Carolyne are well, I hope?"

Savannah frowned, then just as swiftly her expression cleared. "Oh yes, they're fine. This isn't about them. It's . . . about this." She reached into her reticule and withdrew an envelope. "When you came to visit last, I told you I was reading through my father's letters to my mother. The ones he sent during the war."

Maggie nodded.

"In one of his letters—" Savannah halted suddenly and studied the stationery in her hand. When she looked up again, emotion softened her eyes. "Please hear me out before you decide. All right?"

Her curiosity piqued, Maggie nodded again.

"In this letter," Savannah continued, "he references a hurtful conversation he had with my mother one night." Savannah withdrew the letter. "Here . . . I'd appreciate it if you would simply read it for yourself."

Maggie glanced at the missive but didn't take it, feeling more than a little uneasy. "This is a private exchange between your parents."

"It's all right," Savannah softly coaxed. "It's nothing overly intimate, I promise." A tiny smile turned her mouth. "At least . . . not as intimate as some of the others."

Savannah's humor lessening her unease, Maggie accepted and carefully unfolded the pages of the wrinkled stationery. That her dear friend had chosen to share this with her warmed her heart, whatever decision there was to be made.

Dearest Melna,

> *I hope that you will not think I meant to neglect you because I did not write before now. The fact is, we have been marching every day, and by the time night falls I can scarcely spoon the cook's watery broth to my mouth, much less command a pen to paper. But you and the children have been on my heart day and night. You will remember what we spoke of when last we were together, after the children were abed. I ask you again to forgive me for keeping what I did from you. It was most lovingly done. However, I understand how hurtful a revelation it was for you. It was never my intention to add to that past wound, my dearest.*

Maggie turned the page, aware of Savannah watching her. A heavy watermark marred the ink on the time-crinkled page, but Maggie could still make out the words.

Your father was a most persuasive man and even now, I can see the determination in his eyes. Though I know the relationship between the two of you was never the same, I do believe your father entered eternity with overwhelming love for you, and with a desire that you forgive him for the decision he made all those years ago. And I hope, my love, that you will. The longer I fight this war, and the more men I see taken so swiftly from this world to the next, the more I am convinced that harboring unforgiveness is a costly debt. One that is paid over and over not so much by the one needing forgiveness as by the one withholding it.

The ink blotched the page as though the author had hesitated overlong in lifting the pen.

What your father gave me . . . gave you, he did in a spirit of reconciliation, and I hope that in time you will receive his gift as such. Before I left, I placed it with the rest of our valuables for safekeeping.

Maggie looked up, understanding Savannah's cause for excitement now. "Valuables? What does he mean by—"

"Read on," Savannah softly whispered.

I'll adhere to your wishes and will wait to share the story with our entire family once the boys and I return home. But know that this was far more than a simple gesture on your father's part. It was an olive branch intended to heal, and I pray its roots spread deep and wide through our family. I left additional monies in the box as well. Save it if you can. Spend it if necessary. Even if the house is commandeered, it will be safe.

Maggie didn't even glance up this time, eager to finish the letter.

When last you wrote, Melna, you told me you believed without fail that it was God's design for me to see home again. I cling to that hope and your faith in it, for my own grows less day by day. I pray to God that I am wrong. But if I am not, and heaven is soon within my sight, know that with my last breath I will be thinking of you, and thanking God for the gift of your love and for all of our children. Jake and Adam are doing well, fighting bravely, as you would imagine. Though I know they are frightened, as are all brave men, from time to time. I am attempting to keep them safe and am so proud of them both. They send their love.

We all look forward to being home soon.

With deepest affection,
Merle

With Merle Darby's words settling inside her, Maggie felt a familiar weight of grief. But she also felt the spark of excitement and hope emanating from her friend beside her.

"Papa left something behind," Savannah whispered, though no one else was within earshot. "Money, for certain. *If* mother didn't spend it. But also something from my grandfather. Something valuable."

"Do you have any idea where he hid it in the house?" Maggie continued softly.

"No, but I intend to find it! And I want you to come with me."

"But . . ." Maggie searched her friend's eyes, wondering if, in the excitement, Savannah had forgotten the truth of her situation. "The house has already been sold. Weren't whatever furnishings were left sold with it?"

Savannah's gaze clouded. "Yes, but it was something Father left for *us* specifically. Doesn't that mean it would still belong to us? To me, Andrew, and Carolyne?"

Maggie didn't respond as she returned the letter. Not because she didn't know the answer to Savannah's question, but because she hated to dash her friend's hope.

"I'm asking you to go with me, Maggie." Savannah's countenance held a mixture of pleading and admission of guilt. "The new owner, whoever it is, hasn't yet taken possession of the house or the property. He doesn't even know it's there."

"*If* whatever your father referenced is still there, Savannah. Who knows but what your mother might have—"

"She never said a thing about such a box. And she would have . . . if she'd had the chance."

Maggie recalled how swiftly Savannah's mother had fallen ill. She'd been fine one moment, then complained of a severe ache in her head the next. Then she'd collapsed. By the time Maggie arrived at the Darby's house that afternoon, Savannah's mother was already slipping away.

The doctor thought the incident was caused by her heart, but whatever the sickness, it had left Melna Darby unable to move, to speak, and within hours, even to breathe. She'd been gone by the next morning.

"All I'm asking, Maggie, is that you go with me to the house. You don't even have to look for the box if you don't want to. But I haven't been back there since the day I moved us into town, and it would be so much easier if you were with me."

The Darbys' house and estate were a ways from town, about the same distance as Linden Downs. The chances that someone would see them were slim. Still . . . Maggie knew only too well the legalities of ownership when someone else purchased one's family home. Everything became theirs.

Everything. Fair or not.

"I'll go with you," Maggie whispered. "And we'll find that box."

Later that afternoon, heart in her throat, Maggie held Belle's harness as Kizzy settled into the saddle. The girl looked even smaller astride Bourbon Belle than Willie had looked. And with good reason. She was a good three inches shorter and at least ten pounds lighter.

The child was a newborn kitten grasping the reins of a locomotive, and the weight of responsibility Maggie felt for her pressed down hard inside. She prayed she was doing the right thing.

Uncle Bob tightened the stirrups a little more. "You 'member everythin' Missus McGrath told you, child. And you do it."

Kizzy nodded, her dark eyes sparkling. "I will, Uncle Bob."

Maggie reached up and grasped the girl's hand. "Belle has been racing all her life. She knows what to do. Listen to her just like she'll be listening to you."

Kizzy squeezed her hand. "Don't you worry none 'bout me, ma'am. Miss Belle and me, we gonna get along just fine."

Maggie felt the sting of tears. "I know you will. Take it slow the first few times around. Learn her gait. Let her learn your ways too. Remember, sit deep in the saddle. And she doesn't like a tight rein. So keep it loose." Seeing the frown on Kizzy's face, Maggie paused. "What is it?"

"You tell them other girls all these things so many times 'fore they ride Belle? Same as you tellin' me?"

Holding back a smile, Maggie shook her head. "No . . . I don't."

The child's frown deepened to a familiar scowl.

"Because you're the first girl who's ever ridden Bourbon Belle. Besides me."

Without another word, Maggie stepped back and nodded. Kizzy was still smiling as she and Belle circled the track for the third time, and by the fourth, the girl nudged Belle to a canter. The child's seat stayed deep and true, her posture perfect, and Maggie felt a tender pride similar to what she imagined parents experienced seeing their children accomplish something for the very first time.

A tear slipped down her cheek.

But when Belle quickened to a gallop, the mare's stride smooth and true, Maggie pictured herself as a young girl again, astride her first thoroughbred, right here at Belle Meade with Uncle Bob beside her.

"Thank you, Uncle Bob," she said softly, turning to see his own eyes filled with emotion. "For teaching me all you have."

His smile trembled. "And thank you, Lawd," he whispered back, his gaze on the track. "For lettin' me see this day, and another little girl . . . who's learnin' how to fly."

Chapter TWENTY-NINE

Onnie tells me the wolf attacks have become more frequent."

Cullen lifted his head and looked at Maggie across the dinner table, his forkful of creamed potatoes paused midway between his plate and his mouth. She'd been quiet for days on end, and now this.

When Savannah Darby had stopped by the house two days ago looking for her, he'd sent the young woman on to Belle Meade, hoping her visit might be an encouragement to Maggie. But Maggie had since seemed even more brooding.

He followed through on his bite of potatoes, giving himself time to form an answer, and appreciating how the prolonged silence seemed to leech the urgency from her question. "I wouldn't exactly say they're becomin' more frequent." He took a drink of water, the sprig of mint fragrant. "Perhaps more . . . determined, might be a better description."

Her gaze held steady. "I knew of only one incident that occurred almost a month ago. There have been others?"

"Aye."

"How many?"

"I didn't tell you because I don't wish to worry you about it."

She frowned. "How many?"

"One or two happened around the middle of last month." It was a true statement, if not the whole truth.

"What are they getting?"

"Chickens mostly. And a cow. But they also got a young bull."

"They took down a bull?"

He nodded, hoping she wouldn't press for more.

"How many times has it happened since then?"

The clock on the mantel behind him ticked off the seconds.

"Three," he finally answered.

A single dark brow rose. "Which could be construed by some as 'more frequent.' "

Her mocking tone was a gauntlet, and he stared unblinking, determined not to take it up. If only she would put as much energy into mending things between them as she did into trying to pick a fight.

In addition to her rising with the sun every morning—or sometimes before the sun—she somehow managed to sneak upstairs before he did most evenings, change into her gown, and get neatly tucked beneath a nunlike cloister of covers. And this before he even noticed she was missing from the parlor.

Last night, however, he'd caught her watching him in the mirror's reflection as he undressed. He'd curbed a smile at the discovery, not wanting her to know he'd seen.

"So, without my having to ask for a daily accounting . . . How many wolf attacks have there been altogether, Cullen?"

He met her stare. "Seven."

"Seven?" She laid her fork beside her plate. "This has to be stopped. You need to get a hunting party together. I'll go with you, and we'll—"

"There'll be no huntin' party, Maggie."

"But I'm a very good—"

"And certainly not one with a woman along." Seeing her eyes narrow, he held up a hand. "I've already put measures in place. Two men, every night, are keepin' a watch on things."

"Two of our workers?"

"Aye."

She eyed him, and he could see the wheels spinning.

"They're armed?"

Patience thinning, he nodded.

"And do they know how to shoot?"

He exhaled, frustration mounting at her line of questioning—and lack of faith in him. He shrugged. "You know, I probably should've thought of that before givin' them rifles."

Darkness crept into her eyes and promised to sharpen her tongue as well.

"Linden Downs has been my home for far longer than it's been yours, Cullen. I have every right to know what's happening here."

"I agree. But, Margaret . . ." His appetite gone, he pushed his plate away. "It's August already. For nigh onto a month now you've scarcely uttered a civil word to me. Only yes and no, or 'I'm fine, Cullen,' or 'No, thank you, Cullen.' And now you sit here firin' questions and tellin' me how to handle situations as though the only thing I got between my ears is fodder and nonsense. I know what I'm doin' here, Maggie. You need to trust that. You need to trust *me*."

The silence stretched until he thought it would snap.

"And you need to trust me too," she said with unexpected softness.

Miss Onnie chose that moment to return, water pitcher in hand. Wordlessly she refilled their glasses. From her guarded expression, Cullen guessed she'd overheard their argument. He waited until she'd gone before speaking again.

"I do trust you, Maggie," he said quietly.

"No, you don't. If you did, you'd . . ." Her slender jaw worked as if she were tasting the words first. "You would allow me to race Bourbon Belle."

It wasn't as if he hadn't known what was coming. "Maggie, we've been over this."

"No, we haven't. *We* haven't been over anything." Her lovely features hardened. "You simply told me your decision was made, and you wouldn't allow me to do it. Do you have any idea how that feels? What that does to me on the inside?"

"Don't forget who you're talkin' to, love." His smile felt stiff. "I know all about bein' told what I can and cannot do. And if I ever happen to forget, there's plenty of shingles hangin' 'round town to remind me."

Her eyes flickered. With pain, perhaps. Or maybe it was regret over having said that to him. Or perhaps . . . she regretted ever having married him.

Whichever it was, he watched the anger drain from her face even as it drained from him.

Fighting the weight of resignation, he decided to change the subject, intent on salvaging what remained of the evening. "You've been over to Belle Meade more than usual in recent days. Lessons must be goin' well. Nashville's young ladies will be the finest riders in all the South."

Though sincerely meant, the olive branch felt weak in the offering and drew only the thinnest of smiles.

"So tell me," he continued, determined to scale her walls brick by blasted brick. "How many students are you instructin' now?"

Her gaze fell to her plate and she cleared her throat. "I'm teaching eight girls from town."

Only eight? He'd estimated far more based on the time she spent away from Linden Downs. Then it occurred to him . . . Maybe she was only going to Belle Meade so she wouldn't have to be here with him. But that didn't make sense. He was gone most of the day working in the fields.

He tried again, seeing she wasn't going to volunteer anything further. "Do any of the girls show promise?"

A forever second ticked by.

"One girl does," she finally whispered, then stood and dropped her crumpled napkin by her plate. "If you'll excuse me."

She strode from the dining room, the soft swoosh of her skirts overloud in the silence. Bucket raised his head briefly to watch her departure from his place of repose in the corner.

Maggie's boot steps echoed in the hallway as she raced up the stairs, and Cullen closed his eyes. Already weary from a long day's work, he suddenly felt even more so. Especially when he knew that the sure way to end this argument was to tell her the truth of what racing Belle could cost them both.

God, I don't think I can survive her knowin' that about me. Seein' my own shame mirrored in her eyes . . .

No sooner had the thought surfaced than he saw it for what it really was, though he could scarcely believe it. Since when had he become a man on speaking terms with the Lord again? He shook his head. He'd been reading too much of Mr. Linden's Bible lately.

"Let nothin' be done through strife or vainglory." He spoke softly, reciting a verse Mr. Linden had underlined—and that Cullen himself had dwelt on. "But in lowliness of mind let—" Just when he thought he remembered it, the words slipped away.

But he recalled the thought behind the passage just the same. It was about how a person was supposed to respect others and think better of them than they did of themselves.

He opened his eyes and looked in the general direction of their bedroom upstairs. He loved the woman. She was all but driving him to drink, but he still loved her. And hence, wanted to make her happy. But how could he?

"Y'all done, sir?"

Cullen blinked, then noticed Miss Onnie waiting on him.

"Aye." He rose. "We're done." He plucked the sprig of mint from his glass, the taste reminding him of summers back home. He reached the hallway before turning back. "Thank you, Miss Onnie. It was a good dinner."

She nodded. "You welcome, sir."

A few steps more, and Cullen heard his name.

Miss Onnie stood in the doorway. "She young yet, Mister McGrath." Her words came softly. "And she can be a mite headstrong, like her mother was, God rest her soul."

Miss Onnie briefly bowed her head, and Cullen recalled receiving similar counsel from Mr. Linden.

"But she got a heart as wide and deep as her papa's," the servant continued. "And once she give her word, sir, I ain't never seen that child go back on it."

Hearing the intent of her words, Cullen nodded. "Thank you, Miss Onnie. I just have to win her over. Again."

After letting Bucket outside one last time, Cullen extinguished all the lamps save one and carried it upstairs, trying to figure out how to unlock Maggie Linden's heart.

For the second time.

⁂

The footsteps paused on the other side of the bedroom door, and Maggie's heartbeat ratcheted up. Maybe Cullen would stay in his old room tonight, which would be best, considering.

Slowly, the bedroom door creaked open. With her back to him, she hugged the edge of the bed and closed her eyes, not daring to move. Not even when the breeze ushered through the window and stirred the hair at her temple, causing a tickle on her cheek.

The intoxicating aroma of milkweed—sweet, yet spicy with an overtone of honey—filled the room, as did the faint grassy scent of tasseling corn almost ready for harvest. How proud Papa would have been had he lived to see it all. With the exception of this strife between her and Cullen. That would have worn on her father.

The thought undermined her resolve to remain angry, and she squeezed her eyes tighter. She'd already dried her tears and sworn she wasn't shedding another. Not tonight. Not over Cullen.

So why did her throat close tight when the warm halo from the lamp he carried fell across the bed?

He set the lamp on the dresser, then began to disrobe.

She didn't sneak a look at him as she'd done last night. But even without looking, she could hear his movements. She knew his body, his lean muscled chest and broad shoulders. His arms strong, yet capable of such tenderness. She'd always considered herself more boyish in figure, her own body lean and lacking the full curves she knew men found desirable. So it surprised her, the first time they were one as husband and wife, how soft her own body was compared to his. And how well they melded into each other.

Memory kicked in, and her breath quickened along with her pulse. She grew warm beneath the covers. Yet still she didn't move.

How was it she could feel such longing for someone when he'd disappointed her so completely? And due, at least in part, to his determination that she not be hurt. Ironic . . .

In his attempt to protect her, he had wounded her more deeply than he knew.

He turned down the lamp and edged back the sheet. The mattress shifted then shrank by half as he lay down beside her. His thigh brushed against hers, and every nerve in her body threatened to betray her.

As she wrestled between desire and frustration, another possibility for his decision about Belle shook loose. Maybe Cullen wasn't really afraid for her. Maybe the real reason he didn't want her to race was that he believed she wouldn't win. That she wasn't capable of training a champion. The notion sank deep, slicing as it went until it found its mark in an old but familiar wound.

He shifted his weight beside her, and somehow she knew he hadn't presented his back to her as he usually did. He was watching her, his gaze moving over her back, her waist, then downward before making a leisurely journey back up again.

Clenching her jaw, Maggie reminded herself of every reason she shouldn't want him in her bed. He had said no to racing Belle. Then refused to discuss it. He'd shut her out. Completely.

"Maggie," he whispered.

He'd taken what she'd worked for all these years. What she and her father had sacrificed for.

"I miss you, my love."

He'd cast it aside without the least thought for her. He was selfish, prideful, and—

"Please . . . look at me."

Maggie shook her head, the flurry of accusations falling prey to the tension between them. It filled every corner of the bedroom, and she waited with senses heightened for him to touch her, part of her hoping he wouldn't, while the greater part of her prayed he would.

But how would she respond if he did? Would she be able to resist? And if she didn't, would he think her acquiescence meant he was right, and that all was forgiven? Because it certainly wasn't.

The string of moments lengthened, and a single question welled up inside her. She slowly turned onto her back.

"Cullen," she whispered, wondering if he could feel the pounding of her heart.

"Aye?" he said softly.

"I know the real reason you don't want me to race Belle. And it doesn't have anything to do with gambling or what happened with your father . . . does it?"

He didn't speak. He didn't move. Didn't breathe, that she could tell. Surprising her, he turned onto his back, and only their shoulders touched.

Finally he gave a sharp exhale. "No . . . it doesn't, Maggie."

"It's because"—she swallowed against the lump in her throat, the cost of saying the words aloud greater than she imagined—"you don't believe I can win. That I can train a horse and rider to do that. Which is exactly what my mother thought. And told me. Countless times."

She looked over at him, read the set of his profile, the absolute stillness about him, and knew she'd guessed correctly. Turning back, she watched the moonlight chase shadows on the walls and ceiling as the grandfather clock downstairs chimed eleven times, the sound lonely in the silence.

"My mother never thought a proper young girl should ride like I did," she whispered. "Not only did she disapprove of me riding astraddle, she never approved of my training horses to race either. She said it was a man's occupation." She smiled in the dark, not from humor but rather from only now seeing the paradox. "It's comical, really . . . Mother thought I was too boyish, too much like my brothers. And you see me as weak, and fear I might get hurt."

He reached for her hand on the covers, and the emotion in her throat deepened to an ache.

"Margaret Laurel Linden McGrath . . ." His deep voice sounded even huskier in the dark. "You are not weak. You're an extraordinary woman. And it isn't that I think you're incapable of winnin'. It's not that at all. It's more that I—" His grip on her hand tightened.

Hearing the struggle in his tone, feeling it in him, she waited for his next words as if they held life itself.

"I fear what could happen if you *do*."

She closed her eyes as a wave of gratitude poured through her. He believed she could do it!

But then what was keeping him from agreeing to it? A fear of her being hurt didn't seem rational. And yet, considering his past—what happened to his first wife and their daughter—it did make sense. But what mattered most . . .

He believed she could win!

Her thoughts racing, Maggie rose on one elbow to look down at him. "Thank you," she whispered, moving her hand over his chest, touching his face, his mouth, desire for him spreading through her. "Thank you for believing in me."

"Maggie," he whispered, taking hold of her hand. "There are things you don't know. Things I need to say to you, love."

Tasting the memory of his kiss, she moved closer. "No, you don't. At least . . . not right now." She pressed her lips to his, but she sensed a hesitancy in him and drew back, suddenly shy and unsure.

Maybe she should have waited for him to take the lead. This was still new to her, after all. "I'm sorry," she whispered, tucking her hair behind her ear. She leaned back. "I thought it would be all right to—"

With something akin to a groan, he took her in his arms, pressed her deep into the bed, and kissed her the way she'd wanted him to. His mouth tasted of mint and his skin was warm. The solid feel of his chest against hers was heady. His mouth left hers and ventured downward and, pulse racing, she pressed her head back into the pillow, weaving her fingers through his hair.

After a moment he sought her mouth again and, breathless, she met his. She began unbuttoning her gown and he assisted, adept at the skill even in the dark. Lying skin to skin, his hands gentle and wonderfully possessive, Maggie wrapped her arms around him.

"Closer," she whispered, and gave a soft moan when he complied, and more.

Closing her eyes to the shadows dancing across the ceiling, she moved beneath his touch and gave herself to her husband.

Chapter THIRTY

I know what we're doing is questionable, Maggie. Some people might even say it's wrong."

Maggie looked over at Savannah astride the mare beside her and found her friend's lovely expression riddled with guilt. "Do you still want to do it?"

Savannah reined in her mount, and Maggie followed suit. Bourbon Belle obeyed, while making it clear by a toss of her head that she didn't want to.

Savannah winced, her focus on the road that led to the farm that had once been her family's. "Finding that box is all I've thought about since reading the letter. I need to know if it's still there, and what my father left for us."

Maggie smiled. "I think I'd feel the same. So . . . onward."

Savannah grinned. "Want to race? Like we used to?"

Enjoying this side of Savannah, which she hadn't seen in a very long time, Maggie leaned forward and patted Belle's neck. "I'm afraid it wouldn't be much of a fair fight, as they say."

Savannah glanced down at Duchess, the pretty little sorrel Cullen had saddled for her that morning. "Of course it'll be fair." Her grin widened. "Especially if I start first!"

Savannah slapped the reins, and Duchess took off in a plume of dust.

Maggie laughed, holding Belle in check while knowing as well as Savannah did that Duchess was no match for the thoroughbred. Maggie waited a full minute before finally giving Belle the signal the blood horse lived for.

And they flew.

Belle rounded the bend, and Maggie spotted Savannah and Duchess up ahead. Evidently so did Belle. Because even without Maggie's urging, the thoroughbred thundered forward, hooves pounding, the mare's natural instinct to race taking charge. Maggie gave the mare her head.

Belle overtook Duchess and passed her in a blink.

Maggie's skirts whipped behind her in the wind and, as the former Darby home came into view, she thought of the Peyton Stakes in October, two months away, and about how every day for the past two weeks she'd waited for the right moment to tell Cullen what she was doing. Or hoped to do, if Kizzy's parents agreed. Kizzy didn't even know about the race yet. And wouldn't—unless her parents were in favor.

All the girl knew was that she was being taught how to ride. Which was the truth. Because if Cullen—the legal owner of Bourbon Belle—held fast to his decision, and Maggie failed to find a way to persuade him otherwise, that would be all Kizzy would be doing. Learning how to ride.

Reaching the home, Maggie reined Belle in and heard the rhythmic beat of Duchess's hooves coming up the drive.

The house looked much the same as Maggie remembered. Only lonelier, with the grass gone to seed and the weeds leggy and wild.

She'd always admired the stately look of the place. The double porches—first story and second—that wrapped around the house like a warm hug. Those porches had hosted so many dinners, conversations, and evenings spent reading and rocking, often long after the sun had started its nightly journey.

But it was the scent that transported her back in time . . .

Maggie breathed deeply of honeysuckle on the vine and remembered all the summer afternoons she and Savannah had sat right there on the front porch, clumps of those fragrant flowers in their laps. And amidst giggles and secret telling, they'd gently tugged the style from the center of the petals to catch the sweet nectar on their tongues.

She could still see Jake and Adam, Savannah's older brothers, and their long, lanky legs taking the porch steps in twos. Their laughter was etched in her memory, just like that of her own brothers.

It seemed like yesterday, and yet another world away.

Savannah reined in beside her, her cheeks flushed, breath coming hard, and her smile radiant. Until she looked at the house. The flush of joy gradually ebbed from her expression, replaced by a sheen of longing so keen and sharp it almost hurt Maggie too much to look.

"I remember, at the first of the war, my father reading in the paper what President Lincoln said about the skirmish between the states. That it wouldn't last long." Savannah shook her head. "So many times I've wondered . . . if the men who took us to war had known the cost from the very beginning, would they still have done it?"

Maggie reached over and squeezed her friend's hand, having had much the same thought. She waited for Savannah to dismount then did likewise, looping Belle's reins over the post.

Maggie started for the porch steps.

"Where are you going?"

Maggie turned. "To the front door." It came out more like a question than a statement, and Savannah shook her head.

"I don't have the key anymore, Maggie. They took it from us. They tend to do that when one's house goes to auction."

Feeling more than a little foolish, Maggie knew Savannah meant nothing hurtful by the statement, but still . . . it stung.

"They simply showed up one day," Savannah continued. "Mr. Drake and his men. They told me we had an hour to gather clothes and personal family mementos. Anything of real worth was to be left behind to pay the debt." She sighed. "They left for a short time, and I gathered what I could. Thankfully, shortly after Mother passed, knowing we were going to lose the house eventually, I'd gone through most of the personal items and put them in boxes. But at the last minute I carried Mama's table, the one you saw, out of the house and put it beneath the willow at the back of the property. I came back a few days later and got it."

"You never told me that," Maggie whispered. She could imagine only too well Stephen Drake acting the bully. "I would have helped you."

Savannah shook her head. "You and your father were having your own struggles. I didn't want to add to them."

A gentle wind rustled the leaves in the bowers formed by the oak and poplar trees overhead, and brought welcome cool in the heat of day.

Savannah gestured, tentative hope brightening her eyes. "My hope is that one of the windows down here is unlocked. We never locked the one by the kitchen. Let's go see!"

Swept up in Savannah's optimism, as she'd always been, Maggie followed. They checked the kitchen window then all the windows on the ground floor, to no avail.

Everything—doors included—was locked up tight.

Standing on the back porch, they both stared at the grimy pane of glass filling the upper half of the door, and Maggie wondered if her friend was having the same thought.

Savannah ran a hand along the edge of the glass. "I remember the day Papa supervised as Jake put this new pane in. Jake and some of his friends broke the old one playing ball. Jake worked for weeks to pay Papa back." Savannah looked over at her, then slowly shook her head. "I don't think I can."

Maggie looked at the adjacent windows, but felt Savannah's silent sanction and nodded. "Well, then I say we try what my older brothers did on school nights when they were supposed to be in bed asleep."

Question—and a glimmer of mischief—replaced Savannah's somberness.

"Follow me!" Maggie tugged on her arm.

They ran like schoolgirls around the side of the house and to the base of an ancient oak.

"Maggie, you can't do it. You're . . . a married woman."

Maggie winked. "I'm a married woman, yes. But one who can still climb trees!" She reached down and pulled the hem of her skirt up between her legs, then tucked the hem into her waistband and promptly curtsied. "I'll be up—and hopefully inside—before you know it."

She'd climbed this tree a hundred times, albeit not in recent years, and the limbs she remembered as easy to scale proved a tad more challenging than she'd anticipated. Still, she made it to the second-story porch railing and climbed over.

Winded but triumphant, she waved down to Savannah then set to work.

She knew this house as well as her own, and began first with the windows to what had been Mr. and Mrs. Darby's bedroom. They wouldn't budge. She started to move on, but what she saw within the room wouldn't let her.

Savannah's parents' bedroom furniture, just as she remembered it. Handed down from Mr. Darby's parents, she recalled. The dresser, the settee, the wardrobe . . . everything just as Savannah had been forced to leave it. And for the same reason that would have cost Maggie Linden Downs—unpaid back taxes and loans in default.

If not for Cullen.

The past week of truce between them had been so welcome after the tension of weeks prior. But she knew this peace wasn't wholly authentic, because they still hadn't confronted the differences between them.

And they would be forced to soon enough.

She moved on to the boys' room, checking for broken panes as she went, knowing how fragile panes of glass could be. What a shame if one were to break. But . . .

No broken panes. Not even a crack.

"Nothing yet?" Savannah called up from below.

Maggie peered over the edge, mustering a hopeful expression. "Not yet, but I have one room to go!"

She walked around to the windows that looked into Savannah and Carolyne's room and peered inside. How many nights had she spent in that bed, dreaming out loud with Savannah? Or standing before the dresser mirror, brushing her hair?

She pressed her face closer to the window. There . . . Savannah's silver hairbrush, comb, and mirror—the complete vanity set, a gift from Savannah's maternal grandmother—still on the dresser. *Oh, Savannah . . .*

Maggie hurt for all her friend had lost. Possessions that couldn't even begin to compare with the loved ones she'd had to say good-bye to. But still, pieces of a life that was gone.

And same as she'd discovered earlier, these windows wouldn't budge either.

She knelt and peered inside, just a pane of glass away, at the window latch. She doubted she could break it without Savannah hearing, and even if her friend didn't hear, she'd see the broken glass once Maggie let her inside. Unless she cleaned it up quickly, which she could if—

Maggie stood, realizing this wasn't her decision. She walked back to the porch railing. "I'm sorry, Savannah," she called down. "The windows are all locked."

Savannah stared up, and in the silent exchange that followed Maggie felt the weight of her friend's decision hanging between them. She honestly didn't know what she would do if she were in Savannah's situation. That's one thing she'd learned in recent months: a person couldn't guarantee what she would decide in a given circumstance until she was in it. Until the decision was hers alone. Until she'd counted the cost.

Savannah slowly bowed her head, and when she finally lifted her eyes a moment later, Maggie read her answer.

"This isn't my home anymore, Maggie," Savannah said, her voice wavering. "I accepted that once." She took a deep breath, her chin trembling, her gaze traveling over the house. "I need to accept it again."

Chapter THIRTY-ONE

You talkin' 'bout my Kizzy, ma'am?" Disbelief clouded Odessia's expression as she pulled dry laundry from the line, the final days of August proving just as hot during the past week as the ones that came before. "Ridin' your fine horse . . . in a race?"

Maggie nodded, catching the scent of fresh soap and sunshine from the clothes. "That's precisely what I'm talking about, Odessia. I know this is something you'll need to discuss with Mr. Ennis, and also with Kizzy. I haven't mentioned anything about the race to your daughter. And there's always the chance she might not want to participate."

But even as Maggie said it, she knew the probability of that was nil. Kizzy was more at home on a horse than most people were in their parlors. Riding was in the girl's blood. To stay.

"She good enough for that, Missus McGrath?"

Maggie couldn't hold back her smile. "Oh, Odessia . . ." Her eyes watered. "Your daughter is beyond good. She's one of the best riders I've ever seen. Uncle Bob agrees."

"Uncle Bob seen her ride?"

Maggie nodded. "He's been helping me teach her at Belle Meade."

Odessia's jaw dropped as her hand went to her hip, and Maggie knew instantly where Kizzy had learned the gesture.

"Lawd, just wait till Ennis hear this." Odessia smiled, then her expression turned pensive. "But ain't all the riders in them races boys, ma'am?"

"Yes, they are. Or have been. However, the Thoroughbred Society's rule book says nothing about requiring jockeys to be male. Your daughter would be the first girl ever."

Odessia said nothing for a moment. "But ain't it dangerous? Ridin' that way. I heard tell of boys gettin' hurt real bad. Or worse."

Maggie was struck by the depth of concern in the woman's eyes. It felt familiar somehow. Then she realized . . . she'd seen the same look from her own mother. "There are certain dangers involved in racing. And in riding. We work to minimize them, of course. But the risks must be weighed and considered carefully."

"And you say my Kizzy would be the first." Odessia folded one of Ennis's shirts and placed it in the basket, her eyes wary. "Ain't always good bein' first at somethin', Missus McGrath. It come with a price."

"Yes, it does," Maggie said softly. "Which is why I came to you first and am asking you to speak with your husband about it. Then together you can decide whether you want to share it with Kizzy . . . or not."

Odessia picked up the basket of clean laundry, and Maggie followed her around to the front of the cabin and up the steps to the porch.

"What if Ennis and me say no, ma'am? What then?"

Maggie heard the skepticism in the woman's voice, and tried to mask the disappointment from her own. "Then that will be the end of it. I will never mention it to Kizzy, and she will never know. You have my absolute word on that, Odessia."

Odessia regarded her for a moment then gestured toward the door. "'Fore you go, ma'am, I wanna show you somethin' Kizzy did."

Maggie hesitated only briefly before following her inside. After her eyes adjusted to the dimness, she saw Odessia holding out a piece of paper.

"Kizzy been drawin' her whole life, Missus McGrath. Mostly in the dirt, sometimes on a piece of slate with chalk, when we got it. But Ennis, lately he got the children some paper and pencils, and my daughter, she been drawin' everythin' in sight! But this be her favorite thing to draw, ma'am."

Odessia held up the picture, her expression softening, and Maggie's throat tightened with emotion.

"That's me?" Maggie asked.

"Mmm hmm . . . Ridin' Miss Belle. Two o' you all she talks 'bout these days, ma'am."

Maggie sighed. Kizzy's giftedness at drawing didn't begin to equal that of her riding, but it didn't matter. It was the smile the girl had drawn on her—and Belle too—that brought one to Maggie's face even then.

"Thank you for sharing that with me, Odessia. And thank you, too, for speaking to your husband."

Maggie turned to leave, then paused and looked around the cabin.

"Looks a mite different since you was last here, don't it, Missus McGrath?"

Still taking in the changes, Maggie nodded. "Yes, I believe that's a fair statement."

"Your husband, he didn't tell you?"

"Tell me what?"

Warmth filled the woman's expression. "Mister McGrath raised all the men's pay. So Ennis and the children and me, we decided to fix up the place. Some of the other families been doin' the same on theirs."

Maggie looked around. "It looks very nice."

No more daylight stabbed its way through the walls and ceiling. The plank wood floor looked new, all boards tightly fitted, no cracks or spaces, the ground beneath the cabin hidden as it should be. In one corner, a proper bed with a mattress. In the other, a sturdy table with six chairs.

"Got me a proper wash bucket for the dishes too." Odessia pointed. "Ennis say 'fore winter comes he gonna rebuild the fireplace and make a hearth big enough for me to cook in proper like. Right over there." She beamed.

As Odessia showed her the rest of the improvements they'd made, Maggie grew quiet, realizing again how far removed she was from a reality only a stone's throw away from where she'd lived her entire life. What she considered normal was more than some people in the world would ever know.

As she walked back to the main house, she looked across the acres of flourishing crops fanning out on either side of the road, with harvest soon upon them, and for the first time in her life she saw the land for what it really was. A gift to be stewarded. At best she was a custodian, and not a very good one at that. Something she vowed to change.

Cullen understood far more about that than she did. And Papa had seen that quality in him, no doubt. Her father had always had a way of seeing into people. She peered up into the cloudless blue, hoped heaven was listening, and mouthed a silent thanks.

Odessia had agreed to speak with Ennis that evening, then to let her know their response. If the couple said yes, and Kizzy was in agreement, then there was only one more person Maggie needed to speak with.

And despite the man's kind and generous nature, he would be the most difficult to persuade of all.

∽

Wondering if a man's heart had ever beat straight out of his chest, Cullen rolled onto his side and pulled Maggie close, her back velvety soft against him. The quickness of her breath encouraged a satisfied smile, which broadened when she reached for his hand and held it close to her chest. So close he felt the solid beat of her heart.

"I love you, Maggie," he whispered and kissed the crown of her head. What he felt for her in that moment was so much more than anything he'd imagined when first making that promise to Gilbert Linden. A promise Cullen knew he'd never regret.

"I love you too," she answered, shuddering against him, her voice surprisingly fragile.

"What's wrong, love?" He rose up and smoothed the hair back from her face. She turned into the pillow, but he cradled her cheek, urging her back—and felt the trace of tears. Dread swept through him. "Did . . . I hurt you?"

She hiccuped a breath that sounded a little like a laugh. "No . . . of course not."

Relief flooded him. "Then what is it?"

Her hand tightened on his. She took a deep breath, then exhaled. "I simply never expected to . . . care for you like I do."

He laughed and turned her to face him. "We're goin' to have a good life, Maggie. You and me." He kissed her, tasting the salt of happy tears.

She deepened the kiss and slipped her hand beneath the covers.

He smiled against her mouth. "Are you tryin' to kill me, woman, or just—"

A sharp screech from somewhere outside broke the kiss, and Bucket awakened with a growl at the foot of the bed. A half second later, the hoot of an owl followed on its heels—right outside the window, from the sound of it—and Maggie laughed softly.

She snuggled closer. "Well, that about scared me to—"

"Shh." Cullen sat straight up, a cold tingle needling up his spine. Bucket growled low.

"What's wrong?" Maggie whispered, rising beside him.

Cullen put a finger to her lips, listening as eternal seconds ticked passed. Then, in the distance . . .

A shrill scream.

He bolted from bed and grabbed his shirt and trousers, aware of Maggie pulling on her gown then fumbling in the wardrobe. Once dressed, he pulled on his boots and grabbed the rifle from beneath the bed.

He strode to the hallway, Bucket running ahead, barking. "Stay in the house, Maggie. Come and lock the door behind me."

"Cullen." She huffed, pulling on her boots, then hurried to catch up. "If you think I'm going to—"

"I don't have time to—"

"I'm your wife. And I'm coming with you!"

Biting back a response, he raced downstairs and into the central parlor, jerked open the top desk drawer, and emptied a box of cartridges into his pants pocket.

Behind him, Bucket barked and clawed at the front door.

"Cullen!"

He turned and spotted Maggie by the front window, her father's Sharps rifle in hand and an erie glow rising on the horizon over the cabins.

Chapter THIRTY-TWO

As soon as Maggie stepped onto the porch, she smelled the smoke and heard the distant crackle of flames. Cullen set off for the cabins, and Bucket raced past him. She followed, rifle in hand.

"Stay close," Cullen called back. "You understand?"

"Yes!"

Wearing her gown and a long riding coat, the quickest things she could put on, she gathered her skirt and ran as fast as she could, barely able to keep up.

They crested the hill and saw chaos below.

Cabins alight with flames, at least four structures that she could see; people running, screaming, children crouched together in the common area. A volley of rifle fire sounded, and Cullen turned, pushing her to the ground and covering her body with his.

A handful of seconds, and they were running again.

The first person Maggie recognized from a distance was Onnie, then Cletus. The couple was first in a line of young and old spanning the short distance to the creek, passing buckets of water to douse the fires.

As she came nearer, lungs burning, Maggie realized that one of the cabins ablaze was Ennis and Odessia's. She searched the crowd for their faces, for Kizzy and her brothers, but she didn't see them anywhere.

"Follow me!" Cullen yelled and cut straight through the fray.

The heat and smoke from the flames thickened the stagnant summer air and gave the night an unworldly feel. But it was a woman's shrill scream that turned Maggie's blood cold. Up ahead a crowd had gathered, and Maggie spotted Odessia among them.

But not until she got closer did Maggie see the two bodies swinging from a limb far above. Both with arms tied behind them, one with legs still thrashing, fighting for life. The other, lifelessly still as it swayed back and forth.

"No!" Odessia let out a wail and went to her knees, and Maggie felt her own heart do the same as the terror she'd dreamed about—and that young Willie had lived—drew a devastating breath.

Cullen turned, anger hardening his features. "Stay with her!"

He ran for the tree, where other men were already scrambling to climb up. But whatever evil had done this had chosen its instrument well. The ancient oak was tall, and the limb sturdy and high. Twenty feet from the ground at least.

Maggie looked up at the man still struggling—*Ennis!*—saw the fight leaving him, and feared they wouldn't reach him in time.

Groaning, Odessia grabbed hold of Maggie's gown, tears streaming. "Please, help him!"

Maggie looked up to see Ennis's body all but still, and something inside her raged. Gently pushing Odessia away, she stepped forward and cocked the lever of the rifle, felt the chamber load, and took aim.

But it was too hazy. The smoke too thick. What if she missed?

"Do it!" a voice whispered from somewhere close behind.

Rifle tucked against her shoulder, Maggie raised the barrel again, centered the sights, and finger on the trigger, she squeezed. The shot split the night and the rope snapped. Ennis's body dropped to the ground with a sickening thud, his right leg twisted at an odd angle.

In a blink Odessia was there, working the rope from around his neck. Maggie ran and dropped to her knees beside them.

"Ennis!" Odessia called his name over and over, framing his face in her hands.

Maggie closed her eyes, and though words wouldn't come, she prayed with everything in her, the rage from moments before rising like a vicious tide. Then she heard a cough. A ragged, choking sound . . .

And she opened her eyes to see Odessia cradling her husband's head in her lap while another woman worked swiftly to remove the ropes from his wrists. Ennis's breath came in short, wispy gasps as Odessia stroked his face.

Maggie felt a warm hand on her back and looked over to see Cullen kneeling beside her. His hand encircled the nape of her neck, and he kissed her hard on the forehead then brought his face close.

"Your father told me you could shoot," he whispered, his breath shaky. "But *that* . . ."

He moved closer to see about Ennis and said something to Odessia that Maggie couldn't hear.

Maggie heard a familiar jingle and turned to see Bucket trotting up to her. "Hey there, boy." She hugged his neck, relieved to see the dog was all right.

Cullen returned a minute later, and Bucket immediately went to his heel. Maggie didn't mind one bit.

"I need to check on the others." Concern layered his voice even as anger showed in his features. "The two men patrolling tonight were beaten then knocked unconscious. Will you stay with Odessia and Ennis a while longer?"

Maggie nodded. "Of course."

"I've sent for a doctor." A shadow crossed his face. "He should be here within the hour, then we'll know more." He ran a forefinger along her jaw. "You're quite a woman, Mrs. McGrath. I hope you know that."

With quiet pride she watched him work his way through the small community, speaking and helping where he could, while only a short distance away aging timbers, turned to kindling with time, cracked and surrendered with meager resistance to the flames.

Movement from the corner of her eye drew her attention and, though not wanting to, she lifted her gaze. The second body still hung from the limb, his back to them, swinging to and fro, the man they were too late to save. If only they'd—

Maggie squinted, then stood and moved closer. It wasn't a body at all, at least not one made of flesh and blood. This man was stitched from flour sacks stuffed with hay. But why would anyone do such a—

The body turned on the rope until it faced her. She read the words painted in bright red letters on the chest, and the reality of her world—and Cullen's—came into greater and crueler focus than ever before.

Chapter THIRTY-THREE

Hours later, as dawn stretched pink and purple over the horizon, Maggie sat with Odessia on the porch of a neighbor's cabin as Dr. Daniels tended Ennis inside. She hadn't seen Dr. Daniels since he'd attended Papa, but it was good to know the man didn't hold the same prejudices as others in this town.

"More coffee?" Maggie filled Odessia's cup without waiting for a response. Onnie was up at the house brewing it as fast as she could, with Cletus serving as deliveryman.

Odessia turned a grateful smile in her direction and started to speak, then her eyes welled up, and she simply reached over and covered Maggie's hand on the arm of the rocker.

Still upset by events of the night, Maggie did her best not to show it. No loss of life, thank God, but several people—children included—had suffered burns in the fires, and everyone was visibly shaken.

Of the four cabins consumed, three that her grandfather had built were reduced to smoldering rubble—including Ennis and Odessia's—while a fourth cabin, recently constructed, sustained only minor damage. Five wagons loaded with supplies and tools had been sitting near the cabins and had also been set ablaze. She'd overheard Cullen telling one of the men that all of it would have to be replaced before harvest could commence.

After seeing to the people here, she and Cullen had returned to check on the house and the outbuildings. Belle and Levi were fine, to her great relief, as were the rest of the animals. This community, not the animals, had been the target of the hatred.

This, and her husband.

She spotted Cullen walking toward her and felt Odessia give her arm a nudge. Not needing any more encouragement, Maggie rose and went to him. She slipped her arms around his waist, and he pressed her against him. Her body shook with emotion held too long inside, and he led her around to the side of the cabin.

"Come here, love," he whispered, and he pulled her to him again, closer this time, and cradled her head beneath his chin. The solid feel of him, the man he was, the husband he was to her, poured fresh strength into her.

"Why?" she whispered against his neck. "Those hateful words."

His arms tightened around her. "Hateful words from hateful people. We'll get past it."

"I don't want to get past it. I want it to stop."

He sighed against her hair, and she could well imagine his thoughtful expression. "It won't ever stop, Maggie. Not completely. But we can change things, together. It'll take time, and a lot of provin' ourselves to people. But it can be done." He drew back slightly. "We're livin' proof of that, now aren't we?"

He placed a chaste kiss on her cheek, but the firm grip of his hands on her promised more.

They rejoined Odessia on the porch to see Kizzy there, along with her brothers, Jobah and Micah.

"Like I told you earlier"—Odessia pulled each child to her in turn—"Papa gonna be all right. Doctor with him right now, helpin' get that leg straight again."

The boys accepted the assurance easily enough, but Kizzy didn't look convinced.

"Your children did well, Odessia." Cullen gripped Jobah's slender shoulder. "Just like you taught them."

Micah's eyebrows shot up. "We ran and hid in them woods, sir. And didn't come out 'til it was safe."

"That's good, son," Odessia whispered. "That's *real* good."

"Your father's a very brave man." Cullen met each child's gaze. "Not many in the world like him."

Maggie caught the look he gave her, and she thought of her father and the relationship the two of them had shared, and her heart opened to him even more.

Kizzy linked arms with her mother. "But is it my fault, Mama? What happened to him?"

"No, child." Odessia smoothed her fingers over the girl's brow as if trying to erase the lines of worry. "Why you say that?"

"'Cuz o' what we talked 'bout last night. And all you said 'bout how it's full o' danger."

Kizzy looked up, and Maggie went stock still inside.

Odessia brushed a kiss to her daughter's brow and gave Maggie a knowing look. "No one heard that talk but us, Kizzy."

"So I can still ride Miss Belle in that race if I want to?"

Maggie closed her eyes, certain she felt the porch shift beneath her, along with her world.

"We ain't gonna talk about that anymore this mornin'." If Odessia's tone didn't put an end to the discussion, her expression did. "Your papa's what's most important right now."

Feeling Cullen's stare, Maggie couldn't bring herself to look at him.

"Odessia?"

The doctor appeared in the doorway and invited them inside, but Cullen gripped Maggie's upper arm.

"Odessia, you and your children go on in first. Mrs. McGrath and I will follow shortly."

Waiting until they'd gone inside, Maggie forced her gaze upward. "Cullen, I can ex—"

"Ride Belle in what race?" he asked softly. Too softly.

"I was going to speak with you about it. I simply hadn't found the—"

"The right time to bring it up to me. Well, now seems as good a time as any."

Reading the hurt in his eyes, she knew she'd underestimated the wound that hiding this from him would cause. For them both. "Nothing is settled. Kizzy asked me to teach her to ride, which I agreed to do. And I never, ever expected her to be what she is."

"And what would that be exactly?"

The hardness in his tone cut right through her. "She's a born rider, Cullen. Even Uncle Bob says so. He says he's never seen—"

"You have him workin' with you on this too?"

"No. Not like you think." She touched his arm, and while he didn't pull away, the way his muscles stiffened said her touch was not welcome. She removed her hand. "I promise you, it hasn't been like that."

"How long have you been teachin' her?"

A sick feeling churned inside her. "About . . . three weeks."

His mouth tipped, but not in a smile. "The same time things started gettin' better between us again. Imagine that."

Seeing the conclusion he was drawing, and remembering that

first night of being together again after being separated for weeks, Maggie felt the sick feeling sink and fan out inside her. "No, Cullen. I would never do that. I would never use . . . *that* like a game. Or a way to—"

"We best get on inside and see to Ennis and his family."

"But, Cullen, I—"

He reached around her and opened the door, then stepped aside and waited for her to precede him.

~

Later that day, Ennis lay sleeping in a neighboring cabin, and Cullen eased down into a chair by the bed, his focus drawn to the angry, swollen welt encircling the man's neck. His appreciation for Ennis and the fact that his employee—and friend—was still alive after what he'd been through made the plank wood structure surrounding them feel a little like holy ground.

But his anger at whoever had done this made him crave justice and wish he could help mete it out.

Although he didn't know for sure who was responsible—he'd personally spoken with every family that worked at Linden Downs, and no one had seen any of the men's faces—he did know quite a few people who would wish him harm, as well as harm to those who worked here.

And at the top of that list—Stephen Drake.

Cullen would've liked nothing more than to find a link from Drake to what happened here, and then pay the man a short visit on a dark night. At least that's what he would've done a few years back. He would've taken Ethan with him too. And his older brother would've been itching to go.

Cullen stared down at his hands clasped between his knees. Oh, what he'd be willing to give right now to know what Gilbert Linden would do in this situation. Fighting a battle when you were the only one in the fight was one thing. But fighting when others could get hurt—or die—because of your actions was something else.

Especially when it was your job to protect them.

In the past few hours, two moments kept repeating themselves in his mind: Maggie standing there, all alone, taking aim and shooting that rope clean through with one shot. And discovering she'd been deliberately misleading him.

He heard her voice coming from just outside. She'd walked down here with him, though the walk had been as silent as the grave. He'd started wondering today if they were ever going to have more than five minutes of peace between them. It was an exaggeration, of course, brought on by weariness and fatigue.

But still the question weighed on him.

"Mister McGrath . . ."

Cullen's head came up. "Mr. Ennis." Smiling, he stretched out a hand, making all but the final step of the journey.

Ennis's grip was surprisingly strong, considering, and Cullen noticed the rope burns on his wrists too.

"Doc tol' me the bone is sound, sir." Ennis's voice, usually clear and deep, had taken on a raspy quality. "Just broke clean through. But that means it heal right up. He say I be back, good as new, in three months. Maybe less."

"That's good to hear. I don't think Linden Downs could run without you now."

The comment drew a smile from the man.

Cullen knew the doctor had administered something for his pain, but still, he could scarcely believe the man before him had been hanging by a rope earlier that morning. A man of lesser strength and muscle wouldn't have survived. And glancing again at the reddened welt left by the noose, Cullen could scarcely believe Ennis had.

He noticed a cup of tea and a half-eaten bowl of field peas with a slice of cornbread on a nearby table, and gestured to it. "Want to try and eat the rest? Knowin' your wife, she won't be lettin' you leave anythin' behind."

Ennis nodded and washed down a few spoonfuls of peas with measured sips of water. Then he paused, spoon resting on the covers.

"Hangin' there like that, sir . . ." Ennis gently touched his throat, as if making sure the welts were really there. "Seein' my Dessie cryin', the world 'round me slippin' away . . . I ain't too proud to tell ya . . . I was scared."

A tiny knot gathered at the base of Cullen's throat. "Any man would've been. Includin' this one."

Ennis held his stare. "I thought I's gon' die, sir. And I kept thinkin', what's gonna happen to my wife and my young'uns, growin' up in such a place. If my young'uns get a chance to grow up."

Cullen started to offer assurance that they would. But he'd learned this world didn't come with assurances. And just because you believed in the Almighty didn't make you immune to all the wrongdoing in the world.

Sometimes, backward as it sounded, the more you believed, the more trouble seemed to come your way.

"I've asked this of everyone else, Ennis, but I need to hear it from you too. Did you see the men's faces? Is there anythin' you saw that could be used to help to identify who did this?"

Ennis closed his eyes, as if trying to relive the horrific ordeal. "They grabbed me from behind. And all of 'em, every last one, was wearin' a white hood . . . coverin' their whole head." He sighed. "I'm sorry, sir. But I didn't see nothin'."

Cullen handed him the cup of tea, and Ennis sipped.

"I'm sorry," Cullen whispered, the scene coming back to him in sickening detail. "It shouldn't be like this. This shouldn't have happened."

Ennis stared into his cup for the longest time. "You and me, sir. We real different. But we also got some sameness to us. In a way, you was hangin' up there with me too."

Only after the fact did Cullen realize his hand was at his throat.

A couple of the men had climbed the tree and taken down the second "body" along with the remainder of the ropes, wanting no visible reminders left behind. But whether visible or not, he'd never be able to wipe from his memory the image of Ennis hanging there, or the words *white nigger* painted in bright red letters across the chest of the figure hanging beside him. Certain parts of life got captured inside you, whether you wanted them to or not.

"Your wife, sir." Ennis's voice grew even softer. "She come with you this evenin'?"

Hearing what the man wasn't saying outright, Cullen glanced toward the cabin door. "She's sittin' outside with Odessia. I'll get her, if you'd like."

"Please, sir."

Cullen crossed to the door, and Maggie must have heard him, because she peered up, eyes expectant. But the light in them quickly extinguished when meeting his.

"Mr. Ennis would like to see you."

She rose and followed him inside, as Bucket started to do as well, but a quick snap of Cullen's fingers sent the dog back to his place on the porch.

As soon as Ennis saw Maggie, the powerfully built mountain of a man began to weep. No sound, no shudder broke the strong line of his shoulders, only silent tears slipping down his cheeks.

Maggie claimed the chair by the bed.

"Missus . . . McGrath," he said between tattered breaths. "What you done for me today . . ." He paused as if needing to gain his composure. "Thank you, ma'am."

Cullen noticed the man's hand move on the bedcovers as though Ennis wanted to reach out. But he didn't. Instead, he fisted his dark hand tight.

"You're welcome, Mr. Ennis." Maggie's voice broke, and she briefly bowed her head. "I'm just grateful I didn't kill you."

As quickly as Ennis's tears had come, so did his laughter. "You sure can shoot, ma'am. Where'd you learn to do that?"

Maggie smiled and gave a little shrug. "I grew up with four older brothers."

"Mmmm . . ." Ennis regarded her. "Well . . . I thank you again, ma'am. Took courage to do that."

Maggie quickly shook her head. "I was scared out of my wits. I don't think I could've done it without that person behind me urging me on."

Cullen looked down at her then back at Ennis.

"'Bout my daughter, Kizzy, ridin' for you, ma'am. I know how—"

"Why don't we save that conversation for another day, Mr. Ennis," she said quickly, rising from her seat. "For now, let's focus on you getting well."

By the time Cullen retired that night, Bucket barely making it up the stairs ahead of him, Maggie was already abed. Cullen was surprised to find her lamp still lit, and Maggie sitting up reading her father's Bible.

His gaze was drawn to the woman like an ill-fated moth to flame, and he intentionally turned his back to her as he undressed. He gave the collie one last pat then climbed into bed, careful not to meet Maggie's gaze.

He turned toward the wall.

Neither of them had slept since the night before, and he knew she was weary. So was he. Yet somehow he also knew sleep was a long way off.

She turned the page, the crinkle of the paper distinctive to him now, and he wished he'd thought to look at what part of the book she was reading. But he wasn't about to turn over and look now.

After a few minutes she laid the book aside and blew out the lamp.

She settled beside him, not intentionally touching him, he didn't think. But not going out of her way to avoid it either.

As they'd perfected through many a night, they lay in the darkness. Still. Silent. He still couldn't believe she'd tried to go behind his back like that. After he'd expressly told her he—

"I'm sorry, Cullen."

The direction of her voice told him she was lying on her back, probably staring at the ceiling he knew only too well.

"It was wrong of me to approach Odessia about Kizzy without speaking to you first. My thought was that if—"

"If they said yes, then I would have to do the same."

Bucket's soft snores from the corner of the room filled the brief silence.

"That was partly it," she continued softly. "The other part being that I didn't have a jockey yet. So why would I approach you again about something you'd already said no to, when I couldn't have moved forward even if you had said yes."

He followed her logic, but still didn't like that she'd circumvented him. Or tried to. Even as the thought came, so did the unwelcome reminder that he wasn't being completely truthful with her either.

Night sounds drifted in through the window. The spirited chirrup of crickets, the lonely coo of a mourning dove.

"I know you're angry with me." Her tone carried no blame. "But I want you to know how proud I was of you today. And also how"—she took a quick breath—"how proud I was to be there with you. As your wife."

Cullen closed his eyes, her words like a balm. But her actions still a barb.

She shifted positions and he did the same, moving to his back since she was faced away from him. Another dance they were good at. Sadly so.

Scenes from last night kept returning, pushing away any chance of sleep, and he pictured again, in his mind's eye, Maggie standing there, rifle gripped and aimed at the rope. Then he remembered . . .

"Are you still awake?" he asked softly, already knowing the answer.

"I am."

"You told Ennis today that you couldn't have done what you did without someone behind you urgin' you on."

"That's right," she said.

"Maggie . . . there was no one standin' behind you. I saw you myself. You were all alone."

She turned onto her back. "But I heard a voice. I know I did."

"And . . . what did it say?"

"It said . . . do it," she whispered with an intensity that sent a chill skittering up his spine.

The silence lengthened.

"Do you believe me?" she asked a moment later.

He weighed his answer before speaking. "I'm not sayin' you didn't hear somethin'. But what I *am* sayin' is that you were standin' there by yourself."

The weather vane atop the roof squeaked as the wind sent it turning.

"Maybe I was," she finally whispered, her tone not the least argumentative. "But I know this . . . I wasn't alone."

Chapter Thirty-Four

Finished with breakfast early the next morning, Maggie waited for Cullen to come downstairs and join her at the table. Things needed to be said, and she needed to say them while she still had the courage.

Wordlessly, Onnie refilled her cup with coffee, steaming hot like Maggie liked it. And just like Onnie had been doing for years. Not only for Maggie but for her parents and brothers as well.

"Thank you, Onnie." Maggie cradled the warm cup in her grip. "For all you do for me. And thank you as well for all you did yesterday to help after the fire."

Onnie paused in the doorway. "You welcome, Missus McGrath."

It still sounded a little odd to hear Onnie call her by that name. After all, Onnie had known her since before she was born.

"And thank *you*, ma'am"—Onnie's expression softened—"for what you did for Ennis and his family. I's so proud o' you when I heard what you done."

Surprised by the woman's admission, Maggie was also humbled by it.

"I know, ma'am, that your—" Onnie stopped suddenly, then looked away as if she'd come close to embarrassing herself. "I know that your husband will be hungry, ma'am. I'll get his breakfast."

Hearing Cullen's footsteps on the second-story landing, Maggie sensed that what Onnie had said wasn't at all what she'd planned on saying. "What is it, Onnie?" she asked softly. "If there's something you want to say, please say it."

Onnie stepped closer. "All I's gonna say, ma'am, is that I know your mama didn't much care for the ridin' and shootin' you did growin' up. But I think if she was to see you today . . . she be right proud of you."

Taken aback, Maggie didn't quite know how to respond. "Why, thank you, Onnie," she finally managed. "That's . . . very kind of you."

Onnie dipped her head and returned to the kitchen, and Maggie didn't know what surprised her more. That Onnie had shared something so personal, or that she simply didn't believe Onnie was right. No matter how she wished it were true.

"Good mornin'." Cullen nodded to her as he took his seat, looking handsome as always, though not well rested.

"Morning, Cullen. Onnie's getting your breakfast." Bucket padded up to her, and she gave him a good scratching between his ears.

"Thank you."

The tense silence had followed them from the bedroom, but Maggie knew how to fix that. She took a steadying breath.

"Cullen, I need to say something to you, and I need you to hear me out before responding." Even sitting across the table from him, she felt his guard go up.

He merely tilted his head, as if demonstrating his willingness to comply with her wishes.

"What I'm about to say, I don't say lightly. I've given this much thought, and I think it would be best if—" The words caught against the tangle of emotion in her throat, but she forced them past it, thinking again about the likelihood of what happened to Ennis happening to Kizzy. No dream was worth that. ". . . If I stopped giving Kizzy riding lessons, and if we told Ennis and Odessia that we've decided not to enter Belle in the Peyton Stakes."

There, her heart was racing, but she'd said it.

Cullen looked as genuinely surprised—no, shocked—as she'd imagined he would be. And she felt an even greater loss than she'd anticipated.

But after experiencing what she had over the last thirtysome-odd hours, she knew there were far more important things in life than training thoroughbreds and winning races. Even if a part of her still felt as if every moment of her life had been preparing her to do just that.

∞

Cullen watched her walk serenely away from the table, so composed, so seemingly at peace. So unlike the passionate and opinionated woman he knew so well, and loved the same.

"Here you are, Mister McGrath." Onnie set a heaping plate of scrambled eggs, fried potatoes, ham with red-eye gravy, and toast before him. Having awakened hungry, he could hardly wait to dig in. And yet—

He couldn't allow Maggie to say something like that and then just walk away without any discussion. Not when he knew how much this meant to her.

"This looks delicious, Miss Onnie. But if you wouldn't mind keepin' my plate warm for me for just a few—"

"Cullen!" Maggie's scream came through the open windows from the direction of the stable.

Cullen pushed back his chair and was out the door before Miss Onnie could respond.

Following Maggie's desperate cries, he raced to the stable and found her standing over Bourbon Belle. The thoroughbred lay on her side in the stall unmoving, her belly distended.

Chapter THIRTY-FIVE

Cullen gently pushed past Maggie and knelt beside Belle, the scene all too familiar and yet another world—and lifetime—away. "Hey, sweet girl." He spoke softly to the horse, running a hand over the mare's swollen belly. The thoroughbred responded by lifting her head, or trying to.

Behind him, Maggie drew a shuddering breath. "What's wrong with her, Cullen?" She knelt and cradled the side of Belle's face, her hand trembling. "I came in and found her like this."

"Was the door to her stall closed?"

"Yes." Maggie wiped her cheeks.

"And to the stable?"

She nodded again, fresh tears starting.

Cullen leaned down and pressed an ear to the mare's belly. "Her breathin's faint and rapid." He checked the nostrils then the mare's mouth. "She's got discharge comin' from her nose, and the hay 'round her mouth is soppin' wet."

Maggie looked from him to Belle. "What does that mean? What are you saying?"

He saw the fear in Maggie's eyes. "I think someone's poisoned her."

"But—" She hiccuped a sob. "But why? And *how*?"

Cullen rose. "You fed her the usual grain last evenin'?"

"Yes."

"What about yesterday mornin'?"

"The same. And the same before that. As I do every day."

He peered down the line of stalls and quickly accounted for Levi and the other horses. "Whoever did this seems to have had a specific target. And that target appears to have been Belle."

"But why would anyone want to hurt her?"

"Why would anyone want to hurt any champion racehorse?" He saw the hurt slip into her eyes and regretted it. That hadn't been his intention.

What she'd announced moments ago at the breakfast table had both pleased and troubled him. He knew the affection she had for this horse. And for racing. But there was a side of racing that wasn't all integrity and honor.

"But Belle isn't even racing right now, Cullen. And her name isn't on the roster to run in the Peyton Stakes either."

"I understand that. But you have to ask yourself, Maggie . . . Are you doin' anything right now that would make someone think you *might* be plannin' to enter Belle into the race come October?"

He didn't have to wait long for her answer. It showed clearly in her face.

He checked the grain bin outside Belle's stall, scooping handfuls of grain and sifting through it.

She came alongside. "What are you looking for?"

"Anythin' out of the ordinary." He returned to the stall and started rummaging through the hay covering the dirt floor, mindful of the thoroughbred and her powerful hindquarters. This couldn't be happening again, could it? *God, please . . . Don't make this woman pay for my mistakes.*

Maggie knelt beside him. "If you'll tell me what you're looking for, I can help."

"It looks a lot like nettle leaves. And bein' the start of September, it could have little white flowers on it."

She started searching. "And does this plant have a name?"

"White snakeroot." He glanced up to see question in her features. "Ever heard of milk sickness?"

She stilled. "Yes. A lot of people died from that here in the early years."

"It comes from snakeroot. Folks either eat meat or drink milk from an animal that's ingested the plant, then they get sick. It usually takes a couple of days after the animal has eaten it before the signs show up." He looked back at Belle. "But this has all the signs of snakeroot."

"How do you know all this?"

"Because I've seen it before. Back in London."

She frowned.

He glanced away, wishing he had another choice, but knowing

he didn't. She deserved to know the truth, and all of it. Not right now, but soon. "I worked in stables when I lived in London. I saw it there. There's more I'll tell you, but right now time is important. The sooner we get Belle help, the better. I'll ride into town and—"

"No," Maggie said quickly. "I'll ride to Belle Meade."

"For Uncle Bob?"

She grabbed a saddle. "For Rachel. She helps Uncle Bob doctor the horses there."

Cullen grabbed the saddle from her. "I'll go. You stay with Belle. She loves you, Maggie. You're her whole world."

Tears filled her eyes. "And she's a big part of mine."

⁂

Maggie stood just inside the stall beside Cullen as Rachel examined Belle. Maggie had never spent much time around Rachel Norris, but Uncle Bob considered Rachel's gifts of healing to be straight from the Great Physician himself.

The woman's delicate hands moved over Belle's body with tender expertise. "You find any trace of snakeroot?"

"Nay, we didn't. But I've seen before what it can do."

Rachel nodded. "Same as me, Mister McGrath."

Maggie stole a look beside her at Cullen to see him already watching her, his eyes warm with understanding and concern.

Rachel stood, her dark brown curls flowing about her shoulders, her skin the color of well-creamed coffee. But it was the woman's startling blue eyes that Maggie found the most revealing. Eyes that told an all-too-familiar story in a single glance.

"You love this creature, Missus McGrath."

"I do," Maggie whispered.

Rachel slowly smiled. "She knows it. And she counts on your love. She be needin' it, too, if she's to pull through this."

"If?" Maggie's chest ached.

"Judgin' from the signs, I'm thinkin' the poison's been in her body for at least a full day." Rachel glanced back at Belle, who moved from trembling to lethargy based upon the moment.

"The night before last," Maggie whispered, studying Cullen, wondering if he was having the same thought.

"Aye . . ." His eyes narrowed. "There was plenty of time while we were down there for someone to get to her."

Maggie turned back to Rachel. "Two nights ago—"

"I know what happened here," the woman said softly. "We all know." She looked at Cullen. "And my guess would be the same as yours, sir. They slipped the snakeroot into her stall and into her grain." Rachel gestured to the bins outside the stall. "They need to be emptied and washed, and all the grain burned. We don't want another animal sufferin' the same fate."

"Aye. I'll see that it's done, Mrs. Norris. Anythin' else you need?"

"What herbs I need that I didn't bring, I'll get from my cabin. But blankets would be appreciated."

"For Belle?" Maggie asked.

"For me." A dark brow rose. "Times like this, I stay with my patient, Missus McGrath."

"Thank you," Maggie whispered, grateful, but hurting every time she looked at Belle. "Do you think she'll make it through?"

Rachel's hand on her arm was warm and strong. "Every creature on this earth been given a time to be born and a time to leave this land of death and move on into true life. I can't change that for Belle any more than I can change it for you, ma'am." The gentleness of her smile reflected her healing nature. "At best, I can be an instrument in the Lord's hand for his good and perfect will. Just like you were . . . for Mister Ennis."

Maggie thought again of the voice she'd heard so clearly behind her that night.

Rachel knelt by Belle and opened her satchel. "I'll do my best to heal your beloved Bourbon Belle, all while prayin' that my will is in accord with the Almighty's."

Chapter THIRTY-SIX

Following a restless night, Cullen stood on the front porch Monday morning and watched as dawn broke cloudy and gray over the hills. An unease gnawed at him. The rain that started as a sprinkle shortly before midnight had become a deluge and now poured from the roof of the house and outbuildings.

He'd welcomed the moisture earlier in the season, but with harvest upon them, rain was now more foe than friend. Odd how quickly that relationship could change.

Bucket gave a little whine beside him, and Cullen sighed. "My feelin's exactly, boy."

He caught sight of Maggie through the open stable door. She'd insisted on staying with Belle last night, even though Rachel was there. So of course he'd stayed with her.

He doubted she'd gotten any more sleep than he had. Every twig that broke in the night, every whoosh of the breeze rustling the pines, brought his senses to alert and his hand to his rifle.

He'd doubled the number of men keeping watch each night to four, but if whoever did this came back in greater number . . . How could he protect this much land? This many people?

Though he was no closer to discovering who had set the fires and poisoned Belle, he assumed they were one and the same. All any of the workers could tell him was that they'd seen men in white hoods. Cowards hiding behind masks.

He'd reviewed the ledgers for the farm last evening, and replacing what was lost in the fire would swiftly devour what limited cash remained—while still demanding more. It would mean buying on credit, which he loathed.

But he couldn't harvest without wagons, and he needed lumber and supplies to replace the five that had been burned. Judging by the moat forming between the house and the stable, it would take three to four days for the fields to dry up enough to get a wagon through. So they had time.

A punishing thought arose . . .

If he hadn't built the cabins for the workers at the first—if he'd chosen something more practical like canvas tents for the time being, which would still have been far and away better accommodations than they'd had—then he would have the money he needed right now to replace the wagons. It didn't help remembering how Maggie had questioned him on that particular decision.

And also how, when she'd accused him of approaching General Harding to buy Belle, he'd insisted the farm was doing well. But it had been, then. And would be again, once the crops were harvested.

But he simply couldn't admit to her that the ledgers were running so lean. Gilbert Linden had entrusted him with the land and his daughter, and Cullen still aimed to protect both.

The rain let up a little and he made a dash to the stable, Bucket trotting behind. At the last minute the collie dashed through the door in front of him then promptly stopped and shook, sending droplets of water in all directions.

Cullen knifed a hand through his wet hair, oddly comforted by the smell of damp horse and hay that punctuated the confined space. An acquired preference, no doubt. The steady drum of rain on the tin roof reminded him of the low rumble of a train crossing a trestle, but the repairs he and the men had made on the roof earlier in the summer were holding well.

As of two hours ago Bourbon Belle still showed no improvement, but Rachel had warned them it could take days before they knew which way things would go. Rachel Norris was a hard woman to read, but he'd played enough poker in his life—and won—to know the odds weren't in their favor.

He peered into Belle's stall and found Maggie sitting close beside the mare, stroking her head. Maggie didn't look up, apparently not hearing his approach.

Every time he thought of what losing that horse would do to her, the anger that had ignited inside him two nights ago burned hotter and deeper.

"How is she?" he asked.

Maggie's head came up, her eyes red-rimmed and weary. "Much the same. Rachel left a while ago to get a special concoction of herbs for a poultice. Belle's got some swelling in her lower neck here." She tenderly traced the area with her hand. "Rachel says a poultice will help."

He studied the two of them for a moment, remembering the first time he'd seen Maggie and Belle racing across the field. Two beauties who seemed made for each other . . .

He squinted, noting a new addition decorating the stall wall. A picture. Drawn by Kizzy, he guessed. Maggie had told him about the girl's artwork. This one depicted Belle standing in a field with a ribbon around her neck. Not hard to figure out the inspiration behind that one.

But surely by now the girl knew there would be no racing. And no ribbons.

When he'd relayed the news about Belle's condition to Ennis last night, Ennis said nothing about whether they'd planned on allowing Kizzy to race or not. But Cullen's guess was that even if they had been, what had happened to Ennis had changed the man's mind.

All jockeys were children of freedmen. But boys, not girls. Personally, he'd never allow his own daughter to do something so dangerous. He didn't think Ennis would either.

"I'm sorry this happened, Maggie. And I'm sorry it happened to Belle."

Culpability shadowed Maggie's gaze. "Do you really think this happened because someone thought I had plans to race her again?"

The question landed like a punch to his gut. "I don't know. And trust me when I tell you . . . I didn't say that to hurt you."

"I know," she said softly. But her tone lacked conviction.

He stepped inside the stall. "But I do know there are people in this town who will do anythin' not only to win but to make sure others don't. And I'm not only speakin' about racin' thoroughbreds."

She searched his gaze. "The other night. When the cabins burned. That was . . . the 'wolves,' wasn't it."

It wasn't a question. "Aye . . . I didn't want to worry you. You, or the rest of the women and children."

His gaze went to Belle then back to Maggie, and he wondered if the guilt suddenly prodding him was of his own making, or if Maggie had intended the statement to assign it to him.

Either way, the sense of responsibility weighed heavy.

"Forgive me, Maggie, if I was wrong in not tellin' you."

She shook her head. "I don't know that it would have made any difference, Cullen. We can't be everywhere at once, can we?" She leaned down and kissed Belle on the bridge of her nose.

Sensing movement from the corner of his eye, Cullen jumped a little when he saw a hooded figure standing in the doorway.

"Mister McGrath." Rachel removed the hood of her dark cape, setting free a mass of curls. A basket laden with herbs hung from her arm. She moved closer and knelt by Belle, then smoothed a hand along the horse's neck. "She's restin' some better. That's good. I'll be grindin' up herbs for a while, Missus McGrath. I suggest you get somethin' to eat and take a rest."

"I'd rather stay here. With her."

Rachel stood. "If your constitution grows weak, Missus McGrath, Belle will know. And that will only add to her burden." She removed her cape, her dress beneath surprisingly dry. "Go with your husband. I'll be here with her."

Reluctantly Maggie stood, reaching out for the wall to steady herself. "I won't be gone long."

Cullen slipped an arm about her waist as they ran to the house. He opened the door for her and barely caught Bucket before the collie, soaking wet, darted inside.

"Stay," Cullen commanded, and the dog dropped to the porch, head on his paws, soulful eyes pleading.

Miss Onnie met them in the foyer. "Lawd, you two are soaked clean through." She made a tsking sound. "I got you a bath 'bout ready, ma'am. Was gonna come outside and get you. Thought it would feel good to you 'fore you eat somethin'."

Maggie nodded. "Thank you, Onnie. And . . . maybe I'll be hungry later."

"You best be. I makin' some eggs and grits for breakfast. Then a crusty chicken pie with peas and carrots for dinner, just the way you like it."

Maggie sighed. "That was Oak's favorite, remember?"

Cullen glimpsed the shared bond of loss as it moved from Maggie's face to Miss Onnie's.

"Yes, ma'am, I 'member. I think 'bout your brothers near ever' day, and see 'em all over this house. Now . . ." The woman nodded toward the washroom by the kitchen. "You run on and get yourself warm while I finish in the kitchen."

Maggie started up the stairs.

Cullen touched her arm. "Where are you goin'?"

"To get some clean clothes."

He steered her back toward the washroom. "I'll get those, you go ahead and get in the tub."

Apparently too weary to put up a fight, she did as he said.

A few minutes later, he knocked on the door.

"Come in."

He did, but felt a little awkward doing so, with Miss Onnie staring at his back from the kitchen. Reminding himself he was married to the woman in the tub, he closed the door behind him.

Eyes closed, Maggie reclined in the claw-footed porcelain tub, her long hair wet and hanging over the back. Steam rose from the water, filled to within inches of the rim, so though the rest of her was lost to his sight, his memory still worked fine.

"I'll leave your clothes right here."

"Thank you."

He turned to go.

"Cullen?"

"Aye?"

She looked back at him. "I've told God that . . . if he'll let Belle live, I'll never race her again." Unshed tears welled in her eyes. "And I won't care. And I won't feel cheated." Tears spilled over. "I just want her to live."

He crossed to the tub and knelt down. "I want her to live, too, Maggie. But I want her to run again. I want to see you ridin' her like you did that day you nearly scared me outta my wits. Your arms spread wide and her hooves scarcely touchin' the ground."

Her smile hinted at the girl she'd once been. "My brother, Oak, called that *soaring*."

"Then I want to see you and Belle soar again. That's what *I'm* askin' God for, Maggie."

Thank you, she mouthed, then lifted her hand from the warm water and covered his on the rim of the tub. "You said you had more to tell me about white snakeroot. And about London."

His gaze dropped from her eyes to the water, and his smile came slowly. "I'll do that, I give you my word, and I'll answer all of your questions. But right now . . . with you in that tub and me in the room alone with you, the last thing I want to do is talk."

Her face flushed a lovely shade of pink, same as her bare shoulders and other curves.

"So why don't you finish in here, and I'll go change from these wet clothes, and we'll continue this conversation later."

Cullen had barely finished his first helping of scrambled eggs and ham and was anticipating a second when Maggie posed the question again. He politely declined when Miss Onnie came offering more.

As Miss Onnie refilled his coffee cup, he took a long drink of water, a sprig of mint giving it a cool, fresh taste, and he decided the straightforward approach was best. He waited until it was just the two of them again.

"The reason I know so much about white snakeroot is because my older brother, Ethan, used it to poison a horse in London. And he was paid a goodly sum to do it."

Maggie leveled a stare as if she were waiting for him to admit he was only jesting. When he didn't, her expression paled.

"Did you know what your brother was doing?"

"Of course not. All I knew was that somethin' wasn't right. I should have followed my gut and found out what was happenin'. But I owed Ethan so much."

"You owed him money?"

"Not money, Maggie. I owed him my life." Cullen fingered the rim of his plate. "Our father loved the bottle. You know that already. But when he drank, he got mean. Meaner than he already was. He'd come home from the pub in the mood to give a thrashin'. Only once did he give that to my mother." He remembered her beautiful face all cut up and bruised, but he spared Maggie those details. "After that, Ethan and me, we decided from then on we'd take the beatin's. Not our ma, nor our sisters either. But Ethan . . ." Emotion tightened Cullen's throat. Despite all the heartache Ethan had caused him, he still loved his brother. "Ethan was bigger and stronger than me, always was. He took the beatin's in my stead. Every last one of 'em."

Compassion softened Maggie's face.

"I'm not tellin' you this so you'll feel sorry for me, Maggie. I'm tellin' you because I'm responsible for what happened."

"You didn't poison that horse. Your brother did."

"Don't you see? I knew Ethan was in trouble. I knew he owed those men a lot of money. But I was tryin' my best to change my own ways, to make a life for me and Moira and our sweet little Katie. So instead of goin' to Ethan and demandin' he tell me what he was doin', I just looked the other way. Until it was too late."

"What do you mean . . . too late?"

"London's racing commission—"

She held up a hand. "The horse was a thoroughbred?"

"And a racer." Cullen looked her in the eyes. "The stallion that stood to win the Belmont Stakes that season."

Her jaw slipped open.

"I don't know how," he continued, "but the commission traced the act back to Ethan. And then to me, likely because I'd helped get him a job in the stables where I worked. The job that allowed him access to Aristides."

"The stallion he poisoned."

He nodded. "Which belonged to some rich American who lived in New York City."

The muted clang of pots and pans drifted from the kitchen.

"The commission issued warrants for our arrest. But Ethan—he disappeared. Like mornin' dew, here and gone. And I haven't seen or spoken to him since."

"So the commission, they blamed you."

"Aye. If I'd stayed I would've gone to prison. And Moira and Katie, with no family left, no one to care for them . . ." He sighed. "I thought I was savin' them by comin' here. But with the way everythin' turned out . . ."

"You did the right thing in leaving London, Cullen. You weren't at fault. And there's no way you could have known what would happen on that ship."

He studied the mint leaf floating in his glass. "And now you know why I was so determined that you not race Belle. And that I not serve as your front, as it were."

"Because if anyone found out, and then reported you . . ."

"It would cost me, and therefore you too, everything." He studied her across the table. "So you see, Maggie, I'm the last man in the world you'd want representin' you to the Nashville Thoroughbred Society."

She leaned forward. "Do you have any idea where your brother is now?"

"Somewhere far away from London. That's all I know."

"And the horse," she asked softly. "Did he die?"

Cullen shook his head, and heard an audible breath thread her lips.

"But he never raced again."

Chapter Thirty-Seven

At the lumberyard the next morning, Cullen paused outside the door of the warehouse to knock the mud and muck from his boots. The sun hot on his back and the skies stretching a cloudless blue overhead all but guaranteed to dry the rain-drenched fields as he'd hoped. Two or three days, and they'd begin harvesting the crops at Linden Downs. And it was none too soon for him.

Inside, he spotted the proprietor in the back and gestured. The man seemed to hesitate, then held up a hand, indicating he'd be right there.

Cullen eyed the shovels on one wall, then picked a couple and placed them by the front counter. Once the crops were sold at market, Linden Downs would be back on firm financial footing again, and he'd feel more confident about the future.

As it was, he hoped Mr. Blake, the proprietor, would remember how good a patron he'd been when he'd purchased the loads of lumber for the new cabins earlier in the summer. Because as it stood now, the cash in his pocket would scarcely cover the few tools he needed to replace. All of the lumber and supplies to build the wagons, he would have to buy on credit.

"Them's good shovels, for sure. The best, if you ask me."

Cullen turned to see a man sitting atop a barrel in the corner, his hair shock white, his face shriveled and marked with time.

Cullen nodded. "Thank you, sir. I appreciate the recommendation."

The man's thickish eyebrows shot up. "I hear Irish on your tongue, son!" Then he grinned, revealing the absence of a few teeth.

Hearing only curiosity in the man's tone, Cullen laughed. "That you do, sir. You wouldn't be hailin' from my island, too, now would you?" Cullen was only jesting with him, since the man's accent was thick with the South.

The gentleman's brow furrowed. "Why no, son. I was born right here." He eased off the barrel as though his legs, bowed as they proved to be, might break if given too much to bear at once. "Been here all my life, nigh onto seventy years now."

Seventy years? From the look of the man's gnarled hands and hunched shoulders, those years hadn't been easy ones. Cullen wondered if time hadn't thieved a measure of his sanity along the way.

The man kept worrying at something tied around his frail wrist, and Cullen finally caught a glimpse of it. A piece of string.

"Good day, Mr. McGrath. What can I do for you?"

Hearing the proprietor's voice, Cullen tossed the old-timer a parting nod then turned. "Mr. Blake, good to see you again. I'm needin' a load of lumber and supplies. I've got my list here." He handed it to him.

Blake read through the items. "This is quite a list, McGrath."

"Hey, Blake, this the best string you got?"

Both Cullen and Mr. Blake looked over to see the older gentleman holding up a ball of twine.

"Yes, Jessup." The proprietor sighed. "That's still the best string I got."

Jessup grinned, his eyes nearly lost in the wrinkles. "Well, good to know. Still, think I might look around a little more first."

Blake turned back to Cullen and, as if hearing the thread of Cullen's thoughts, he shook his head. "Fortysome-odd years," he whispered, "Jessup Collum's been the caretaker over at City Cemetery. Rumor has it he ties strings about the wrists of dead folks before he buries them . . . just in case one of them wakes up." He gave Cullen a look. "People say he's a bit touched in the head, but he's harmless enough." He refocused his attention on the paper in his hand. "This constitutes a sizable purchase."

"Aye, sir, it does. We had some trouble at Linden Downs the other night. Cabins were burned, along with wagons loaded with supplies I need for harvest."

Blake glanced away. "I'm sorry to hear that."

"Thank you." Hearing the man's sincerity, Cullen also sensed by his lack of curiosity and hesitance to meet his gaze that the news wasn't new to him. And he didn't like the feeling that accompanied the discovery. "So, as I said, I'm here for these items. I've got cash to cover part of it." He hesitated. "A small part. So I'll need to purchase the rest on credit. But I'll pay my debt—with interest, of course—as soon as

I've harvested. Should be no more than two to three weeks before you get your money."

Blake fingered the list in his hand, a faint smile struggling to take hold, and failing. "I thought you were a cash-only patron."

"I usually am." Cullen eyed him. "But I failed to set aside money for the cost of men comin' onto my land, burnin' my workers' cabins, and settin' my wagons ablaze."

To his credit, Blake winced. "Listen, McGrath, I'm sorry for what happened to you. I truly am, but—"

"Your condolences are appreciated, Mr. Blake"—Cullen worked to contain his temper—"but what I would appreciate even more is to be able to purchase these items on credit. Just this once. I need these supplies to harvest my crops."

"I'm sorry. I wish I could help." Blake returned the piece of paper. "But I can't extend you credit."

Cullen leveled his gaze. "They tried to kill a man that night, Mr. Blake. Hung him right there in front of his wife. That's an image I'll never get out of my head. That, and the children with their arms and legs all burned and blistered from the fire. And all this because of cowards hidin' behind hoods."

Blake lowered his head, but when he looked up again his eyes held warning. "You don't understand how things are around here, McGrath." He lowered his voice. "And what those men are like."

"Oh, I have a fairly good idea." Cullen paused. "Do you know who they are?"

Blake shook his head, glancing around them. "I don't. And you'd do well not to do anything to provoke them."

"Provoke them? I was on my own land!"

Casting another glance behind him, Blake drew himself up. "I sold to you before, McGrath, because you had cash."

Cullen narrowed his eyes. "And an Irishman's word to pay isn't good enough?"

"That's not it. I sold to you despite knowing others wouldn't like it. If it were up to me, I'd charge the whole lot of it for you. Gilbert Linden was a good friend, McGrath, and an honorable man. As are you. But I'm only part owner of this place. The lesser partner. And my business associate has made it clear he's not in favor of certain decisions I've made. I'm truly sorry, but I have workers to take care of, too, McGrath. And a family. As well as a business to run."

Cullen eyed the list in his hand. "You're the only lumberyard in town, Mr. Blake." When Blake didn't answer, Cullen returned the list to his pocket. "May I ask, then, is your business partner here? Perhaps I could speak with him?"

"He's not. But it wouldn't do you any good. And if he gets wind that I've sold to you again, even in cash, it won't go well for me. But I want you to know"—he looked as though what he was about to say cost him greatly—"I don't hold to his opinions about people, McGrath. Or to how so many folks feel about foreigners around here. Which is why I'm willing to do what I can for you. In cash."

Able to see the man's situation, Cullen also saw his own, and so much more. "An honorable man, and a friend to us both, once told me that the time is comin' when a man will have to boldly stand for what he believes, or everythin' he holds dear will be taken from him. And from those he loves."

Blake's jaw hardened, the muscles working, and Cullen could see his struggle. And couldn't fault him for it. Wasn't he wrestling with the same thing himself?

A moment passed, and Blake finally shook his head, and Cullen felt his own conviction edge up a notch. He strode to the door.

"McGrath?"

Cullen paused, not turning back.

"What everyone is saying is that your wife . . . she shot the rope clean through. Is that true?"

Cullen turned and read disbelief in Blake's eyes, then saw the old-timer waiting for an answer as well. He felt a surprising smile come to his face. "That she did. And with only one shot fired."

"It weren't his time," the old-timer whispered, fingering the string around his wrist, his eyes surprisingly clear.

Thinking about Ennis and the voice Maggie had heard, Cullen reached for the door. "No, Mr. Collum, it wasn't. Good day, gentlemen."

Cullen stopped briefly by the mercantile for a handful of items Maggie had requested. The outcome of his conversation with Mr. Blake still roiled inside him, as did the counsel from his late father-in-law.

How did a man *boldly* stand for what he believed, when standing so boldly could very well end up costing him the people and property he sought so hard to protect?

Not for the first time, he wished he could have another evening—or a hundred of them—to sit with Gilbert Linden and pose questions, glean from his wisdom.

With no lumber, building the wagons themselves wasn't an option. He could buy the wagons—at much greater cost—if someone would sell them to him. And only if they would allow him to buy them on credit. And he already knew the answers to one, if not both, of those questions.

Every farm in the area was harvesting, or soon would be, so borrowing wagons for the next two to three weeks wasn't an option either. No, they'd simply have to make do with the one wagon they had left. Which meant harvesting the crops would take much longer, and a portion of the produce would overmature or even mold in the fields, which would lower—or negate—the market price.

Just thinking about telling Maggie sent his mood from bad to worse. He recalled on their wedding night how she'd told him she viewed their marriage as a business arrangement. He huffed a breath. Some business partner he'd turned out to be.

He joined the queue to pay for his items, realizing how much Maggie's opinion of him mattered. Far more than she likely knew. A man needed the respect of his wife as much, if not more, than he needed her love.

When he'd left the stable earlier that morning, Maggie and Rachel had been attempting, with meager success, to coax Bourbon Belle into standing. The thoroughbred could barely support her own weight, and when she did, her rear legs seemed ready to buckle.

Witnessing the pain in Maggie's eyes tore at him. And watching what was happening to Belle—this magnificent blood horse struggling to walk when she'd once been the envy of the wind—brought to mind the stallion Ethan had poisoned and what the animal must have suffered. It disturbed him in a way it hadn't before.

Perhaps because it was more real to him now, seeing Belle endure it—and having confessed the truth to Maggie. How could his brother, the defender, the protector, have done such a thing?

After paying for his items, Cullen returned to the wagon and placed the crate in the bed, eager to get home, though not eager to explain to Maggie the outcome of his trip. Imagining the disappointment in her eyes felt like a blunt knife shoved between his ribs.

Riled all over again, he started to climb up to the buckboard when he caught a whiff of tobacco and stilled—instinct yanking hard at his memory.

The scent had a distinctive sweetness to it.

It took him a moment, but he finally placed it. That night, the night Maggie thought she'd seen someone outside, he'd smelled the same scent as he'd walked back to the house.

The sweet-smelling tobacco grew stronger, and he reached into the wagon bed under the guise of looking for something, all while scanning the passersby and reminding himself that plenty of men smoked tobacco, sweet varieties included.

But somewhere among them, Cullen knew, was one man who had come onto his land, onto his front porch, and frightened his wife, a woman who didn't frighten easily.

Cullen's gaze snagged on a man, and held. Some ten paces past the wagon, the fellow seemed to be in a hurry, and hanging from his mouth—a cigar.

Watching his progress, Cullen pretended to check the items in the crate, then followed him down the street, the sweet scent wafting back on occasion.

Cullen hadn't seen the man's face straight on, and he didn't recognize him from behind. He followed the stranger on foot, and after four blocks began to wonder whether he was simply wasting his time.

The fellow paused. Cullen did likewise.

The man took one last puff on the cigar and exhaled, smoke pluming about his head. He searched the street one way, then turned, and Cullen saw his face. He recognized him, he was certain of it. But from where? The way the man stood—cocksure and assuming—seemed a little familiar, as did the way he dropped the cigar and ground the butt out with his foot.

Bonnie Scotland. This was the fool that day with the whip! Cullen struggled to remember his name.

The man continued down the street until he'd nearly reached the corner, then he ducked inside a building. Cullen closed the distance, his familiarity with the area quickly narrowing the likelihood of where the man—Grady Matthews, that was his name—had gone.

So when Cullen found his suspicions confirmed, it wasn't so much a surprise to him as it felt as if a missing link had suddenly found its place.

And his earlier anger felt tame by comparison.

Chapter Thirty-Eight

"Come on, girl," Maggie whispered, gently tugging Belle's lead rein, encouraging her to try to stand. Even Bucket issued a soft whine from where he lay watching a few feet away. Maggie tugged harder. "You can do it."

Lying on her side, Bourbon Belle looked up at her with eyes so dark and full of love and confusion that Maggie had to choke back a sob. She never should have put Kizzy on Belle to begin with. Maybe Cullen was right. Even though she never formally stated that she was training Kizzy to race, in her heart she was.

Anyone else looking on would have assumed that's what she was doing. But except for Uncle Bob, who at Belle Meade would have taken notice of such a thing? As soon as that thought occurred, another followed. General Harding entertained many important visitors. They came and went without Maggie's notice.

But apparently one of them had noticed Belle and Kizzy. What other explanation could there be?

Unless . . . the evil behind Ennis's hanging and setting fire to the cabins and wagons had turned its wandering eye to Belle, too, and did this as yet another way to hurt, destroy, and instill fear.

Not knowing the reason, and with silent tears slipping down her cheeks, Maggie pressed her forehead to Belle's. "I'm so sorry," she whispered, hoping somehow this beautiful, magnificent animal knew how much she had enriched her life. How much Belle had freed her in a way she would have never known without her.

The emotion Maggie sought to hold back moments earlier broke through. She moved to one side, where Belle could see her unobstructed. "Thank you," she said softly, her hand so small against the side of Belle's head, "for letting me soar."

"Is she . . . d-dyin', ma'am?"

Maggie looked up to see Kizzy standing in the stall opening, the girl's lower lip trembling, her face awash in tears.

Wishing she could offer encouragement, Maggie simply lifted a shoulder and let it fall. "I don't know. But I pray not."

Kizzy's breath came staggered. "I's prayin', too, ma'am. We all is."

Maggie held out a hand, and the girl sank down beside her in the hay. Bucket moved closer, silent but attentive.

Kizzy stroked Belle's head. "You's a pretty girl." The child's voice, usually so full of spunk and sass, sounded small and scared. "You's strong too," she whispered, then leaned down and kissed Belle on the nose.

Belle blew out a breath and briefly raised her head, and Kizzy's eyes went big. But not as big as Maggie's felt.

"Go on," Maggie urged. "Keep talking to her."

As Kizzy leaned close, Maggie reached over and got a lump of sugar from the shelf and slipped it into Kizzy's hand. The girl held it to Belle's mouth, but the mare simply snorted in response.

Kizzy wiped off her hand and tried again, this time acting as if she was eating it first before she offered it to Belle. But the outcome was the same.

"I'm back, Missus McGrath."

Maggie peered up at Rachel, who smiled at the scene of Kizzy lying beside Belle in the hay, all cozied up and quiet.

"I see Miss Belle has her a visitor." Rachel laid her basket of herbs aside.

Maggie glanced back. "I think Belle's happy to see her. How is Mr. Ennis?"

Rachel retrieved her mortar and pestle. "That man got a strength in him there ain't hardly a word for. 'Cept maybe *God*."

Maggie smiled. "His wife, Odessia, has that same strength."

"Mmm hmm . . ." Rachel pulled the herbs from her basket and began grinding them in the mortar. "God did right in bringin' them two together."

Maggie studied her grandmother's wedding band on her left hand, and thought of everything that had happened in Cullen's and her lives to bring them together at this point. So many beginnings and endings, too many to count. And was God aware of them all? Did he orchestrate them?

Or did he present different paths, ones he permitted, and then leave room for each person to decide which one to take?

She wasn't certain, but after recent months, she'd begun to think perhaps it was a blending of both.

"I's there when they jumped the broom together."

Rachel's comment pulled Maggie back.

"'Nother lifetime ago now." Rachel sighed. "Long 'fore any of they children come along."

"When I was a girl," Maggie said, speaking softly, "I used to hide down by the cabins and watch when the couples would have the broom ceremony. Mary Harding would come with me too. We grew up wishing we could get married that way. We thought it was so special."

Rachel stilled. "Special?"

Sensing from the woman's tone that she'd said something wrong, Maggie sobered. "Well . . . yes. I suppose it was because the ritual was so different from ours."

Rachel held her stare, then gently laid aside the pestle and mortar and brushed off her hands. "It ain't your fault, ma'am. You was just a girl then. But now that you older, I think it's important you know."

Maggie grew aware of Kizzy listening too.

"Reason why all them couples jumped the broom back then—me and my husband, Ennis and Dessie—we did it 'cuz we wasn't allowed to get married. Only free people get married, Missus McGrath."

The woman's soft smile wasn't the least bit cruel or mocking, quite the opposite. So why did Maggie feel cut open and laid bare?

"Marriage give a couple rights over each other, and them rights ran straight against the way things used to be. So we chose to do somethin' that would show we was as close to married as allowed . . . by the folks who owned us."

Her heart in her throat, Maggie could almost feel the soft flurry against her face as memory upon memory was shuffled and reordered, and as truth shed light on the hushed whispers and giggles of little girls hiding in the woods behind the cabins. The very same woods where Jobah, Micah, and Kizzy had hidden when men came to burn their home and murder their father.

Sometime later Maggie peered through the open door of the stable and knew something was wrong the minute Cullen jumped down from the wagon. His expression was fierce, his demeanor brusque. And the wagon bed . . . empty, but for a small crate.

Leaving Belle to Rachel's care, she joined him outside where Bucket was already greeting him, the collie's tail wagging and tongue lolling. Cullen gave the dog a quick pat, but didn't seem at all eager, Maggie noticed, to meet *her* gaze.

"We'll have to make do with the wagon we've got," he announced. "But we'll manage." With a cursory glance, he grabbed the crate of items from the mercantile and carried it into the house, Bucket romping behind him.

Her stunned silence short-lived, Maggie followed. "I don't understand. I thought you were going to the lumberyard to get supplies to build new wagons."

"I did. Blake said no." He set the crate down on the kitchen table with more force than necessary, and Onnie stared between them. Cullen strode back outside, dog on his heels.

Maggie cast Onnie an apologetic look and hurried to catch up with Cullen. "But why? Were they out of lumber?"

"They have plenty of lumber, Maggie."

"And yet you came home with nothing."

He began unhitching Levi from the wagon, his movements quick and sharp. "As I said, we'll manage."

His ire prodded her own, and Maggie reached for patience worn thin by sleepless nights and concern over Belle. "Papa purchased from Mr. Blake for years. It's not like the man to turn away business."

Cullen said nothing.

She moved a little to one side in order to see him better. "Did you explain to him why you were there? And what happened here the other night?"

"Aye, I did."

"And what did he say?"

He blew out a breath. "The man said he was sorry, Maggie! And then he said no. That's it! Now, I've got work to do."

Taken aback by his sharp tone, Maggie felt her shoulders go stiff. "So how are we going to harvest the crops in time if we don't have but one wagon?"

"As I said, we'll make do. And we'll work as fast as we can."

"Make do?" She came alongside him. "You keep saying that. But if the crops are left too long in the field, they'll begin to rot and—"

"That's why we'll work as fast as we can."

Frustrated and tired, Maggie quickly decided what needed to

be done. "I know Mr. Blake very well, Cullen. I'll go see him first thing tomorrow and—"

"Oh—" His laughter was brittle. "That's just dandy! Exactly what a husband wants . . . for his wife to go beggin' on his behalf."

"Begging?" She looked up at him. "I said nothing about going to beg. All I said was that—"

"He wouldn't lend me credit, Margaret!" The muscles worked in his jaw. "*That's* the reason I came home with no lumber."

"But . . . why are you buying on credit? We've always paid for everything with—"

She read the answer in his eyes, and suddenly it all made sense. The reason he wouldn't look at her. Why he didn't want to answer her questions. He wasn't angry. He was embarrassed. And . . .

They were out of money.

She tried not to let the shock—and disappointment—show in her expression, but knew from the way his eyes darkened that she'd failed miserably. "Cullen, I—"

"I don't want to discuss it now, Maggie."

"But we need to. If Linden Downs is having financial trouble again, then I—"

"We're *not* havin' financial trouble. I just need to get the crops harvested, then we'll be fine."

She started to ask again how he proposed to do that without the proper equipment, when something else occurred to her. "I have some money. Saved from my lessons. It's not much, but it might be enough to convince Mr. Blake to—"

"Sakes alive, woman!" His voice was harsh, but the look in his eyes held entreaty. "Can't you see I don't want you worryin' with this? You've got enough to deal with. I don't want your money either," he added hurriedly. "And I certainly don't want your pity. What I want is for you not to look at me as if I've lost what's most dear in the world to you. That all but slays me."

Tears pooling too close to the surface in recent days threatened to rise, but Maggie kept them at bay.

"I swore to your father to protect you, Maggie. To keep you—and this land—safe. And I aim to keep that promise. On both counts. No matter the cost. I owe him that much, at the very least."

He grasped the lead rein and led Levi into the stable, and Maggie let him go. Moved by what he'd said, one thing in particular stood out above the rest. He'd said it with such conviction and emotion.

She walked back to the house and into the kitchen. Onnie was outside in the back, and Maggie poured herself a glass of water, her hands shaking. She brought it to her lips, but her quickness of breath made it impossible to drink.

She set the glass down.

I owe him that much, he'd said.

Cullen had made a promise to her father. He'd also made a promise in marriage to her, however contractual that promise had been at the time. So which promise was it that held him here . . . that kept him in her bed? Was it one of obligation? Or one of the heart?

She thought they'd been making a home together. A life. One with a difficult and unexpected start, to be sure, but still . . . Her stomach cramped, yet she wasn't hungry. If his promise to her father was what was truly keeping him here . . .

She brought the glass to her lips and drained the contents dry. It scared her how much it hurt to think that *her* heart was the only one wrapped up and bound tight by vows they'd made in haste and with the wrong intention . . . but which, somehow, her heart—and conviction—had come to embrace.

She closed her eyes, a defeated little laugh escaping. A business arrangement. That's what she'd told him their marriage was. And yet now it was so much more. For her anyway.

With a steadying breath, she retraced her steps outside and saw Cullen standing by the well. She strode toward him then slowed. A hat? Since when did Cullen wear a hat?

Then he turned, and she took a hasty step back. It wasn't Cullen. It was another man. A man who looked very much like—

"Ethan?"

She heard Cullen's voice behind her and looked back to see shock on her husband's face reflecting what she felt. Yet his swiftly gave way to an altogether different emotion, one she'd seen on his face before, the night of the fire. And it didn't bode well.

Chapter Thirty-Nine

Cullen could scarcely believe his eyes. "Ethan," he whispered a second time, even as a deep-seated anger, seething and white hot, shot up through him.

Seeing his brother again after all this time, after so much had changed, unleashed a thousand different memories—some happy, some painful, most somewhere in between and sewn so thickly into the fiber of who he was, he'd never be able to extract this man from his life.

And Ethan's smile, same as it ever was. So carefree and jaunty. Cullen strode toward him.

"Cullen, m'boy!" Ethan grinned and welcomed him with outstretched arms. "Look at ya! All filled out and—"

Cullen drove his fist square into Ethan's mouth. His brother's head popped back and the hat went flying. Wide-eyed, Ethan staggered back a step, blinked—once, twice—then landed with a thud on his seat in the dirt. Blood trickled down his chin.

Knowing his fist should be aching from the blow, Cullen barely felt it, his body on fire, shaking with all the rage he'd felt the day he'd buried Moira and Katie in the briny deep. Rage and grief roiled inside him, unlikely partners, each one feeding the other.

Eying him, Ethan wiped the blood at the corner of his mouth. "Now that's a mighty fine welcome for your brother!"

"Get up."

Ethan smiled. "I will not. You'll just wallop me again." He smiled, his teeth tinted red. "I taught you well, lil' brother. That's quite a punch."

"I said . . . *get up*."

Ethan's humor faded, and Cullen readied for what was coming.

Ethan stood and charged. But Cullen moved at the last minute and caught his brother in the rib cage. Cullen heard the air go out from him, but not before a curse did too.

Seeing movement off to his right, Cullen caught sight of Maggie, hand at her throat, her expression stricken.

The blow from behind sent him sprawling, relieving his lungs of air.

"Never turn your back on the other fella, Cullen." Ethan hauled him up by the back of his shirt, wheeled him around, and delivered a well-placed blow to his jaw.

Pain exploded through the right half of Cullen's head. He blinked, the world spinning.

"But maybe," Ethan continued, smiling that smile, "there are a few lessons you still need to learn from your—"

Cullen caught him beneath the chin with his left, then—thinking of that stallion again, and of Belle—he smashed his fist into Ethan's jaw. His brother toppled even as the pain in Cullen's hand sent him to his knees. He'd forgotten his brother's granite jaw.

"And you," Cullen said, working his hand, shaking off the sting, "need to keep your trap shut when you're fightin'. That's always been your weakness."

On his back in the dirt, Ethan laughed, unmoving. And Cullen was glad to see it. He didn't think he could take any more right now.

He looked over at Maggie again, still standing where she'd been, and read concern—and confusion—in her expression. He shouldn't have spoken to her the way he had earlier, and knew an apology was owed as soon as he could get her alone.

He stretched out a hand to his brother, but Ethan eyed him as if not trusting the gesture.

"Truce," Cullen said softly.

Ethan matched his gaze, then accepted, his iron grip every bit as familiar to him as were his brother's features, so similar to his own, or Ethan's wild shock of red hair, which was decidedly not.

Ethan dusted off his britches and exhaled, then shot a look at Maggie. Appreciation—and more than mild interest—warmed his expression, and Maggie frowned and looked away.

"So, lil' brother." Ethan turned back, his eyes bright. "I guess I deserved that beatin' after what I put you through. You and Moira both," he added softly.

Just hearing her name on his brother's lips brought a lump to Cullen's throat.

Ethan looked around. "So where is she? And that sweet little Katie? I have somethin' for 'em both in my pack."

The emotion clenching Cullen's throat made it impossible for him to speak, and he knew better than to look over at Maggie.

Watching Ethan digging into his pack, Cullen closed the distance between them. "Ethan," he said softly.

"It's in here somewheres. I'll find it."

"Moira's gone," Cullen whispered, his eyes burning. "So is Katie."

Slowly Ethan straightened, a tiny doll clutched in his hand. He searched Cullen's expression, his own full of disbelief. "W-what are you sayin' . . . they're *gone*?" He looked around. His gaze settled again on Maggie, this time absent anything but dread, then dragged its way back to Cullen's.

Cullen took a deep breath then gave it gradual release, letting the silence pressing in from all sides whisper the answer to his brother so he wouldn't have to.

Ethan's eyes filled. His lips moved, but no words came.

"They died on the voyage here. On the ship."

The doll Ethan was holding trembled in his grip as tears slipped down his stubbled cheek.

"I looked for you," Cullen continued, "after everythin' that happened. But you were gone. They came after me then, and aimed to lay the blame at my feet." He didn't want to be cruel, but the truth needed to be said.

Ethan shook his head.

"So I couldn't stay. Not knowin' only prison awaited. So Moira and me, we decided to get away before the authorities came."

Ethan held up a trembling hand then looked down at the doll. "I'm sorry, Cullen," he whispered, his rugged shoulders shaking. "I'm *so* sorry." He reached for the well beside him, grabbed hold of the rock wall, and sank down, head in his hands, and wept.

Chapter Forty

So how did you find me?"

At Cullen's question, Maggie sneaked a look across the dinner table, wondering the same thing.

The depth of Ethan's reaction a while earlier when he'd learned about Moira and Katie's passing had been both unexpected and heartbreaking. Such tender emotion for so rugged a man. Especially a man who had done what he did to that stallion.

No matter how she tried not to, every time she looked at Ethan McGrath, that's what she thought about.

When Cullen had made introductions between them, the surprise in Ethan's expression had been revealing. Ethan had taken the opportunity to wash up before dinner, so this was the first opportunity the brothers had to speak to one another without fists flying.

Watching them now, Maggie felt as though she was examining two sides of the same coin.

Hunkered over his plate, Ethan finished chewing a bite of pork roast before answering. "I was at a pub in town last night. Heard about a skirmish at a local farm. Somethin' 'bout the owner bein' Irish, and how someone had stitched together a body and wrote"—Ethan's gaze met Maggie's then quickly fell away. "Wrote somethin' not quite so favorable 'bout an Irishman on it before hangin' it from a tree. And I thought to myself, 'That could be my lil' brother they're talkin' 'bout.' And sure 'nuff—" He speared another bite of meat with his fork and raised it in triumph. "I was right!"

"But how did you know where to look, Ethan? How did you know I was here in Nashville?"

"I didn't. I just kept thinkin' 'bout what Moira told me. 'Bout her wantin' to come to Tennessee."

Cullen's eyes narrowed. "Moira told you about Tennessee?"

"Aye." He skewered a roasted potato. "She said what she'd heard of the place made her think of home, or somethin' close to that."

"That its hills are as green as those of home," Cullen whispered, as though quoting.

Ethan's eyes came open. "Aye! That was it."

Cullen leaned forward. "When did she tell you this?"

Ethan grew quiet, his expression more serious, as if only now detecting the earnestness in his brother's tone. "I think it was the last time I saw her. Right before I left London. For good," he finished, his voice barely audible.

Cullen eased back in his chair, his features steeped in memories another world away. And in another woman. "She must've known that you were leavin'." He gave a humorless laugh. "Moira knew it before I did."

"I never said a thing to her, Cullen. I swear. I wouldn't have involved her."

"You didn't have to. Moira could see into a person. And she read you, Ethan."

"But why would she tell me somethin' like that?"

"Because likely she knew that when you left, they'd come for me. Then we'd have to leave. And even knowin' how angry I was with you, she still wanted you to know where we were goin'."

Ethan didn't speak for the longest time. "You were so angry."

Cullen locked eyes with him. "And I've been angry with you ever since. From the day I walked into the stall and saw that stallion on its side, unable to breathe. Until today when I looked up and there you were."

Seconds passed before Ethan spoke again. "I'm sorry, little brother. If I could take it all back, I would."

"But you can't." Cullen sighed. "And neither can I."

Ethan rested his forearms on the table. "I've learned my lesson, and I aim to do better than I ever have."

"Leavin' me to answer for your actions? Runnin' away from what you did? Then hidin' who knows where for over a year now . . . That's what you call learnin' your lesson?"

Ethan's features clouded. "I wasn't hidin' for the past year, Cullen." His mouth tipped the slightest bit, but the look in his eyes was grave.

"I've been in prison. I got wind they'd arrested you. That's what the papers said, anyway. But it was all a ruse." He exhaled and leaned back in his chair. "But by then, they had me."

Maggie looked over at Cullen and saw the same surprise on his face that she felt.

Cullen stared. "So you came back after all?"

"Aye. I couldn't let you take the blame. And the only reason I'm here now is because I knew every crooked trainer and jockey in London, and I handed 'em all over to the London Thoroughbred Society. Well, at least the worst ones," he added with a wink. "Else they would've let me rot in there for good."

Maggie studied Cullen's contemplative expression, wondering what he was thinking.

Discovering Ethan had served time in prison for what he'd done should have eased her own misgivings about the man, but it didn't. She still didn't trust him. And frankly, didn't want him at Linden Downs.

But Linden Downs wasn't only her home anymore.

She looked between the two of them. So similar, yet so different.

She remembered Cullen telling her how much bigger and stronger Ethan was, but Cullen was every bit as broad-shouldered and muscular as his brother. Perhaps the months Cullen spent working the docks in Brooklyn had evened that score . . . even if other scores seemed yet to be settled between them. The fighting her brothers had done was tame by comparison.

Seeing the emotion on Cullen's face when he'd spoken of Moira and Katie's passing fed her newfound doubts. Of course he'd loved his first wife and their child dearly. He wouldn't be the man she loved now if he hadn't. Still . . .

She wished she knew if he was with her because he truly loved her, or if his affection was rooted in a hastily made promise. Or if it was merely because he'd needed a place to hide.

Her appetite gone, Maggie confined her gaze to her dinner plate.

"How long have you been in town?" Cullen asked.

"I was here several weeks back. But when I couldn't find you, I moved on to other towns. Eventually got into Georgia. Pretty country down there too."

Head bowed, Maggie felt a nudge of realization at Ethan's admission. That day in town, weeks ago, when she thought she'd seen Cullen . . . It must have been Ethan.

As the silence lengthened, so did her discomfort, and she decided to take advantage of the opportunity. "If you'll both excuse me . . ." She pushed back her chair and rose, causing Bucket to rouse from his corner. "I need to check on Bourbon Belle."

Cullen stood, and Ethan quickly followed suit.

Ethan cleared his throat. "Even though I don't know what kind of creature belongs to such a name, I like it, Mrs. McGrath."

Maggie's smile came from obligation. "Bourbon Belle is my horse, Mr. McGrath. She's a thoroughbred." She could feel Cullen's stare. "And she was poisoned four nights ago."

Every trace of levity slid from Ethan McGrath's face, and the silence from a moment earlier couldn't begin to compare to the heaviness blanketing the room.

"And whoever it was," Cullen added with a weight in his voice, "used white snakeroot."

"You know who did it . . . don't you? Who poisoned your wife's horse. Who started the fire, and tried to kill that man."

Cullen looked over at his brother sitting beside him on the darkened porch, the night quiet around them, the moon slowly retreating behind the clouds. "I have a fairly decent notion," he answered, reaching down and rubbing Bucket, who was sprawled beside him.

Ethan's brief laugh was telling. "For you to say somethin' like that, you've got more than a decent notion, brother." He leaned forward in the rocker, his voice lowering. "Tell me, and I'll pay them a visit for you. I'll pass along your desire that they never set foot on Linden Downs again."

"No." Cullen shook his head.

"But you said yourself . . . these men, they won't be givin' up 'til they've gotten their way."

"It's not as simple as payin' someone a visit anymore, Ethan. Not when you have people you're responsible for, and when those people can be hurt because of somethin' you've done. Come against you or me"—he exhaled—"and we can hold our own. But my workers, my *wife* . . ." He looked toward the stable, where Maggie and Rachel were caring for Belle. "I can't take care of situations the way you and I used to."

So many opinions he'd held earlier in life weren't so steadfast anymore. Changes were going on inside him that he didn't understand, nor could he ignore them.

Cullen rose and walked to the railing, pausing close to where he'd stood with Gilbert Linden that first afternoon. How long ago that day seemed now, yet how deep a love for the man's land—and his daughter—had taken root inside him.

"I can be civil, you know," Ethan said, joining him at the rail.

Cullen laughed. "Your definition of civility and mine have always stood a bit at odds. And I'm guessin' that after this past year, your definition has changed yet again."

Ethan shrugged in a way that usually accompanied a wry grin, but the truth of his features was lost to the shadows.

A breeze carrying a surprising touch of cool even for September stirred the night air and shushed the limbs of nearby maple and oak, causing their leaves to tremble. Bucket stood and stretched, then trotted over and settled by Cullen, heaving a sigh.

"Was your time in there . . . hard?" Cullen asked softly.

"Aye, it was. I've done a lot of things in my life, Cullen, but spendin' time in prison was somethin' I'd not wagered on doin'. But what I did was wrong, and I know it. I knew it then too. But—"

"You had men after you."

"Aye . . ." Ethan looked away. "And I had a debt I couldn't begin to pay."

Cullen turned to him and waited for his brother to meet his gaze. "But we made good money, Ethan. They paid us well, those wealthy London lords with their blood horses and grand estates soaked in ancestral money. The extra they slipped us on winnin' days alone was more than our own da made in two years of sproutin' potatoes."

"And you squirreled away every bit of yours. Didn't you, lil' brother?"

A thread of sarcasm weighted Ethan's tone, something that, when they were younger, had made Cullen hesitant to cross him. Now it only made him realize how different their choices had been in recent years.

"Aye, I did," Cullen answered. "Every penny. Or at least every penny Moira and I didn't need to keep the cupboards stocked."

Wordless, Ethan stared into the night, the hum of crickets softening the harshness of the silence.

Even so, the ease between them warred with the tension, and Cullen realized his love for his older brother—and his gratitude for what Ethan had done for him—had sought, time and again, to lessen the distance between the choices they'd made. But even love's tendency to be blind couldn't set things to right that were blatantly wrong.

Cullen gripped the porch rail before him. "When did it start?"

"The gamblin'?" Ethan asked.

Cullen nodded.

"Four years back, or thereabouts. Came so natural to me." He laughed. "But I always was more like our da than you. You got Ma's strength and smarts. Me, I got Da's bent toward weakness and discontent."

"That's not true. You're a—" What he'd started to say—*a good man*—he couldn't, not knowing what he knew. "You were a good brother to me."

"Cullen." Ethan's voice held authority. "I *am* our da. I gambled away a small fortune. I wasted so many years lovin' women while half the time I didn't even know their names, much less remember bein' in their beds. I drank 'til I couldn't remember where I was, much less who I was. Because the more I saw him in me, the more I ran. And the more I ran, the more I realized I couldn't get away from it." Ethan bowed his head. "It felt as if the part of me that somehow knew better than to do those things did them anyway. And what I knew I should do, I didn't. Instead, I became everything I had hated about him. Only now I hated it in myself too."

Some distance away, the lonely howl of a wolf cut through the quiet, reminding the night of a far less gentle side.

As Ethan's confession settled inside Cullen, he felt an inexplicable familiarity about it—as well as an equally overwhelming love for his brother.

"You're not alone in your struggles, Ethan. Nor in hatin' parts of yourself. I still fight the temper I learned from our da, too, among other even less desirable traits. But I've learned somethin' in the past few months, somethin' the man who sold me this land taught me."

"Margaret's father?"

Cullen nodded. "Part of bein' able to move on is found in lettin' go of the past. And for us, that means lettin' go of the hate we had for our father. It's not hurtin' him anymore. He's gone. It's only hurtin' you and me . . . when we hang onto it."

Pale yellow lamplight illuminated the open door to the stable, and Cullen recognized Maggie's slender frame as she walked by. What he wouldn't give to see Bourbon Belle whole again. Odd, when he thought about it, considering he'd been so against Maggie's desire to race the mare.

Which he still was. That hadn't changed.

But seeing Maggie so burdened with concern for the thoroughbred wore on him. As did their cross exchange earlier in the day concerning the wagons and harvest.

He gazed out over the sleeping fields ready for reaping and saw, again, the image of Grady Matthews slipping into Stephen Drake's office. Drake was behind what had happened the other night, including Belle's poisoning. Cullen knew it, even if he didn't have evidence.

After all, a sweet-smelling cigar wasn't exactly proof. So why did Ethan's suggestion of paying someone a visit still hold appeal?

"She doesn't like me, you know," Ethan said, frustration in his voice.

Seeing Ethan staring in the same direction he was, Cullen smiled, not surprised his brother had picked up on Maggie's less than exuberant welcome. "She doesn't know you well enough yet to know she doesn't like you. She simply doesn't like what you did. And I can't say I blame her. Can you?"

Ethan said nothing, only stared at him, then strode into the house.

⁂

Maggie stirred, awakened by a shift of weight on the mattress. She opened her eyes and was surprised to see Cullen already up, and without the faintest hint of light in the sky. Her first thought went to Belle, and she pushed herself up.

"Is everything all right?" she whispered, feeling a sinking inside her. She should have stayed in the stable last night, but Rachel had insisted she rest.

"Everything is fine," Cullen assured her softly, gesturing. "Go back to sleep. I'm sorry I awakened you."

Chilled by the cool morning air, she took advantage of the warmth he'd left behind in the bed and huddled deeper into it. Rachel was right. She *was* weary and, based on Belle's lack of progress in the last four days, was readying herself for the worst.

She watched Cullen dress in the dark. He pulled on his trousers and reached for his shirt in the wardrobe. She knew the future of Linden Downs weighed on him just as Belle's future weighed on her, if not more so. Because if they lost Linden Downs, it wouldn't be only the two of them losing their home. So many other lives were involved now.

And here in the darkness before the dawn, the time that had held some of the loneliest moments in her life, hope struggled to find a foothold.

Wanting to ask him a question, she hesitated, remembering his frustration with her yesterday. Yet her need to know outweighed the possibility of that recurrence. "So . . . do you know yet when you'll begin harvesting?"

"Today."

She waited, wanting him to say more. But after a full minute had passed, she assumed that was all.

"You'll harvest with one wagon?" She tried for a blameless tone, with only marginal success.

"We'll harvest with what we have, Maggie."

Hearing the curtness in his voice, she knew she'd gotten all the information she was going to get on that subject for now.

He sat on the edge of the bed and tugged on his boots.

"Cullen?" she whispered.

"Aye?" he answered, focused on his task.

"How long is Ethan planning to visit?"

He stilled, and she sensed he'd seen through her not-so-subtle phrasing of the question—and part of her was ashamed. After all, Ethan was his brother.

She'd lain in bed last night, door open, listening to the low murmur of their voices drifting up the stairs and wishing she could hear more. It was silly, but she was almost jealous of their history together and how interwoven their memories were.

Cullen stood. "He asked me last night how long he could stay."

Maggie was grateful the darkness masked her chagrin. "And . . . what did you tell him?"

An endless pause filled the space.

"I told him I'd have to discuss it with you. After all . . . Linden Downs is *our* home, Maggie."

Grateful, she hugged her pillow tight, hoping he wouldn't pursue the discussion now, yet already knowing what her vote would be. But she also knew her vote would come at a cost.

Then again, so would having Ethan McGrath live with them.

"Go back to sleep," Cullen said quietly as he crossed to the door. "I'll be back in a while."

She heard Bucket stir at the foot of the bed, then the sharp snap of Cullen's fingers.

"Stay, boy."

"But . . . where are you going?" *And without Bucket.*

"I have business in town. I'll be back soon." He closed the bedroom door behind him before she could ask again.

Chapter Forty-One

The doorknob rattled, followed by a telling creak, but Cullen didn't move from where he sat in the corner, unseen, in the darkness. The shadowed figure closed the door, crossed the office to the desk, and dropped a briefcase unceremoniously on top. Then one by one, the man lifted each of the window shades, allowing entrance to a demanding sun.

"A little late comin' in this mornin', wouldn't you say, Mr. Drake?"

Stephen Drake whirled, a startled expression contorting his florid face, a reaction Cullen enjoyed perhaps a little too much.

Drake quickly recovered. "Mr. McGrath . . ." Shaking his head, he smiled and made a *tsking* sound. "Forced entry into a place of business. Not unexpected from your kind. But still, against the law." Drake crossed to the desk, opened a side drawer, and pulled out a pistol, then aimed it square at Cullen's chest.

Cullen stood. "Call for the authorities. They won't find a busted lock or jimmied window anywhere. Just a man who arrived a bit early to speak to the Tax and Title Office Manager about his land, and who found a door that opened with very little resistance."

Cullen took a step toward him, and Drake cocked the gun.

"You should have left town when I told you to, McGrath."

"And you should do a better job of hidin' your gun."

A shadow crossed Drake's face. He uncocked the pistol and checked the chamber.

It was Cullen's turn to smile. "You'll find the bullets. Eventually."

"My men will—"

"Will be back in about an hour, at least I believe that's the order you gave them a moment ago." Cullen nodded toward the front window, through which voices could be heard even now. "Seems nothin's very private these days."

"I don't know what you hope to gain by coming here, McGrath. But whatever it is, you won't get it. And I'm not afraid of you." He laid the gun aside as if proving his point.

"I would hope you're not. After all, we're goin' to be neighbors. For a very long time."

Drake leveled a stare. "I seriously doubt that."

His patience thinning, Cullen crossed the room, knowing how differently this "meeting" would be going right now if Ethan had come in his place, as his brother had begged to do. "I'm goin' to speak slowly for you, Drake, so you'll be sure to understand. At times you Southern men seem to be weak in your listenin' skills, among others." All levity drained from him. "I'm here to give you fair warnin'. I know it was you and your men who visited my farm a few nights back."

"You have no proof of that."

"You're right, I don't. But I've got somethin' better. Two things, actually. I've got my gut. And my gut tells me you're rotten through and through. I smelled the putridness on you the first time we met. And second, I've got my land. Paid for outright, deeded to me. And there's nothin' you can ever do about that."

Drake smirked, his eyes going dark. "You ignorant Irish dirt grubber. You cannot begin to comprehend who I am or what power I have in this town. In this state!"

"That may be true, but whatever power you may have, along with the other cowards runnin' 'round at night in those fancy white hoods, I'm here to tell you that if you step foot on my land again with the intention of doin' harm, I'll show you no mercy. Same as you showed Mr. Ennis."

The heat in Drake's features cooled by a degree. "I don't know what you're talking about."

Desperately wanting to put his fist through the man's face, Cullen struggled to hold his temper in check. "Consider you and your men warned, Mr. Drake. You come onto my land again, you come in daylight, on a horse, straight up my drive. You come in the dark of night, you die."

"Do you know what men in this town would do to you if you killed me?"

"To know you're dead, they'll have to find your body. And hear me well, Drake . . . I won't be wastin' good rope for the likes of you."

Cullen got as far as the door.

"Funny how you think you know people. Take Margaret Linden, for instance. I've known her all my life. Pretty enough as a girl. But once she blossomed into womanhood . . ." Drake whistled low. "Even more beautiful, wouldn't you say?"

Cullen's grip tightened on the doorknob.

"Oh, I knew her father had a certain . . . softness for Negroes." Drake laughed softly. "But until you came to town, I'd never pegged pretty little Maggie as being a nig—"

The words scarcely left Drake's tongue before Cullen lifted him by the throat and shoved him against the wall. For the first time Cullen glimpsed a glimmer of fear in the man's eyes. He tightened his grip, and Drake's eyes widened. Why was it some men only understood force?

Tasting the bitterness in his mouth and seeing his whitening knuckles around Drake's throat, Cullen eased his grip, then let go.

Drake slumped against the wall, his breath coming hard. "You'll regret this . . . McGrath. I give you . . . my word."

Cullen looked at him. "I've seen you up close, Drake. You're not nearly as good a liar as you think you are. And your word is worth nothin'." He strode to the door. "Now stay off my land."

A blistering sun beat down on the fields, belying the earlier cool, and Cullen wiped his brow with his shirt sleeve. Bucket lay panting beneath the shade of the wagon, attempting to stay cool. At this rate they'd never get the crops harvested and to market, much less get it done before the quality of the yield began to suffer.

Even with everyone helping to pick the corn, transporting each load from the field to the barn with only one wagon took too long. He shielded his eyes and scanned the gentle rise and fall of green in all directions.

To have come this far only to fail now seemed even worse than if the crops hadn't come in well at all.

It was near sundown by the time the wagon returned with the last load of the day, and when Cullen saw for himself how little they had stored in the barn, he wished he *had* put his fist through Stephen Drake's face that morning.

But when he spotted Maggie walking toward him from the stable, tears streaming down her face, an even greater depth of disappointment nearly drove him to his knees.

Then she smiled—*smiled*—and the wave of dread building inside him lost its momentum, rendered powerless in the wake of fresh hope.

"Come and see," she whispered, voice shaky. She took hold of his hand. "I started to send word to the fields an hour ago, but I wanted to show you in person."

He grasped her hand and followed, Bucket trailing behind, tail wagging. And he felt an answer to her prayer—and his—coming to fruition, even if another was not.

He entered the stable and saw Belle standing in her stall, regal and beautiful, eyes bright and tail swishing, and he knew that even if that mare never ran again, she would always serve as a reminder for him to never give up.

Maggie brought her face close to Belle's and kissed the horse on the bridge of her nose. Belle whinnied and tossed her head, causing Maggie to stagger backward a step.

Instinctively Cullen reached to steady her, letting his hand linger at the small of her back.

"She's going to pull through," Maggie whispered, her tone rich with hope and love.

But Cullen looked into the thoroughbred's large, dark eyes and saw the heart of a champion, and knew—with a quandary of emotion—that Bourbon Belle was going to do a lot more than simply pull through.

Question was . . . what would he do then? Because he knew his wife. And he also knew the dream she'd supposedly given up still beat steady and strong inside her, whether she fully realized it or not.

Chapter Forty-Two

Two mornings later Maggie rose with the sun and felt the lingering sting of grateful tears when she saw Belle waiting and watching for her at the stall door.

"Morning, pretty girl," she cooed softly.

With fluid strokes she ran the curry brush over Belle's coat, treasuring each familiar pass.

Rachel Norris had returned to Belle Meade last evening, and Maggie was certain Bourbon Belle wouldn't have made it without the woman's healing qualities. After harvest was finished, and if finances allowed, Maggie planned on speaking with Cullen to see if they couldn't do more for Rachel than the modest amount the woman had charged.

Outside, the workers gathered for another day of harvest, young and old doing their part. Maggie heard Cullen's voice over the throng, as well as Bucket's gleeful bark.

"Mrs. McGrath?"

She turned and looked behind her. "Mr. McGrath . . ." She tried to resist the frown that rose every time Cullen's brother came near.

He paused outside the stall. "Is it all right with you that I'm here?" A tentative smile touched his mouth. "Cullen told me about her progress, but I been wantin' to see it for myself. If you don't mind."

Feeling pride akin to a first-time mother's—but protectiveness, too, Maggie stepped aside and gestured an invitation. She was surprised it had taken Ethan this long to work up the courage to visit the stable. The man asked after Belle at least twice a day.

Still, it wasn't as though she'd encouraged him to come.

Ethan stepped inside the stall, his timidity making him appear even larger somehow. Belle turned her head to eye him, and Maggie watched Belle, knowing horses were excellent judges of character.

Ethan held out his hand and the mare sniffed it then licked his palm.

Cullen had told her last night as they lay in bed that Ethan was doing the work of nearly three men, carrying bags of corn and bundles of tobacco on foot from the farthest fields back to the barn. And from what she'd seen herself, the workers seemed to like Ethan as much as they did Cullen.

And she had yet to see anyone Ethan couldn't talk to. In that regard, as in so many others, the brothers were much alike.

"She's a beauty, Mrs. McGrath."

"Thank you. Yes, she is."

Cullen hadn't yet broached the subject of whether she was in favor of his brother living here indefinitely, and she hadn't brought it up either. Her vote was the same as it had always been. At least on most days.

"I'm so glad she's better," he said softly, his voice tinged with emotion. He looked at Maggie. "I'm sorry for what I did. In London, I mean. It's important to me that you know that."

Maggie studied him. "Thank you, Mr. McGrath."

He turned to leave, then paused. "Do you think—"

Maggie tensed, hoping he wouldn't ask what she thought he was going to ask.

"—you might consider us goin' by our Christian names with each other? Seein' as we're family and all?"

Witnessing his gentleness with Belle and the mare's obvious calm with him, Maggie felt a slight softening toward him. "I believe we could do that . . . Ethan."

The man beamed. "Thank you . . . Margaret."

He took his leave, and a handful of minutes later, Maggie heard a distant hum outside. If she hadn't known better, she might have thought it was street traffic. She strode to the door of the stable and saw a group of workers staring down the road. She spotted Cullen among them and moved closer to see what they were watching when a swell of cheers arose.

Coming up the drive was General William Giles Harding himself, followed by four . . . no, five . . . no, *six* wagons.

General Harding guided his black stallion to where Cullen stood. "Mr. McGrath, I hear you're in need of wagons for harvest, sir. And though this doesn't begin to settle the debt I owe you for Bonnie Scotland, it's my hope that you'll accept the loan of these wagons and consider them yours until such time as you can replace them."

Maggie knew her husband well, and even though Cullen shook the general's hand and expressed his hearty thanks, she knew the loan of these conveyances from General Harding of Belle Meade Plantation himself meant more to Cullen than he let on.

Because with them, Linden Downs had a fighting chance again.

"Mrs. McGrath." General Harding directed his attention to her. "My daughter tells me that Bourbon Belle is doing much better now."

"She is, sir."

"Glad to hear it. By chance will you be running her in the Peyton Stakes? And before you answer, my hope is that you will. And I'm certain, if Fortune had a voice, she would say the same."

Feeling Cullen's gaze, Maggie smiled up at Mary's father. "I'm afraid not, General. I've decided—" She caught herself. "My husband and I have decided not to race Bourbon Belle again." Her smile faltered the tiniest bit. "I believe that's for the best."

General Harding eyed her, and though the man offered no verbal contradiction, she knew he did not agree.

❧

Mid-September brought cooler mornings and the promise of approaching fall, even as a persistent summer still grappled to maintain its hold. But with onset of evening, when the light was nearly spent and a watermark of color framed the hills to the west, the northerly breeze tipped its hand to the coming victor.

Cullen stood on the front porch appreciating the night sky, hair still damp from washing, a satisfying fatigue in his back and shoulder muscles. He'd enjoyed what was likely his last trip to the creek, as the weather would soon be too cool for bathing there. He briefly leaned down and rubbed Bucket, the dog still panting from their game of fetch on the way back.

Gilbert Linden had sorely spoiled this dog, embarrassingly so. And Cullen was determined to follow in the man's footsteps.

Thinking of Mr. Linden stirred a sense of gratitude inside him, and he closed his eyes for a moment, imagining the man still standing there beside him, staring out across the land he'd loved.

Thank you, sir . . .

The silent utterance left him and lifted upward. How far a journey it had, he didn't know. Or when it would get there. Or if. But the magnitude of the gift he'd been given wouldn't let him keep silent.

Cullen peered upward, the moon a pale thumbnail against the evening sky, and he thought of another gift, a far more precious one. One that Mr. Linden was also responsible for having given him. Or at least, for having made the introduction.

Thank you too . . . Sir.

Father God is how Mr. Linden had always addressed the Almighty in prayer, but the term *father* didn't feel quite right to Cullen. So he hoped *Sir* was acceptable, at least for now.

Five days into harvest with an additional six wagons, and the future of Linden Downs looked considerably brighter. Between the rain-logged fields and beginning the reaping with only one wagon, they'd lost valuable time. But they would make it up in the next three weeks, Cullen was determined.

As was Ennis, as the foreman had told him during Cullen's recent visit to check his progress. Cullen missed Ennis's leadership in the fields, and their friendly banter in general.

Bourbon Belle's future also appeared brighter. Each day the thoroughbred seemed to gain more strength and vitality, as did the mare's lovely mistress.

Cullen scanned the cloudless purple gray overhead and exhaled a satisfied breath.

"That was a deep sigh."

Surprised at the voice, Cullen felt Maggie's arms come around his waist from behind.

He turned to face her and nuzzled her neck.

Chuckling, she playfully pushed him away. "Your hair is still wet!"

He laughed and pulled her to him again, the softness of her curves awakening his desire. He kissed her, and she tilted her head to better meet his mouth. Fatigue forgotten, Cullen lifted her by the waist and her arms came around his neck. She gave a soft murmur. Then the creak of the front door sounded.

Ethan stepped out and, seeing them, smiled. But Maggie stiffened and indicated for Cullen to set her down. He did so, and she hastily put distance between them. Cullen slipped her a wink, but her serious expression said she didn't find it amusing.

He'd told her before that Ethan didn't care, but that hadn't altered her opinion. Miss Onnie occasionally catching them in a kiss was apparently one thing; Ethan seeing them was another.

But Cullen had a feeling that Maggie's opinion of his brother went far deeper than mere self-consciousness.

Ethan shot him a look. "Miss Onnie has dinner 'bout ready."

"Thank you, Ethan." Maggie smoothed the front of her dress and went on inside.

"If you two have any appetite left," Ethan finished beneath his breath.

Cullen smiled at his brother's comment, even though he knew Maggie's aloofness bothered Ethan.

Ethan nodded in the direction Maggie had gone. "I'm tellin' you, Cullen, your wife just isn't warmin' up to me."

"She will. Give her time."

"Maybe I need to be movin' on, like I told you before."

Cullen gripped his older brother by the shoulder, feeling more like the elder lately than the younger. "No, Ethan. Your place is here with us, I know it. The Almighty led you here, don't you see that?"

"The Almighty?" Ethan gave him a funny look. "The two of you are on regular speakin' terms now, are you?"

Cullen laughed and held the door open, casting a last glance out across the fields. "Let's just say I recently learned that there's always a conversation goin' on. It's just me who's sometimes stubborn of hearin'."

That night Cullen awakened from a dream, the sounds still so vivid within him—the drum of rain on an angry ocean and the clap of waves as they beat against the ship's hull.

He shook his head to clear the cobwebs of sleep, his mind willing but his body lagging behind. He looked beside him at Maggie, the echoing drumroll of rain from his dream drowning out her soft breaths. She began to stir, and he realized . . .

He was either still in his dream, or—

Cullen bolted from bed and raced to the open window. The plank wood floor slippery beneath his bare feet, he pushed back the rain-soaked curtains as a flash of lightning inflicted a jagged scar across the night sky. Thunder rolled overhead—the clap of waves against the ship's hull from his dream—and a torrent of hail beat down from the heavens like a drum.

Chapter FORTY-THREE

Cullen reined Levi in at the crest of the hill and struggled to come to grips with the scene around him. Laid bare by morning light, the fields looked more like those belonging to winter than summer, and could almost be described as beautiful—if they didn't hold such devastation.

Bruised, battered, and broken, crops that had rivaled his height yesterday were flattened. Once proud stalks of corn now bent and leaning, others snapped clean in two, dotted the landscape as far as he could see, the ears themselves buried in patchwork blankets of hail.

He dismounted and picked up a piece of ice the size of a hen's egg. Two inches in circumference at least, and bitter cold when gripped tightly in his palm. A moment passed, and water leaked from his fist as his fingers and hand started to go numb.

He opened his fist again to find the ball of ice still hard as a rock, for the most part stubbornly unchanged.

From somewhere behind him came the telling plod of hooves. A moment later Ethan appeared beside him.

"I'm so sorry, Cullen. I-I've never seen anythin' like this in my life." Ethan placed a hand aside his head, as if viewing the aftermath was causing him a physical ache. "It's like the hand o' God reached down to smite the land."

Cullen lifted his gaze from the fields and peered up into the azure blue stretching in all directions above him, and felt so small and insignificant by comparison. So much more so than he'd felt yesterday when the financial future of Linden Downs had been secure.

In a matter of minutes, what had taken weeks and months to nurture into growth had been snuffed out like a bothersome wick. He didn't have to put pen to paper to know how damaging this would be to the farm.

And to his wife.

∽

"Have you lost your mind, woman?"

Seeing how angry Cullen was, Maggie steeled herself, her rationale at the ready. "Cullen, listen to me." Seated in the chair opposite his by the hearth, she leaned forward. "I've been thinking about this for several days now. Long before the hailstorm yesterday. I know I said I'd given up on the idea, and I truly thought I had. But . . . with everything that's happened, it makes perfect sense."

"Not to anyone with half a brain. Nay—" He shook his head. "I'll not entertain this idea from you, Maggie. Not now. Not *ever*."

"But, Cullen, you should see Belle run. She's not as fast as she used to be yet, but she will be. I know it. Even Uncle Bob says that—"

He exhaled. "Please, Maggie, let's not—"

"—he says he believes she'll be running like the wind in no time."

"Listen to me . . ." Cullen knelt by her chair and gripped her gently by the shoulders. "Don't you understand . . . You mean the world to me, woman. And I cannot and will not allow you to race Belle yourself. The very idea of a grown woman bein' out there—"

"But this is our chance, Cullen. Our crops are gone. You said yourself last night that you don't know how we'll be able to keep paying all the workers, much less keep the farm. If we race, and we win—"

He shook his head, and she cradled his face in her hands.

"—then we will have secured Linden Downs for years to come. And if we don't win, then—" She shrugged. "We're no worse off than we were before."

"That's not true, Maggie. And I'm not ever goin' to say yes to this, so what I'm sayin' now is just for the sake of argument. What if somethin' *were* to happen to you as you raced? Accidents happen all the time on the track. What then?" He searched her eyes. "What would I do? I don't think—" He took a breath, his grip tightening on her shoulders, but not enough to hurt, and his voice dropped to a whisper. "I don't think I could handle losin' everythin' I hold dear a second time."

Feeling a stinging behind her eyes, Maggie kissed him. "Nothing is going to happen to me, Cullen."

"You're right, love. Because you're not racin' Belle at the Peyton Stakes."

A knock sounded on the front door, and Cullen went to answer it.

Maggie recognized Dr. Daniels's voice and heard Cullen inviting him in. It had slipped her mind that he'd arranged for the physician to stop by and check on Ennis and the other two men who had been beaten. She rose to welcome the doctor, and her world swam. She quickly reached behind her for the chair and sat back down.

"Maggie?" Cullen was beside her in a heartbeat. "Are you all right?"

"I'm fine." She attempted a lighthearted laugh, which would have sounded more convincing if the room had ceased its swirling.

Dr. Daniels knelt beside her and pressed two fingers against the underside of her wrist. "Your pulse is quite rapid, Mrs. McGrath."

Maggie read concern in Cullen's expression and attempted to give him a reassuring look.

"I assure you, Dr. Daniels. I'm quite well."

"And I believe you're well, too, Mrs. McGrath. But just the same, I'd like to make certain of it." The doctor rose. "So if you'll allow me to examine you, we can ascertain your wellness together."

Chapter Forty-Four

Cullen paced outside the bedroom, all efforts to listen through the closed door having failed. Then he heard Dr. Daniels's sober voice.

"You may come in now, Mr. McGrath."

Hand on the latch, Cullen hesitated, then gave it a push, his heart racing as if he'd run to the bluff and back. Maggie was seated on the edge of the bed, her head bowed, and Cullen's heart went to his knees.

Then she looked up.

Her hand moved to her midsection and she smiled, and Cullen felt the dread that had tightened his chest fall away. He looked to the doctor to be sure, and when Daniels gave a single nod, Cullen went to Maggie, knelt beside the bed, and lifted her hand to his lips.

"Oh, love . . ." he whispered.

"I believe I'll give you two a moment together, Mr. and Mrs. McGrath, and see you downstairs."

Cullen smiled, his gaze locked with Maggie's. "Thank you, Dr. Daniels. We're much obliged to you, sir."

The door creaked.

"And may I say," the doctor added, "how very happy I am for you both."

The latch clicked, and Maggie's smile trembled. Cullen leaned in and kissed the place where her hand had just rested, the place where their precious child—he could scarcely believe it, even now—was safely nestled.

Maggie slipped her arms around his neck. He drew her up and held her, her head cradled against his chest, her arms tight around him, and he realized yet again that as long as he had those he loved, he had everything. All else could—and would—come and go. But this . . .

He kissed the crown of her head and felt her sigh against him. *Thank you, Lord.*

This was everything.

Two months. That's how far along Dr. Daniels had estimated she was with the baby yesterday. Maggie paused just inside the stable and gently pressed her hand against her abdomen.

Cullen's child.

Every time she thought about it, it felt as though someone had lit a match inside her. Even if it did mean surrendering any possibility of riding Belle in the Peyton Stakes. Dr. Daniels had been quite clear in his instructions as he'd left the house yesterday, and Cullen had been relieved to hear them.

"Mrs. McGrath, while I'm not an old-school physician who implores confinement and bed rest for a woman in your condition, I do urge you to use good sense. Continuing your riding lessons is fine. However, *your* riding is not."

She continued on to Belle's stall, surprised when she saw Kizzy inside, standing on a stool, rubbing Belle down with the curry brush.

"Good morning." Maggie let herself in.

"Mornin', Missus McGrath." The girl didn't look up. In fact, she didn't look in Maggie's direction at all. She just kept brushing short, smooth strokes along Belle's side.

What was the child up to?

Then Maggie saw it. The pile of pennies on the shelf. And her heart clenched tight.

"Kizzy," she said softly, and tried to take the brush from her hand.

"No, ma'am!" The girl jerked back. "I wanna do it. I—" Her voice caught. She gave a little gasp as she turned. "I do whatever you say, ma'am. You just gotta keep teachin' me. You done *said* you'd teach me."

Seeing the girl's tears encouraged Maggie's own. "Kizzy, I wish I could. More than you realize. But—"

"I can get more money. I heard Papa say the boss done lost lots of it. I can find me a job, and then give you—"

"Oh sweetheart, it's not about the money. You don't have to pay me anything."

Big tears rolled down the girl's cheeks. "Then why ain't you teachin' me no more? I see Belle runnin' in the fields again. I know she gettin' better." She paused. "Is you gonna be teachin' them other girls still?"

Maggie hesitated, then nodded. "But that's different, Kizzy."

The girl's eyes darkened. "I ain't no different from them."

"Oh yes you are, Kizzy. You're a born rider. God gave you a gift. Those other girls could spend a lifetime learning how to ride, and they would never ride like you do."

The child sniffed and said nothing. Then her tiny hand went to her hip. "I wanna ride Belle in that race comin' up, ma'am. She and me can win. I know we can."

Maggie shook her head. "There are people . . . bad people who might hurt you if you rode in that race."

Kizzy hopped off the stool. "I ain't afraid of 'em."

Maggie touched the tip of the girl's chin. "No," she whispered, thinking about the scar on Ennis's neck. "But I'm afraid for you. So there will be no race for you. Or Belle."

Cullen held out the potato, and Maggie could scarcely believe what he'd just told her.

"This is how it came out of the ground?" she asked.

"Well, it was a little dirtier, but aye." His mouth tipped in a smile.

She took the potato and studied it—nary a blemish or bad spot on it. She eased down into one of the rockers on the porch. "They're all like this?"

"So far. We're harvestin' them right now."

"So the man in town was right."

"Aye. As was your father."

Loving Cullen for crediting Papa, she looked up again. "So what does this mean?"

He claimed the rocker beside her, and Bucket chose a spot between them. "It means that while we lost the corn, the tobacco, and most of the cotton, we do have potatoes. And they're the finest potatoes in all of Nashville. Maybe even Tennessee. Which will surely count for somethin' at market." He laughed softly.

"What's so funny?"

He took the potato and turned it in his hand. "An Irishman havin' the best potatoes."

He took hold of her hand, and she covered his.

For all the disappointment in recent days, there had been far more joy. She rested her hand on her midsection. For the time being, she and Cullen had agreed to keep the news of the baby to themselves. She couldn't help but wonder at the events of recent days, and at how—even in the face of such misfortune, there was so much good, so much to look forward to. Regardless of her not racing Bourbon Belle again.

But Kizzy . . .

The girl had been brokenhearted after their conversation yesterday, which Maggie understood only too well.

Cullen leaned forward in the rocker, and Maggie followed his line of sight to see a wagon coming up the road. Not the main road to the house, but the road coming from the workers' cabins.

Seated on the buckboard were Cletus and Odessia, which was enough to pique Maggie's curiosity. But when she spotted Ennis in the back of the wagon on a makeshift bed, that brought her out of her chair. Cullen too.

They met the wagon as it pulled up, and Cletus nodded.

"Is everythin' all right?" Cullen asked.

Odessia climbed down, with Cullen's assistance.

"My husband and I would like a word with you, sir. You, too, ma'am."

Cullen shook Ennis's offered hand. "We would've come down if you'd asked."

Sweat dotted Ennis's brow, and he mopped at it with his kerchief. "I know that, sir, but I ain't wantin' to take the chance that Kizzy'll hear what I got to say. That girl . . ." He smiled. "Once she hears you say somethin', even if you's just talkin' things through, she take it as a vow."

Maggie felt her face go warm.

Wincing, Ennis shifted on the pallet. "I guess I best come right out and say my piece."

Cullen nodded encouragement.

"I know your wife done told my daughter there ain't gonna be no more teachin' and no racin'. But my wife and I talked things through real good, and . . . Well, sir, we here to ask if your wife would keep teachin' our daughter. And then if"—Ennis's focus shifted to Maggie—"if she be good enough, ma'am, if you might put her in that race. Ridin' Miss Bourbon Belle."

"No," Cullen said almost before Ennis could complete the thought. "I'm sorry, but that's out of the question. My wife and I have discussed it too, at great length, and it's too dangerous for your daughter. We can't be party to it."

"I figured you was gonna say that, sir. And I respect you for it."

Maggie noted Ennis wiping the sweat from his forehead again. She'd assumed his perspiration stemmed from pain, which it well could. But judging from the dread—and determination—in his eyes, his nervousness seemed rooted more in what he was about to say.

"But my daughter already know what it's like to be beaten by a white man. She know what it's like to watch her papa get beaten too. And worse. She done seen things, sir, all my children have, that I'd give my life for them not to see. Or feel. But that ain't a choice I get to make."

A silent tear slipped down Odessia's cheek.

"I want my daughter to grow up strong, Mr. McGrath," Ennis continued. "And happy. And doin' what she love. And she *love* to ride, like you know already. But mostly sir, I-I just want my little girl to grow up."

A knot lodged at the base of Maggie's throat and, even without looking over at Cullen, she sensed a similar response in him.

The muscles in Ennis's jaw worked something fierce. "And if my family stays here, sir, in this town, in this state, with the way things is . . . there ain't too good a chance of that happenin'."

The man shifted on the pallet again, his grimace telling a story words couldn't. "One more thing, sir . . . We's grateful for what you done for us, bringin' us here to Linden Downs. But we left what little we had to come here. You lose this farm, sir, and we lose everythin' too. And we's back in Shantytown."

Odessia blinked and wiped her cheek. "I done checked around some, and we know what a jockey gets paid. But I know too," she added hurriedly, "that Kizzy ain't no jockey like them boys that been ridin' 'fore they could walk. But we's wonderin', Mr. Ennis and me, if you was to let Kizzy ride Miss Belle, and if they was to win . . ." Odessia twisted a worn handkerchief in her grip. "If you'd give us half of regular jockey pay."

"That way," Ennis continued, "we have us enough money to go west, sir, and start over new. And our children, maybe they can have a life different from this one here."

Maggie slipped a look at Cullen. He held the man's gaze, his struggle mirrored in his troubled expression.

Then Cullen looked at her, his eyes discerning, and she willed for him to read every thought, prayer, and dream in her heart concerning Kizzy and this family.

Finally Cullen shook his head. "There's no way we can agree to half of regular jockey pay."

The faint hope in Ennis and Odessia's eyes faded.

"But if you're willin' to take full pay—and a bonus, if we win—then we've got ourselves a deal."

Chapter FORTY-FIVE

In less than ten hours, at six o'clock sharp, the gunshot would sound, and Belle and Kizzy would be racing around Burns Island Track. Just thinking about it sent goose bumps skittering up Maggie's arms, even as the tangle of nerves that had been her near constant companion over the past month coiled a little tighter.

But Kizzy was ready. She knew it. So was Belle.

A chilled breath of fall stirred the bedroom curtains, the risen sun brilliant against a depth of cloudless blue. The perfect day. Kizzy hadn't seemed a bit nervous last night, but Ennis and Odessia were. Maggie saw the trepidation behind their smiles.

But the girl was fearless, as Uncle Bob had commented in their final practice yesterday at Belle Meade. "That child got more spunk and grit to her than anybody her size has a right to."

And Maggie knew the girl was going to need every bit of both.

Kizzy was a gifted rider, but she'd never ridden in a real race before. And to have her first race be the Peyton Stakes . . . To say it was an ambitious goal was putting it mildly. But Belle knew the ropes.

All Kizzy needed to do was exactly what she'd been doing. Be an extension of Belle and let the thoroughbred fly. If things went as Maggie expected, Kizzy wouldn't need to worry about the other riders once they were out of the starting gate, because Belle would already be several lengths ahead.

Maggie finished buttoning the front of her emerald green riding habit, the skirt slightly more snug fitting than the last time she'd worn it, yet not so much that anyone would notice. She smoothed a hand over her abdomen.

The nausea she'd been experiencing upon awakening each

morning had tapered in recent days. She found that eating something before her feet ever touched the floor helped, so she'd taken to keeping a small stash of Aunt Issy's lemon cookies in the drawer of her bedside table.

Feeling the tiniest swell beneath her palm, she smiled, wondering if Aunt Issy's cookies weren't at least partly responsible.

The creak of a floorboard drew her gaze to the mirror above the mantel, and her smile took an intimate turn.

Cullen ducked through the doorway and came to wrap his arms around her from behind. "Guess who's downstairs with the Linden Downs racin' silks."

Maggie felt a blush of excitement—and relief. "I can't wait to see them!"

She'd never doubted Savannah could do it. But she'd begun to wonder whether her friend would be able to do it in time. Savannah was sorely overworked, she knew. Every minute of her friend's day was spoken for, between sewing and caring for her younger siblings.

She'd met with Savannah nearly a month ago now, and together they'd chosen the colors and the design for what Kizzy would wear today.

"Miss Darby says she's sorry it took her so long, and she'll make any last-minute alterations on the spot. I've already sent for Kizzy."

"Thank you." Maggie leaned into his strength, enjoying this rare moment alone. It seemed as if there was always someone else around these days.

He searched her eyes in the mirror's reflection even as his hand spanned her midsection. "You haven't told her yet," he said softly.

Maggie averted her gaze.

"You need to tell her, love."

"It isn't as easy as that, Cullen. Besides, you and I haven't told anyone yet. Well, outside of Onnie and Cletus."

"And Ethan."

She frowned.

"He and I were talkin' late last night in the stable, and he asked, in a roundabout way."

"A roundabout way?" She raised an eyebrow.

"Said he'd noticed you seemed . . . different lately."

Maggie found that impossible to argue with. She certainly *felt* different. And yet, her opinion of Cullen's older brother remained largely unchanged. Something about the man simply didn't sit well with her.

Cullen kissed the top of her head and turned her in his arms. "Savannah Darby will be happy for you, Maggie. Your friend's got a kind heart."

"I know she does. She's one of the kindest people I've ever known. But it'll also make her sad, in a way." Maggie fingered the buttons on his shirt. "And I dread doing that."

A telling look moved into his eyes. "She's goin' to know soon enough. And then what will you say when she asks why you took so long to tell her?"

Maggie sighed, knowing he was right.

Cullen fingered the ivory point plat lace on the worn lapel of her suit jacket, and Maggie wished she'd had the money to enlist Savannah's skill for a new riding habit as well. But she wasn't about to ask Cullen for money for such a luxury, not with funds so tight.

Besides, even though she wasn't the superstitious type, she'd worn this riding habit for every one of Belle's wins. Maybe it would bode well for them today.

Cullen kissed her forehead. "We're about ready to load up Bourbon Belle. If ever a horse was eager for a race, I'd say it was her."

"I'll be right outside after meeting with Savannah. I know I'll see Belle again at the track this afternoon, but I'd like to see her here too. So please don't leave before I come out?"

"I wouldn't dream of it."

As they made their way toward the stairs, Maggie spotted Ethan's still-closed bedroom door—at half past eight, no less—and she paused on the second-story landing. "About your brother . . ."

Cullen's expression became guarded, and she chose her words carefully.

"Sometimes when I rise very early, I'll notice his bedroom door is still open and his bed unslept in. Do you think he's . . . doing things he oughtn't?"

Cullen cradled the side of her face. "I wouldn't worry. Ethan's always been a bit of a late nighter, if you know what I mean. I also think he's learned his lesson in that regard."

She didn't know *exactly* what he meant, but having had four older brothers, she had an inkling. And Cullen's cloaked expression kept her from pressing the issue.

Once Maggie reached the foyer, she heard Kizzy's excited squeal. And when she turned the corner into the central parlor, she realized why.

"Oh, Savannah . . ." Maggie looked at Kizzy strutting around the room in her dusky blue racing silks with burgundy trim. "They're beautiful."

Kizzy beamed. "I like 'em 'cuz they's trousers."

True enough, they looked identical to the shirts and trousers the other jockeys wore. And were a perfect fit on Kizzy's lithe frame.

At Odessia's urging, they'd decided not to flaunt the fact that Kizzy was a girl. Odessia had braided her daughter's hair tight against her head, and the jockeys' names were never listed in the program—only the thoroughbreds—so no worry there.

But once Kizzy slipped her cap on—which the girl did as though on cue—any question regarding gender was removed.

She looked like a boy. Same as another young girl Maggie remembered. Only, *that* young girl would never have had the opportunity to do what Kizzy was doing today. Sad, how the color of one's skin so defined the path of a person's life. Both in freedom for opportunities, and in boundaries.

She prayed, especially in light of the recent war, that it wouldn't always be that way.

"Missus McGrath, I gonna run show my mama these. She out back of the kitchen with Miss Onnie. That all right?"

Maggie smiled. "Yes, but please don't get them dirty."

Kizzy went running.

"Maggie . . ." Savannah's tone was tentative. "I apologize that it's taken me so long to finish the silks." Savannah grew teary and gave a little laugh, then waved a hand like she always did when she became emotional and wished she hadn't. "My new employer can be a tad demanding."

"A tad?" Maggie blew out a breath, remembering that day in the shop. "Mrs. Adelicia Acklen Cheatham of the Belmont Estate can be a *tad* demanding—or seemed such when you sewed the new silk draperies for her parlor. But your employer," Maggie exhaled, "she's Attila the Hun in bloomers!"

Savannah's laughter bubbled up, and Maggie's did too. Oh, but it broke Maggie's heart to have to tell her friend her wonderful—yet painful for Savannah—news.

"Savannah, I've been intending to—"

Her friend held up a hand. "One more thing!" She reached behind the settee and withdrew a box. "When we bought the material for the racing silks, I saw another cloth of the exact color that day, and

I thought it would be lovely on you." Savannah placed the box on the cushioned seat, then looked down at Maggie's emerald jacket and skirt, and smiled. "I wish I could have paid for it myself. But I couldn't. So I approached your husband, and he was more than willing to pay for it all."

Maggie felt her mouth slip open. She glanced through the front window to see the culprit himself walking into the stable. "That man . . . He never said a thing to me."

"As well he shouldn't have. I threatened him within an inch of his life if he did." Savannah nodded to the box on the settee.

Cherishing her friend, Maggie untied the string and removed the lid. Seeing the garment within—or rather, a master seamstress's work of art—Maggie tried to give voice to the gratitude in her heart, but the words wouldn't come.

She withdrew the jacket from the box and held it up.

The garment was dusky blue, the same shade as Kizzy's racing silks. But the fabric had a more substantial, luxurious feel, and a lovely paisley corduroy collar in burgundy and earthy tones of green that complemented the blue. The same swatch of corduroy embellished the edge of the sleeves.

"Savannah, this is stunning."

Savannah's smile was pure pleasure. "I so enjoyed sewing this for you, Maggie. Especially knowing what an important day this is. And—" She reached for her satchel and withdrew a small pair of scissors, a needle, and some ivory thread, and laid them on the side table. "I also know how some owners of thoroughbred racehorses can be about following the same routine or wearing the same clothes as they did the time before when their horse won, so . . ." She gestured to the lace on the lapels of Maggie's emerald green jacket. "I want to transfer the lace from your old jacket to your new one. So you'll have a bit of past wins with you today too." She grinned. "So hurry up and let's see it on you!"

Excited, Maggie raced up the stairs to the bedroom. Savannah followed. With the door closed, Maggie began undressing, noticing how her friend surveyed the room. The same room where they'd lain awake at night as girls, giggling.

The room now bore definite masculine touches. Cullen's second pair of boots by the wardrobe, his shirt hanging from the desk chair. And by the wash basin, his razor and shaving cup, which the man remembered to use maybe every third day.

Maggie laid her jacket on the bed.

"He seems like such a good man, Maggie. Your father chose well."

This time it was Maggie's turn to come close to tears. "Yes, Cullen *is* a good man. And I pray every day, Savannah, that God will bring someone just like him into your life."

Savannah raised a dark blond eyebrow. "You mean a tall dark Irishman who's as kind as he is handsome?"

Maggie's eyes widened, then she giggled, slipping off her skirt. *This* was the Savannah she'd grown up with. The feisty, spirited Savannah before the war. "And to think," she whispered, "I couldn't stand the man at first."

Savannah shook her head. "I'm proud of you, Maggie. Proud of what you're doing today too."

"Can you be there? Is Attila giving you the time off?"

With a faint smile, Savannah shook her head. "But I'll be cheering for you and Belle and Kizzy from a few blocks away."

Maggie stepped into the skirt Savannah held out for her. And no sooner did she reach around on the waistband to button the closure than she remembered—

Maggie pulled on the fabric.

Savannah frowned. "Is it too small? I followed your last measurements."

"No, it's fine!" Maggie tugged. "I've simply gained a little weight, I think."

"Well, it's about time. Marriage must be agreeing with you if that's the—"

Savannah stopped midsentence. She looked at Maggie, then at the skirt, then at Maggie again, her expression one of joy—and woundedness. "You're with child," she whispered.

"I was going to tell you, Savannah. I promise. I simply—"

"I'm so h-happy for you, Maggie." Savannah bit her lower lip until Maggie feared she'd draw blood. "I truly am," she said, choking back a sob.

"Oh, Savannah . . ." Maggie reached out to her, but Savannah held out a hand.

"Take off the skirt, and I'll fix it. I can move the button over a little for today. Then I'll make the alteration so you can wear it a while longer." Her smile trembled. "I'll wait for you downstairs."

The door closed and Maggie dressed again in silence. A few minutes later, she returned to the central parlor with the ensemble to find Savannah waiting, needle and thread at the ready.

She reached for the skirt, and Maggie handed it to her, then knelt beside her chair.

Maggie took Savannah's hand. "I don't know why things worked out so differently for me. I do know"—her throat tightened—"that it's *not* because I'm a better person than you, or more kindhearted, or anything *more*. Because you're the most courageous and loving woman I've ever known. And you're my dearest friend, Savannah Darby."

Tears traced Savannah's cheeks. "And you are mine . . . Maggie McGrath."

Through the years, Cullen had witnessed hundreds of thoroughbred owners at this precise moment, seeing their horses for the last time before they would send them to the track.

But never before had he struggled with his emotions as he did while watching his wife with Bourbon Belle.

The thoroughbred—magnificent in beauty, over a thousand pounds of sleek muscle and bridled strength—stood stock still and stared intently at the diminutive young woman, whose features had taken on a look of reverence.

"I love you, Belle," Maggie whispered. "And I could not be more proud of you."

Maggie teared up, and Cullen realized why she'd wanted to do this here instead of at Burns Island.

"So when you run later today, when you and Kizzy fly around that track, remember that. And know how grateful to God I am that he allowed us to belong to each other."

Maggie kissed the mare. Belle's nostrils flared as the animal huffed a breath.

Kizzy joined them a minute later, dressed in her silks—and enjoying them, judging by the way she strutted—and Cullen realized Odessia and Maggie were right. Dressed this way, the child really did look like a boy. No one would even have cause to question it.

So why did he have this gnawing feeling in his gut? And where was Ethan? He'd promised to help today, to make certain Belle was protected and so was Kizzy. Yet he hadn't shown hide nor hair of himself since yesterday afternoon.

Ethan had taken to disappearing for spaces of time in recent weeks. Cullen wondered if his brother was privately seeking justice for what had happened at Linden Downs. He didn't inquire after Ethan's whereabouts, but every time he caught sight of Ennis hobbling around on crutches, and saw the deep scar on the man's neck, Cullen couldn't help hoping that was what his brother was up to.

Yet considering what was happening today, and how Ethan had given him his word he would be here . . .

Cullen hoped his brother wouldn't let him down—again.

Maggie hugged the girl tight. "Your mother and I will follow shortly."

"Why you cryin', ma'am? This ain't a sad day."

Maggie tapped Kizzy's nose. "Remember everything Uncle Bob and I taught you."

"Done told you I would." Kizzy scampered up onto the bench seat beside Cletus, who seemed as excited as the little girl.

Minutes later, with Belle secured in the trailer, Cullen kissed Maggie good-bye and climbed up to sit beside Kizzy, still trying to shake off the nervous edge. He nodded to the four workers accompanying them on horseback to take the lead.

Up ahead a throng of people walked up the road from the cabins, and when they looked in the direction of the trailer, and Kizzy waved, they sent up a cheer.

"Don't be too long," Cullen said, looking down at Maggie.

"We won't. There's just one more thing I need to do."

Chapter Forty-Six

The noon hour, and Burns Island Track was already abuzz with activity. Cullen briefly reined in to let a wagon pass, and he sensed Kizzy taking everything in. The little girl had talked continually since they left Linden Downs, but now she was all eyes.

Tents crowded both sides of the road leading to the track, vendors vying for space to hawk their wares, while inside the gates, men worked feverishly to prepare the stands and the dirt track. And all of this for the most important two minutes of thoroughbred racing in Nashville for the year.

Even now a cool breeze blew across the field. Perfect conditions. But still, Cullen felt a gnawing in his gut.

Then he realized . . .

This was his first time back inside a track since London. Though he'd once relished this part of his life, he'd thought it forever behind him.

But he knew he had no reason to worry. Ethan had paid the debt for his crime back in London. His brother's slate was clean. As was his own.

Now if only Ethan would follow through as he'd said he would.

After maneuvering the trailer into the stable area and getting Belle unloaded and into a stall to rest and get oriented, Cullen left Kizzy and the mare in the care of Cletus and the other workers and turned to go check in.

"Mr. McGrath!"

Cullen turned to see General Harding a few stalls down and went to greet him. "Good afternoon, General."

The older man's firm grip defied his age.

"Good to see you, McGrath." Harding nodded past him. "Uncle Bob told me you'd decided to run Belle today. I must say I'm glad." He leveled a stare, his eyes sharp. "To me, racing isn't so much about winning as it is about making a stronger, better thoroughbred. Bourbon Belle has Vandal's blood coursing through her veins. And Fortune here"—Harding gestured to the stall beside him with the pretty bay mare—"is in Epsilon's lineage, another of my champion stallions. So regardless of who wins today, I learn something that helps me in the long run."

"So you won't be mindin' then, if Belle takes home the purse?"

Harding's long, thinning beard trembled when he laughed, and Cullen judged it had grown another half inch since he'd last seen the man.

"I never said that, Mr. McGrath. I like to win as much as the next man. But still . . . I wish you luck."

Cullen shook his hand a second time. "One more thing, sir . . . I thank you again for the loan of the wagons during harvest. What the hail didn't get, I was able to get to market because of your generosity. "

Harding shook his head. "I pay my debts, Mr. McGrath. And I still owe you a sizable one for what you did for Bonnie Scotland. I won't forget it."

"Consider the debt paid in full, General."

The look Harding gave him clearly said the man didn't. "Have you learned anything more about the men who burned the cabins that night? Or about who poisoned Belle?"

Wishing he had firm evidence instead of simply a gut hunch and the aroma of a sweet-smelling cigar, Cullen shook his head.

"While I do not agree with what's been done to my beloved South, I abhor violence of this nature, Mr. McGrath. It is our right—and *duty*—to protect those who work for us, as well as to protect our property and our land." Harding extended his hand again. "Now if you'll excuse me, I have a meeting to attend. Best of luck to you today, McGrath."

"You as well, General Harding."

Feeling both confirmed and slightly admonished, Cullen took the stairs to the second floor, which housed offices for the Thoroughbred Society. He withdrew the registration documents from his shirt pocket.

A bespectacled young man peered up from behind the counter. "May I help you, sir?"

"Aye. Name's Cullen McGrath. I'm here with Bourbon Belle. She's in the stable." He slid the papers toward him.

The clerk looked down at his ledger. "Ah yes, Mr. McGrath, I see your name right—" He paused and looked back at Cullen, then unfolded the documents. The young man nudged his glasses farther up the bridge of his nose as he read, then he peered up again. "You say you're here with Bourbon Belle."

"That's right."

"And . . . you're the legal owner of the thoroughbred."

"Aye," Cullen said more slowly, hearing a question in the youth's tone. "I am."

The clerk hesitated, then shuffled through the papers a second time before sliding them back toward Cullen. "By chance, do you have proof of your ownership, sir?"

"Proof?" Cullen felt the unease he'd dismissed earlier returning, but this time with anger in tow. "I presented proof a month ago when I registered the mare for the race. I brought in my deed to Linden Downs and showed it to the clerk here at the time."

The young man nodded. "Yes, sir. But in a race with a purse this size, the Nashville Thoroughbred Society mandates that ownership of each thoroughbred entered to run be verified. A request was sent to verify your ownership of Linden Downs, and a response was promptly received. However, it's noted here that no official papers were submitted for the thoroughbred." The clerk pointed to the ledger, leaning back a little as he did. "And in reviewing the official deed to Linden Downs, the deed contains no mention of the blood horse either. Only the land itself."

The heat in Cullen's chest rose to his throat, and he worked to keep his voice even. "And where exactly did you send this request?"

"To the Tax and Title Office, sir. They always work hand in hand with the Thoroughbred Society on this issue."

"And no one thought to contact me directly about the matter?"

"W-why yes, sir, of course we did. A letter was sent to you as well. It was posted on"—the clerk trailed a finger across a line of the ledger—"September thirteenth."

Wishing again that he'd put his fist through Stephen Drake's face when he'd had the chance, Cullen took a deep breath, the situation quickly coming into focus. He'd never thought to ask Gilbert Linden for Bourbon Belle's official papers. With good reason—he hadn't known what the horse was worth until after Linden's passing. And by then, everything at Linden Downs was his. If not on paper, then in effect.

Yet he knew Gilbert Linden had listed everything in detail—including livestock and horses—in the deed. They'd both reviewed the document to make certain that—

No. His memory peeled back another layer.

The information hadn't been included in the deed. Mr. Linden had included it in the letter he'd written. The letter the woman in the office had included in the file that day.

Cullen refolded the papers and stuck them in his pocket. "Give me half an hour, and I'll be back with the proof you need."

"Oh, I'm sorry, sir, but—"

Cullen turned back, and the clerk's face paled.

"Even if you could provide proof . . . which I'm certain you can," the young man added quickly, "I'm afraid the date for submitting additional documentation has passed." He winced. "I'm truly sorry, sir, but your mare isn't permitted to race in the Peyton Stakes."

"It's coming true, Papa," Maggie whispered, looking down at his grave. Bucket sat a few feet away, watching her. "Belle is running today in the Peyton Stakes. Just like we dreamed."

Her gaze trailed the line of wooden markers. Her family, all resting at her feet. But not really. They weren't there, she knew. That thought always brought both hope—and loneliness.

"I wish you could see the race, Papa," she whispered. "And be here with me, cheering Belle on. You worked so hard for this."

As she turned to leave, she paused and studied her mother's name on the grave—Laurel Agnes Linden—and wondered if her mother's perspective about her infatuation with racing, and with horses, would have changed, even the slightest bit, if she could have seen Belle race—and win.

Not that it mattered now, Maggie told herself as she walked back to the house. And yet . . . it did.

"Bourbon Belle *will* be runnin' in the race today, sir." Anger made the words come out harsher than Cullen had intended. "So you best tell me how we can work together to make that happen."

The clerk stared, eyes wide. "I'm s-sorry, Mr. McGrath, but I've got rules to follow. I can't just go changing them for one person and not the next."

Understanding the man's situation, Cullen also understood his own. "What's your name, son?"

"Thomas." The clerk audibly swallowed. "Thomas Fulton."

"Mr. Fulton." Cullen felt his eyes narrow. "I'm tellin' you, I never got that letter. And I'm not leavin' here 'til you tell me how we're goin' to fix this."

"I reckon that the only way to fix it, sir"—Fulton swallowed audibly—"would be for you to request a meeting with the Thoroughbred Society."

"And how do I do that?"

"You . . . file a written request, Mr. McGrath. With the appropriate documentation. To be presented at their next meeting."

Cullen exhaled through clenched teeth, imagining having to tell Maggie that Bourbon Belle wasn't going to race.

"But if you want," Fulton said hurriedly. "I can interrupt their meeting to see if—"

"Their meetin'," Cullen repeated.

The clerk nodded. "Yes, sir." He stood. "If you'll stay here, I'll—"

"Take me to that meetin', Mr. Fulton."

Cullen followed the young man down the hallway to a set of double doors, where Fulton reached for the knob.

"I believe I can take it from here," Cullen said.

"But sir, it's a closed meeting, and—"

Cullen stared.

Fulton nodded. "Yes, sir."

Hearing the hasty retreat of steps behind him, Cullen gathered his shredded patience and opened the door.

Chapter FORTY-SEVEN

All eyes in the room turned to Cullen. But it was the smug triumph Cullen read on Stephen Drake's face that ignited his anger. Cullen strode down the side of the table to where the man was seated.

"Mr. McGrath!"

General Harding's commanding tone sliced through Cullen's determination and stopped him where he was. Cullen scanned the faces of the men around the table—thirteen at a glance—and found Harding seated at the head, a haze of cigar smoke in the air.

But not a trace of sweetness.

The general's expression held both curiosity and censure. "How may we help you, Mr. McGrath?"

Still seeing red—and *feeling* Drake's arrogant conceit—he focused his thoughts on Maggie and reached for calm beyond his nature. "I have an issue, sir. To bring before the board."

Drake glanced back, his expression taunting. "This is a closed meeting, McGrath. You'll have to wait until next month to—"

Cullen reached for him, wanting to—

"Mr. Drake!"

Cullen froze, and Stephen Drake looked to the head of the table.

"*I* am addressing our guest, Mr. Drake." General Harding tilted his head. "If I require your assistance, sir, I'll not be hesitant to ask for it."

Drake said nothing, but Harding's subtle reprimand helped ease Cullen's temper.

"Now, Mr. McGrath," Harding continued, chastisement still edging his tone. "I assume by your manner of entrance that your issue with us is of an urgent nature."

Cullen nodded. "Most urgent, sir. I was told just now by Mr. Fulton that my mare, Bourbon Belle, won't be allowed to participate in the race today due to lack of proper documentation." Cullen summarized the situation, taking the opportunity to familiarize himself with his audience.

A few of the men's faces he recognized—business owners in town—but the rest were new to him. And none overly sympathetic, judging by their scowls.

"So," Harding continued, "you never received the letter, Mr. McGrath."

"Nay, I did not. If I had, I would've provided what was needed."

Harding nodded. "Which I find most believable, considering what is at stake today." Harding's attention returned to the left side of the table. "Mr. Drake, these issues are handled through your office, are they not?"

"Yes, General Harding," Drake answered, sitting taller. "Just as this one was. I wrote the letter myself and sent it via courier to Linden Downs."

"Via courier?" Harding asked, his hands steepled beneath his chin. "Is that the usual manner such documentation is delivered?"

Drake cut a look at two men sitting across the table from him. "I was simply making sure it was handled correctly. And in a timely manner."

"Which I believe it *was*," the man seated opposite Drake offered.

"As do I," another offered. "The rules clearly state, Harding, that all entrants must—"

"I am well aware of the rules, Mr. Sadler." Harding's expression held warning. "My father, John Harding, established this organization, after all. And he did so on integrity . . . and honor."

Cullen felt a shift in the room, a silent challenge. And a reckoning of loyalties.

Harding leaned forward. "Your horse is running in the race today, Mr. Drake. Is he not?"

Drake stiffened. "Yes . . . as you already know, General Harding."

Harding nodded again. "I believe our regulations state that the owner of a thoroughbred denied permission to race must be given opportunity to provide the required proof."

Harding turned to the gentleman directly on his right.

The man, pamphlet at the ready, flipped through the pages, then stopped. He gave a consenting nod. "Section seventeen, General. Would you like for me to read it aloud?"

"That won't be necessary." Harding sat back in his chair. "So, Mr. McGrath . . . consider this your opportunity."

Tempted to feel relief, Cullen knew better. Because he knew Stephen Drake. "Mr. Gilbert Linden, my late father-in-law, penned a letter listing the details of the transfer of Linden Downs into my ownership. The letter clearly states that the land and everything on it, all livestock and horses—which includes Bourbon Belle—belongs to me. That letter was filed with the Tax and Title Office at the time the back taxes and fees were paid in full."

Harding's attention swung back to Drake. "Is that correct, Mr. Drake?"

"We received the deed for the land, General Harding. But sadly, there was no letter such as Mr. McGrath states." He shook his head, his regret having all the appearances of truth.

Cullen instinctively started for the man again, then caught himself. If he wanted even the slightest chance of racing Belle today . . .

He steeled his temper. "General Harding, that's simply not true. If you'll allow me to go get my wife, she will confirm that there is—or was"—he met Drake's gaze—"a letter from Gilbert Linden. She read it herself, as did the woman in the office."

Drake exhaled. "So now we're expected to take a woman's word over a man's?" He laughed. "That's the way of the Irish for you, gents!"

A few of the men laughed along with him. The rest looked at General Harding, who merely took a piece of paper, turned it over, and began to write.

The room was silent, the scratch of the fountain pen the only sound.

After a moment General Harding finished, and from the flourish of his hand, Cullen could only guess the man was making his signature.

"There we are." Harding blew against the paper, waiting for the ink to dry, then slid it down the table in Drake's direction. It landed squarely in front of the man.

Cullen read it over his shoulder, and his gratitude toward William Giles Harding increased yet again.

Harding rose from the table. "Gentleman, I had the privilege of speaking with Gilbert Linden myself, *after* this transfer of ownership occurred, and I can confirm without hesitation that it was Mr. Linden's wish—no, his determined desire and understanding—that Linden Downs, in its entirety, was at that time—as it is today—under the ownership of Mr. Cullen McGrath. And I have penned an affidavit stating such."

Drake gripped the paper in his hand. "But this doesn't mean McGrath can race Bourbon Belle in the—"

"It does, in fact, mean precisely that, Mr. Drake. Because the only question was about Mr. McGrath's ownership of Bourbon Belle. And I have confirmed that. Unless, of course, you judge *my* statement and signature as inadequate to provide proof."

The question hung like a saber set to slice sinew from bone. And though a few of the men seemed to be calculating the cost, none seemed willing to pay it. Save one.

"There is another issue, General Harding." Drake glanced back at Cullen. "Two, actually." The conceit in his tone conveyed the man's enjoyment of the moment.

Harding settled back into his chair, the creak of aged leather somehow complementing the thinning patience in his demeanor. "And may I assume you plan to enlighten us on these points, Mr. Drake?"

"With pleasure, General Harding. The jockey McGrath has set to ride Bourbon Belle today . . . is a girl."

Shocked grumblings shot up from around the table, along with disapproving looks. Cullen began to think Ethan's original plan to silence Stephen Drake might have been the better idea.

"Gentlemen!" Harding raised his voice, but even *his* expression held objection. "Is this true, McGrath? Your jockey, the young boy I just saw downstairs . . . is actually a girl?"

Cullen ignored the faint snickers. "Aye, sir, she is. And while it's unconventional, I admit, as far as I can see there's nothin' in the rule book that states a girl can't be a jockey." Sensing further objection, he quickly continued. "My wife's former jockey, as you know, was a lad. But his family was forced to leave town after a black man was hung and the remainin' community was threatened with the same retribution if they didn't leave town as well." Cullen looked pointedly down at Drake. "That seems to be a relatively common bit of advice newcomers of certain creeds receive when arrivin' in this city."

More protests arose, but the slam of Harding's palm on the table silenced them all.

"We will proceed with order, gentlemen! And anyone who cannot, I invite to take his leave. Immediately."

The silence simmered.

"Mr. McGrath," Harding continued, "you are correct, sir. And I do *not* need to consult the rule book in this regard. I know without fail there is nothing in the regulations about a girl riding in a race, for the very reason that it is understood that jockeys are boys. Jockeying is a dangerous occupation. It takes skill and strength and a quickness of reflexes females simply do not possess."

"Hear, hear," several of the men murmured.

Cullen held back his smile as best he could and included the entire gathering in his glance. "Once you see the girl," he said, "I think you'll change your mind."

"And what if she gets hurt, Mr. McGrath?" a much older gentleman asked. "What happens then?"

"The very same thing that will happen if a boy gets injured . . . sir."

Feeling the silence turning the tide against him, Cullen knew he had to do something. "Are you all afraid to let a girl race against the boys?"

The men laughed in unison, even General Harding, though not as heartily as the others.

Cullen allowed himself the faintest smile. "I remember a time when no one thought a female thoroughbred could beat its male counterpart. But, if I'm not mistaken, that's happened a time or two. Right here in Nashville." *And, Lord willin', it will happen again today.*

The laughter quieted.

Aware of Harding watching him, Cullen hoped what he'd said hadn't pushed the general too far.

Drake leaned forward, and Cullen, knowing what was coming, decided to beat him to the punch.

"Somethin' else you need to know, gentlemen, that I'm sure Mr. Drake here was about to tell you . . . is that my brother poisoned a thoroughbred at a track in London over a year ago. And that for a time I was wanted for the crime as well."

This news drew only solemn stares.

"But what Mr. Drake doesn't know—and doesn't *want* to know—is that I had absolutely nothin' to do with the incident. My name has been cleared. And my brother . . . He's spent the last year in prison, payin' for what he did. He came out a changed man too." Though, in a way, Cullen wondered if Ethan wasn't still paying.

General Harding met Cullen's stare and held it. "Mr. McGrath." He sighed. "You have made quite an impression today, sir."

Cullen could tell the impression wasn't wholly favorable.

"Gentlemen." Harding glanced at his gold pocket watch before returning his focus to his colleagues. "The past hour has brought many topics of discussion. But as I see it, only one that requires any response from our society as a whole—and with ever dwindling time to make it. And that question is: will we allow a girl to race in the Peyton Stakes?"

Drake started to speak again.

But Harding raised a hand. "Mr. McGrath, if you would be so kind as to step out in the hallway for a moment while we discuss this issue further."

Not liking the subdued nature of Harding's tone, Cullen did as the man asked. But he paused just before closing the door and stepped back inside, feeling as if Gilbert Linden were right beside him. "Somethin' else I want you to know, gentlemen. My name is on the record as bein' trainer to Bourbon Belle, just like Gilbert Linden's was. But my wife, Linden's daughter, Margaret Linden McGrath, is the *real* trainer for the thoroughbred. And always has been."

Harding's eyebrows shot up.

"Margaret raised the mare from a foal. My wife's late father, a man I grew to greatly admire in a very short time, indulged his daughter's dream. And I nearly made the tragic mistake of not doin' so. So, should you see Bourbon Belle flyin' 'round the track later today, just remember . . . That'll be the work of females, gents. And that'll sit just fine with this Irishman."

Chapter Forty-Eight

"How long has Mr. McGrath been gone, Kizzy?" Maggie asked. It was nearly three o'clock, and she and Odessia had already been waiting with the girl for over an hour.

Standing on a stool in the stall, Kizzy stroked Belle's head. "He done left soon after we got here, ma'am. Ain't seen him since."

Maggie exchanged a look with Odessia, who sat beside her in the fresh hay, her expression pensive.

Kizzy leaned down to scratch her leg, and Maggie caught a brief glimpse of the welts just above the child's ankle. The thin scars, perfectly matching the tail end of a whip, rekindled Maggie's anger, as did thinking about Ennis and all this family had endured.

She rose and brushed off her skirt, and just then heard Cullen's distinctive brogue. She stepped out into the aisle and felt a flush of pride at the mere sight of him.

She met him halfway, and as he got closer his smile widened.

He picked her up in a hug. "It's good to see you, Mrs. McGrath."

Holding her tight, he stepped inside the empty stall neighboring theirs and kissed her soundly before putting her down again. Blushing, Maggie glanced outside the entryway to see if anyone had seen them. Her husband's soft laughter, along with the pleasure in his eyes whenever he touched her, all but silenced that prim voice of warning inside her.

"Is everything all right?" she asked. "Kizzy said you've been gone almost since you got here."

"Everythin's fine. Registration details just took longer than I expected."

His tone was convincing enough, but the tiny lines at the corners of his eyes seemed more pronounced and made her wonder if something had gone awry.

"You look beautiful, Maggie." His gaze moved over her.

Pleased that he thought so, she smoothed a hand over her new riding habit and gave a formal curtsy. "Thank *you,* sir, for your kindness."

He offered an exaggerated bow that drew a giggle from Kizzy, who was watching over the top of the stall. Cullen tweaked her little nose.

"In just a while," he said, taking Maggie's hand, "it'll be our turn on the track to get warmed up. Let's get Kizzy and Belle ready."

A while later, at Cullen's insistence, Maggie led Belle onto the track, Kizzy astride the mare. Cullen, Odessia, and Cletus followed, and Maggie paused to look around, taking it all in. How different it looked to see the racetrack from the ground again instead of from a bird's-eye view up on the ridge.

Already spectators were arriving, and the breeze carried a luscious blend of aromas from vendors cooking food for purchase outside the gates. The scents ranged from sweet to spicy and everything in between.

Maggie was certain she smelled fresh-popped corn, and her mouth watered. But it wouldn't be right to eat in front of Kizzy, who had had so little today, much less in the past week, all in an effort to make the girl as light as possible on Belle.

Maggie had promised to make the child Aunt Issy's lemon cookies following the race. Likewise, Onnie had promised her *sweet* sweet potato sticks, one of the woman's specialities. And Maggie knew Kizzy would hold them both to it.

Kizzy shielded her eyes in the midafternoon sun. "This be bigger than the practice track at Belle Meade, Missus McGrath."

"Yes, it is." Maggie stared up into the empty stands. "But think about this: it's also easier in a way. Think of how many turns you and Belle have to make at the track at Belle Meade to cover the same distance. There aren't nearly so many turns here."

Kizzy nodded as though comparing the two in her head. "I'm thinkin' we can go even faster here!"

Maggie exchanged a look with Cullen, who'd come alongside them.

"That's what every jockey thinks . . . at first. Remember what we talked about on the way here." Cullen laid a gentle hand on the girl's shoulder. "Fast off the mark, then steady and smart. You don't want to push Belle until the very end."

"Yes, sir, I know. Uncle Bob done told me the same thing." The child got a sassy look about her. "Over and over," she finished beneath her breath.

Cullen poked her in the ribs, and Kizzy giggled. Even Odessia laughed at that.

Watching Cullen with the girl, hearing them jest with each other, warmed Maggie's heart and gave her a glimpse of the father he would be. And had been, she remembered.

She went to stand with Odessia and Cletus as Cullen led Kizzy around the track. "I wish Ennis could be here with us."

"I don't," Odessia said softly, then firmed her jaw in such a way that Maggie almost felt as if she'd misspoken. "My husband, ma'am," Odessia continued, "he's strong in his body and in his mind. But his heart—that man's heart is all wrapped up in me and these kids." Odessia laughed, but it had a desperate sound about it. "Anythin' else were to happen to our little girl—" She firmed her lips. "I'm sorry, Missus McGrath. I shouldn't borrow trouble, I know. That's what Ennis always says."

"You're worried about your daughter, Odessia. And that's understandable. But I truly believe she'll be fine. I've never seen a—"

"A better rider," Odessia filled in for her. "Or more gifted, especially so young. Ain't that what you was gonna say, ma'am?" Not a hint of sarcasm tainted the woman's voice, only deep concern. "Missus McGrath, I don't want you to think that I ain't grateful for what you and your husband are doin' for my baby girl. And it ain't that I don't think she can do it neither." Her voice caught. "I think she can. And *will*." A tear slid down her cheek. "But—"

Maggie took hold of her hand. "But even when you know someone can do something—" She paused, seeing the love welling up in Odessia's eyes, so similar to another love she'd seen and been so blessed to know. "Even when you think they should, sometimes you're still a little frightened for them when they do."

Odessia nodded. "It's 'cuz you love 'em so much."

Oh, Papa . . . Maggie's eyes burned with the memory, her voice scarcely coming. "And you can't imagine your world without them."

❧

"Ladies and gentlemen!" Using a speaking trumpet, a man in the two-story wooden tower overlooking the field called out instructions.

"It's time," Cullen whispered, looking at Maggie and seeing in her eyes the same exhilaration, hope, and worry that roiled inside him.

"Twenty minutes," the man in the tower announced, "until the race begins. Everyone who is not a horse or a jockey or a trainer in some capacity *must* leave the staging area at this time."

The comment drew laughter from racing entrants and spectators alike.

Odessia hugged Kizzy tight. "Baby, you do everythin' Mister and Missus McGrath and Uncle Bob done told you to do, you hear me?"

"You's squeezin' me too tight, Mama!"

But Cullen noticed that the little girl didn't struggle to get away.

He reached for Maggie, and she came into his arms seemingly without a care of who was watching. But everyone else around them was hugging too.

"They're going to be all right," he whispered in her ear. "Both of them."

Maggie nodded, her arms briefly tightening around his waist. Then she knelt before Kizzy. "I'm so proud of you, Kizzy. You're going to do so well."

"I's gonna win, that's what I's gonna do, ma'am!"

Maggie laughed and kissed the top of the girl's cap. Then, with a last look, she made her way with Odessia to their seats in the stands. Cletus and the other workers gathered in the Negro section at the far end of the track, but Cullen had purposefully listed Odessia as Maggie's personal maid, to allow her to accompany them.

He helped Kizzy onto Belle, the girl's weight so inconsequential he wondered how the mare even knew the child was in the saddle.

Cullen felt the stares and gathered that the news of Belle's jockey being a girl had spread.

"Mr. McGrath—"

Hearing the familiar voice, Cullen turned to find General Harding beside him—along with Grady Matthews. If only Cullen had proof, he'd tell Harding his suspicions about the man right now.

"I came to wish you and your jockey godspeed," Harding said, shaking his hand. "And to tell you how well I thought you handled yourself today. Certain individuals can be . . . more difficult than others, and those were volatile subjects."

"Thank you, sir. I appreciate that."

Harding smoothed a hand over Belle's haunches. "She's a beauty. I look forward to seeing her run. And I sincerely hope she feels none of the effects from her recent illness."

Grady Matthews stepped forward and also gave Belle a pat. "Glad she's doin' better, sir. Snakeroot's a hard thing for a horse to pull through."

Cullen held Grady's gaze, his spine going stiff. "Aye, Mr. Matthews. It certainly is."

The two men left, and Cullen waited until Harding was a few feet away before calling out his name.

The general returned. "Something wrong, McGrath?"

"Just thought I'd let you know I figured out who poisoned Belle."

Harding's eyes narrowed.

Cullen glanced in the direction Grady Matthews had gone. "There are only four people who knew Belle was poisoned by snakeroot. Me, my wife, my brother, and Rachel Norris."

It didn't take long for understanding to move into General Harding's features. The man turned and looked at Grady Matthews standing beside Uncle Bob and Fortune, Harding's own prize-winning thoroughbred. Then the older man turned again and searched Cullen's face.

Cullen nodded. "And he didn't act alone. I know that much."

"Men like that never do."

The thunderous look that came over Harding's face made Cullen glad they weren't enemies.

"You have my solemn vow, McGrath. I'll get to the bottom of this."

"And I'll gladly help you, sir."

Harding returned to his party and Cullen pulled his focus back, hearing the man in the tower starting to call for the horses by position.

Cullen had hoped for the rail, but they'd drawn fifth place out of eight. So it would be a few minutes yet before they took the track.

"You all right, sweetie?" he asked Kizzy, noting she'd grown quiet.

The girl nodded, but said nothing.

Cullen scanned the crowd, still thinking perhaps Ethan would show as he'd promised. But instead of seeing Ethan, he spotted the one man he wanted to see least of anyone in the world, and he was walking straight toward them.

"McGrath!"

Acting as though they weren't merely acquaintances, but good friends, Stephen Drake extended a hand, which Cullen ignored.

"I just came by to say may the best horse win." Drake smiled, then placed a hand on Kizzy's calf.

The girl sucked in a breath.

Drake peered up. "How are you, darlin'? Ready to ride?"

Cullen jerked Drake's hand away, shoving the man back in the process. "Don't touch her!"

But Kizzy was already shaking. And Drake was grinning.

"Good luck, McGrath." He laughed as he walked away. "You're going to need it."

"Position three," the man called from the tower. "Fortune, from Belle Meade Plantation. Take your place."

"Kizzy, are you all right?" Cullen peered up and searched Kizzy's expression, but the girl wouldn't look at him.

She just kept reaching to pull down the hem of her trousers, her little hand shaking. And that's when Cullen saw the deep welts encircling her thin calves. A repulsive thought hit him like a jab to the gut, quick and explosive, and white-hot anger flashed through him. *Oh God, I'll kill him . . .*

"Kizzy, listen to me. Whatever that man did to you—"

She wouldn't look at him.

"Position four," the man called from the tower. "Rose at Dawn, from Rosemont Hill. Take your place."

Cullen reached up and drew her down, mindful of the other owners and their jockeys and workers nearby, waiting to be called. Kizzy's thin arms locked around his neck like a vise. Her whole body shook. His eyes watered, and he felt people staring.

"Look at her," a man said to his right. "She's afraid."

"I *told* you girls weren't fit to ride like this!"

"What was he thinking? Putting a little girl on a blood horse!"

"Kizzy," he whispered against her ear. "Can you hear me?"

Her shoulders started to tremble. But she nodded.

"Listen to my voice, Kizzy, and only my voice." He cradled the back of her head, the feeling of her arms around his neck so painfully familiar to him, and yet so distant. "I've got you, love. That man will *never* hurt you again. He will never come *near* you again. I'll make certain of it."

Her tears were wet against his neck.

"You're safe now. You're safe." He whispered it over and over again.

"Position five," the man called out. "Bourbon Belle, from Linden Downs. Take your place."

Holding Belle by the harness and Kizzy in his arms, Cullen walked to the starting mark.

Chapter Forty-Nine

Hearing the jeers from those around them and those coming from the packed stands, Cullen positioned Bourbon Belle on the starting mark. The thoroughbred pawed the dirt, antsy to run, but he held Belle's harness tight.

"Steady, girl," he whispered. "Wait . . .

"Aw . . . look at the little girl who's—"

Cullen pierced the jockey in position four with a look, and the young boy fell silent and turned his eyes back to the track.

"Kizzy," Cullen whispered, the girl's death grip having loosened on his neck. "You don't have to do this if you don't want to. We can walk off the field right now—you and me and Belle. And I won't be the least bit angry with you. Neither will Mrs. McGrath. But I do need to tell you somethin' . . ."

Face buried in his shoulder, she gave a little nod.

"There are moments in my life I wish I could go back and do again, but I can't. Because once a moment is past, it's past. There's no gettin' it back. And this is one of those moments for you. As hard as it is right now, as much as I wish we could stop it and start it all over again . . . we can't. If you don't do this now, Kizzy, you may not get another chance."

He nudged her gently with his shoulder, urging her to look at him.

She drew back, her eyes puffy from crying. She looked past him to the crowd. "They's sayin' I can't do it." She looked back at him. "And I ain't sure I can neither."

Cullen smiled. "If there's anyone who can do this, Kizzy, it's you. You and Belle were made for each other."

The girl gave him a weak smile then reached out to touch Belle.

The horse tossed its head, resisting the restraint, but Cullen kept a firm grip on them both.

He could only imagine what Maggie and Odessia were going through up in the stands, and he prayed for wisdom to know what to do. If he forced this child to race when she wasn't ready, and she was injured, or worse . . .

But he knew how courageous and strong she really was. And if she *was* ready and just didn't know it, if she couldn't see through the haze of fear and sadness right now, if she missed this chance to change not only the path of her life but that of her family—and in a far less impactful way, his and Maggie's, and that of Linden Downs—he felt as though he'd be failing her if he didn't help her see the opportunity for what it was.

The jockey riding the thoroughbred in the sixth position took his place beside them, and Cullen heard the announcer calling for the seventh—and next to last—thoroughbred.

"Sir, you *must* leave now," Cullen heard behind him, and he turned and nodded to the field official.

"Kizzy . . ." He looked her in the eyes as she sniffed and wiped her nose. "The best way to beat somebody is to show them who you are, and to succeed by doin' what they say you can't."

The little girl blinked, her dark eyes clearing.

"So tell me, little one. Do we walk off the field together now? Or do you get in that saddle and show this crowd of people who you are and what you and Belle can do together?" He chucked her gently beneath the chin. "Either way, you're a winner to me."

⁂

"What's wrong?" Odessia whispered. "Why she off the horse, ma'am?"

Standing along with everyone else, Maggie shook her head, barely able to force out the words. "I don't know." But the last five minutes had felt like the longest minutes of her life. Watching helpless as Kizzy had fallen into Cullen's arms and then as he *carried* her onto the track.

Wishing she could go to them, yet knowing she couldn't, Maggie saw an official approach Cullen for a second time. The two men exchanged words, somewhat heated, judging by Cullen's stance, and now, from what she could see at this distance, he was talking to Kizzy, and the girl was wiping her eyes.

"Oh, no Lawd . . ."

Maggie looked beside her at Odessia. "What's wrong?"

The woman's chin shook, but the fierceness in her dark eyes told Maggie the emotion didn't stem from tenderness. She trailed Odessia's gaze down to the field, but still didn't see what the woman was looking at.

"Position eight," the announcer called from the tower. "Dixieland, from Drake Estates. Take your place."

Spectators clapped in response, and from the field Stephen Drake turned and waved back toward the stands.

Odessia bristled. "That man be the devil himself," she said in a voice so low Maggie could scarcely hear.

Maggie looked from her, back to Drake, then to Kizzy. Realization crept in, then sank deep and hard. She swallowed. "The scars on her legs?"

Odessia nodded. "He got a side to him, ma'am . . . More animal than man."

The bitter taste of bile rose in Maggie's throat. "Did he—" But she couldn't say it.

Odessia turned and read the question in her eyes. "No, ma'am. My baby was lucky there, I guess." Angry tears brimmed. "He didn't want her to . . . visit with him in the shack like he did them other girls. He say she was too homely." Her voice caught. "He liked to hurt her with the whip instead. Say he liked the way she cried. Ennis got us away from him just 'fore the war ended." Odessia looked back toward the field. "Took my baby three years 'fore she could cry again with somebody seein' her. She just held it all inside."

Loving the child even more now than she had before, Maggie looked back to see Kizzy throw her arms around Cullen's neck again, and in a heartbeat she felt all the hope she'd had for today—and for the years of dreaming about this day—fall away.

And yet the disappointment wasn't as great as it would have been if Odessia hadn't told her what she had just now.

"I's so sorry, Missus McGrath," Odessia whispered beside her.

Maggie turned to see Odessia's head bowed. The woman was crying, and Maggie was surprised she wasn't crying herself. No doubt she would. But at the moment she was too stunned.

"It's going to be all right, Odessia," she heard herself saying, knowing the woman's tears were due only in part to disappointment for her and Cullen, but also, if not more, for the loss of what this meant for the woman's own family. "Odessia . . ." Maggie took hold of her hand, and Odessia's closed tight around hers. "It truly is going to be—"

Then Maggie heard Kizzy's name, coming toward them like a wave from the far side of the field. *Kiz-zy! Kiz-zy! Kiz-zy!* And emotion balled tight at the base of her throat.

Maggie lifted her head to see Kizzy astride Belle, and Cullen nowhere in sight.

She searched the sidelines for him and found him looking up into the stands as though he were searching for her. She waved big, still clutching Odessia's hand, and Cullen stilled and waved back. Then he smiled and gave her a smart little salute. *Just like Papa.*

"She back on the horse, ma'am!" Odessia said, breathless. "She back on!"

Maggie laughed, fledgling hope taking its first steps. "Yes, she is!"

Odessia's grip tightened. "If that child got this far and didn't see it on through, I'd be hearin' 'bout it 'til the day I die!"

Maggie smiled.

"Looka there, Missus McGrath." Odessia pointed. "It be all the people from home, ma'am. From Linden Downs."

Maggie looked and, sure enough, she spotted Cletus and Onnie congregated with a sea of others at the end of the track, by the very last turn.

Odessia started clapping and chanting her own daughter's name along with them, and Maggie joined in.

In the tall wooden tower on the track, a man waved a large red flag, and the din of voices and cheers from the stands gradually quieted even as the swell of Kizzy's name rose in the distance.

"Ladies and gentlemen"—the announcer's voice could scarcely be heard over the hum of anticipation—"the horses are on their marks! Get set . . ."

The gunshot sounded.

The horses on the track bolted forward and Maggie watched, the emerging hope within her grappling for purchase as Belle quickly fell into sixth place, only two from last.

Cheers rose from the spectators and drowned out Kizzy's name as well as the pounding of hooves on the track. The horses hadn't gone twelve lengths before Belle had fallen into seventh place. And no wonder . . .

Maggie reached into her pocket for her father's spyglass, telescoped it out, and seconds later had Kizzy in her view.

She was crouched too low, and she was gripping the reins too tightly. The child was scared. And worse, Belle knew it.

"Relax, Kizzy," Maggie whispered, knowing the girl knew better. "Stand up a little more in the saddle."

Fortune, General Harding's mare, already leading, pulled ahead another two lengths. Dixieland, in second, vied hard for first. And by the time the thoroughbreds came into the first curve, Belle was gaining, but still two lengths behind sixth place.

The race was one and a half times around the track, but if Belle didn't find her stride soon . . .

"What's wrong, Missus McGrath?" Odessia said beside her. "Why ain't Belle and Kizzy goin' fast like I seen 'em do?"

"Kizzy's scared. And Belle feels it. Belle won't break loose until Kizzy lets her know it's all right."

A third of the way around the track, and Belle looked like any other thoroughbred, running smooth as silk, dirt flying up behind her. But she simply wasn't running like Belle.

The cacophony of cheers rose all around them, everyone on their feet.

"Come on, baby." Odessia let out a moan. "You was born for this. *Lawd, please,* You gotta say it to her for me. Whisper it to her, Jesus. 'Cuz she can't hear me right now."

Maggie lowered the spyglass and watched, heart in her stomach, as Fortune and Dixieland continued to battle for first, a good six lengths ahead of the others. To have come all this way . . .

But it wasn't all Kizzy's fault, she reminded herself. Belle had been sick, after all, recovering from the poisoning.

She squinted.

In a flash, or so it seemed, Belle overtook the horse in sixth place, then was passing the fifth when the jockey edged over, trying to nudge Kizzy out. Kizzy stiffened and Belle's pace slowed, making them even with fifth again.

Maggie's jaw firmed. "Don't let him do that to you, Kizzy."

Belle pulled a length ahead, and Maggie raised her spyglass. Kizzy and Belle came into view, and Maggie's heart filliped to life again.

Kizzy's form was perfect, crouched just as she'd been taught, steady as a rock, with the reins loose, her slender legs absorbing the motion. Beneath her, Bourbon Belle ate up the distance, the mare's hooves crushing into the soil.

Over halfway around the track, Fortune and Dixieland still fought for first, while Belle's shoulders rippled with strength as the mare thundered into fourth place.

Maggie lowered the glass, her breath quickening as memory gave her a taste of what Kizzy was experiencing in that moment—her heart thudding as the mare surrendered to what every instinct in the horse's sleek-muscled body commanded it to do. To *run*. The wind in Kizzy's face, the freedom that only riding like that could bring . . .

"Let her fly, Kizzy," Maggie whispered, then raised her voice along with everyone else's, barely hearing herself above the fray. *"Let her fly!"*

Hooves flashing, Belle pushed forward until she was tied neck and neck with Rose at Dawn, the mare in solid third since the race began. Making liberal use of the riding crop, the jockey riding Rose at Dawn whipped his horse repeatedly about the haunches.

But when Maggie saw Kizzy flinch, her body went hot. "No!" she screamed, but her voice was lost amidst the shouts of others who had apparently seen the infraction too.

Take charge, Kizzy. You know what to do.

Maggie glanced ahead. Fortune and Dixieland had almost reached the starting point again, which meant only another half length of the track remained in the race. And Belle was still a good eight lengths behind them.

Come on, Belle. You can do it, girl. There was still time.

Maggie quickly searched for Cullen below and found him standing stock still, watching the track. Then the cheering that seconds before had been thunderous turned into a deafening roar, and she looked back to see Belle leaving Rose at Dawn behind on the final curve, her strides powerful and fluid, making the other mares look languid by comparison.

Nerves taut, Maggie counted seven lengths between Belle and Fortune, who narrowly held the lead, Dixieland still fighting.

Belle's hooves seemed to barely touch the ground.

Maggie held her breath. Five lengths separated the horses, then four, then three as Bourbon Belle—both beautiful and ferocious—closed the gap on the homestretch.

Odessia's hand crushed hers as in a blink Belle flew past Dixieland then overtook Fortune. Then left them both behind. Belle and Kizzy crossed the finish line in a blur, and the crowd erupted.

But it was seeing Kizzy stretch her arms out wide and lift her face to the sky that brought Maggie's laughter bubbling up, along with a flood of happy tears.

Odessia, crying and laughing herself, turned to her. “What she doin’ out there, ma’am?”

Maggie exhaled a shaky sigh, barely able to catch her breath. “She’s soaring, Odessia. Your daughter is *soaring*!”

Chapter FIFTY

"On behalf of the Nashville Thoroughbred Society, it's my honor to present you, Mr. Cullen McGrath, with this handsome silver cup." General Harding transferred the trophy to Cullen, who straightaway shared it with Maggie beside him, her smile radiant. "And my personal congratulations on Bourbon Belle winning the inaugural Peyton Stakes."

Harding reached over to shake Cullen's hand as applause rose from spectators still crowding the stands.

"Congratulations, Mr. McGrath. That was a fine race."

"Thank you, sir."

"Except for the last twenty seconds," Harding added discreetly, glancing down the track toward the finish line.

A slow smiled turned Cullen's mouth. "Actually, the last twenty were among my favorite."

Harding laughed beneath his breath.

Kizzy, all grins astride Bourbon Belle, seemed more subdued than usual, which wasn't surprising considering all that had happened.

Two men stepped forward with a garland of pink roses and draped the flowers across Kizzy's lap. The floral blanket extended down Bourbon Belle's sides, nearly touching the ground.

General Harding addressed the crowd once again. "The roses are a gift from Mrs. Adelicia Acklen Cheatham, and were cultivated in her conservatory at the Belmont Estate here in Nashville." Harding peered at the piece of paper in his hand. "According to the notes given me, this species of rose was actually grafted for and named on behalf of Mrs. Cheatham. It's called the Adelicia Rose."

The gathering responded with more applause.

Cullen's gaze swept the crowd, looking for someone specific—and snagged on Ethan, standing off to the side. His brother signaled, indicating he wanted to speak with him, and Cullen nodded. His frustration with Ethan had greatly lessened in light of the win. But it lingered nonetheless.

"And finally, last but certainly not least . . ." General Harding smiled and tucked his notes into the breast pocket of his coat. "The winning purse of *thirty-five thousand dollars*"—his voice took on added gusto—"the largest purse to date in Nashville racing history, is being held in guarantee for you at the First Bank of Nashville."

Cheers rose, and someone toward the back—from the Irish contingent, Cullen felt certain—yelled, "Hip hip!" to which people responded in unison, "Hooray!"

"Hip hip!"

"Hooray!"

"Hip hip!"

"*Hooray!*"

A crush of race day well-wishers—many of whom had begun celebrating early, judging by the whiff of ale he caught on their breath, which didn't smell half bad—pressed in for a chance to get a better look at the silver cup. But to Cullen's relief, the throng on the field quickly thinned.

He hugged Maggie again, still sharing the weight of the trophy between them.

"Can you believe it?" he whispered.

"Aye," she said with an Irish accent that was almost convincing—"that I can, Mr. McGrath."

He smiled, and heard Kizzy and Odessia laugh behind them.

"Mrs. McGrath . . ."

They turned to see General Harding approaching with his daughter, Mary.

"General." Maggie offered a curtsey, then accepted a hug from her friend.

"Mrs. McGrath, I wish to offer my personal congratulations to you as well. Your husband here informed the board members of the Thoroughbred Society today at our meeting that you, in fact, are responsible for training this magnificent horse." Harding motioned to Bourbon Belle. "Well done, my dear."

Surprise lit Maggie's expression. "Why . . . thank you, General. That's most kind of you."

Cullen caught the look of appreciation she sneaked his way.

"Actually, it's not 'kind' at all." Mary linked her arm briefly through Maggie's. "It's simply true. I'm so proud of you, Maggie!"

The general turned to Cullen. "McGrath . . . remember when I said I still owed you a debt for what you did for Bonnie Scotland?"

Cullen nodded. "Aye, sir. I do."

Harding looked pointedly at the silver cup, a glint in his eyes. Then looked back at Cullen. "Consider my debt paid in full, son."

Cullen laughed, then spotted Ethan striding toward him, looking as though he had something he wanted to discuss. Which, having an idea of what Ethan had been doing lately, Cullen preferred to do in private.

Cullen cocked his head, indicating he'd meet his brother in the stable.

Maggie put a hand on his arm. "You attended the Thoroughbred Society's board meeting today?"

Cullen nodded, then handed her the trophy, pretending to almost drop it. She gave a gasp, then smacked him on the arm when she realized he was jesting.

"I'll tell you all about it later, I promise." He smiled, then glanced toward the stable, sobering. "But right now I need to speak with Ethan."

She looked in that direction, her expression telling. "He finally showed up, I see."

Hearing the distrust in her voice bothered him. Although he knew she had reason for it, she also didn't know everything about his brother.

He kissed her cheek. "Wait here. I'll be back shortly."

He met Ethan just inside the stable, and his brother promptly wrapped him in a bear hug.

"Hello, little brother. Or should I say, my *rich* little brother." Ethan slapped him on the back. "I'm proud of you, Cullen!"

"Did you see the race?"

"Aye." Ethan pulled a piece of paper from his pocket. "And all the speech-makin' right after. You and General Harding seem to be thick as thieves."

"He's a good man, despite bein' rich." Cullen glanced at the paper in his brother's hand.

Ethan held it out. "Consider this my gift to you, brother. My way of sayin' thanks for what you done for me back in London. And for any pain my actions caused you."

Hearing the sincerity in his voice, Cullen unfolded the paper then looked up. "A list of names?"

"Not just names." Ethan lowered his voice. "Names of the men who visited Linden Downs that night."

Cullen looked at the list again, and his eyes narrowed. "How did you come by this?"

"I was civil, I give you my word."

"How did you come by this list, Ethan?"

"In case you haven't noticed, I get along with people quite well. 'Specially the freedmen. And there are those among 'em who know what's goin' on. Some of 'em still work for the men on that list. What's more . . . I know who poisoned Belle. I found some snakeroot in the man's bunk at Belle Meade."

"Grady Matthews," Cullen said quietly, and his brother nodded. Movement at the far end of the stable drew Cullen's attention. The person he'd been looking for. "Excuse me, brother." He returned the list. "There are a few things I need to tend to."

Cullen strode past him and went directly to Stephen Drake.

"What do you want, McGrath? Just because you win a race, you think you're—"

Cullen punched him hard in the gut, and Drake doubled over.

"That's for poisonin' my horse. And this—" Cullen drew the man up by the shirt, then landed another blow in his side. Drake went down in the dirt. "That's for hangin' Ennis."

Gasping, Drake cursed him and called him names Cullen hadn't heard since he'd left England.

"And this last one"—Cullen dragged him up again, easily deflecting the man's blows—"is for the little girl." A crunch of cartilage beneath his fist, and Drake cried out, holding his nose.

"McGrath!"

Cullen turned to see General Harding standing behind his brother.

Harding's expression was fierce. "What do you think you're doing?"

"I'll tell you what I'm doin', General." Leaving Drake writhing on the ground, Cullen walked back to them. "I'm makin' sure this man remembers poisonin' my horse. And hangin' my foreman in front of his wife before he set my cabins ablaze. And I hope to God he remembers this the next time he even thinks of takin' a whip to a little girl." Cullen's breath came hard. He grabbed the piece of paper from Ethan and held it up with a bruised fist. "Some men only understand this kind of language, General. Like the men on this list."

Cullen handed him the paper.

Harding's gaze moved over the page. After a long moment, he looked up. "These are the men who visited Linden Downs that night?" he said quietly.

"Aye," Cullen answered. "It took some doin', but my brother here scouted them out."

Harding looked over at Ethan.

"Some of these men were sittin' right around your table this afternoon, General," Cullen continued.

Harding winced. He took the piece of paper and folded it carefully. "Do you trust me, Mr. McGrath?"

Cullen stared.

"I said, do you trust me . . . Mr. McGrath."

"Aye," Cullen finally whispered. "I do."

"Then let me take care of this in my own way."

"But, sir, I—"

"If you mete out justice as you've done here now, you'll only be making it harder for your own people, McGrath. And your workers. Don't hear me saying that what you did here wasn't deserved." Harding glanced past him. "But we have other ways of dealing with things like this. Let me do that for you. *Please*."

Cullen shook the sting off his fist, aware of Ethan's close attention and of Harding's lengthening patience. Slowly, he nodded.

Harding offered his hand, and Cullen shook it, wincing, his own still tender.

"Thank you, Mr. McGrath. And may I say . . . I knew Gilbert Linden all my life. He was a fine man, and I believe he chose very wisely. I hope we'll be neighbors for many years to come."

"As do I, sir." Cullen sighed. "As do I."

Harding turned.

"One last thing, General."

The man looked back.

"Understandin' how most people in this town feel about the Irish, I'm wonderin' . . . Why is it you're different? That you've been so decent to me. Don't be gettin' me wrong, I'm grateful. I'm just . . . curious."

Looking away, Harding took a moment to answer, and when he did, his expression was tender. "My late wife was a McGavock, Mr. McGrath. Scotch-Irish blood flowed through her veins, and her grandfather had a brogue as thick as the mist on the heathlands."

Epilogue

May 13, 1870

Still half asleep, Maggie turned onto her back in the bed, the endless warble of a mockingbird outside the window far too chipper for so early an hour. Dawn's first light cast the bedroom in a silvery mist, but the night seemed reluctant to renounce its hold. So she snuggled deeper beneath the covers and hugged her pillow, drifting on a wave somewhere between wakefulness and slumber.

The distant mewling of a kitten—so soft, so sweet—tugged at her heart, and she reached beside her for Cullen to—

The space was empty. But lingering warmth told her he hadn't been gone long. She yawned and stretched, the fog of sleep slowly clearing. Then she smiled, realizing she'd been dreaming.

She smoothed a hand over her all but flat stomach, then raised up in bed to see Cullen standing over the cradle. The same cradle her grandparents and parents had used through the years.

"What are you doing?" she whispered.

"Watchin' him sleep," he said softly.

She lay back down, the fullness in her breasts telling her it wouldn't be long until their son was awake again. As though the thought summoned him, little Gilbert let out a whimper. That sounded much like a kitten . . .

She sighed, smiling. "You intentionally woke him."

"Nay, I did not."

But Cullen's soft laughter hinted otherwise. He cradled their son against his bare chest and returned to bed, leaning down to kiss her before tucking the babe between them.

Cullen brushed a finger over Gilbert's tiny, perfect hand and the baby immediately grabbed hold. "Strong little fella."

Maggie smiled and kissed the crown of her son's head, breathing in the scent of him, fresh from heaven.

Bucket rose from his place by the hearth, shook the sleep off, then trotted to Cullen's side of the bed.

"Mornin', boy." Cullen rubbed the collie between the ears, and the dog peered up—alert and inquisitive—before promptly lying back down again.

Maggie laughed softly. "So much for being interested."

Nestled there in a warm cocoon with her men, as she thought of them, she counted her blessings again. Too many to name. Too many not to try.

The past winter had been one of the coldest anyone could remember, but awakening to snow blanketing the fields, sparkling like crushed diamonds in the morning light, had inspired an appreciation within her for the seasons—and for Linden Downs—she'd not had before.

How could you live somewhere your entire life and not see it for the blessing it was? But realizing that instilled a sense of anticipation at what God would reveal in coming months and years, and of his orchestration through it all. *Oh Lord, open my eyes to all you've given me, and to all you are. You* alone *are my shelter, my strong tower* . . .

Cullen had read a passage from her father's Bible a few Sundays ago that had held that nugget of a truth, and it had been with her ever since. They'd begun attending church together, too, at a newly formed Irish and freedman congregation on the outskirts of town. Each service was an adventure.

Long before winter's chill set in, new cabins were built to replace the ones that burned, and Cullen saw to it that all the cabins—both old and new—were, as he put it, "Worthy of keepin' out the cold and keepin' in the warm." Hence, every cabin had a wood-burning stove and plenty of blankets on the beds.

Under Cullen's direction, the men had enlarged the stable, and already work was underway on a new barn. Despite the winning purse, Cullen was spending wisely, frugally. Papa would have been so proud. So much for which to be thankful, so much to look forward to. And yet . . .

A sadness mingled with her joy, and she dreaded what the coming week would bring.

Gilbert wriggled, issuing a hungry cry, and Maggie unbuttoned her gown and pulled her son close. The sweet sounds he made as he nursed, his little mouth working, entwined her heart to his in a way she'd never imagined possible.

"You're both so beautiful," Cullen whispered, trailing a finger along their son's cheek. He met her gaze. "How're you feelin', love?" he asked softly.

In the days following Gilbert's long and difficult birth, exhaustion had been a close companion. But in the past six weeks, Maggie's strength had slowly returned.

Cullen never left her side during her labor. The sweetest image she carried from those seemingly endless hours, besides the moment she'd first laid eyes on their son, was when she'd looked over to see Cullen on his knees beside the bed, head bowed, hands clasped.

And any lingering question about what kept him at Linden Downs—whether his promise to her father or his love for her—had been silenced for good.

"I'm feeling much better," she whispered, smoothing a hand over his chest. She'd missed intimacy with him in recent weeks. She read another, unvoiced, question in his eyes and felt a tightening in her throat. "But I dread saying good-bye to Ennis and Odessia. And Kizzy and her brothers."

He brought her hand to his mouth and kissed it. "It's provin' harder for me to accept too."

It comforted her to know he felt the same about Ennis and his family leaving later that week.

Along with paying Kizzy the regular amount a jockey earned for riding in a race, Cullen had included a generous bonus to Ennis and Odessia that secured the opportunity for the family to go west, as Ennis wanted. Thanks to Uncle Bob, the couple already had a contact in Colorado, a Mr. Cooper and his wife who had a ranch some distance from Denver.

Cullen had arranged for a wagon and horses for Ennis and Odessia as well. And in addition to enough lemon cookies to see the family clear to Colorado, there was a special surprise awaiting Kizzy on the morning of their departure . . . Spunky, a pretty little buckskin mare, whose name fit the girl to a T.

How quickly people once strangers to you could become like family. Especially when they really *were* family. Maggie thought of Ethan . . .

It was a wonder how a baby could melt the heart of even the roughest man. And Uncle Ethan was a puddle when it came to Master Gilbert Cullen McGrath.

"He's a little bruiser, this one," Ethan had said earlier that week. "Got the McGrath chin for sure. And look at that fist, would ya? No one'll be messin' with him."

The past few months had brought a truce—then peace—between her and Cullen's older brother. Then that peace had somehow unfurled into a warmth of affection she never expected to feel for him.

Learning what he'd done for her last fall had certainly helped. All the nights he'd been gone or had come in late, he'd been keeping watch—over Bourbon Belle, Kizzy, the workers—before the race, and then long after.

And the list of men—all of whom were being held accountable for what they'd done—was due to Ethan, Cullen told her. But she knew the credit was properly shared between the two men. Because Cullen had never given up on his brother, and what Ethan had done for her was in response to that love.

She'd lost four brothers to the war, but God in his mercy—and humor—had seen fit to give her another. One she'd not expected, but would cherish.

The baby finished nursing, and she sat up in bed, held him to her chest, and patted his back until a gentle gurgle of air worked its way up and out. Then she pushed back the covers.

"I'll take him." Cullen returned Gilbert to the cradle, smiling as he stood there, rocking it gently back and forth. Then he reached for his shirt. "It's still early. You sleep on. I'll wake you later, when Onnie has breakfast ready."

"But . . . what if I'm not sleepy?"

Cullen stopped, one arm in a shirt sleeve, the other not, and looked at her. She let her smile come slowly.

His gaze moved leisurely over her body before finally seeking her eyes again, and the darkening in his own fanned a flame inside her. He slipped off his shirt and lay back down. Her gown, still open, drew his focus, and even before he touched her she felt the heat of his desire.

His kiss was hungry and deep and she wrapped her arms around him, disappointed when, a moment later, he drew back.

"Patience, love," he whispered, then unbuttoned her gown the rest of the way, kissing her as he did. He covered her body with his.

Later, as the sun rose and light gradually seeped into the room, Maggie lay in the crook of his arm, her pulse slowly finding its rhythm again, and she realized—no, *knew*—that no matter who came and went in her life, this man, this child God had given her . . . *they* were her home.

And always would be.

A Note from the Author

Dear Readers,

Thanks for taking yet another journey with me.

The inspiration for *To Win Her Favor* had its start in a question: How does prejudice influence our lives and choices? In the nineteenth century many Americans harbored animosity toward foreigners, and though I wanted to give an accurate historical perspective on the issue (specifically about the Irish in Nashville), I didn't want to *only* give a historical perspective on prejudice. Because heaven knows, its insidious nature is alive and well.

So it's my prayer that—as you read the story—you took the same journey I did in exploring your own heart even as you experienced the stark reality of prejudice in Cullen's and Maggie's journeys. We have a long way to go in healing the prejudicial wounds in this country, in this world, and that healing will only come through the powerful presence and name of Jesus Christ and in having a relationship with him. He can change hearts. He can move mountains.

The story also grew out of the many historical accounts I've read about marriages of convenience in the 1800s, and how the struggles these couples endured—and the unexpected blessings they encountered—shaped their commitment to each other and what they learned about *real* love.

History fascinates me, and a lot of true Nashville and Belle Meade Plantation history is woven into this novel. What's some of the actual history, you ask? The thoroughbreds in the story—Bonnie Scotland, Vandal, and Bourbon Belle—are names of real horses that lived at Belle Meade, and many current day Kentucky Derby winners (including the famed Secretariat) trace their lineage back to Bonnie Scotland and Belle Meade in the 1870s.

The following characters were based on people who actually lived:

the Harding family, Uncle Bob Green, Rachel Norris, and Adelicia Acklen. And in all of my novels, I include cameos from characters from previous novels. Did you catch who they were in this novel? If not, you might want to check out *A Beauty So Rare* and *Within My Heart*.

I invite you to visit www.BelleMeadePlantation.com for more information about the estate, the people who lived there, and the blood horses whose lineage still dominates the thoroughbred racing industry today.

You can also tour the grounds and mansion of Belle Meade Plantation with me by visiting my website (the Belle Meade Plantation novel page under Books) and by viewing several two-minute video vignettes we filmed on location at Belle Meade.

As I wrote this novel, a secondary character in *To Win Her Favor*, Savannah Darby, thoroughly captured my heart with her courage and strength in the face of insurmountable struggle. So much so that I wanted to write her story, and have done so, in *To Mend a Dream*.

To Mend a Dream is part of a novella collection comprised of four Southern love stories. The collection titled *Among the Fair Magnolias* releases in July 2015. I hope you'll join me as we revisit the Darby Farm and characters from this novel, and discover whether Savannah's deep longing for her family home, lost in the war, is ever fulfilled.

Until next time ...
Through Jesus, our true shelter and strong tower,

Psalm 61:3; Galatians 3:28

Discussion Questions

1. How would you describe Cullen's and Maggie's personalities? What are their biggest strengths and weaknesses? And their biggest differences from one another?
2. Were you able to put yourself in Cullen's place? Did you feel the prejudice and bias he experienced? Were you able to identify with Maggie's "fall from grace" in a social sense? Which character did you identify with most and why?
3. How did you feel about Gilbert Linden's "offer" to Cullen? How do you think you would fare with an arranged marriage? Would you trust your parent to choose for you?
4. Maggie was initially very resistant to the idea of marrying Cullen. Not surprising. Discuss her reasons for finally agreeing. Put yourself in her shoes. What would you have done?
5. In chapter 10 Maggie reflects on God's presence in her life, or perceived lack of it. Have you ever felt as though God were punishing you for a choice you made, as Maggie did?
6. In chapter 11 Cullen reflects on little turning points in life. What are these as he defines them? Have you experienced something similar?
7. In chapter 16 Maggie is thinking about childhood memories and experiences that shaped who she became, who she is. What were those experiences? What childhood experiences have shaped you (for good and bad)?
8. In chapter 17 Cullen talks about hardships in his life. What were some of the hardships in his life and how did they affect him? Why do you think God allows hardships in our lives?
9. This novel delves into the issues of prejudice in the nineteenth century. Do you believe the same issues exist today? Which issues? Cullen shares with Maggie that people are rarely what

they appear to be (from outward appearance). Do you agree or disagree?

10. Mr. Linden told Maggie that through the years he's had to "let go of her" in a sense. Discuss that conversation that occurs at the beginning of chapter 19.
11. In chapter 33 Cullen reflects on vengeance and what it can cost a person. Did you agree with the actions he took toward Stephen Drake? Do you think he should have done more? Less? What would you do if faced with the same challenge of protecting those you love?
12. In chapter 38, Maggie wonders at all the events that led to her and Cullen being together. What is your opinion of God's orchestration in peoples' lives? Do you believe in coincidences? Is there an incident in your life that you're convinced had divine intervention?
13. In chapter 41 Ethan and Cullen are discussing life choices on the front porch. Read Romans 7:14–25 and discuss the similarities between Ethan's "excuses" for sinning and what Paul says. Do you relate to the same struggle? How?
14. Kizzy is a character Tamera quickly fell in love with as the story unfolded. What are your thoughts about Kizzy? Were you familiar with horse racing in the nineteenth century and how all the jockeys were young black boys? Would you allow your young daughter to ride in a race like Kizzy did?
15. Do you have a favorite scene? What is it about that scene you liked best?

Would you be willing to send Tamera a picture of your book club? She'd love to feature you on her Facebook page. Send the picture to TameraAlexander@gmail.com with your name(s), your group's name, and the city where you're located. Be sure to hold up your books!

Acknowledgments

Over the years many people have supported and influenced my writing. My family (Joe, Kelsey, and Kurt) have always been at the top of the list. Closely following are my parents. Mom went home in 2009, but there are days when I'm certain I can still hear her cheering me on, a part of that "great cloud of witnesses" the writer of Hebrews tells us about. Dad continues to be such an encouragement to me, too, as is his sweet wife, Esta.

My agent, Natasha Kern, manages the business side of my writing career with such grace and integrity. I wouldn't want to walk this road without her.

I'm grateful to my team at HarperCollins Christian Publishing (Zondervan/Thomas Nelson) for partnering with me in this writing endeavor. It truly takes a team to write a book, and I've been blessed to work with some fabulous people in this industry who have graciously shared not only their expertise and talent, but their lives as well. Special thanks to Daisy, Ami, L.B., Katie, Jodi, and Becky. I appreciate my entire HCCP team.

Thanks also to numerous friends who have lightened my load and carried me in prayer during the writing process. Thank you to Lea Sullivan (and her father, Robbie) for sharing her story about finding a little puppy in a five-gallon bucket and naming it so appropriately.

Thanks to Carl and Heather Cartee for naming your four sons so creatively and for letting me borrow their names (Oak, Ezra, Ike, and Abe) for Maggie's older brothers.

Author and friend Deborah Raney, my writing critique partner for twelve years and counting, is my first reader and lends such insight to my first draft. The ladies of Coeur d'Alene are truly the sisters I've always wanted but never had. Our July retreats are a highlight of my year, and a glimpse of heaven.

The folks at Belle Meade Plantation (Alton Kelley, Jenny Lamb, John Lamb, and Joanne Hostettler-Floyd, and so many others) always issue me such a warm welcome, and I'm forever grateful to them for allowing me access not only to the mansion and grounds but to the Harding family's letters and personal histories, as well as those of the former slaves who lived and worked at the plantation both before and after the Civil War.

Thank you to you, the reader. I spend much of my time in the nineteenth century with characters who are as real to me (sometimes more so) as real people. So it's a magical thing when—after these characters have inhabited my heart for so long—a book is finally published, and I hear from you saying that you love them the same. You make my joy in writing complete.

My prayer is that, as you read, you'll take a step closer to Christ. Because truly, it's all about him.

Aunt Issy's Lemon Cookies

Cookie ingredients

4-1/4 cups unsifted all-purpose flour
1 tsp. baking soda
1 tsp. cream of tartar
1 tsp. salt
1 cup (1/2 lb.) butter, softened
1 cup confectioners' sugar
1 cup granulated sugar
2 eggs
1 cup oil
1 tsp. lemon extract
1 tsp. grated lemon peel

Icing Ingredients

3-1/2 cups confectioners' sugar
7 Tbsp. freshly squeezed lemon juice

Cookie Directions

In mixing bowl combine flour, baking soda, cream of tartar, and salt. Set aside. In larger mixing bowl, beat softened butter and both sugars on medium until well blended. Beat in eggs, one at a time, until dough is light and fluffy. Add oil, lemon extract, and lemon peel. Beat until well mixed. Gradually add dry ingredients to creamed mixture and beat until well blended. Wrap and chill for several hours.

Preheat oven to 325 degrees. Grease cookie sheets or line pans with parchment paper. Divide dough into thirds. Work one part at a time and refrigerate the rest. Roll a heaping teaspoon of dough into a ball and place on baking sheet. Flatten into a 2-inch circle with the bottom of a glass dipped in granulated sugar.

Bake 8 to 10 minutes or until lightly golden at the edges (careful not to overbake). Let stand on baking sheet for 2–3 minutes before removing. Makes 7 dozen rich and crisp old-fashioned lemon cookies.

Icing Directions

Combine sugar and lemon juice to make a stiff paste. Set bowl over a pan of hot water to warm icing to spreading consistency. Keep the pot over low heat while frosting the cookies, as the paste will stiffen as it cools.

Special thanks to Katie Rawls and her Aunt Issy for sharing this treasured family recipe.

An excerpt from *To Whisper Her Name*

Prologue

August 17, 1863

In the hills surrounding the Union-occupied city of Nashville . . . First Lieutenant Ridley Adam Cooper peered through the stand of bristled pines, his presence cloaked by dusk, his Winchester cocked and ready. Beads of sweat trailed his forehead and the curve of his eye, but he didn't bother wiping them away. His focus was trained on the Negro hunched over the fire and what he was certain—if his last hour of observation proved true—the slave had hidden just over the ridge.

Best he could tell, the man hadn't spied him, else he wouldn't be going about making supper like he was. Beans and pork with biscuits and coffee, if Ridley's sense of smell proved right. *Real* coffee. Not that foul-tasting brew the Rebs scalded over an open flame until it was sludge, then drank by the gallons.

Rebs. His brothers, in a way, every last one of them. Two of them the blood kind. And yet, the enemy. He hoped Petey and Alfred were all right, wherever they were.

A northerly breeze marked evening's descent, but the air's movement did little to ease the sweltering heat and humidity. Someone raised in the thickness of South Carolina summers should be accustomed to this by now, but the wool of the Federal uniform wore heavy, more so these days than when he'd first enlisted.

Yet he knew he'd done the right thing in choosing the side he had. No matter what others said or did. Or accused him of.

Ridley felt a pang. Not from hunger so much, though he could eat if food was set before him. This pang went much deeper and hurt worse than anything he could remember. *God, if you're listening, if you're still watching us from where you are . . . I hate this war.* Hated what this "brief conflict"—as President Lincoln had called it at the outset—was doing to him and everyone else over two bloody years later.

And especially what it called for him to do tonight. "At any cost," his commander had said, his instruction leaving no question.

Jaw rigid, Ridley reached into his pocket and pulled out the seashell, the one he'd picked up on his last walk along the beach near home before he'd left to join the 167th Pennsylvania Regiment to fight for the Federal Army. The scallop shell was a tiny thing, hardly bigger than a coin, and the inside fit smoothly against his thumb. With his forefinger, he traced the familiar ridges along the back and glanced skyward where a vast sea of purple slowly ebbed to black.

It was so peaceful, the night canopy, the stars popping out one by one like a million fireflies flitting right in place. Looking up, a man wouldn't even know a war was being waged.

When his commanding officer had called for a volunteer for the scouting mission, the man hadn't waited for hands to go up but had looked directly at Ridley, his expression daring argument. Ridley had given none. He'd simply listened to the orders and set out at first light, nearly three days ago now. Ridley knew the commander held nothing personal against him. The man had been supportive in every way.

It was Ridley's own temper and his "friendly" disagreement with a fellow officer—a loud-mouthed lieutenant from Philadelphia who hated "every one of them good for nothin', ignorant Southerners"—that had landed him where he was tonight. The fool had all but accused him of spying for the Confederacy. Their commander had quashed the rumor, but the seed of doubt had been sown. And this was the commander's way of allowing Ridley to earn back his fellow officers' trust again, which was imperative.

Ridley wiped his brow with the sleeve of his coat, careful not to make a noise. He'd tethered his horse a good ways back and had come in on foot.

He didn't know the hills surrounding Nashville any better than the rest of his unit, but he did know this kind of terrain, how to hunt and move about in the woods. And how to stay hidden. The woods were so dense in places, the pines grown so thick together, a man could get lost out here if he didn't know how to tell his way.

They'd gotten wind of Rebels patrolling the outlying areas—rogue sentries who considered themselves the law of the land—and his bet was they were searching for what he'd just found. So far, he hadn't seen hide nor hair of them. But he could imagine well enough what they'd do to a Union soldier found on his lonesome—especially an officer and "one of their own kind" to boot—so he was eager to get this thing done.

Gripping his Winchester, Ridley stepped from the tree cover, still some thirty feet from the Negro. He closed the distance—*twenty-five feet, twenty*—the cushion of pine needles muffling his approach. *Fifteen, ten* . . . But the man just kept puttering away, stirring the coffee, then the beans, then—

Ridley paused mid-step. Either the Negro was deaf . . . or was already wise to his presence. Wagering the latter, Ridley brought his rifle up and scanned his surroundings, looking for anyone hidden in the trees or for a gun barrel conveniently trained at the center of his chest. It was too late to retreat, but withdrawal of any kind had never been in his nature, as that cocksure, pretentious little—he caught himself—*lieutenant* from Philadelphia had found out well enough.

He tried for a casual yet not too pleasant tone. "Evening, friend . . ."

The man's head came up. Then, slowly, he straightened to his full height, which was still a good foot shorter than Ridley. He was thicker about the middle, older than Ridley too. In his thirties maybe, or closer to forty, it was hard to tell. The Negro was broad shouldered, and judging by the thickness of his hands and forearms, Ridley guessed that years of hard labor had layered a strap of muscle beneath that slight paunch. He hoped it wouldn't give the slave a false sense of courage.

"Evenin'," the man answered, glancing at the stripes on Ridley's shoulder. "Lieutenant, sir."

Not a trace of surprise registered in his voice, which went a ways in confirming Ridley's silent wager. The man's knowledge of military rank was also telling.

The Negro's focus shifted decidedly to the Winchester, then back again, and Ridley couldn't decide if it was resignation he read in the man's eyes or disappointment. Or maybe both.

Ridley surveyed the camp. Neat, orderly. Everything packed. Everything but the food. Like the man was getting ready to move out. Only—Ridley looked closer—not one cup but two resting on a rock by the fire. He focused on the slave and read awareness in the man's eyes. "How long have you known I was watching?"

The Negro bit his lower lip, causing the fullness of his graying beard to bunch on his chin. "'Bout the time the coffee came back to boilin' sir."

"You heard me?" Ridley asked, knowing that was impossible. He hadn't made a sound. He was sure of it.

The man shook his head, looking at him with eyes so deep and dark a brown they appeared almost liquid. "More like . . . I *felt* you, sir."

A prickle skittered up Ridley's spine. Part of him wanted to question the man, see if he had what some called "second sight," like Ridley' s great-grandmother'd had, but the wiser part of him knew better than to inquire. He had a job to do, one he couldn't afford to fail at. Not with his loyalty to the Union being called into question by some. "I take it you know what I'm here for."

There it was again, that look. Definitely one of resignation this time.

"I reckon I do, sir. It's what all them others been lookin' for too." The slave shook his head. "How'd you find me?"

Only then did Ridley allow a hint of a smile. "I don't know that I can say exactly. We got rumor of horses being hidden in these hills. I *volunteered*, you might say, and then just started out. I followed where my senses told me to go. Where I would've gone if I was hiding horses."

The man's eyebrows arched, then he nodded, gradually, as if working to figure something out. He motioned to the fire. "Dinner's all ready, Lieutenant. Think you could see fit to eat a mite?"

Ridley looked at the pot of beans and meat bubbling over the flame, then at the tin of biscuits set off to the side, his stomach already answering. The man was offering to feed him? All whilst knowing what he was here to do? Ridley eyed him again, not trusting him by any stretch. Yet he had a long journey back to camp, and the dried jerky in his rations didn't begin to compare. "I'd be much obliged. Thank you."

They ate in silence, the night sounds edging up a notch as the darkness grew more pronounced. The food tasted good and Ridley was hungrier than he'd thought. He'd covered at least seventy-five, maybe a hundred miles since leaving camp in Nashville.

Just four days earlier, Union headquarters had received rumor of a slave out in these hills, reportedly hiding prized blood horses for his owner. Word had it the horses were bred for racing and were worth a fortune. Ridley would've sworn they'd confiscated every horse there was in Nashville when they first took the city. But he'd bet his life that the man across from him right now was the slave they'd heard about.

He lifted his cup. "You make mighty good coffee. Best I've had in a while. And this is some fine venison too."

"Thank you, sir. My master, he got the finest deer park in all o' Dixie. Least he did 'fore them no-good, thievin'—" The Negro paused, frowning, then seemed to put some effort into smoothing his brow, though with little success. "I's sorry, sir. I 'preciate all your side's tryin' to do in this war, but there just ain't no cause for what was done at Belle Meade last year. 'Specially with Missus Harding bein' delicate o' health, and Master Harding packed off to prison like he was. Them Union troops—" He gripped his upper thigh, his eyes going hot. "They shot me! Right in the leg. I's just tryin' to do what I's been told, and they shot me straight on. Laughed about it too. And here we's thinkin' they come to help."

Reminded again of another reason he hated this war and why the South no longer felt like home and never would again, Ridley held the man's gaze, trying to think of something to say. Something that would make up for what had been done to him. But he couldn't.

Ridley laid aside his tin and, on impulse, reached out a hand. "First Lieutenant Ridley Adam Cooper . . . sir."

He knew a little about the slave's owner—General William Giles Harding—from what his commanding officer had told him. To date, General Harding still hadn't signed the Oath of Allegiance to the Union, despite the general's incarceration up north last year at Fort Mackinac—a place reportedly more like a resort than a prison—and the lack of compliance wasn't sitting well with those in authority. Not with Harding being so wealthy a man and holding such influence among his peers. It set the wrong precedent. Union superiors hoped the outcome of this scouting mission would provide General Harding with the proper motivation he needed to comply with the Union—or suffer further consequences.

The Negro regarded Ridley—the crackle of the fire eating up the silence—then finally accepted, his own grip iron-firm. "Robert Green, sir. Head hostler, Belle Meade Plantation."

Also From Tamera Alexander

Pink is not what Eleanor Braddock ordered, but maybe it would soften the tempered steel of a woman who came through a war—and still had one to fight.

Plain, practical Eleanor knows she will never marry, but with a dying soldier's last whisper, she finds fresh purpose. Impoverished and struggling to care for her ailing father, Eleanor arrives at Belmont Mansion, home of her aunt, Adelicia Acklen, the richest woman in America. Adelicia insists on finding her niece a husband, but a simple act of kindness leads Eleanor down a different path—building a home for widows and fatherless children from the Civil War.

Archduke Marcus Gottfried has come to Nashville from Austria in search of a life he alone has determined. Hiding his royal heritage, Marcus finds work as an architect, but his plans to incorporate natural beauty into the design of the widows' and children's home run contrary to Eleanor's wishes. Through their collaboration on the home, Marcus and Eleanor find common ground—and a love neither of them expects. But Marcus is not the man Adelicia has chosen for Eleanor, and even if he were, someone who knows his secrets is about to reveal them all.

A Beauty So Rare
A Belmont Mansion Novel

About the Author

TAMERA ALEXANDER is a *USA Today* bestselling author whose richly drawn characters and thought-provoking plots have earned her devoted readers worldwide, as well as multiple industry awards. After living in Colorado for seventeen years, Tamera has returned to her Southern roots. She and her husband make their home in Nashville where they enjoy life with their two adult children who live nearby, and Jack, a precious—and precocious—silky terrier. And all of this just a stone's throw away from the beloved Southern mansions about which she writes.

Tamera invites you to visit her at:

Her website: *www.tameraalexander.com*
Her blog: *www.tameraalexander.blogspot.com*
Twitter: *@tameraalexander*
Facebook: *tamera.alexander*
Pinterest: *Tamera Alexander*

Or if you prefer snail mail, please write her at the following postal address:

Tamera Alexander
P.O. Box 871
Brentwood, TN 37024

Discussion questions for *To Win Her Favor* and all of Tamera's books are available at www.tameraalexander.com, as are recipes to accompany your reader group's gathering.